SHADOWLAND

GORDON STEVENS

SHADOWLAND

MACMILLAN
LONDON

First published 1992 by
Macmillan London Limited
a division of Pan Macmillan Publishers Limited
Cavaye Place London SW10 9PG
and Basingstoke

Associated companies throughout the world

ISBN 0 333 57530 X

1 3 5 7 9 8 6 4 2

A CIP catalogue record for this book is available from
the British Library

Phototypeset by Intype, London
Printed and bound in Great Britain by
Mackays of Chatham PLC, Chatham, Kent

For twenty-eight years and eighty-seven days,
from the night of Saturday, 12 August/
Sunday, 13 August 1961,
the Berlin Wall divided a city
and symbolized a world.

It was breached on the evening
of Thursday, 9 November 1989.

During that time
most people came to accept its existence.
This book is dedicated to the handful who did not.

Especially the men and women of Tunnel Fifty-Seven.

And most especially Wolfgang Fuchs,
escape organizer *extraordinaire*.

Heidi Fuchs, political prisoner, escaper
and escape helper.

And Peter Schulenburg, tunneller and courier.
Betrayed, arrested and sentenced to eighteen years'
imprisonment in East Germany.

The fiction is mine, the truth is theirs.

GORDON STEVENS
Berlin

Erich Honecker (head of the East German
Communist Party) lies on the beach in the Baltic.
The sun rises above the early morning mist.

'Good morning, dear Sun,' says Erich.

'Good morning, General Secretary,' says the sun.
'I wish you a pleasant day.'

'How kind of you, dear Sun.'

The sun smiles.
'General Secretary, my only wish is to please you
and to serve the Party. I am delighted that my
greeting makes you happy.'

In the evening, as the sun sets, Honecker looks up.
'Thank you, dear Sun. I've had such a pleasant day.'

The sun looks down and smiles again.
'Kiss my arse, you old fool. I'm in the West now.'

East Berlin underground joke, October 1989

AUTHOR'S NOTE

IN DECEMBER 1943, eighteen months before the end of the Second World War, the foreign ministers of the United States, Britain and the Soviet Union met in Moscow to decide the fate of Germany after Hitler. The consensus was to divide Germany into zones of occupation, at first three then four to include the French.

In London the following year a similar agreement was reached to split Berlin, the symbol of Hitler's Germany, into four sectors, each controlled by one of the Allies, even though the city lay in the centre of the Soviet zone of occupation. The Russians reached the city in April 1945, the Americans and British in July and the French a month later. By then the Cold War was already taking grip.

In 1948 the Western powers decided to rebuild the economies of their zones as a bulwark against communism. In June the Russians blocked off all road and rail access to West Berlin and tried to starve it into submission. The Western response was the Berlin airlift. For almost a year all food and coal which the city needed was flown in, aircraft landing during one period at the rate of one every minute.

In the summer of 1949 the blockade was lifted. That year Germany was formally divided into two countries, the Federal Republic in the West, and the Democratic Republic in the East.

Throughout the 1950s an increasing number of people left the East. In 1960 two hundred thousand crossed to the West, mostly through Berlin after the border between the two countries had been closed. In the summer of 1961 the figure rose monthly, almost weekly: seventeen thousand in May, twenty thousand in June, thirty thousand in July.

On the night of Saturday 12/Sunday 13 August 1961 East Germany sealed off its half of the city and laid the first blocks of the Berlin Wall.

The Wall itself was four metres high, made of interlocking

concrete sections, each reinforced, the top rounded to prevent hand-holds. It was placed two metres east of the border line, allowing a footpath west of the Wall which belonged to the East, with concealed doors to allow access to the path.

The death strip, on the east side of the Wall, was some forty metres wide. At the foot of the Wall was a stretch of raked sand, to show footprints of intended escapers, next to it a five-metre-deep vehicle ditch, then a fifteen-metre stretch of grass, followed by a patrol road for Frontier Troop vehicles, a second grass strip, and a trip-wire, releasing flares if activated. On the eastern side of the death strip were two more walls: an inner mesh fence and an outer concrete wall to restrict viewing. Houses and streets immediately east of the Wall were restricted to trusted Party members.

The entire area was illuminated by floodlights, with watch-towers positioned so that every section of the death strip could be seen from at least one tower. The grass stretches were frequently mined, with machine-guns and grenade throwers activated by trip-wires in some sections.

By the time of its fall three thousand people had been arrested trying to cross it, and nearly two hundred killed.

On the night of Thursday 9 November 1989, the Wall was opened up.

Even today, no one has explained why.

NOTE ON HISTORICAL CHARACTERS
AND REFERENCES

ULBRICHT, WALTER (1893–1973). Fought on communist barricades Leipzig 1919, organized German Communist Party against Hitler. Spent Second World War in Moscow, then sent by Stalin to run Berlin in 1945. Deputy Prime Minister, East German Democratic Republic, from 1949. Chairman of Council of State following abolition of the presidency 1961–71.

HONECKER, ERICH (born 1912). Membership of Communist Youth Movement aged fourteen, full membership at seventeen. Organized activities of young communists against Nazis. Arrested by Gestapo in 1935 and sentenced to ten years' hard labour. Freed by Red Army 1945 and joined Ulbricht faction in Moscow. Central Committee member 1946. As security minister in the politburo, organized construction of Berlin Wall 1961. Designated successor to Ulbricht 1967. Leader of SED and chairman of Council of State 1971–89.

MIELKE, ERICH (born 1907). Joined German Communist Party aged fourteen. At age twenty-one implicated in murder of two policemen and fled to Moscow. Soviet agent in International Brigade during Spanish Civil War. Entrusted with political police and security responsibilities in Soviet zone 1945. From 1957 head of State Security. Politburo member from 1976.

MfS. Ministry for State Security, sometimes known as the Stasi.

KRENZ, EGON (born 1937). Former head of East German Communist Youth Movement. Central Committee secretary for security, youth affairs and sport. Assumed to be Honecker's chosen successor. Key conspirator in 1989 politburo plot.

SCHABOWSKI, WALTER (born 1929). Former editor of Party newspaper *Neues Deutschland*. Party chief of Berlin. Key 1989 politburo conspirator.

KHRUSHCHEV, NIKITA SERGEYEVICH (1894–1971). First Secretary Communist Party of the Soviet Union, the CPSU, 1953–64. Involved in Cuban missile crisis, though introduced certain internal reforms in Soviet Union.

BREZHNEV, LEONID ILICH (1906–82). First Secretary (after 1966 General Secretary) CPSU 1964–82. Hardliner. Replaced Khrushchev in 1964 coup.

ANDROPOV, YURY VLADIMIROVICH (1914–84). Head of KGB 1967–82. General Secretary CPSU 1982–4.

CHERNENKO, KONSTANTIN USTINOVICH (1911–85). Interim, and almost geriatric, General Secretary CPSU 1984–5.

GORBACHEV, MIKHAIL SERGEYEVICH (born 1931). General Secretary CPSU 1985–91. Instigator of glasnost and perestroika.

SHADOWLAND

EAST GERMANY

AIR CORRIDOR →

FRENCH SECTOR

To HAMBURG

Tegel

EAST BERLIN

BERLIN

AIR CORRIDOR →

BRITISH SECTOR

Gatow

WEST BERLIN

Tempelhof

SOVIET SECTOR

GLIENICKER BRIDGE

AMERICAN SECTOR

POTSDAM

AIR CORRIDOR →

To HANOVER and MUNICH

EAST GERMANY

BERLIN 1945 – 1989

BRITISH ZONE

BERLIN

POLAND

WEST GERMANY

EAST GERMANY

FRENCH ZONE

AMERICAN ZONE

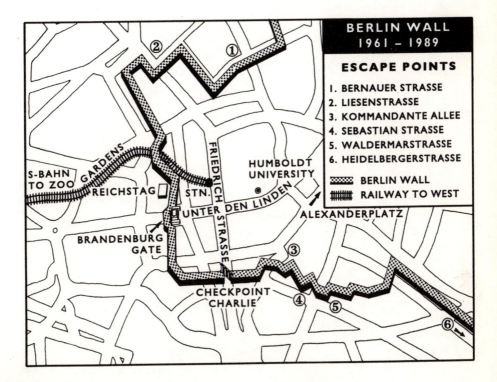

BERLIN WALL
1961 – 1989

ESCAPE POINTS

1. BERNAUER STRASSE
2. LIESENSTRASSE
3. KOMMANDANTE ALLEE
4. SEBASTIAN STRASSE
5. WALDERMARSTRASSE
6. HEIDELBERGERSTRASSE

▨▨▨ BERLIN WALL
▥▥▥ RAILWAY TO WEST

S-BAHN TO ZOO

GARDENS

REICHSTAG

FRIEDRICH STRASSE STN.

HUMBOLDT UNIVERSITY

UNTER DEN LINDEN

BRANDENBURG GATE

ALEXANDERPLATZ

CHECKPOINT CHARLIE

PROLOGUE

THREE IN the afternoon. East Berlin, November 1989.

In an hour the light would begin to fade and the people would begin to gather.

The General was eighty-two years old and had headed State Security for the past thirty-two of them. He was thinly built, with sharp eyes which now darted round the conference table at the men he had recruited over those years. The men who had served him well and been rewarded with control of the country and seats on the Collegiate. All old now, except the two.

He looked again at the photograph. 'Who is he? Find him for me.'

Four in the afternoon. Bonn, West Germany.

The Chancellor sat behind his desk, the light fading and the reports already coming in from the East. Leipzig, where it had begun. Magdeburg, Halle, Dresden.

'How many?'

'How many where?'

'Berlin.'

'A hundred and fifty thousand.'

'And he's there again?' There was something about the man in the photograph which haunted him.

'Yes.'

The Chancellor turned to the two people in the world he most trusted. 'Who's behind him and what do they want?'

Washington. Eleven in the morning Eastern Standard Time, five in the afternoon Central European.

The shadows hanging like ghosts in the recesses of the Oval Office, and the reports updated constantly.

'Karl-Marx-Stadt, Plauen and Erfurt on the move.'

'Berlin?'

'Two hundred thousand.'

Satellite intelligence reporting major troop and tank movements in East Germany. Signals picking up heavy traffic between Moscow and Berlin. The Pentagon arguing readiness and the State Department counselling caution. Strategic Air Command querying Defcon Three status and recommending upgrade to Two.

The three men and one woman watched and waited. If the President moved too soon he would provoke the Soviets; too late and he risked going into history as the man who allowed his country to be caught with its trousers down.

Three weeks to Thanksgiving and the Macey's parade, the President suddenly thought, then the run-in to Christmas.

'Go to Defcon Two.'

The next report came in. 'A quarter of a million on the streets of East Berlin and growing.'

'What did Trotsky say about Berlin?'

'It was Lenin.' The woman was blonde, in her early forties, a power-dresser, padded shoulders and slim gold necklace. 'The world was Europe, Europe was Germany, Germany was Berlin.'

And Berlin was the Wall.

He picked up the photograph. The man was in his early fifties, strong features but gaunt-faced, as if he had had little to eat. His hair was neatly combed, the style old-fashioned, and he wore a suit, collar and tie, also old-fashioned. The man who had changed it all, the man who had brought the world to the brink of God knew what.

The fourth quarter, the President remembered his college football days. Ten seconds on the clock and somebody going for the big one. One hell of a play, whatever it was.

'So where do we start looking for him?'

At the beginning, the Director of Central Intelligence might have said, but did not.

BOOK ONE

CHAPTER ONE

THE BOY was thin for his age. He sat on the man's shoulders, fingers gripping the jacket collar, and looked at the crowd around them. Tonight they should not have come, the woman knew. Tonight they were right to come because of who and what they were. She controlled the shiver and glanced at her son.

Berlin, September 1948.

Three years since the victorious Allies had divided Germany into zones of occupation, and Berlin, deep in the Soviet zone, into Allied sectors.

Three months since the rift between the Allies had become the Cold War, since the Russians had sealed off the west of the city and tried to starve its people into submission. Since the Western Allies had begun to airlift to West Berlin the food and coal it needed to survive.

Three weeks since the agitators from the East had first tried to stop the councillors from the West taking their seats on the one council which – officially at least – still governed the city.

The sky was blood-red, the first purple darkening in the east. At five in the afternoon they had begun to make their way to the Place of the Republic in front of the remnants of the Reichstag; by seven, as the first politicians began to speak, the square was packed and the people had spread to the sides and spilled into the Tiergarten behind.

The seasons were changing, the unpredictability of summer giving way to the calm of early autumn; yet still the August mood clung on, still the electricity hung in the air and the expectation in the streets.

The woman was in her mid twenties, dark laughing eyes but the skin drawn tight on her face so that her cheekbones were prominent, as if from too little food or too much work. Her clothes were the same, clean and freshly ironed yet thin and worn.

The sky was darker and the red deeper, the purple drawing

over them. The speakers' voices were distorted by the loudspeaker system, almost unreal.

'Heavy?' Lutz was in his late twenties, the age Hans-Joachim's father would have been. His face was lean and grey with tiredness.

'Heavy enough.' Viktor was older, in his early fifties, bigger build.

Lutz reached up and lifted the boy on to his own shoulders.

The council meeting that morning had been scheduled to meet at noon in the City Hall on Parochialstrasse, in the Soviet sector. At eleven the Party agitators had arrived, at first in small groups then in trucks and marching columns. Before the councillors from West Berlin could take their seats the mob had occupied both the chamber and the public gallery. That evening, the news had spread through the city: there would be a demonstration at the Reichstag.

The last speech finished and the crowd began its march, past the Brandenburg Gate towards Postdam Platz. Even when those at the front were four hundred metres past the Gate those at the rear had still not left.

Above the Gate, fluttering in the night sky, Christina saw the Red Flag. In Pariserplatz beyond, the People's Police watched them, some sitting in trucks and others standing, staring sullenly at the marchers. The section of the crowd in front roared and she looked up, saw the figure trying to climb a column of the Gate, trying to reach the Red Flag and tear it down. She laughed and looked again at her son, saw the other movement, casual, almost haphazard. In the Pariserplatz one of the People's Police raised his rifle and squinted along the barrel, as if taking aim at the man halfway up the column.

The section of crowd in front of her reacted immediately, the hunger and frustration and anger suddenly focused, the thin frayed strand of reasoning suddenly snapping. Breaking left, towards the Gate. Not sure why, even less sure what they would do.

The first shots were ragged, disorganized, almost lost, the second echoing in the evening. The frustration of the crowd becoming an anger, the trickle of men closing on the Gate suddenly becoming a tide, surging forward. Those in front unaware what was happening, those behind sweeping those in the middle into the East, some of those in front trying to stop, others carrying the rest with them.

Lutz saw Christina trying to reach them, strained to seize her hand, touched it, felt Hans-Joachim slipping from his shoulders and grabbed his legs. Christina was carried away from them, still holding out her arms, being swept towards the Gate. Viktor pushed his way through, trying to reach her. More shots, more organized this time, more disciplined. Lutz could still see Christina, further away from him now, through the Gate and into the East. Viktor almost to her, reaching for her. Hans-Joachim gripping Lutz tight and screaming for his mother.

The surge from the back was stronger, more determined, the men pushing the women and children aside, trying to reach the People's Police. Shots again. Someone struck Lutz from behind. He felt himself falling forward, the boy catapulting from his shoulders, and fought to maintain his hold. He was on his knees, the crowd around him, over him, but the boy still there. The sky disappeared above them and the crowd swallowed them. He gripped the boy's leg with his left hand and reached up with his right, grabbed a coat, skirt, trousers. Did not care what, who. Began pulling. Someone seized his shoulders and pulled him and Hans-Joachim up. He held the boy tight and looked again for Christina, saw Viktor wave that he could see her and that Lutz should get the boy clear. He banged against a column of the Gate and slid into the space behind. There was another volley of shots, longer this time, almost continuous, and the pace of the tide slackened momentarily. He dipped his shoulder and pushed sideways. The anger was rising again, a fresh charge beginning. He knew he was about to be swept into the East and braced himself against the storm of bodies round him, his back to them and the boy clutched in front of him. The crowd was beating against him, arms and elbows thudding into his back. Then suddenly he was clear, could not believe it.

'Where's Mum?' The boy was almost speechless with fright.

'Mum's all right, Uncle Viktor's with her.' They sat on the ground, tight against each other, the boy too terrified to cry and Lutz trying to draw the breath back into his lungs. 'We'll wait for them at home.'

By the time they reached Bremerplatz it was dark. The rubble was still piled in the middle of the square and the houses still standing around it were like broken teeth against the sky, their frames torn apart by the bombing. Lutz pushed open the door of the hallway, the boy balanced on his right hip, and felt for the light switch. There was no power. Carefully he edged his way up the stairs, keeping to the outside and looking up for the candlelight beneath the door. The flat would not last for long, they all knew: even in summer the walls and ceilings were buckling and in winter they ran with wet where the rain poured through what remained of the roof.

The kitchen was empty, the bedroom which Christina and her son used through a twisted door off it, Viktor's next to it. The table in the middle of the floor was scrubbed clean and the single photograph hung above the fireplace.

Lutz sat Hans-Joachim on the sofa where he himself slept when he stayed the night, and lit a candle.

'Where's Mum?'

'Mum and Uncle Viktor will be back soon.'

He knelt down, took off Hans-Joachim's coat and shoes, and carried him into the next room. 'It's all right, I'll stay with you.' He lowered the boy on to the bed, covered him with a blanket, and lay down beside him, his arm round him. Hans-Joachim curled into his body and held his shirt.

They both heard the sound.

Christina stood in the doorway. Her coat was torn and her face was white. She did not see Lutz, saw only her son and ran to him, collapsed to her knees and held him tight.

Thank God you're safe, Lutz told her. Where's Viktor? he wanted to ask. He left them together and went back to the kitchen. The room was cold. He lit the fire and made coffee, heard her soothing the boy. The electricity came on and Christina came into the kitchen. Even before he stood she crumpled against him, shaking. He sat her down, spooned the saccharin into her coffee and wrapped her hands round the cup.

'Where's Victor?' she suddenly asked.

'He'll be back soon.'

Christina was trembling again, the hot liquid splashing on to her skin. Lutz took the cup from her and wiped her hand.

'The People's Police began shooting. Some people were wounded. I thought I'd lost you and Hans.'

He led her back to the bedroom and told her to sleep.

The night was cold. Lutz sat at the table, a blanket wrapped round him, and stared at the door. At two o'clock, perhaps three, Christina came out of the bedroom and sat opposite him.

'Viktor?' The shock had gone from her voice.

'He signalled me to look after Hans-Joachim then went through the Gate after you.'

'Oh, my God.' Her elbows were propped on the table and her face was in her hands.

'You didn't see him?'

She shook her head. 'I hardly saw anything, didn't know what was happening. Nobody did.' It was her turn to comfort him. 'Don't worry. He'll be okay. He's an old soldier.'

It was four in the morning, still dark outside. He stood up and pulled on his coat.

'Where are you going?'

'To look for him.'

'Wait another hour. It'll be light then. I'll come with you.' She reached across the table and held his hand. 'He'll be back by then, you see.'

The drizzle was settling on the city. At five Christina took Hans-Joachim to the people upstairs; by six she and Lutz were back at the Brandenburg Gate. The morning was grim-grey and raw-cold, the Red Flag hung limply and the trucks of People's Police were lined along the edge of the Soviet sector. They left the Gate and walked to the Franziscus Hospital. The corridor inside the main entrance smelt of disinfectant and the nun was seated at a desk just inside the doors.

'We're looking for someone who was at the Gate last evening.'

'I'll get the doctor.'

There was a way she spoke which suggested that they were not the first that morning. They nodded their thanks and sat on a wooden bench along the side of the corridor. The couple opposite were cold and thin, huddled together. Their faces were colourless and the stubble on the man's face was specked with steel. The woman's coat was threadbare and she sat hunched as if she had forgotten what it was like to be carefree and warm. It was only when the woman looked at her that Christina realized she was staring into a mirror.

The doctor came down the stairs to their right and sat beside them. He wore a crumpled grey suit and carried a brown file. 'You're asking about someone who might have been injured at the Brandenburg Gate last night?'

They nodded again.

'You were there?'

'Yes.'

'So was I.' He opened the file. 'Name?'

'Viktor Wischenski.'

He scanned the sheet. 'He's not with us.' He closed the file. 'Three people were dead when they arrived. We don't know who they are.' Even the care he took could not diminish the impact.

'Where are they now?' It was Lutz who asked.

'The morgue. The attendant doesn't start till eight. I'll take you myself.'

Not Viktor, Christina knew. Not Viktor who despite his massive frame and big furnace-worker's hands sometimes collapsed coughing, scarcely able to breathe, from the day in 1918 when the thick yellow-grey clouds had drifted over the trenches and he had breathed in the mustard gas. Not Victor who had fought with the volunteers against the Russians during the last desperate days of 1945 in the forlorn hope that the Americans would get to Berlin first; who had protected them after, found food for them when there was no food to find. Not Viktor who had taken Lutz as a friend when he had come home from the camps.

The walls of the mortuary were tiled white. There were shallow gullies in the floor from the marble slabs to the drain in the corner, the lights hung above the slabs and the surgical instruments were laid neatly along a shelf at the side. Even though the room had been meticulously scrubbed the smell hung in the air, penetrating the pores of their skin and settling in their hair.

The bodies lay side by side, covered with separate white sheets, the contours visible and the cloth smudged with a dirty red. Christina and Lutz stood inside the door, unsure what to do. The doctor raised the top left corner of the first sheet, looked at the face, then turned to them and shook his head. 'Female.'

He raised the top of the next sheet and turned to them, not speaking. Lutz left Christina, stood by the doctor, and forced himself to look down. The bullet had entered the neck to the left of the windpipe. The hair was plastered over the forehead, the shirt was torn open and the suit was stained brown.

He shook his head.

The doctor lifted the corner of the last sheet. The eyes were closed, the mark of a rifle butt was embedded across the face and the shirt was stained a dark, almost brown, red where the bullet had struck the chest. Lutz turned away and felt his jaw clenching, the hint of tears in his eyes anyway. Christina was by his side. He held her arm above the elbow, to support her, support himself. She looked down and searched beneath the sheet. The hand was cold and stiff. She held it tight and tried to bring the warmth back into it.

'I'll need some details.' The doctor's voice was comforting, the bureaucracy helping them, giving them something to do.

'Of course.'

The photographer came to the flat at four. His newspaper had been given the address by the hospital and wondered if there was a photograph they might borrow. Christina took the picture of Viktor from the wall above the fireplace and gave it to him.

'You *will* return it; it's all we have of him.'

'Of course.'

The article appeared the following morning: the details of those who had died, as well as more descriptions of the shootings and condemnations by the politicians who had addressed the crowd that night.

The photograph of Viktor Wischenski was in the centre. In it he was gaunt-faced, as if he had had little to eat. His hair was neatly combed, the style old-fashioned, and he wore a suit, and collar and tie, also old-fashioned.

At two the next afternoon, in the cemetery near Südstern, he was laid to rest. The suit in which he was buried was the one he had worn the day the photograph had been taken and the weather was like the morning after he had died, cold and raw, the drizzle settling over the headstones and the mound of earth at the side of the grave running wet.

The two men who waited shuffled uncomfortably as the hearse entered the graveyard and came slowly towards them, the head of the horse drawing it bowed and its legs plodding with weariness, the knot of people behind it small and lost – Christina, Hans-Joachim and Lutz, the families from the upstairs flat, and one person from downstairs.

'This is how the city remembers a man who died for it.' The doctor's voice was bitter.

'Politicians.' The photographer echoed the sentiment.

When the funeral was over Christina would ask him if he would photograph the grave; the following day, when he brought the print to the flat, she would ask him for two more. The afternoon after that, whilst Lutz and Hans-Joachim walked in the city, Christina would sit alone in the kitchen and write two letters, the first giving the full details of Viktor's death but the second, for fear of censorship or reprisal, stating only that Viktor had met his death on the evening of Thursday, 9 September. When she had written them Christina would fold them tightly and put them in the envelopes, between the two sheets of stiff card protecting the photograph of the grave in the cemetery near Südstern. Then she would walk to the Kurfurstendamm and post them.

The committal ended and they looked for the last time at the simple wooden coffin, the boy standing between Christina and Lutz and holding their hands, and the rain dripping from the trees. Lutz nodded and the workmen began to shovel in the soil. When the task was finished he knelt and placed the simple wooden cross at the head, the words in white lettering on it.

Viktor Wischenski. 1894–1948. That he never be forgotten.

The others had gone; Christina and Lutz walked away, then hesitated and turned back, stared at the boy. The rain was running down his face, and his lips were tinging blue with wet and cold. His hands were clenched tight and they saw his mouth moving but could not hear his words.

'Don't worry. I won't let them forget. One day I'll make them all remember.'

BOOK TWO

BOOK TWO

CHAPTER ONE

THE COUPLE were in their early thirties. The man carried a case, brown leather and battered, the belt round it saving it from falling apart, and the woman carried the child, two perhaps three years old, weighing heavily on her arms and unsure what was happening.

Hans-Joachim Schiller watched them. There were so many now, every day all day it seemed. Sometimes into the evening, even at night. Some being stopped and taken away but most just staring ahead and walking. Sometime the authorities would stop it, they all knew. Sometime they would have to stop it.

Berlin. Saturday, 12 August 1961.

The couple passed him and turned for the reception camp.

The party began at ten that evening. At two he left and returned to the flat on Vorbergstrasse which he shared with the other students from the Free University of West Berlin. By two thirty he was asleep, the city still and quiet. He woke at three, abruptly and violently, the madman hammering on his door and shouting for him. He stumbled out of bed and across the room. The man outside was a student from his department, the sweat was pouring from his face and he could barely speak with breathlessness.

'Quick,' he managed to say. 'Now.'

The lights round the Brandenburg Gate had been switched off. They stood and waited, the small crowd behind them and the noises in the dark in front of them. Berlin enjoying itself, Hans-Joachim thought, Saturday night going into Sunday morning and the city asleep, at a party or trying to find its way home from one. The dark of the night gave way to the ink-grey of first dawn and they saw the trucks of the People's Police and the squat outlines of the water-cannons. In Ebertstrasse squads of workers from the east were digging up the road, the rumours began. A train had been stopped and turned back at Staaken, the S-bahn had been cut off.

The light grew stronger. They're dividing the city; Hans-

Joachim heard the gasp behind him. They're building a wall through Berlin.

At ten that morning he left the flat, took the S-bahn to Lehrter Bahnhof, and spent the next hours prowling the line between East and West. In Bernauer Strasse, in the French sector to the north, the Russian sector ended at the front walls of the houses on the east of the street, the families looking out of their doors and talking to neighbours as if it was a normal Sunday morning. At the bottom of Friedrichstrasse, in the American sector, the coils of wire were stretched across the old borough boundary. He watched as a group of students returning from the East and unaware of what had taken place had their identity cards checked, two allowed through the opening in the barbed-wire and three turned back. In Heidelberg-erstrasse, further south, the Soviet sector extended across the street to the front walls of the houses in the west. Already troops and workmen from the East had laid a roll of barbed-wire along the street, leaving just enough space for those who lived in the housing to the west to walk along the inside of the pavement, the families from either side looking across the wire at each other and shrugging their shoulders both in disbelief and the sure knowledge that the disruption was only temporary and would soon be over.

Everything was as unreal as the tanks facing each other at the Brandenburg Gate, he thought. He left the area and returned to the Gate. The mood of the crowd there was changing, growing angry. Not simply with the soldiers and workers of the East, but with the Allies in the West, the rumours already growing. In Britain Prime Minister Macmillan and Foreign Secretary Douglas-Home were in Scotland grouse-shooting and saw no reason to return to London. In France President de Gaulle was also in the country for the weekend. In America President Kennedy had determined that there was no reason for immediate action. Even West Germany's Chancellor Adenauer had decided not to come to the city.

Conrad and Rolf from West Berlin; he remembered the other students with whom he shared the flat. Kurt from the East.

By the time Hans-Joachim returned to Vorbergstrasse it was early evening. The Moritz was on the corner. The café was single-fronted, half a dozen tables on the pavement outside. The barman recognized him and nodded to the room at the back. Conrad and Rolf were seated at one of the tables, other students from the university around them.

'Where's Kurt?'

'He's all right.'

Hans-Joachim called for a beer and sat down.

'He went to a party in Pankow.' Pankow was in the east of the city. 'Came back this morning. When he saw what was happening he made a run for it and got through.'

'Where's he now?'

'Checking on other friends from the East.'

The following morning Hans-Joachim was at the university by eight thirty. In the first lecture that morning he tried to estimate how many were missing, in the second the same. At eleven, when he met the others for coffee, the numbers were mounting. Five students from his class alone, three from Rolf's physics seminar. Four students from the West had girlfriends in the East. Three, slightly older, had wives and children in the other half of the city or in East Germany.

That afternoon the mayor of West Berlin, Willy Brandt, was scheduled to address a demonstration in front of the town hall in Schöneberg. Hans-Joachim Schiller did not attend. Instead he walked again along the line which had suddenly divided the city, pacing quickly and anxiously, hands in pockets and shoulders hunched, his hair wet in the drizzle and hanging over his forehead.

In Heidelbergerstrasse the number of Volkspolizei had been increased and the wire barrier appeared to have been strengthened. At the bottom of Friedrichstrasse, the wire had also been reinforced, East German Grepos, border guards, manning the passageway through.

By the time he reached Bernauer Strasse it was seven in the evening. The front doors opening on to the West had been locked, the keys taken and the shutters were fastened. Yet still no one believed what was happening – the impression was vague but accurate – still people appeared to believe that when the city woke the next morning the events of the weekend would be reversed. He stood under a lime tree, not quite sure why, and waited. The evening drew on, the light fading and the drizzle harder, the street empty. He heard the noise and saw the movement. Thirty metres away the window opened and the head peered out then disappeared. He waited again. The window opened and the man dropped down, then turned, hands held up. The bundle which was passed to him was small and well wrapped. The woman dropped down and they hurried into the shadows on the west side of the street.

This is my Berlin, the anger was almost subconscious, this is what they're doing to my city and my people.

During Sunday night and Monday – officially, at least, though he knew that such figures were almost certainly an underestimate – twenty-eight people had escaped across or through the wire into West Berlin. On the Monday afternoon came the first wounding at the new border, an East Berliner bayoneted by guards as he tried to flee along the railway tracks alongside Kopenhagener Strasse.

The following morning, without questioning why, Hans-Joachim Schiller went again to Bernauer Strasse. Overnight the feeling that the division was merely temporary had evaporated: already workmen were cementing breeze blocks against the inside of windows and doors on the ground floor. In the windows on the upper floors the wooden shutters were closed. The crowd watched for a while, then drifted away.

The shutters on the first floor opened slightly and the face looked out, then the shutters closed. The workmen were almost at the house where the escape had taken place the previous night. The shutters opened again, slightly wider and he saw the woman. She was in her sixties, white hair, her eyes staring and frightened. The crowd gathered suddenly, knew what she was going to do, someone shouting at her, someone else running. Stay quiet, he urged, don't alert the authorities. The woman opened the window. The crowd was growing, waving at her to come, someone shouting again. Bolt the door, Hans-Joachim wanted to tell her, jam something against it so they can't get in. The fire-engine braked on the edge of the crowd, the firemen running through and spreading out the safety net below the window.

Jump now, someone, everyone was shouting. Look down, one of the firemen told her. There's a small balustrade below the window. Get on to that first.

The woman nodded, still terrified, and climbed out of the window, feet feeling for the balustrade.

Now just let go. The firemen were looking up at her, the crowd willing her on. She tried to release her grip but froze.

They heard the crash as the door was broken and saw the woman look away from them and back into the room. The Vopos were suddenly in the window, grabbing her wrists. The crowd began shouting, yet no one moved. The woman's feet slipped off the balustrade, the scream splintering the air and her body dangling, then the Vopos began to haul her in.

Still nobody moved to help.

Hans-Joachim bulldozed through, past the firemen, and pulled himself on to the sill of the window below the woman. 'Hold me in place.' The woman's feet were just above him. He stretched up and felt someone hold his legs to keep him in position. Someone else jumped on the sill beside him and reached up. His fingers caught the woman's ankle and locked around them, the Vopos at the top pulling up, he and the man beside him pulling down. He felt her body beginning to move, then the three of them fell back on to the safety net.

The crowd was cheering, gathering round the woman, the firemen checking that she was not injured. Hans-Joachim Schiller left Bernauer Strasse and went for a beer.

The Moritz that evening was packed with students discussing the latest escapes from the East and the details of those with friends or relatives on the wrong side of the wire, the increasing lists of students suddenly missing from the university. Hans-Joachim sat quietly, listening to the others.

It was not his responsibility, he knew some would have said, his responsibility was to the sacrifices Christina and Lutz had made to get him to university; his responsibility was to get a degree and a good job. Not his responsibility at Bernauer Strasse that morning, he knew they would also have said.

At eleven, when they returned to the flat, the others continued the discussion. The curtains were pulled and the door locked. In many ways the debate was little more than a repetition of the many which had taken place in the café that evening. Whether the division of the city was temporary or permanent. If temporary how long it would last; if permanent what could be done to help those stranded on the other side.

Either he opposed the Wall or he did not. Hans-Joachim made up his mind. If he opposed it then he should do something about it.

'The wire is temporary, they'll soon begin to replace it with concrete blocks. We therefore begin by looking for places along the wire where the guards are thinly spread.' He divided the border between the two cities into three sections and allocated one to each of the others. 'Recce tomorrow, we'll discuss possibilities in the evening and I'll check them out the day after.' There was no point hanging around, no point wasting a chance once they'd spotted it. 'We start bringing people out as soon after that as we can. We'll only be able to use each point once, the other side will close it down as soon as they see what we've done.'

Friends of friends, he would reflect in the years to come. And when they were out he would go back to his studies.

'Contact with people in the East.' He turned to the next point. 'The communists are allowing people through the crossing at the bottom of Friedrichstrasse. I'll check tomorrow.'

The American troops were one side of the wire and the East Germans the other, sometimes staring at each but more often appearing to ignore the presence of the other side. Already the Allies had given the crossing a name – Checkpoint Charlie. Checkpoints A Alpha and B Bravo were points on the autobahns into Berlin from the west.

Hans-Joachim Schiller left the U-bahn station and crossed Kochstrasse into Friedrichstrasse. No one else was going through, no one else was even going near the crossing. He walked past the Americans and stopped at the wire.

'Where do you think you're going?'

'Visit friends.'

'Where?'

'Weissensee.'

'Identity.'

Hans-Joachim produced his West Berlin card from his wallet. The Vopo examined it and shook his head. 'No West Berliners.'

He returned the card to his wallet, walked back to the station and took the U-bahn to the university. The refectory was busy, the student he was looking for sitting with a group in the corner. Hans-Joachim bought a coffee and sat down. The group began to leave.

'A word, Max.'

Max Steiner was studying law. He was the same height as Hans-Joachim though a lighter build. His hair was blond, slightly long.

'Trouble?'

It was almost as if Max knew, Hans-Joachim would think later. As if he was waiting to be asked or was planning something himself.

'There are a number of people in the East who might want to come out. We're thinking of helping them.' The two had known each other for eighteen months. 'They're not allowing West Berliners over. I tried this morning but was turned back.'

'So what do you want with me?'

'You're from Stuttgart.' You're from the West. Therefore you don't have a Berlin identity card. Therefore they might let you through.

It would only be in the years which followed, when the world had changed and he and Max with it, that he would reflect on the naïvety of the moment.

'Why not?'

It was what he had known Max Steiner would say.

The American tanks were parked to the west of Checkpoint Charlie, a convoy of Red Army trucks facing them in the East. Hans-Joachim watched as Max Steiner crossed the road and approached the wire. A bus passed along Kochstrasse, the traffic in front of it stopping it at the junction, fumes and black smoke belching from its exhaust. By the time the bus pulled away Max Steiner was the other side of the crossing and walking hands in pockets up Friedrichstrasse. Hans-Joachim went to the Oasis bar on the corner of Zimmer Strasse, on the left as he looked at the crossing. The wire ran down the centre of the street, one half of Zimmer Strasse in the East and the other in the West. From the window he could look up Friedrichstrasse. He ordered a beer and waited for Max to return.

An hour later the West German sauntered back down the road, showed his identity card at the crossing and was allowed through. Hans-Joachim let him pass the bar, checked that he was not being tailed, then followed him to the station.

'Any problems?'

'Not yet.'

The meeting that evening lasted two hours, the five of them grouped round the table in the kitchen and examining the map of the city and the possible crossing points which Conrad, Kurt and Rolf had prepared. At the beginning there were seven sites, by the end the selection had narrowed to three.

'I'll check them out in the morning. By evening Max should have made contact with the people in the East. We'll bring them out on Friday.' Hans-Joachim turned to the West German. 'You're the one taking the risks. You have first choice.'

The law student shook his head. 'Kurt is East. He has family there. He has the choice.'

'My brother.' There was no hesitation.

Hans-Joachim nodded and turned to Conrad.

'My girlfriend.'

Hans-Joachim knew her well. 'Rolf?'

'My girlfriend as well.'

Hans-Joachim made his decision. 'Three's enough for the first run, till we know what we're doing.' He did not ask whether the others agreed. 'Give Max the details.'

The State Security Lada was parked at one end of the road, two lorries of the People's Army at the other, and the Vopo patrol on the pavement opposite. Max tried to remember whether he had met Conrad's girlfriend at any of the parties, and if so what she looked like, and knocked on the door.

The young woman who opened it was blonde, about his age.

'Hello, Ursa.' He recognized her immediately. 'I'm a friend of Conrad's.'

'How is he?' The fear showed in her eyes.

'He's fine. He'd like to see you.'

She understood why he had come. 'I'd like to see him.'

'Tomorrow. The junction of Karl-Liebknecht Strasse and Spandauer Strasse, on the hour starting at ten. I'll meet you and tell you what to do.'

The second address was in the housing complex on Karl Marx Allee, formerly Stalin Allee, where the building workers had begun the rising of '53. Tomorrow, five past the hour under the railway bridge over Karl-Liebknecht Strasse at Alexanderplatz, he told Kurt's brother.

The last address was off Willi-Bradel Strasse. The junction of Karl-Liebknecht Strasse and Memhard Strasse, he told Rolf's girlfriend. Every sixty minutes starting at ten past ten.

The Brandenburg Gate was in front of him, soldiers and People's Police everywhere. He hurried along Unter den Linden and turned left down Friedrichstrasse, making himself walk slowly and trying not to attract attention. Even before he came to Checkpoint Charlie he saw the way the Vopos were looking at him, the Americans on the opposite side. He handed the Vopo his ID and waited.

Rolf's girlfriend won't come tomorrow, he suddenly thought. She won't betray me but she doesn't have the need for freedom that will make her risk her life. The Vopo gave him back his card and waved him through.

The meeting that evening was again in the flat on Breslauer Allee, Hans-Joachim leading the briefing. 'The cross-point is on Kommandante Allee. Max makes the contact between ten and ten past ten, and gives them their instructions. They meet at twelve, on the corner with Beuthstrasse.' The street map was spread on the kitchen table. 'From there they get a good view of the wire. I'll be opposite, behind the embankment. I'll stand once, at five past twelve exactly, to show them that I'm ready and to confirm the cross-point.'

The sense of unreality hung in his mind. Max didn't really cross the wire today. Tomorrow we go to the lecture rooms at the university as we always do. Tomorrow we don't really begin to bring men and women out from the East.

'The guards are normally a hundred metres apart, fifty to sixty metres either side of where I'll be. Sometimes they talk, or walk away to the next guard on the section so that the distance is increased.' He turned to Max. 'Your people should wait till this happens. Once I see them break I'll open the wire for them to come through.'

'Code words?'

'Johnson.' The following day the American Vice-President and the former military governor were due to arrive in West Berlin. 'The reply is Clay.'

Kurt, Conrad and Rolf left for the bar on the corner.

'Why, Max? Yesterday morning, when I asked you. Why did you agree?'

Max Steiner looked at him. 'My father always said he was

opposed to Nazism but he still served in Hitler's army. I always told myself that if I opposed something, I would do something about it.' He shrugged. 'I object to the Wall. Simple as that.' What about you? The question was implicit.

'Anger. My city and my people.' They began to go downstairs. 'What else is it, Max?'

'Rolf's girlfriend. I don't think she'll make it.'

'You mean she won't make it through the wire?'

'No. I don't think she'll make the contact.'

'Tell me.'

The morning was humid, the thunder in the air. At eight fifteen Hans-Joachim showed Max the cross-point, then the two men caught the U-bahn to Kochstrasse. The previous afternoon the first death by shooting had occurred on the Wall.

'The contact is at ten, they come over at twelve. You cross back out at eleven. I don't want you in the East if anything goes wrong.'

They left the station and walked into the daylight. The crossing at the bottom of Friedrichstrasse was a hundred metres away.

'No risks, Max. If Rolf's girlfriend turns up, don't make the contact.'

'Let me decide when I get there.'

'Up to you, but you know what I think.'

Max crossed Kochstrasse and walked into Friedrichstrasse. American jeeps on right and left, the crews looking at him and the Vopos opposite already picking him up. He came to the wire. The Vopo was a sergeant, older face. Leaner and harder. He knows what I'm doing, Max thought, knows what's going to happen. He gave him his identity card, not speaking. The policeman looked at it and turned it over in his hand. Run while you have the chance, the thought shot through Max's brain. The policeman gave him back the card and nodded him through.

Everything was suddenly different, the guards looking at him more closely and the nerves tighter in his stomach. He walked up Friedrichstrasse and turned right along Unter den Linden. The police and army were everywhere. Don't forget the Stasi, he reminded himself, the State Security agents and informants scattered on the streets like confetti at a wedding. He walked on, working out a cover in case anyone stopped him. It was thirty minutes to the first contact. He went to a café behind the university and asked for black coffee.

The nervousness was swelling inside him. Never again, he promised himself. He paid for the coffee and walked to Karl-Liebknecht Strasse. Time moving so slowly, now suddenly so fast.

The woman looked up from the shop window and saw him. He crossed the road and shook her hand.

'Twelve o'clock. The corner of Kommandante Allee and Beuthstrasse. Possibly two other people there, one male one female. The code word is Johnson, reply Clay. The wire is fifty metres away and the crossing point is straight in front of you. The guards are normally sixty to seventy metres either side. There's a small embankment in the West; the contact will show himself at five past twelve exactly then hide behind the embankment. You decide when to go. The contact will open the wire as soon as you make your move.'

If they see her, he suddenly thought, if they don't think they can get to her, they'll shoot her.

'You understand?'

The woman nodded.

'Code words?'

'Johnson, reply Clay.'

'Good luck.'

She began to walk away, then turned back. 'How can I thank you?'

Bloody crazy, he thought. 'Buy me a beer on the K'damm.'

Four minutes past ten, Kurt's brother waiting beneath the railway bridge near Alexanderplatz. Nine minutes past, the junction with Memhard Strasse. No Rolf's girlfriend. Go now, he felt the relief, looked round. Twelve minutes, almost fifteen, time going so slowly. One more minute, Max told himself, give her one last chance.

The embankment was slippery and the gradient sharper than Hans-Joachim remembered; the stinging nettles at the bottom and the houses thirty metres behind him. Twelve o'clock. Kurt with him, chatting apparently idly, Conrad and Rolf in the alley between the houses. He still did not believe it was real, still did not believe what he was about to do. It was five past twelve; he stood and walked casually to the top of the embankment. The houses opposite were grey and colourless and seemed so far away. The guards to the right were a hundred metres away, further than normal, those to the left eighty, ninety, talking to others further along. He turned to go back down the embankment and saw them.

A man and woman, running. Out of the grey into the open. They're coming; he slid down to the wire. Christ, they're bloody well coming. The wire-cutter was in his hand, Kurt beside him, pulling the strands back. The man and woman were clear of the building, forty metres away, thirty. He heard the shouting from the right and knew the guards had seen, those on the left turning. His fingers were wet with sweat, the cutters slipping. The man was in front, running for his life. Kurt pulling the wire and taking the strain from it. Hans-Joachim cut through the last strand and they pulled the gap open, the barbs slicing through their gloves, Kurt's hands red and the blood flowing from them. The first body was coming through, hands out, barbs tearing at his coat. Conrad pulled him clear, someone else suddenly behind him, Rolf pushing them away and clearing space. The guards were shouting, sprinting. The girl was through, summer dress ripping on the wire. The guards suddenly so close. Time to go, get the hell out. They began to let go the wire, Conrad and Rolf already pulling the two escapers away from the wire and up the embankment.

Hans-Joachim saw the third figure. A girl. Slow motion. Seeing the guards but still coming. Coat and dress floating in the wind and hair streaming behind her. Don't leave me, he saw the look on her face, don't let me down. Not one of theirs, he knew, not Rolf's girlfriend. The guards were too close, the girl not going to make it. Go back, he wanted to shout, get back to the houses and they might let you go. *Wait for her and they'll get you both.* He began to turn. *Leave her and you'll make it another day but her face will accuse you for ever.* She was still running, her hands stretching out and the realization on her face.

Hold the wire; he heard his own shout, felt the slack as Kurt began to let go then the tension as he pulled tight again. The girl saw, the slow motion suddenly gone. The wire was cutting through his gloves; he heard the sound of shouting, imagined the burning in her throat and the thudding in her ears. She was coming through, her face and dress a blur. The guards were at the wire, reaching for her, the barbs threatening to entangle her. She was grabbing his hands, pulling herself through, legs torn as they hauled her clear. More people, clustering around them, slapping them on the back. Someone at the top of the embankment cheering.

Hans-Joachim hurried the woman out of sight and into the houses.

I'm sorry about Kati, Max told Rolf that evening, I waited fifteen minutes after the appointed time but she didn't show. Rolf nodded and smiled. You still helped, Hans-Joachim reminded him, you still did your job even when you knew she wasn't coming. Of course, Rolf Hanniman replied.

It was five days to Christmas. The night before Hans-Joachim and Max had sat in the flat and wrapped the parcels: the dolls and small toys for the girls, the perfume for Inga and the whiskey for Rudi. Dangerous, but they owed them.

After Kommandante Allee they had brought three more groups through the wire, then the East Germans had tightened security and strengthened the Wall: the concrete barrier, the death strip and the watch-towers.

For two months after that they had brought people through Checkpoint Charlie using forged West German identity cards, the student Rudi Fischer developing and printing the photographs in the kitchen of his flat in East Berlin and Hans-Joachim and Max applying them to the ID cards while Rudi's wife played with his two daughters in the room next door.

One day we'll get you and Inga and the girls out, they had told him.

Then the East Germans had changed the system, introduced currency exchange forms, one copy given to the person entering East Berlin and checked against a duplicate as they left.

No worry, they still remembered Rudi had said. You'll get us out when you can.

The jeeps were pulled into the right side of the road just before the twin barriers of barbed-wire, the Americans stamping their feet, their parkas pulled tight against the rain and cold and the M16s on their shoulders. Facing them, on the other side of the wire, were the troops of the East German People's Army, the Grenztrabants and trucks behind them and the AKMs hanging from their straps.

Max Steiner walked past the Americans and joined the thin queue of men and women waiting nervously at the barrier. The line shuffled forward; he stepped into the control hut and handed over his identity card and Deutschmarks. The guard checked the photograph, stamped the visa and currency exchange form, and nodded him through. Ten minutes later Hans-Joachim presented the false ID card to the guards and followed Max Steiner up Friedrichstrasse.

The buildings were bleak, police, army and Stasi everywhere. In the shops along the Kurfurstendamm, he thought, the windows were bright and busy and stocked with goods, the coloured lights along the streets. They left Friedrichstrasse, the Brandenburg Gate to their left, and cut across Unter den Linden.

Rudi Fischer would be alone, hunched over the glass of beer at the corner table in the café on Munzstrasse, every pore and cell of his body telling him not to do anything which would single him out yet his eyes darting up the moment anyone pushed the door open. The contact at twelve noon, Hans-Joachim and Max had told him: if they had work for him, if he needed to contact them in a hurry. Security vital, they had insisted: he should always come to the café alone; he should never bring his wife or daughters.

They turned into Munzstrasse.

The girls' faces stared at them through the café window and the Vopo Lada was parked at the next junction, two policemen in it and a third standing on the corner opposite. They divided, Hans-Joachim checking the streets to the left and rear, Max those to the right and front, then met again a block in the direction from which they had first approached the café.

'Five minutes.' Max crossed the road and entered the café, not acknowledging Rudi or his family. The girls looked cold and hungry, as if they had not eaten. He checked the rear then came back through. Hans-Joachim was waiting two blocks away.

'The toilets are empty. There's a door to the street at the back, locked but the key's in it. There's a window in the cubicle, bit tight but you'd get through.'

Hans-Joachim crossed the road and went into the café, choosing a table away from them, but where he could see Max in the doorway opposite, and ordered a schnapps. When the waiter brought the drink Hans-Joachim thanked him then went to the toilets. Thirty seconds later Rudi joined him.

'Stasi.' Rudi spoke almost before the door was closed, the panic showing in his voice as the fear showed in his eyes. 'Came for us two days ago. I was out, Inga was collecting the girls from some friends.'

'How'd you know?' Instinctively Hans-Joachim checked the window.

'Some neighbours warned her. She waited for me down the street.' He was slightly calmer. 'I checked yesterday and this morning. They're still there, in a car, probably in the flat as well.'

There was a noise from the café. Hans-Joachim turned, expecting Max to burst through with a warning.

'Where are you staying?'

'Friends the first night, other friends last night.'

'Tonight?'

He saw the way Rudi shook his head and wished he had not asked. The thoughts were spinning in his brain; Hans-Joachim tried to settle them, organize them into some semblance of order.

'Why did the Stasi come for you?'

'No idea. Perhaps it was something I said, did. Perhaps Inga. Perhaps it was an informant.'

Rudi was beginning to disintegrate again. Pull him together, Hans-Joachim thought; tell him something, anything, that will stop him falling apart and endangering the entire organization.

'It's all right. We're taking you out tonight. That's why Max and I came over today.' Don't ask me why we've brought you a bag of presents if what I'm telling you is the truth, Rudi, don't ask me how I'm going to get you out. Don't ask me anything. 'When did the girls last eat properly?'

'Yesterday.'

Hans-Joachim pulled some money from his pocket. 'Stay until two thirty.' Keep them off the streets as long as possible, away from where the Stasi will be looking for them. 'After that you take one of the girls to the cinema and Inga takes the other to the pantomime.' The Stasi would be looking for a family of four, not two pairs. 'Be back here at five thirty.' Don't give Rudi any options, just give him orders. 'I'll meet you at six. Then we go over.'

They returned to the café, Hans-Joachim allowing Rudi twenty seconds before he followed him. He waited five minutes then paid the bill and left. Even before he had crossed the road Max Steiner saw the look on his face.

'What the hell have you done?'

'I told Rudi we're bringing them out tonight. I told him that's why we came across today.'

It was raining again; they turned their collars against it and hurried along Unter den Linden.

'Why?'

Hans-Joachim told him.

'How?'

'The ladder.'

He knew what Max would say. That they hadn't tested it, hadn't even recceed the section of the Wall where they might use it, checked and re-checked the schedule of the guards.

'Where?'

'Heidelbergerstrasse.'

'As good a place as any.'

Thanks, Max, he wanted to say. They turned down Friedrichstrasse.

'What time?'

'All being well we'll come across at seven.'

The rain was harder, their trousers were sodden and their shoes were saturated. They split, passed through the checkpoint, and met again on the U-bahn platform at Kochstrasse.

'So what time do we go over again?'

'He's expecting *me*, Max, there's no reason for both of us.'

'In that case I'll be on the ladder.'

'Thanks.'

By the time they reached Vorbergstrasse it was almost two. Both the flat and the bar on the corner were empty. They took a cab to the university and divided.

The seminar ended at three. Max Steiner waited till the lecturer left and followed him to his study.

'You have a car with a roof rack which you said I could borrow.' Max came straight to the point. He was wet through; neither he nor Hans-Joachim had dried themselves or changed clothes, and the water still dripped from his coat.

'Yes.' The lecturer dropped the notes on to his desk and sat down.

'I need it now.'

It was the last day of term. 'I'm Christmas shopping with my wife.'

'I need it now.'

'When will I get it back?' The lecturer reached in his pocket and handed Max the keys. No questions, they had agreed, never any answers.

'When I've finished with it.'

Conrad and Kurt were in the library; they saw Hans-Joachim through the glass door, collected their books and joined him.

'Where's Rolf?'

'Refectory.'

It was gone three, the afternoon already edging black. They stopped briefly for Max to change his clothes then drove to the flat, waiting while Hans-Joachim also changed.

'There's a problem, we go tonight. The cross-point will be the northern end of Heidelbergerstrasse, the start point is the bottom of Widenbruchstrasse. The distance from there to the Wall is sixty metres. This afternoon you and Max hide the ladder in one of the courtyards off Heidelbergerstrasse. You return at quarter to seven and check that the area is secure. I collect the escapers and bring them to the start point. Unless something's wrong, you stand by every thirty minutes. On the hour and half-hour precisely Max signals by torch from the top of the Wall that everything's ready, then he stays in position for thirty seconds. If everything's secure in the East I bring the escapers over when I see the signal. If not, you conceal the ladder again and wait for the next half-hour.'

'What about the watch-towers?'

'Luck.' There was nothing else he could say.

'How many escapers?'

'Four.'

'Adults?'

'Two adults, two children.'

The other three guessed but did not ask.

'And once you've got the signal from Max, you'll tell them to run?' They all knew what Rolf meant. 'You won't bring them across the death strip yourself.' You can't, the understanding was clear.

'I don't know.'

Heidelbergerstrasse was quiet, two men sitting in the bar on the corner, a streetlamp above the doorway and a second fifty metres along, above what had once been a baker's shop, their pools of light barely meeting, the Wall down the centre of the street and the cobbles gleaming wet, the blocks of flats grey and massive, almost colourless.

Max drove the car into the street and switched off the engine. The window-front of the baker's shop was blocked up, the name faded on the wall above it. As he stepped from the car the searchlight on the watch-tower to their left swept along the top of the Wall. They unloaded the ladder, paints and brushes and carried them through the hallway and into the courtyard. The smell of cooking came from the flats around them, the lights were sparkling from the windows and someone was singing, a child crying. They covered the equipment with a tarpaulin and left.

Checkpoint Charlie was bleak, forbidding. Hans-Joachim crossed through and hurried up Friedrichstrasse. The top of the street was busy, two men selling Christmas trees on the waste ground below the S-bahn station. It was already dark. He took a tram along Unter den Linden and an S-bahn from Alexanderplatz to Treptow Park.

The streets were badly lit and the pavements and roads poorly maintained, some of the houses still suffering from the bomb damage of a quarter-century before. He began to walk down Elsenstrasse and changed his mind: there was no point risking everything at this stage, especially if the Vopos stopped him and found he was carrying West German papers. Someone was cooking potato and onions. He breathed in the smell and knew how he could get Rudi and his family to the Wall. At least it had stopped raining.

By the time he returned to Alexanderplatz it was almost six and the shops were closing. At a stall near the station he bought two shoppings bags, from another loaves of bread to stick out of the tops, then he took a tram to Friedrichstrasse and bought a Christmas tree from the men under the bridge there.

The café on Munzstrasse was almost empty; Rudi and his family were sitting at a corner table, the plates of soup untouched in front of them, the girls too exhausted with fatigue and the parents too nervous. Wrong table, Hans-Joachim thought; if you're hiding the last place you sit is in the corner. He greeted them as if they were old friends, put the tree and bags down and called loudly to the waiter for a coffee.

'It's arranged. We take the S-bahn to Treptow Park, then walk. When we're in place we wait for a signal, one flash from a torch. When we see that we'll know there's a ladder in position.' What do I do then? Do I go with them or do I leave them to themselves?

'And when we see the signal Rudi and I run with the children?' Inga answered for him.

Thank you, he wanted to say. 'Yes.' Don't ask me about the guards in the watch-towers, don't ask me about the searchlights and the machine-guns. 'Someone else will be there to help you.' You know about the searchlights and the machine-guns, so why don't you ask me why I won't be crossing with you? What motivates you so much that you are prepared to risk even your children on the death strip?

'Why the Christmas tree and the shopping?' There was almost a laugh on Inga's face, brave but superficial, hiding the sadness for her children and her fear of what she would do that night.

'Sometimes they stop people in the streets close to the Wall; if we're carrying a Christmas tree it might look as though we belong there.'

They paid for the soup and left.

The S-bahn station at Treptow Park was quiet. By the time they began walking it was five to seven, the girls staggering with exhaustion and cold and their parents shivering with fear. They turned off Elsenstrasse towards the streets which bordered the death strip. Pity there wasn't more street lighting, make them less suspicious.

The headlights came past them, the car slowing. You live on Kunger Strasse, he whispered to Rudi and Inga, number fifteen. Knew that if they were stopped the information would be checked and they would be finished. The headlights were almost past them. Slowly he turned, as if he was interested rather than almost paralysed with fright. Green Lada. Vopos. The driver wound down his window, the car barely moving. Three men, driver and two passengers, the man in the front passenger seat looking at them and reaching for the radio. The girl holding Rudi's hand waved and showed the driver her doll. The man wound up his window and drove on.

Seven o'clock. Rolf signalled that the street was empty and they carried the ladder out of the hallway and placed it against the Wall. The night was colder, ice forming in the gutter and the cobbles slippery. Kurt and Rolf held the bottom in place and Max climbed to the top. There was almost a metre clearance. At least, he thought, they had got their measurements right, at least they could swing the other section into the East. Watch-towers on right and left, but no movement. He took the torch from his pocket, pointed it towards Widenbruchstrasse, and switched it on, the cardboard tubing taped to the end directing the beam and reducing the risk of it being seen from either side. Ten seconds, fifteen. No reaction from the towers but nothing from the gloom on the far side. Twenty-five seconds, thirty. He switched off the torch and waited to see the figures. A minute, already too long. He climbed down and they carried the ladder back into the courtyard.

Seven twenty. Hans-Joachim crouched in the rubble, only the lights of West Berlin in front of them. West Berlin, the watch-towers and the death strip. Seven twenty-five. He smiled at the girl closest to him and ruffled the hair of her doll. Twenty-seven.

Max pulled the tarpaulin off the ladder.

Twenty-eight.

'Ready?'

Rudi and Inga nodded, held the girls close to them.

Twenty-nine.

The signal from Conrad that the street was clear, the ladder through the hallway and against the Wall.

Seven thirty. Finger on switch, exerting pressure. Hans-Joachim's hand up, ready to wave them on. Rudi and Inga half crouched, child each.

They all heard the noise, the kick-start of the motorbike engine. The patrol left the watch-tower on their left, rider plus pillion, both armed. Cruising slowly and deliberately. Down, Hans-Joachim urged the others. Down, Max signalled to the men below. The family dropped back into the rubble, Max already off the bottom rung and the ladder scraping back into the West. The motorcyclist purred past them, then swung right and back along the cobbles at the foot of the Wall.

'Next time,' Hans-Joachim whispered.

The sky had cleared, the night suddenly and bitterly cold and the stars bright, the children beginning to cry. One minute to eight.

'Ready?'

They nodded.

Eight o'clock. They saw the speck of light opposite, almost lost in the night.

'Go.'

Inga was up and running, the child in her arms in front of her and her coat flapping, headscarf slipping.

'Go, Rudi.'

Inga heard and slowed, realized Rudi was not with her. She stopped, looked back.

'For Chrissake go.'

The man was frozen, his daughter in his arms, unable to move. Inga was putting the other girl down, subconsciously, not aware of what she was doing. As if they were already in the West, Hans-Joachim thought, as if they were on the bloody Kurfurstendamm. The woman was turning back to help her husband, the girl standing in the middle of the death strip, thumb in mouth and doll hanging from her hand.

The searchlight flicked on and swung towards them.

Hans-Joachim cleared the rubble and snatched the girl from Rudi's arms. 'Come on.' He passed Inga and scooped up the second child, one under each arm. The searchlight was coming round and there was the sound of running behind him. He looked back and almost stumbled, saw Inga and Rudi coming after him. Halfway across the strip, thirty metres to go.

The beam of the searchlight passed over the rubble where they had hidden and flicked off.

Hans-Joachim reached the ladder, Inga and Rudi tight behind. Max was at the bottom, inside the death strip. He took the first girl and scrambled half up, passed her to Rolf, astride the Wall, then pushed up the second. Inga after her, Rudi behind. Hans-Joachim was bent double, panting. Max hitched him up and followed him over.

In the night to the south they heard the sound. One volley, silence, then a second. Some poor bastard being shot, Hans-Joachim Schiller thought, some bastard doing the shooting.

CHAPTER TWO

THE NIGHT was cold, the spotlights glaring from the bridge over the canal a hundred metres to the left and the tower a hundred to the right. The border itself ran down the canal. The trees were spaced along the eastern side, three metres of rough grass and mud dropping sharply down to it, the allotments behind and the houses behind the allotments. The first layers of barbed-wire were stretched across the top of the allotments and the second along the bank itself. Yet still they tried to get through, the corporal thought, still they tried to slither through the wire and across the stubble of vegetable stumps, then through the next layer, down the bank and across the sixty metres to West Berlin on the far side.

The corporal was a little over twenty years old, tall, his uniform the green of the Frontier Troops. He and his men had come on duty at four, at six he had made the first tour, at eight he left the barracks and drove south to the section of the Anti-Fascist Wall assigned to his unit.

The rain had stopped and the sky was clear. He stopped the Grenztrabant, pulled the greatcoat tight round him, picked up the AKM, and walked past the bridge, keeping to the shadows. The boys would be out somewhere, hunched in pairs and trying to keep warm, some of them looking for the figures who tried to flit through the defences but most hoping to Christ that if anyone tried tonight they would choose a different section of the Wall.

The fog settled under the bridge and spread in fingers along the canal. Two of the boys beside the tree, the NCO noted, outlines lost against its shape, another two by the next. One of the guards motioned for him to be silent and pointed along the bank.

The woman was almost naked; as he watched she stepped out of her dress and laid it at the top of the slope, the man already in the water and the guards at the second tree also looking. The woman slid down the bank and into the water. There was the faintest sound of splashing and the couple began to swim, the man

42

already pulling ahead and the woman swimming slowly, weakly. The water in the canal was black and freezing cold, the surface oil beneath the bridge a hundred metres to his left shimmering green and the fog drifting towards them. The man was fifteen metres from the east bank, forty-five to the west. The NCO nodded and the lamps flashed on, the harsh glare of the search beam picking out the woman immediately. She turned, frightened, her body flashing white as she rolled over and looked up, then she raised her hand and indicated to them that she was giving in. The beam swept from her and scanned the canal, looking for the man, the fingers of fog suddenly thicker, curling down the centre of the waterway. The searchlight picked up the man, still swimming, trying not to make a noise. Twenty metres from the East, forty to the West. Less than ten before the fog would save him.

'Halt or we fire.'

The NCO's voice echoed across the canal. The man looked back, blinded by the lights, then turned again and saw how close the fog was.

'Over his head.'

The first shots echoed the night. The man half turned then kept swimming. The fog thinned momentarily and the NCO saw again the outline of the canal bank in the West.

'Over his head again, but make it closer.'

The guard next to him raised his AKM and pressed the trigger, the water two metres in front of the swimmer churning white then black again. The man was still swimming, arms working frantically, the fog suddenly thickening and closing again on the canal. The guards to the NCO's right waited, AKMs on automatic.

'Take him.'

It was what they had taught him at the tiny red-brick school off Marienbergplatz, then in the Free German Youth movement and the GST, the militaristic Society for Sport and Technology. That one day he would be called upon to protect the fatherland.

The fog faded into the black as quickly as it came, and the swimmer knew he had lost, hoped it was not too late. He turned, arms raised as best he could to show his surrender, and began to swim back.

'Okay.' The NCO nodded and watched as the search lamp followed the man's progress back to the East and the guards dragged him up the bank.

Where the hell's the woman? he suddenly thought.

The lamps swung across the oil green of the water again, closer to the eastern bank. Nothing, nobody. The woman broke surface, screaming, drawing the freezing water into her lungs, then sinking again, arms flailing and hands and fingers still reaching up. The guards were laughing, not understanding, bundling the man up the slope. The woman surfaced again, more briefly, then her head dipped under. Christ, the NCO swore to himself, she's going to bloody well drown. He pulled off his greatcoat, jerked the magazine from the submachine-gun, unhooked the arm strap, and slid down the bank. The woman surfaced for the last time and he threw her the strap. She saw his outline against the dark and held on. The water was round his waist, the mud of the canal sucking him in and the water suddenly up to his chest. He pulled her in and passed her up to the boys, then scrambled up the bank himself. The woman was shivering, arms folding round her body. He picked up his greatcoat, draped it round her, and looked her in the face.

They all knew what he was going to say. Just like the corporal, they would tell everyone later, made sure the story was passed to the other patrols. A good one, Langer, one of the best.

'Next time you choose my sector, make sure you can swim first.'

Compared to the cold outside the barracks were warm. The NCO pulled off his uniform, left it dripping on the floor, and stepped under the shower.

The formalities after the incident at the canal had taken six hours: the handing over of the prisoners and the preliminary reports, then the bastards from State Security had become involved. Why didn't you shoot the male swimmer when you had the chance, one of them had asked, why give him two warnings?

I'm cold and wet and tired; the corporal's reply was already circulating round the Frontier Troops guarding the Wall. You've got two live bodies and they can tell you far more than two dead ones. I haven't had a hot drink for eight hours and if it's all the same to you I'm pissing off to get warm.

He turned up the pressure on the shower head and enjoyed the hot needles. In the barracks outside a door opened and he heard the captain's voice.

'Good job this evening, well done.'

Typical officer, he knew the section would be thinking, share the credit when the news was good, keep his head down when the shit hit the fan.

'Yah,' he bellowed so they could all hear. 'The boys did a good job tonight.'

He heard the door shut as the captain went out, and slumped to the bottom of the shower, letting the water run in rivulets down him and thinking of the moment he had killed the swimmer in the canal. The man was still alive, of course, being interrogated in some cell in the MfS prisons somewhere in the city. As good as killed, though; he had given the command, only circumstance had decreed that the man had lived. Orders, he told himself, not even surprised that it did not concern him, he was only doing his duty. Three more days, he told himself, then he would begin his Christmas leave, then he would be home in Leipzig.

The woman left the factory and took the tram to the Nicholai-kirche, the Church of St Nicholas, then hurried through the maze of side streets which formed the Old City, across Marienbergplatz and Rosenstrasse, and turned into the small courtyard, the gates always open at the entrance and the cobblestones in the centre. Sometimes Eva Langer looked twenty; at other times the lines etched deep into her face and she seemed older than her forty-five years.

The flat was small, up a short flight of steps to the left of the courtyard; the kitchen, which also served as a sitting room and where Werner had slept as he had grown up and before his grandparents had died, and the two small bedrooms off it. The day before she had bought the Christmas tree and put it in the corner where she always put it, decorated the rooms as she and Werner always decorated them.

The woman from one of the other flats was waiting for her. 'Telegram.' She waved the envelope. 'From Berlin.' Everyone knew Werner, everyone in the local branch of the Party talked of the great things which the future held for the boy from the courtyard. 'Arrived at eleven, I said I'd give it to you.'

'Werner's due home today.' Eva smiled at the woman. 'Anja's meeting him at five.'

She slit open the envelope and saw the words.

*

The station was crowded, the excitement in the air. The woman had arrived an hour early, spending the time looking at the arrivals board above the main concourse and checking the number of the platform at which Werner's train would arrive. She was tall, in her late teens, with blue eyes and long blonde hair, her coat draped round her. The Berlin express pulled in and she waited, scanning the crowds as they poured off, her excitement almost like nerves. The last of the passengers left the train and she felt the confusion, almost the panic. No Werner: perhaps she had missed him, perhaps he had not seen her in the crowd. Eva would know, Eva was like a friend. She left the station and caught the tram to Rosenstrasse. It was getting dark, she hurried – almost ran – into the courtyard and up the steps to the flat.

Eva was sitting at the table in the middle of the kitchen, the fire flickering and the photographs on the wall. She looked up and saw Anja. She doesn't know, she thought; all this time she's been at the station and there's another telegram waiting at her home.

'I'm sorry. His leave was cancelled. I've only just heard myself.'

CHAPTER THREE

THE WINDOW had been broken for two weeks. It was on the third floor, the apartment block overlooking Liesenstrasse in the French sector, to the north of the city. Overlooking the Wall. It was mid February, the snow was lying on the streets and the wind was cutting from the north and east.

Hans-Joachim Schiller started the engine and they pulled out. The second-hand Volkswagen mini-bus had been donated by the father of a student whose girlfriend they had helped escape. It was the way the organization was operating now: gifts, sometimes a little financial assistance, more often items and equipment they needed or which might prove useful. The list of those waiting to escape was growing, yet the rate of escapes was slowing. The Wall defences were becoming more secure, more brutal, and each time they exploited an opening they closed it for ever. More time now had to be spent researching the Wall, making their checks before they even laid the most basic plans of an escape. They turned into Bernauer Strasse and stopped for coffee.

There were three addresses which Hans-Joachim Schiller and Max Steiner had decided might be of help, either because they could be directly involved in an escape or because they overlooked the Wall and could therefore be used in an attempt to spot its weaknesses: the first in Liesenstrasse, a second in Sebastian Strasse and a third in Boyen Strasse. That evening, when they checked, there was a light in the flat in Boyen Strasse and they eliminated it from their list; in Sebastian Strasse and Liesenstrasse, however, the windows remained dark and black.

The following morning, Sunday, they drove to Sebastian Strasse, parked the Volkswagen, and made their way into the block and up the stairs to the flat. The building smelt of must and stale cabbage. Max knocked on the door and they waited. The door opened and a woman faced them.

'I'm sorry to trouble you. Is Bruno in?' He had worked out his story in advance.

The woman looked confused. 'No Bruno lives here.'

'I'm sorry. I must have made a mistake.'

They left Sebastian Strasse and drove to Liesenstrasse. On the third floor the doorbell on the left had a name beneath it, on the right nothing. Max knocked on the right-hand door and they waited. Max knocked again. Still no reply.

The caretaker lived on the ground floor. He was in his sixties and carried himself like an ex-soldier. They apologized for troubling him on a Sunday and said they understood there was an empty flat in the block. He grunted, took a set of keys from a board just inside his door, and led them up the stairs, limping slightly, his irritation at being disturbed on a Sunday clear. The flat was at the back, on the wrong side of the building.

'Where'd you get that?' The reference to the man's limp in Hans-Joachim's question was obvious.

'France. The Falaise pocket.'

'Seventh Army. August '44.'

The caretaker nodded.

'My old man was with the Afrika Korps: 21st Panzer Division.'

The caretaker unlocked the door. Good lads, he looked at them differently. Knew about the old days. Square shoulders, both of them tall and straight-backed, stood with authority and knew what they wanted. Not like some he saw on the Kurfurstendamm nowadays. Like himself when he'd been their age.

'What about the flat at the front?'

'Bit big. Planning a family or something?'

'If that's all right with you.'

There was the faintest touch of conspiracy in the reply. Just like himself when he had been their age, the old soldier confirmed. He locked the flat at the rear and took them to the one they wanted.

'Be down in ten minutes.'

The caretaker left them. They stood in the window and looked out. Liesenstrasse was beneath them, the pavement on the opposite side, then the Wall, beyond it a cemetery. Even in the iron-hard cold of a February morning there were people tending the graves. On the right as they looked was a small chapel, red-brick and slightly dilapidated, close to it a watch-tower. Hans-Joachim felt the nervousness in his stomach and concentrated on the details.

48

The border itself was formed by the old cemetery wall, four metres high, the guards patrolling in pairs inside it. On the right as they looked at it, the watch-tower was not simply *close* to the chapel, it might actually be obscured by it if the position in the cemetery was right, the weakness covered by the patrols. On the left, a hundred, possibly a hundred and thirty metres away, the view from the next watch-tower might be obscured when the trees had some foliage. Along the base of the wall, rolls of barbed-wire prevented anyone getting within two metres of it, the guard patrolling in pairs next to it.

They locked the flat and went downstairs. By twelve the apartment was theirs, at one they returned to the Volkswagen and made their daily tour, looking for weaknesses and examining where they might use the ladder system again. At two they came to the crossing at Invalidenstrasse. The light was fading fast and the air was beginning to freeze.

The rolls of wire stretched on either side of the small wooden hut just inside the eastern section, joining fifty metres either side with the more substantial concrete wall, the guards stamping their feet and rubbing their hands against the cold. Four men in civilian clothes stood near the wire itself, three in their mid twenties and one older. To their left a couple entered the crossing point from the West; in the East, immediately opposite them, a young man approached the guard hut. Behind him a Grenztrabant of the Frontier Troops stopped and an NCO jumped out.

The couple from the West stopped at the wire and held their documents up for inspection. The man leaving from the East reached the guard hut. Abruptly the NCO came up behind him, caught him off balance, and pushed him inside. Ten seconds later he re-emerged, and began issuing orders to the troops outside. In the ice cold they heard the distinctive crack of the safety catches being unlocked.

The NCO left the hut and walked across the frozen ground to the group at the wire, the discussion between them hard, almost hostile, especially between the NCO and one of them. The older man in the group lit a cigarette, allowing the smoke and smell to hang in the air, then he left the wire and strolled nonchalantly to the guard hut, the others following him.

The NCO watched them then turned to face Hans-Joachim and Max. Even in the narrow gap between the top of his collar and the peak of his foraging cap they could see his face, his eyes. *He's the enemy*, Hans-Joachim thought, *he's the opposition*. The NCO was less than fifteen metres from them, separated only by the wire. Bastard. Don't ever forget his face.

The refectory at the university was almost empty, a handful of students drinking coffee between lectures at the table nearest the door. It was March, almost April, the weather warming. Hans-Joachim Schiller and Max Steiner saw the man the moment he appeared in the corridor outside, knew what he was going to do and what he was going to ask them. He bought a coffee and looked around, welcoming the way they moved a chair for him to sit down.

Michael Madetski was in his late twenties. In the daytime he studied chemistry and in the evenings worked at a café off the Kurfurstendamm. His face was thin and his eyes seemed slightly haunted. His wife was called Gisela, his daughters Monika and Brigita, and they lived twenty kilometres east of Berlin, in East Germany. Since the Wall had gone up Michael Madetski had not seen them.

'I was talking to Rudi. He said I should see you.'

They had told Rudi not to talk to anyone, knew that he would but that he would only give their names to those he trusted.

'What did Rudi say?'

'That you might be able to help me.' The other students left, Michael Madetski glancing over his shoulder at them. 'You know my family are in the East.'

They nodded noncommittally.

'I've saved up some money. Rudi said you might be able to take it to my wife for me.'

'Deutschmarks or Ostmarks?'

'Ostmarks. I got a good rate for them.'

'Careful, Mike. There's only one reason why anyone wants Ostmarks and the Stasi soon find out.'

'I *was* careful.' The fear was in his eyes.

'Okay, Mike.'

'When you see Gisela I also wonder if you could ask her something.'

They knew what.

'Could you ask her whether I should go back, or whether I should stay.'

'What do you really want to ask us, Mike?'

'Whether you can get them out for me.'

The meeting was at three and the politician was forty minutes late. Hans-Joachim Schiller sat patiently, smiling occasionally at the secretary. When he arrived the politician bustled past him, barely acknowledging his presence. Only after another fifteen minutes was Hans-Joachim shown in. The man was seated behind a large desk, a photograph of Chancellor Adenauer on one side and a stack of documents, deliberately placed, on the other. He was overweight, the jowls of fat beneath his chin.

'You've got five minutes.' He tried to appear busy and made no attempt to apologize for his lateness. 'What do you want?' He already knew what his visitor wanted.

'Money. As you are aware, I help people escape from the East. It costs.'

There was something about his visitor which unbalanced the politician. 'What's in it for me?'

No one did something for nothing, Hans-Joachim understood, especially politicians. 'Votes.'

'How?' The man was a Christian Democrat on the opposition benches of the city's House of Representatives.

'You provide the funds, and whoever I get out with that money publicly states his, her or their debt to you when you think fit.'

The politician pretended to hesitate. 'How much?'

Hans-Joachim looked at him, did not answer the question. 'That person or persons will also, of course, be prepared to speak in the West.' Even the least significant Berlin politician had national ambitions.

'How much?' There was weakness rather than strength in the repetition.

'Ten thousand Deutschmarks.' He saw the man's lower lip tremble. 'No questions about who, what, when or how. You supply the money and I give you a vote-winner.' He checked his watch as if he was about to leave.

'Done.'

Max Steiner was waiting at the flat on Liesenstrasse. The two

maintained a presence there, though the only furniture was a pair
of camp beds, a table and three chairs.

'How'd it go?'

'Like a cattle market.'

'What did you expect?'

'Something better, I suppose.'

The next day Max crossed into the East.

The cemetery facing Liesenstrasse was in a box bounded on
three sides by the Wall and to the south by Invalidenstrasse. It
was the first thing he and Hans-Joachim had noticed, the almost
natural trap which it formed.

South of Invalidenstrasse the police and army presence was
noticeable but no more than he expected; once he crossed the
street, however, there were Vopos on every corner, always in pairs,
marked and unmarked Ladas parked deliberately and threaten-
ingly every fifty metres, and plain-clothes agents lounging in doorways. In front of him a couple were taken aside by two Stasi. A
hundred metres away, across what had once been a major road,
he saw the Wall and knew he would not get closer.

To his right a woman turned out of the side road leading from
the cemetery. Casually, taking care not to draw attention to himself, he turned and walked back towards Invalidenstrasse. When
he was clear of the security area he slowed and allowed the woman
to pass him. She was old, almost seventy, grey hair tied back, dark
blue headscarf with white spots and black mac despite the early
spring weather. In one hand she carried a shopping bag, one of
the handles slightly torn, and in the other a watering-can.

'Nice day for paying one's respects.' He stood by the woman
and waited for a line of trucks.

'My husband, he passed on ten years ago. I visit him every
week.' She was lonely and wanted only to talk.

'What sort of flowers did you take him today?'

The trucks trundled on. He held the woman's arm and helped
her across the road.

'I planted some daffodils; saved the bulbs from last year.' She
looked up at him and smiled. 'What about you?'

They walked down Friedrichstrasse.

'I wanted to see the grave of an aunt, but they wouldn't let me
in.'

'Of course not, dear. You need a special pass. Too close to the

Wall, you see.' She rummaged in her handbag and showed him the pass. 'You go to your local priest and he writes you a letter saying that you have a relative in the cemetery. Then you take the letter to the police, and they give you your pass.'

'Thank you very much.'

The woman's face beamed with pleasure.

The meeting between Max and Hans-Joachim that night was in the flat on Vorbergstrasse.

'Access to the cemetery is difficult, but because of that security inside might be weak. The first priority is to see if anyone on the list has a relative buried there.'

'What about forging a pass?'

'Difficult. We'd need one to copy, and there might be a register of passes issued. So if our target was using a false pass and the guards checked, he'd be in trouble.'

Hans-Joachim moved to the preliminary details. 'We use a ladder again, three sections hinged together, one to go up the Wall, the second to go across it and the wire, and the third to drop down the other side. The others can start on that now. There's nowhere close enough to hide it so we use a pick-up truck.'

The East already had people in the West, they were aware, informants to infiltrate political parties and industry, even organizations like theirs, as well as lower-grade watchers who reported on items of even the smallest significance near the Wall.

'The guards will be paying special attention to anyone not familiar to them, therefore the target will have to make several visits to the cemetery before the run. We'll need an observer in the flat and a signal system to the target and the pick-up.'

'Anything on the patrol patterns?'

'Nothing yet.'

The following day Max began contacting those who had asked for names of friends or relatives to be put on the escape list. The details he sought from them seemed innocuous; most had been included merely to camouflage the one item he needed. Age, address, occupation, sport, whether or not they could drive or had access to a vehicle, family background. Plus details of the areas of East Berlin where they or their families lived. Where relatives lived or had been buried. After two weeks he had a short-list of three, after another four days he had made his decision.

The escaper would be Jurgen Bley. He was nineteen years old

and an engineering student. There was one other person on the list with a relative buried in the cemetery. What distinguished Jurgen Bley, however, was not simply that his escape had been requested by his girlfriend in the West, but that her father was a senior executive on a national magazine. And that the magazine might assist in the cost of escapes in return for exclusive interviews with the escapers. It was an aspect which appealed to neither of them, but one which both knew they would have to come to terms with if they were to continue.

The weather was changing again, late April, the afternoons sunny and the evenings slightly lighter. That Sunday Hans-Joachim went for lunch in the flat off Bismarckstrasse where his parents lived and where he remembered growing up. Christina was tall, like himself, and good-looking, her figure well preserved. The following year she would be fifty. Lutz was slightly taller and two years older.

'So how's the university?'

The flat was on the fourth floor, the lounge large and well furnished. Lutz poured them each a white wine while Christina finished the salad.

'Fine.' Sometimes he wondered if they suspected.

'And the exams went well?'

'I got through them all.' He had missed one of them and persuaded a lecturer who was a friend of Rudi's to cover for him.

When the meal was over they took the U-bahn to the Kurfurstendamm, getting off at Adenauerplatz and walking east along its length. The tables from the cafés had spilled out on to the pavements, families and couples enjoying themselves. At the western end, where the Romanisches Café and the Kaiser Wilhelm Church had once stood, a new block was being built, though the remnants of the church had been allowed to remain as a monument. They turned left, past the Zoo Gardens and the station there with its U-bahn to Friedrichstrasse in the East, and returned to the square in front of what would become the Europa Centre. A group of children were playing on the steps of the church, opposite them a man in a green Bavarian hat was turning the handle of a barrel organ, the music settling on the late afternoon warmth.

Always the children playing, Christina thought, always a man in a green Bavarian hat and a barrel organ.

The K'Damm was crowded: soldiers, civilians and refugees. Even at three in the afternoon the prostitutes were out, hands on hips and smiling. Some of them wore lipstick and looked like the women they were, Christina thought, others were just like herself, desperate for food for themselves and their children.

Berlin, the early summer of 1945. Hitler was dead and the war had been lost.

Beside the rubble of what had once been the Kaiser Wilhelm Church, a man in a green hat turned the handle of the barrel organ, the music settling on the afternoon.

They crossed what remained of the square, hoping there might be bread or potatoes in the area behind the Zoo Gardens.

It was almost a month since the Americans had entered Berlin, yet still there was hardly any food, still Viktor searched each night after work. The black market was beginning to flourish – for a handful of cigarettes or a pair of nylons a person could get anything – but the ration coupon system introduced by the new administration was not working. Even now, perhaps even more now, the children cried with hunger and the women spent their days scouring the city for whatever scraps they could find.

By the time Viktor Wischenski returned that evening it was past ten. During the period when he had gone to fight, two families had moved into the flat upstairs; when he had returned he had said simply that it was not right for even a single room to be empty while so many had nowhere to live, and had moved in with them, sleeping on a sofa in the kitchen.

Christina spooned the potato soup into his bowl while the others waited to see what he had found for them that day. Viktor was killing himself for them and the boys, she thought. They were so used to seeing him as an old man that they no longer noticed how grey and tired he looked. Triumphantly he pulled a loaf of bread from the bag he always carried and placed it on the table.

That night, when he had finished eating and they had gone to bed, Christina lay awake listening to Viktor coughing in the kitchen. There was nothing she could do to help, she thought, nothing any of them could do. In the bed alongside her Hans-Joachim curled into her for comfort, his eyes piercing her and the hunger still in his face. The coughing died away and she waited for the sound of Viktor's breathing.

There were memories from the last days which would haunt them for ever: the sounds of the battle as they hid in the cellar, Viktor Wischenski's face when he returned, the destruction of the city, the body of the first woman spreadeagled white and naked on the rubble in the square after she had been raped.

One memory, however, Christina Schiller clung to rather than pushed away. In the final days, when the Russians were already in the eastern and northern suburbs of the city, one of the women with whom she and Hans-Joachim shared the flat had returned one evening with the single loaf of bread she had been able to find and her eyes flashing, the excitement on her face.

'A special present.' She had taken the envelope and roses from behind her back.

'Tonight the Berlin Opera is giving its last performance.' She had queued outside the Schauspielhaus since nine that morning, spent the last of their money. 'Tonight I'll look after the boys. Tonight you two have your last night out in Berlin.'

Christina had looked at the tickets. 'The opera? You're mad.' Not just the opera. The Berlin Opera, which had played in the most famous cities to the most famous people.

'It's a mad place.'

'But I've never been.'

'Then it's time you went.'

That night, wrapped in what passed for her best coat, the rose in her buttonhole and the sound of the final stages of the Battle of Berlin around her, Christina Schiller had sat in the half-destroyed Schauspielhaus concert hall and waited. There had been few Party members present, mostly ordinary Berliners playing out their last act of defiance. The orchestra had filed in and they had applauded; the choir, more applause. The conductor had taken his place and bowed to them, raised his baton. In the silence they could hear the thud of the guns. That night the Berlin Opera had performed extracts from Verdi's Aïda and Mozart's Magic Flute, then the last movement from Beethoven's Ninth. In the background, when the music stopped, they could hear the thump of the artillery shells in the suburbs of the city. When the performance ended those in the audience with flowers had presented them to the orchestra. The violinist was young, her age, black hair swept back and his evening suit thin and worn. As he stood, violin in hand and breathless, Christina had taken the rose from her coat and given it to him, the man bowing almost formally and thanking her, both of them close to tears.

Two months later the Americans had finally entered the city, but not before the Russians had raped and pillaged whatever they could, and established the German communist Walter Ulbricht as political head of Berlin.

In the still of the night she heard a boy crying with hunger, his mother trying to comfort him. Christina wrapped her arms round Hans-Joachim and did not know where the thought came from, only that it disgusted her.

The Kurfurstendamm the following afternoon seemed full of soldiers and prostitutes. It was only sex, Christina told herself, and she would not have to do it very often, only when they needed food. The woman on the corner was attractive, no make-up. She was looking nervous, seemingly unsure what to do or say, picking at her fingernails and glancing up and down the street. It's your first time, Christina wanted to say. A jeep stopped and the woman got in. Christina saw the way the woman glanced at her as the jeep pulled away, as if she knew Christina understood.

There were vegetables behind the Zoo Gardens but they could not afford them. No food no option, she thought. Better than the children going hungry. Better than

Viktor killing himself for just a loaf of bread. It won't be that bad, you just lie there and let them do it, then you take their money.

When Viktor returned to the flat that evening it was half past seven. In his bag he carried not only half a loaf of bread but some carrots and potatoes. Thank God Viktor Wischenski had found enough food for them all, she almost cried, thank God she wouldn't have to do it.

Max Steiner's first meeting with Jurgen Bley took place behind the Opera House on Unter den Linden, in East Berlin, at three in the afternoon the following Wednesday. His instructions to the escaper were brief and simple: Bley should contact his priest and arrange the pass to the cemetery off Liesenstrasse where his aunt was buried, and they would meet again in two weeks or so. Then he returned to the West and made his way to the flat overlooking the cemetery.

The window was open, Hans-Joachim seated two metres back from it, in the shadow of the room so he could not be seen from outside, the flask of coffee on the floor on one side of the chair and the binoculars on the other.

'There's a pattern beginning. I'm not sure what it is but it's coming.' He stood up and flexed the stiffness from his shoulders. 'Something about the patrols.'

'When?'

'Early days, but I think it's the weekends.'

That evening Max Steiner made contact with Mike Madetski, the following day he crossed again into the East. The morning was warm and dry, and Alexanderplatz was busy. Only when he was sure he was not being followed did he go to the railway station. The journey took forty minutes.

At ten past three Gisela would leave the flat and walk to the school to collect her eldest child. Max knew the family details from Madetski, had studied the one photograph the man had of his wife and family. Her younger daughter Brigita would be with her.

He left the station and walked to the school. The building was almost lost amongst the houses, halfway down the street on the right, the parents already gathering. He stood fifty metres away and waited. The figures came down the road, the woman in a light blue dress, cardigan pulled over it, and the girl in a home-made skirt, both instantly recognizable from the photograph. The mother was talking to the girl, telling her a story, both of them laughing.

'Hello, Gisela.'

She looked up, startled.

'Mike sent me.'

The colour drained from the woman's cheeks. She bent down and spoke to her daughter. 'Sammi's over there. Why don't you play with her?'

The girl ran off, the mother watching till she had joined the others. Are you really from Mike? It was across her face and in her body movements. When will I see him again?

Max slipped the envelope into her hand. 'Mike asked me to give you some money. He's been working hard, managed to save some.'

'How is he?'

'He's fine.' He wondered how he should say it. 'He wants to know whether he should come home.'

'Or?' She glanced again at her daughter.

'Or whether you'll wait until he can get you all to the West.'

'Tell him we'll wait, tell him we miss him.'

The children were already coming out of school, both girls running towards her.

'It may take months. A year, even more.'

'We'll wait.'

He turned to go, knew the image he would take back with him. The woman suddenly surrounded by children but lost and alone.

'What's your name?'

'Harry.'

'Thanks.' A pause. 'Harry.'

Eight days later Max Steiner made his next contact with Jurgen Bley.

'No trouble with the pass?'

'None.'

'Two things.' Max sat forward slightly. 'The first is that you have to establish a routine. We want you to go to the cemetery between eleven thirty and twelve thirty each Sunday, let them get used to you before we bring you over.' The guards changed at twelve, Hans-Joachim had noted, the pattern a little firmer. 'The second is that we want you to check whether you can see the watch-tower at the bottom of the cemetery from your aunt's grave. If you can, then you must choose a grave where you can't, but it has to be close to the Wall. We also want you to go to the Wall,

in a straight line from the grave you choose, and check if you can
see the tower at the top of the cemetery, or whether the trees
obstruct it.'

He saw the concern in the student's face.

'It won't be a problem. Get a watering-can and go to fill it up.
Look at the other graves rather than the Wall; keep your back to
it if you want.'

'When do I start?' Jurgen Bley's stomach was turning and he
fought to keep down the beer.

'This Sunday.'

The morning was quiet. Hans-Joachim sat in the chair, looking
through the open window to the cemetery opposite. It was ten
thirty, the sun dappling in the trees and the people already tending
the graves. Max brought them both coffee, hot and black, and sat
on a second chair beside him.

At eleven the woman with the spotted headscarf knelt by the
grave and began talking to the person buried there, the guards
patrolling the base of the Wall next to the wire glancing across
and one of them smiling at her. If she dropped her watering-can
and ran for the Wall the man would shoot her, Hans-Joachim
thought.

The routine of the guards was mechanical, the lines the patrols
took always the same. In the shadows of the trees they saw the
figure and recognized the escaper. Wonder if he knows we're looking at him, Hans-Joachim watched him, wonder what he's thinking. His own throat was tight, the blood pumping and his nerves
tingling.

The escaper was carrying a shopping bag. Slowly he walked
round the graves, looking at the headstones. The guards at the
Wall glanced across at him, not recognizing him, concentrating on
him. The escaper glanced at a headstone and stopped. Right grave,
wrong position, Hans-Joachim sensed instinctively. Jurgen Bley
looked round and walked on. Ten metres closer to the Wall was
a grave topped by a white marble angel with half-folded wings,
the grave itself neglected and the grass growing untidily around
it. They saw him stop again, look at the name then look around
him, and put the bag on the ground. The guards were still looking
at him. He left the grave and walked towards the Wall, stopping

just short of the rolls of wire, then turned left and went to the small chapel at the bottom of the cemetery and tested that the water was working. The guards turned away and continued their patrol. Jurgen Bley returned to the grave, took out the shears and begin to trim the grass from the base of the angel.

The NCO left the patrols and walked away from the Wall. He hadn't seen him before, Hans-Joachim thought; the man must have come in to the cemetery while he and Max were concentrating on the escaper. The corporal sat down at a bench, took out a letter and began to read it. Hans-Joachim looked again at Bley and saw him tidy the grass trimmings.

'Christ.' He picked up the binoculars, made sure he was seated far enough into the room so that the sun would not reflect in the lenses, and focused. 'It's him.'

'Who?'

'The bastard at the Invalidenstrasse crossing.' He remembered the face, the way the NCO had stared across the wire at them, and passed the glasses to Max.

'You think he's on to us?'

'Who knows?'

In the cemetery the soldier looked up from the letter.

'Girlfriend?'

'If it is, I hope to Christ I never meet her.'

The soldier folded the letter, put it back in his tunic pocket, and walked away.

The following Wednesday Jurgen Bley confirmed that the ground between the angel and the Wall was blind to both towers. What about the corporal who sat on the bench close to you? Max asked him. The man hardly noticed him, the escaper replied, he was too busy reading.

Hans-Joachim saw the opening on the second Saturday in May. It was not that he had not seen it before, rather that it had not existed. Because of this he delayed telling Max until it was repeated on the following Sunday.

'Normally the shifts overlap, the outgoing one stays in place until it's replaced by the incoming. Yesterday it changed.' He had almost forgotten how long he had looked for the break. 'Yesterday the outgoing shift left the Wall and met the incoming guards at the watch-tower by the chapel. For a minute, almost ninety seconds, the Wall was unguarded.'

His excitement infected them both.

'Same today?'

Hans-Joachim nodded. 'Christ knows why. Perhaps there's a game of football, perhaps they have some girls lined up.'

'You think it's just weekends?'

'Yes.'

'So what do we do?'

'Confirm it next Saturday. Go on Sunday.'

The following Wednesday Max Steiner told Jurgen Bley that he was doing well and that all was going to plan.

When? he knew the student was going to ask.

'Possibly this weekend.' He explained the shift system and the weakness which Hans-Joachim had identified. 'Next Sunday arrive slightly early. In the West, immediately opposite the cemetery, is an apartment block. Look for the window on the second floor down, six in from your left. The curtains will be drawn. When they're pulled back the escape will be under way. Twenty seconds after that a ladder will come over the Wall exactly opposite you. When you've started to run, don't stop for anyone or anything.'

At five minutes to twelve the next Saturday Hans-Joachim Schiller, Max Steiner and Rolf Hanniman sat anxiously in the lounge of the flat on Liesenstrasse and waited for the moment the guards in the cemetery would change. At one minute to twelve the two guards left the cemetery and walked quickly to the watch-tower at the side of the chapel. At twelve exactly the incoming guards took their place. By one the rest of the escape team was being briefed.

The night was warm and none of them slept. Dawn was at five, at eight they sat down to breakfast and made do with coffee. At nine Rolf went to the flat on Liesentrasse, the curtains drawn from the night before. At ten Max collected and checked the pick-up, the morning dragging.

Half past eleven, time suddenly speeding up, going quickly. Through the crack in the curtains Rolf saw the student kneel by the grave next to the angel and begin weeding. Fifteen minutes to go. Jurgen Bley took the shears from the bag and began cutting the grass, his back to the Wall. Along the track at the side of the barbed-wire the guards turned and continued their patrol pattern. Ten minutes to twelve. Jurgen Bley worked his way round the

grave, still cutting the grass. Five minutes to twelve. Rolf Hanniman saw how the escaper had planned it. The student stood up,
walked to the other side of the grave and began trimming the grass
again, facing the Wall.

Four minutes to twelve. Michael Madetski took his position.
Three minutes. Hans-Joachim, Conrad and Kurt in place. Two.
They saw the pick-up coming up the road. The vehicle stopped,
engine running. They climbed in the back and pulled off the
tarpaulin.

No signal. Twelve exactly. Still nothing. Max Steiner's fingers
were clamped round the steering wheel and his foot tapped gently
on the accelerator, clutch in. No signal but no shots or shouts from
the other side of the Wall. One minute past, the new shift in
position by now. Two minutes. Rolf came round the corner and
walked past them, shook his head.

'Bastard.'

They had returned to the flat on Vorbergstrasse.

'It was going perfectly. The kid was good, worked it so that he
was facing the Wall at the right time. One minute to twelve,
slightly before actually, the guards slope off and I'm almost pulling
the curtains. Then the bastard shows.'

'Who?'

Hans-Joachim and Max knew.

'Some NCO. Just appears from nowhere. Sees there's no guard
on the Wall and stays there until the new shift comes in. Ructions,
I tell you. Somebody's in for it tonight.'

It was the second weekend in June.

'There's a pattern again.'

The moment Hans-Joachim had entered the flat they had all
known.

'Same?'

'Not quite.'

The evening was warm and the sky a brilliant blue.

'The outgoing shift still waits for the incoming shift to relieve it
at the Wall before it leaves the cemetery. The pattern starts before
that.' He took the beer Rolf passed him and drank from the bottle.

'The bastards are still up to something on Saturday and Sunday afternoons. But because they daren't push off early any more, they talk about it instead.'

It was going to be even tighter than before, he knew.

'There are two guards on duty, always on the move and always making sure every part of the Wall is covered.' He put the bottle on the table. 'At ten to twelve yesterday, for the last patrol of their shift, they changed. They met in the middle and walked back to the top together. Same today. Just once. But enough.'

'So that for the last patrol of the shift the bottom half of the Wall is unprotected?' It was Rolf.

'Exactly.'

'For how long?'

'Twenty seconds, perhaps thirty.'

'So what do we do?'

'Same as last time. Check on Saturday, go on Sunday.'

The night before it had rained. The grass was wet and the knees of his trousers were damp where he had knelt to weed the grave. Jurgen Bley moved slightly so that he could see the Wall and looked up. Ten minutes to twelve, he did not dare check his watch. The guards were coming from the corners of the cemetery, almost at the middle. The last patrol of the shift. Without thinking he put down the trowel and picked up the watering-can. The guards slowed and met, glanced across at him. Bloody stupid, he thought, holding a watering-can after it's been raining. The guards turned and began to walk together up the cemetery, towards the top corner. Eighty metres before they reached the top and turned, he began to count down, seventy-five metres, his eyes suddenly fixated by the Kalashnikovs on their shoulders. Second floor from the top, he remembered the instructions, sixth window from left. He looked at the apartment opposite and saw the moment the curtains were pulled back.

Max Steiner saw the way Michael Madetski's head turned, pulled away before the lookout had moved his hand to take the handkerchief from his pocket. Across the junction, Hans-Joachim, Conrad and Kurt pulling the tarpaulin off the ladder. He reversed the pick-up on to the pavement and slammed on the brakes. First section of ladder already against the Wall, second section going up. The ladder was heavy and awkward, the third section making it difficult. He snatched on the handbrake and climbed to the back. Hans-Joachim pulled himself on to the Wall and hauled the second section up, muscles suddenly straining and heart pounding.

Jurgen Bley saw the ladder and the figure. The guards still walking away.

The second section was in place, just clearing the wire on the other side, the third still hinged back. Kurt handed him the broom and Hans-Joachim leaned out and pushed the section away from him so that it dropped down the other side of the wire.

The guards were almost at the top of their walk, about to turn back.

Jurgen Bley dropped the watering-can and ran. The ladder was swinging in the air above him, sticking out from the wire. He jumped and tried to reach it. Missed. Jumped again, fingers only just grabbing the section and pulling it down. At the top of the cemetery the guards began to turn. Jurgen Bley did not even look, concentrated on the ladder, was scrambling up it before the bottom had even touched the ground. Up the first section, across the top, the rolls of wire beneath him. He was over the wire and on to the Wall. The guards were seeing, running. Hans-Joachim grabbed him and bundled him over into the pick-up. Max was back in the cab, people already stopping in the West, a police car suddenly appearing at the top of the road.

Hans-Joachim felt the elation and raised his arms in victory. In the back of the pick-up the others were dancing, Jurgen Bley bemused, almost in shock, hugging them. Hans-Joachim saw the figure running through the trees of the cemetery and knew who it was.

Got you, you bastard. Said I would and now I have.

CHAPTER FOUR

THE SNOW WAS lying on the streets and the wind was cutting from the north and east. Two o'clock on a Sunday afternoon in February, the light already fading and the air beginning to freeze. Langer left the barracks and drove to the crossing at Invalidenstrasse.

Trouble, he sensed, the boys relieved to see him.

Four men in civilian clothes were near the wire itself; three were in their mid twenties and one older, in his late thirties. A couple were entering the crossing point from the West. In the East a young man – similar age and dress to three of those by the wire – approached the guard hut. In the West, on the opposite side of the wire, two men stood and watched, one big-built and dark-haired and the other blond.

Trouble, he knew for certain.

The couple from the West stopped at the wire and held their documents up for inspection; in front of him the man leaving from the East reached the guard hut. Langer switched off the engine and came up behind him.

There was something about the man, about the men by the wire. 'Inside.' He caught the man off balance and pushed him into the hut, bundled him into a corner and against the wall. 'If he moves nail his feet to the floor.'

He stepped outside again. 'You two, over there.' He indicated a position thirty metres to the left of the hut. 'You two there.' A second position twenty metres to the right. 'Safety off. If those bastards by the wire even touch it, shoot.'

He left the hut and walked to the four men. 'What's up?' He faced the group.

Nothing more needing to be said, the older man knew. He was thinly built, with sharp eyes that missed nothing. One of the younger men reached inside his overcoat to the inner pocket of his jacket, withdrew a leather wallet and opened it for the NCO to inspect.

65

The man was in his mid twenties, thick-set with dark eyebrows, the hair patching between them. Intelligent, thought Langer, more dangerous than the others by far. The fingers which held the identity card were thick and powerful, black hair along them.

Gerhard Meyer, he read. MfS. Ministry for State Security.

Meyer was not one of his team, the older man thought. Meyer was one of those recruited by Moessner, but Moessner was in Moscow and he was looking after the other man's department.

'I suggest you move.' Langer faced Meyer.

'And why do you suggest that?' There was an arrogance in the voice.

The eyes of the older man flicked to Langer.

'Because if anyone tries to escape you're in our crossfire.'

The older man turned and looked at the disposition of the border guards.

'One of yours as well?' Langer indicated the guard box.

The older man took a silver cigarette case from the inside pocket of his overcoat, selected a cigarette and lit it, breathing deep on it and allowing the smoke to hang in the air. 'I'd imagine so, wouldn't you?' He breathed again on the cigarette, exhaling slowly and deliberately.

'I'll leave it to you.' Langer watched as the three younger men walked away and the older man made his way to the hut.

Twenty metres in front of him, on the West side of the wire, the other two men were still watching him. Not Stasi but trouble anyway. Register their faces. Remember them for next time.

'All right your corporal, isn't he?' In the guard hut the older man chose the most inexperienced of the unit and slipped into a familiar routine. 'What did he say his name was?'

'Langer.'

The party to celebrate the birth of the new nation was to be held on the Saturday afternoon. On the Wednesday of that week the government of Walter Ulbricht had announced the formal creation of the German Democratic Republic, thereby finalizing the division of Germany into two countries.

The parents assembled after school, most of them Party members. On the Friday evening they cleaned the walls and scrubbed the floors, and began to put up the first decorations. At eight the following morning they assembled again, some of the fathers who were carpenters beginning to build the stage at one end of the hall, and the rest

– men and women – continuing the decorating and preparing the food. At ten o'clock they stood back to review their progress, some of the mothers coming round with mugs of coffee.

'Thanks for helping. Last night as well.' It was the branch secretary.

'Wouldn't have missed it.' On three occasions the woman had asked Eva Langer to join the Party; each time Eva had made an excuse and declined.

The party began at three, an hour of games, then tea, and a show on the stage they had built that morning, the parents and children sitting in rows on the floor. Anja and her mother sat two rows from the front, the girl's face beaming with excitement, Eva and Werner four rows behind.

The magician was standing against the far wall; his face was painted a deathly white and the black moustache and beard he wore were bizarre and exaggerated. Someone's father: Werner half heard the mother behind him, did not hear the name. He looked back at the stage, then again at the magician. On the far wall one of the older boys pointed to a parent and the magician nodded. The previous act finished and the magician took the stage, the children clapping with delight and anticipation.

Not one of the boys pointing at one of the parents, Werner felt the cold of the shock, one of the bully boys from school pointing at Anja and her mother.

The magician put his hand into the top pocket of the teacher's coat and pulled out a long line of flags, then reached behind the teacher's ear and produced an egg. The children were already rocking with laughter, their parents joining in.

Not Anja, Werner Langer felt the foreboding, not in front of everyone. Eva felt her son fidgeting and saw the way he glanced at the magician then at the other boys.

Anja eats horse-shit. He still remembered the day they had begun to pick on her at school, the way they tipped the meagre contents of her lunch box on the floor, the way no one would sit with her.

She doesn't really eat horse-shit? he had asked his mother that night.

No, Eva had replied.

Then why does her mother collect it on the street?

Because Anja's mother's very poor. She dries it and burns it on the fire.

So why does nobody sit with Anja at school?

What about you, my son? He would never forget the tone of his mother's voice. Do you sit with her? Are you her friend?

For the next hour the magician pulled rabbits out of hats and paper flowers out of handkerchiefs, using boys and girls from the audience as his assistants with card tricks, tearing sheets of newspaper apparently haphazardly and giving them to those who helped him then standing back and clapping as they opened the sheets to reveal the shapes of animals and stars, once a face like his own.

'For my next trick I need someone with plenty of money.'

The parents laughed.

'You madam.' The magician pointed to a woman behind Eva. 'No, you've probably only got ration coupons.'

The parents laughed again.

'You, sir.' The magician pointed to a man. 'No, you'll hit me if I get it wrong.'

The children were screaming with delight, some of the parents almost crying with laughter.

'You madam.'

Anja's mother.

'I need a note.'

Werner saw the terror in Anja's face, the way the boys were looking at her, laughing at her. The woman was searching in her purse and pulling out a note.

'Only one Ostmark. Not much for a lady of your substance.'

The other parents were laughing. Not Anja's mother. Werner saw the teacher offering the magician some notes, any notes, trying to distract him from the woman. The magician was off the stage, bending over her, taking the purse from her.

'Ten Ostmarks. That's better.'

That's all she has. Werner watched Anja's face.

The magician tore a corner from the note and gave the purse back. 'A round of applause for my very attractive assistant.' He made her stand up and turn round as the audience looked at her and clapped. When the clapping stopped he gave her the corner he had torn from the note. 'Look at it. On it you will see the number of the note you gave me. Hold it in the air, keep it there so that people can see it.' She did as he instructed. From his pocket he took an envelope, placed the note in it for all to see, asked Anja's mother to confirm that it was inside, then sealed it and climbed back on to the stage.

'Two more volunteers.'

He called the man and woman he had originally approached, again asking for applause for each, then gave the woman the envelope and asked her to hold it against the light so that everyone could confirm the note was still inside. From his pocket he took another envelope, gave it to the man, asked him to check that it was empty, then instructed him to seal it and hold it so that everyone could see.

Anja's face was white, trembling.

The magician took a cigarette lighter from his pocket, lit it and held it under the envelope the woman was holding.

'Everything okay?' He glanced at Anja's mother, laughing at her the way his son laughed at her daughter.

The flame of the lighter touched the envelope, the paper beginning to singe, suddenly burning. Anja's face was tight with fear.

The magician took the envelope, turning it so that the flames engulfed it, then *faced the man and asked him to open the second envelope. They all knew what would happen, wondered only how the magician had done it.*

'Tell me what's inside.' The magician's tone was confident, exaggerated.

The man peered inside the envelope and shook his head. 'Nothing.'

Anja's face collapsed completely.

'Sorry.' The magician shrugged at her mother. 'I'm sure you won't miss it.' He felt in the inner pocket of his jacket and took out a gold cigarette case. 'After that I think we both need a cigarette.' He offered the man a cigarette and lit it for him.

'Just a minute.'

The magician plucked the cigarette from the man's mouth, examined it, again with a theatrical flourish, and slit open the paper. Rolled inside was a ten Ostmark note, one corner missing. The magician crossed the stage, gave it to Anja's mother and asked her to check the number of the note with the number on the corner she was holding.

'It's the same.' The woman could barely speak.

The magician straightened then bowed, the audience bursting into applause.

Why choose her – Eva saw the way the teacher looked at the magician – why spoil such a good day? She looked at Anja and saw the way she was looking at Werner. Looked at her son's eyes and wished she had not.

The barracks were warm, condensation running down the windows. Langer switched on the television and rested his feet on the bunk in front. Gymnastics, state opera after; he switched channels and sat back in the armchair. The door opened and the group came in, stamping their feet affectedly as if they had spent time outside in the cold, the platoon captain escorting them.

Another visiting party, he knew. Army general, somebody from the politburo and a representative of the mayor's office. Always the same. Except for the fourth man. He swung out of the chair and stood to attention.

'Interesting television programme.'

He remembered where he had seen the man before.

'West Berlin TV?' The politburo member's face showed his astonishment.

Cover yourself, the captain. Cover us both and I'll only have half your ass after.

'Of course.'

In the so-called old days East Germany had listened to West German radio, now they watched its television programmes.

'Name?'

Typical functionary from the mayor's office, Langer thought, ingratiate himself to the senior Party members present even if it meant jumping on some poor squaddie. The others were waiting, the fourth man standing slightly back and watching all of them.

'Cigarette?' The man reached to an inner pocket, took out a cigarette case, opened it, selected one for himself and offered the NCO one, not extending the courtesy to anyone else.

'Thank you.'

The man offered him a cigarette lighter, also silver; Langer lit the cigarette then handed the lighter back.

'You've misunderstood.' He turned to the functionary, not even the slightest hint of apology in his voice. 'I'm a border guard, my job is to stop people fleeing the state.' He was careful not to use the word *escape*. 'One way of stopping people going over the Wall is to find out how others do it. I know how those I arrest try, but I don't have any idea how those who succeed manage it.' He noted the way the fourth man's eyes flicked to the minor official from the mayor's office then to the politburo member. 'Each week West Berlin television carries interviews with those who've left the East, plus details of how they did it. They tell me what I need to know, or at least part of it.'

They stood and watched. A student from the Max Planck High School who had climbed on to the side of the Warsaw-Aachen express as it crossed the viaduct over the River Spree, an engineer who had spotted a security lapse in some allotments in the north of the city, and a second student who had crossed the Wall in the south.

The interviews ended.

'Know what you want?' It was the general.

'For the moment.' Langer leaned forward and made a show of switching channels and the visiting party prepared to leave.

'But you prefer gymnastics.' The man from the mayor's office was pale-faced and wore spectacles.

'All right if you like little girls in white.'

November had been bleak and cold. In December, therefore, the local branch committee had decided that the annual end-of-term party should be special. For this reason the committee had met every week, planning and organizing, and raising funds. In many ways their plans, when finalized, resembled those for the celebrations which had marked the birth of the nation four years before.

On the Tuesday before the party was due, Eva returned from the organizing committee with an official schedule of games and activities.

Seventeen months before, Werner's teacher had bought her a drink as she sat watching the boys playing football in the square near the Nicholaikirche and asked her why she had not joined the Party. Why should I join? she had replied. For the sake of your son, he had told her. That evening, after supper, Eva Langer had gone to the house of the woman who was the local branch secretary and said that she wished to join. Three months later she had been called to the office of the manager at the factory where she worked and informed that she had been promoted. She was unsure whether this was because of her efficiency or her Party membership, but thanked him anyway.

'Mum?'

'Yes.' Eva had settled by the fire and was mending a shirt.

'Is the magician coming?'

'Yes.'

'You know the trick with the money that the magician did?' It had taken him six months to work it out.

'Yes.'

'Do you think he could do it again?'

'I expect so.' She concentrated on the mending.

'Mum.'

'What now?'

'Make sure it's someone else asks him.'

The party began at three, the children excited as they arrived, the afternoon already growing dark and the snow falling from the sky. The hall was warm and brightly decorated, the stage at one end. Games, tea, then entertainment. Werner Langer joined in, behaving mechanically, the nerves eating like worms at his stomach.

The magician arrived, placed his case in the classroom at the side of the hall then stood close to the trestles where the food had been placed. Werner crossed the room, the others running and shouting around him, and stood by the door. The magician was talking to one of the teachers. The boy checked one last time, went into the classroom, and closed the door behind him.

The room seemed cold, quiet, the sound of the party muffled. He felt the pounding in his ears and the churning in his stomach. The magician's case was on the teacher's desk. He opened the locks and lifted the lid. The black coat was across the top. He removed it, not disturbing the folds, and laid it on the desk, making sure there was no dust or chalk which would attach to the coat. The paraphernalia of the magician's trade were laid neatly below: the make-up bag, the packs of cards, the coloured handkerchiefs and paper flowers and flags. He moved the items and saw the gold cigarette case. *The thudding had gone from his ears and the nerves from his stomach; he was aware of every decibel of sound and every movement of air.* He opened the case and saw the cigarettes.

The trick was so simple, he wondered why it had taken him so long to see it. Two switches, both at the beginning, then the apparently random selection of a cigarette at the end. Everything else a smokescreen. There were five cigarettes in the case, neatly and firmly in place. Each cigarette containing a rolled bank-note with the corner missing, he had calculated, the cigarettes placed carefully in sequence according to the denomination of the note inside, each denomination covered.

He checked the door then changed the cigarettes round, changing the sequence but making sure they were packed tightly together with the tops even, as he had found them. Then he closed the cigarette case, placed the other items round it, laid the coat back on top, and closed and locked the lid. The thumping was back in his ears and the nerves in his stomach. He stood by the door and felt the trembling in his hands. Then he opened the door and slid back into the hall.

The tea and games ended and the children and parents sat in rows on the floor facing the stage, clapping the singers and applauding the magician as he took his place. For half an hour he enthralled them with his skills, the card tricks, the paper flowers appearing from handkerchiefs. He's not going to do it, Werner thought. *The hard-boiled egg from someone's ear, the fluffy white rabbit from nowhere, given to a child to hold.*

I need a volunteer with money. You, madam; no, you only have ration coupons. He's going to do it, he's going to do the trick. *You, sir. No, you'll hit me if I get it wrong. Both standing, bowing to the applause. You, madam, you look as if you have plenty of money. Stand and take the applause. The routine was familiar and the pattern slick.* Corner switched while the audience looked at the woman who had given the magician the money; the boy's brain worked coldly and logically. Switch folded paper for note, even switch envelopes. *He tried to see which, saw nothing. Two helpers, man and woman, two envelopes. The fire eating through the envelope with the money, the gasps of horror and the offer of a cigarette from the gold case.*

The magician took the cigarette from the helper's mouth, slit it open, and unrolled the note inside for all to see. Smiling, laughing, bowing to acknowledge their applause. Seeing, realizing. Everyone seeing, realizing. The magician's face turning pink, bright red, purple.

'That's what I call magic.' *They all heard the voice from the back of the hall.* 'Took Frau Hildebrandte's one mark and turned it into fifty.'

The visiting group left the barracks, the wind gusting through the door as they went outside. Werner Langer picked the cigarette from the tin lid which served as the barrack ashtray and looked at the name round the filter. Camel. American, available only in the West.

'The corporal we met earlier, the one with the television set.' It was an hour since the group had finished their tour and fifty minutes since they began to take refreshments in the mess. 'What's his name?'

The incident at Invalidenstrasse when a Frontier Troop corporal had pointed out to a State Security officer that he was in his crossfire, Dieter Lindner could have told the captain. The episode at the canal just before Christmas when a Frontier Troop NCO had told a Stasi lieutenant that he was wet and cold and that if it was all the same to State Security he was pissing off to get warm.

He lit a cigarette, offered the captain another vodka and took one himself.

'Langer, sir.'

Of course, Lindner said, as if he did not know.

The weather in Leipzig was warm and the spring was in the air. Anja's exams had gone well: she had finished the final paper with twenty minutes to spare, enough time to check her answers and add some refinements. In the summer she would graduate, then she would need to find a job. She crossed the square, passed the Nicholaikirche, and hurried to the flat. Her mother was working the late shift; recently Anja had begun to worry about her. Nothing specific, perhaps to do with the hours she worked or the pay she received. A month before she had talked to Anja about moving, said she had received an invitation from relatives to visit them in East Berlin, suggested that the two of them might like to go during the holidays.

The letter from Werner was waiting for her. Anja devoured it, as if it was the most important thing in the world, and replied that evening.

*

73

Langer left the barracks and waited for the driver to pick him up. His last letter to Anja had been short, he was aware. It was as if he was allowing events to control him, he sometimes thought, allowing circumstances to carry him along. It was not too late, he told himself, he would make time, sit down and write a long letter, one in which he believed rather than the factual details with which he made do nowadays. And he would arrange a leave, insist on taking it. The Trabant jeep stopped; he jumped in the front passenger seat and tried to push the worries about Anja aside.

A week before he and his men had been shifted north, to the line of the Wall bordering the French sector. Since then he and the other NCOs had been busy familiarizing themselves with the new ground and trying to anticipate the holes which they had inherited or which their lack of familiarity would create.

The cemetery was cool and quiet. He told the driver to wait at the main gate, walked through, and sat on a wooden bench at the side of one of the pathways running between the graves, looking at the rolls of wire at the foot of the Wall and the apartment blocks beyond it in the West.

The examination results were outstanding, though they did little to lift Anja's spirits. Her mother seemed even less happy in Leipzig than before; she had shown Anja the letter from her sister inviting them both to join her in Berlin. As if to encourage them the woman had mentioned a job vacancy she had seen at the Humboldt University Library and suggested that Anja might wish to apply for it. And there was Werner. Rather, there was not Werner. Perhaps it was the upset over Christmas, perhaps that he had still not received any leave, so that they had not seen each other since he had gone away. And their letters suddenly seemed shorter, still full of facts and information, but somehow missing the feeling which she used to enjoy in them so much.

The Humboldt University Library: she laughed at the thought. The most famous university in Berlin, the most prestigious library in the country. She would never get the job, even if she decided to apply. But if she got it she would be in Berlin, and if she was in Berlin she and Werner could be together again.

She sat down and wrote the letter of application.

The evenings were shortening and the smell of the autumn hung in the air. That summer, in the warm and balmy days of August, when the school was finished and the boys and girls played and swam together in the river, Eva had sat on the bank and watched how Werner and Anja were growing. How the contours of the girl's body were showing beneath her costume, especially when she was wet and her hair was hanging back over her shoulders. How the boys, even those who had once bullied her, looked at her. Yet how she still only saw Werner, how he still only saw her.

Each morning, when they walked to the river, Eva had seen how the two held hands. Casually, almost carelessly, as if they were not even aware of it. Each afternoon, as the sun relaxed them all and they grew tired and listless, she had seen how they draped their arms round each other. Each evening, as they walked back from the river, she saw how they said goodnight, as if they were not really saying goodnight. As if the summer days by the river would never end. Yet the August had gone into September, and now the September into October.

In the cities, towns and villages of Hungary the men and women had risen against the Soviet army and the secret police. On the streets of Budapest the people were celebrating their freedom. On public buildings the Red Star had been hauled down and the national flag hung in its place.

Each night Anja sat in the flat in the dreary grey block where she and her mother lived and listened to Radio Free Europe. The news that the government of Imre Nagy was negotiating with Moscow for the withdrawal of Soviet troops, that already Nagy was talking about the ending of the one-party system and the advent of a full democracy. Each morning she confronted Werner and told him of the day freedom would come for them all.

Monday, 5 November 1956

Eva began work at eight and returned home at six. Werner's grandmother was sitting in the chair by the fire where she always sat and Werner was reading, hunched over the table by the window. The stew Eva had made before she had gone to work that morning bubbled on the stove and the wireless played in the corner next to the fire.

'Bastard.'

She looked up and saw Anja. Her hair was streaked across her face and her eyes were red where she had been crying, yet crystal clear with anger. Werner was standing, turning to face her, trying to ask her what had happened, the girl pummelling his chest and shouting at him as if he bore the responsibility.

'What's up? What's going on?' He tried to hold her arms, tried to stop her.

She tore free and turned to the radio, kneeling in front of it and re-tuning it. Trying to pick up the broadcasts from the West. 'The Russians attacked at dawn. The people are being killed in the streets. The soldiers are shooting them, the tanks are running them over.'

You're being melodramatic, he wanted to tell her. If the Russians have gone into Hungary, he would say later when they walked in Marienbergplatz by themselves, it's because they had to, because they had to protect us all. The Russians are not protecting anyone but themselves, she would flash her anger at him. Who ran down the workers in East Berlin in '53? Who ordered the courts to find the innocents guilty and condemn them to be shot in the grey of the dawn? You're hysterical, he would shout at her, you listen too much to what your mother tells you. You're crazy, she would scream in reply, you only believe what they teach you in school and in the Party meeting and at the youth weekends the Party takes you on.

It's all right, he told her, lifted her up as if his mother and grandmother were not looking at them.

Everything will be fine, she told him, slipped her hands under his arms and round his back as if the two women did not exist.

Anja in Berlin: Langer laughed, was unsure what he was really feeling. Leave in six weeks, he reminded himself, then he would go home. This time nothing would stop him. He folded the letter, put it back in his tunic pocket, and joined the convoy for the cemetery. The weather was warmer, the second week in May.

In front of him the truck with the boys stopped at the watch-tower. He began to pull in behind them then changed his mind and drove on to the iron gate which was the main entrance. Sunday morning, wonder what the old girl with the fancy headscarf is planting today? He parked the jeep and walked into the cemetery.

It was ten minutes to twelve, almost five to. There were no patrols, no troops in sight. He knew what the stupid bastards had done, knew that the outgoing patrol had left the Wall early and was talking to the members of the incoming unit at the foot of the watch-tower. The Wall exposed and unguarded. He stepped forward and took their place.

Twenty metres away the young man left the grave and filled his watering-can.

The two letters to Anja were on the kitchen table. The first was from Werner; even before she opened it she knew what it would say, the things he would talk about. Perhaps he doesn't have time any more, she thought, perhaps my letters to him are the same.

Perhaps it's inevitable. She opened it and tried to tell herself it would be different, felt the excitement. He was coming home on leave. He had arranged it, made sure that nothing would interfere with it. Perhaps they could choose a ring, he suggested, perhaps they should become engaged.

She opened the second. It was from the Humboldt University. Dependent on her passing the final examinations at the end of her course, she was offered a post in the university library, beginning the next academic year.

Her mother was still working. Anja left the block and ran to tell Eva.

Two weeks today and he would be on leave; two weeks today he would be arriving in Leipzig and Anja would be waiting for him. Langer parked the Grenztrabant at the cemetery gates and switched off the engine. The morning was hot, the sun high in the sky. Perhaps we'll walk in the fields, he thought, perhaps we'll swim in the river.

He heard the shouts of the guards and grabbed the Kalashnikov. The woman with the headscarf was standing bemused. The marble angel was on his right, the watering-can discarded halfway to the Wall and the ladder was hinged across the wire, a young man scrambling up and over it, the man astride the top of the Wall pulling him over then raising his arms in triumph.

I know you, know where I've seen you before. Trouble, he had known at Invalidenstrasse. Trouble, he knew again. My day will come, you bastard, and then I'll have you.

The station was hot and crowded. Anja had been waiting an hour. Please not again, she prayed, please may there not be a telegram waiting for me at home. She made her way through the crowd and waited at the end of the platform. Five minutes to go, she was wearing the blue dress she knew Werner liked and her stomach was churning. He'll be in uniform, of course; not for her but for the members of the local branch of the Party; they'd want to talk to him, admire his corporal's stripes and ask him about Berlin, tell him what they were doing in Leipzig. She saw the train, two minutes early, saw the men and women getting off. Saw Werner.

No uniform, plain jacket and open-necked shirt. He saw her and waved. She pushed her way through the crowd and ran to him.

The farewell party for Werner would begin at eight. Eva had arranged the school hall and found a band. Most of the people would be Werner's friends though some would be members of the Party who had been his mother's friends over the years.

She stood in the window, looking down at the courtyard and remembering how Werner and Anja had walked down the street to the tram stop. A young man and young woman. Saw again the way they touched hands and looked at each other, smiling and laughing, almost afraid to smile and laugh. Talking, joking, almost afraid even to speak. Remembered the way their bodies moved and the electricity leapt between them.

August, 1961.

Werner and Anja left the bus and walked towards the fields, the city behind them. The day was hot and the road dusty, Anja's dress as blue as the sky, white buttons, flat shoes. They stopped and faced each other. Kissed. Long, as if nobody else in the world existed. Walked on, drifting apart then together again. The trees hung over the lane and the fields were yellow with corn. They kissed again, longer, harder. Werner slightly taller than Anja, tilting his head slightly, she hers.

The people have a right to leave. But the people also have a duty to stay.

For weeks now they had read and heard the reports of the numbers of people fleeing to the West, argued about it.

Everyone has a right to freedom, to stand on a railway line and want to travel along it. But what if that person is the only doctor in the village? What if he or she goes to the West and the next morning a child in the village is taken ill?

It was as if the conversation did not exist. As if it should exist because it was part of them. They held hands and helped each other over the gate.

That's what the Party tells you to think. What happens when you're in charge of the Party? What will you do when the people want to leave and you're in charge of the tanks?

The corn was tall around them, the perfume from the flowers in the hedge heavy, almost intoxicating. They knelt, facing each other, her arms around his neck.

'Goodbye, Werner.'

Her shoes had fallen off and the cloth of her summer dress was thin and tight. He kissed her again, holding her face, fingers gentle on her cheeks, lips hardly touching, not moving. She kissed him again, mouth open, wet. Felt the way he was shuddering, knew she was shaking the same way. He ran his fingers through her

*hair, kissed her neck, began to unbutton the front of her dress. I'll want you for
ever, Anja. She slipped her arms from his neck, undid his shirt. I love you, Werner.
You cannot ever imagine how much I want you. The cloth slipped from her shoulders,
he slid it off her arms to her waist and ran his hands over her. I cannot imagine a
time when I will be without you. He bent down and kissed her breasts, gently at
first, then harder, opening his mouth and drawing her nipples in.*

'Why goodbye?' He unbuttoned the rest of her dress and folded it off her.

*'Because tomorrow you begin your military service. Tomorrow you go away for
two years. Because although you mean it when you say you'll come back, you never
will.*

*'You won't come back because you're a member of the Party and one day my
politics will embarrass you.'*

*Her arms were tight round his neck again and their mouths were soft and open,
tongues searching. The dialectic, he had once joked, thrown his Marxism at her, the
coming together of opposites.*

'Of course I'll come back.'

The courtyard off Rosenstrasse was warm, the children chattering
on the cobbles in the middle. Werner and Anja walked through
the arch, arms round each other, and up the steps to the flat.

'Welcome home, Werner.' It was one of the men who lived
opposite.

The wallflowers were growing on the steps; they stepped through
the door and into the kitchen. Everything was as he remembered
– the kitchen, the photographs on the wall and the table at the
window where he had done his homework, the tiny bedrooms off
it – but everything was so small, he suddenly thought, everything
so cramped.

Eva had heard them outside, wiped her hands, and stood to
greet them.

That evening Anja's mother joined them for dinner. When the
meal was finished the four of them washed up and then Eva and
Anja's mother left them, knowing they wished to be alone but
unsure how to phrase it.

The evening was warm, the sun dipped behind the roofs but the
room still light. They sat opposite each other, facing across the
table. Langer rose, locked the door, took Anja by the hand and
led her into the bedroom which had been his grandparents' before

they had died. The room was small and tidy, the bed against the wall under the window. He sat Anja on the edge and kissed her, holding her face in his hands, Anja trembling, running her fingers round his neck and through his hair.

He straightened slightly and undid the buttons of the dress, peeling it from shoulders, holding her breasts, bending again and kissing them.

Why didn't you wear your uniform home, Werner? Why haven't you told me the truth about Berlin and what you do there?

He slid the dress to her waist and slipped his fingers inside her pants, eased them off her, Anja lifting herself slightly so that he could do so.

Why haven't I told you that I belong to the Frontier Troops? Why haven't I told you that I protect the Anti-Fascist Wall, that I give orders to shoot if anyone tries to cross it? Why haven't I said that the only reason I could get leave in the first place was as a reward for a job well done?

He undid his shirt and began to undo his trousers. He was kneeling in front of her, her hands on his shoulders.

She remembered the last time they had made love, the only time they had made love. The day Werner had begun his military service. The day Erich Honecker had ordered into action his plans for the Berlin Wall.

He reached down, fingers running across her stomach and through the tangle of hair, expecting her to be wet and open for him, expecting that she would be moving, would be needing to hold him. To run her own fingers lightly along him, hold him harder. To lie back and guide him into her.

'You want to make love?'

'If you do.' Her body was stiff and her voice was strange, distant.

'What's wrong?' He knew what was wrong.

'Once you were mine. Then I shared you with the Party. Now the Party has all of you.'

He straightened and moved slightly so that she could pull on her dress, and did up his trousers.

'I'm sorry.'

'So am I.'

She was right and she was wrong, he told himself. Right that the Party totally owned him, wrong to think that it should be otherwise.

She would take up the job at the Humboldt University, Anja decided; she and her mother would move to Berlin as her mother's sister had suggested. She would not allow the Party to tell her what to do with her life.

CHAPTER FIVE

THE CAR which stopped outside the block of flats overlooking the cemetery at Liesenstrasse was a Lincoln town car. Three of the men who stepped from it, including the driver, wore the uniform of the United States army. They were in their early twenties, two were black and one was white. The fourth man was in his mid thirties and wore a suit.

It was four in the afternoon, the second Thursday in July, the sky a cloudless blue and the sun hot over the flats. The soldiers were in shirt order and the civilian carried his jacket over his arm, his shirt unbuttoned at the neck and his tie undone.

The driver remained standing by the vehicle while the others went inside. The caretaker was waiting for them; Michael Rossini shook the man's hand, slid him three five-dollar bills and followed him up the stone steps to the flat overlooking the street on the third floor. After the heat outside the cool was welcoming. The woman who answered the door was in her late twenties, hair tucked in a bun; from inside came the smell of cooking and the sound of children. When the group left one of the five-dollar bills would be passed to her, though Rossini would return later with the memorabilia of America, the Hershey bars and the baseball caps, which were prized items even in Berlin.

The American sector covered the city boroughs south of Bismarckstrasse and the 17th June. Liesenstrasse, to the north, was in the French sector. For reasons of protocol permission was always requested for units to enter a sector controlled by one of the other Western allies – normally to show new members or visiting politicians interesting places on the Wall. In this instance the visitor was the junior senator from Wisconsin, Martin Schumaker.

'The woman and her family moved in four weeks ago. Before that the assumption is that it was used as the lookout and signal point for the escape over the Wall through the cemetery opposite.'

Rossini led him to the window and handed him a pair of binoculars.

In the graveyard, Frontier Troops were removing the headstones and coffins and repositioning them further into the East, and Alsatian dogs prowled on long leads against the barbed-wire by the Wall itself. Schumaker focused the binoculars and ran over the details.

'Why the mirrors?'

'You'll know as soon as they see us.'

Schumaker nodded and the soldier continued the account.

'Immediately after the escape, the guards at this section were doubled and the dog run introduced. The assumption is that once they've moved the graves back, they'll put up a proper wall here.'

'Who organized the escape?'

'Nobody knows. There are a number of escape organizations, of course, some professional outfits doing it for money; some of the local mafia are also involved. The feeling is that this group did it for political reasons.'

'Why?'

'Money doesn't seem to have been the object. The story later appeared in a West German magazine, which suggests that they needed financing.'

'But nobody knows who they were?'

'Seems not.'

'What about the flat?' Schumaker edged closer to the window.

'Rented in a false name and paid for in cash.'

'And the caretaker knows nothing?'

'That's what he tells everybody.'

Two evenings after the escape the old soldier had been collected by a man he did not know and taken to a bar off the K'Damm. There Hans-Joachim Schiller and Max Steiner had apologized to him for the deceit when they had rented the apartment, and introduced him to the escaper Jurgen Bley, though no names had been used.

'You believe him?'

The guards in the cemetery saw them; whilst some continued digging two others picked up the mirrors and reflected the sun into the window, dazzling them. Schumaker grimaced and waited for an answer.

'He's a Berliner.' Rossini's reply was oblique. 'Listen to him when he talks about *the boys*. He thinks they did a good job.'

'Do you?'

'Why not?'

The square was empty. It was early evening, the first chill of autumn in the air. During the afternoon it had rained, so that a few leaves now lay wet and sodden in the gutter or stuck to the pavement. There was just enough light; Rossini took the Nikon from his shoulder and shot off six frames.

The houses round the square were five-storey and fashionable, most of them divided into apartments, the goods in the shops at street level high class and expensive, as were the cars parked outside them. He shouldered the camera and looked for number twenty-eight.

Michael Rossini was the image of his father as a young man, a little over six feet tall and athletically built, dark hair parted on the left and eyes that smiled. At school and college he had excelled both at his studies and at sport; when his draft was over he would study law, though it was not his intention to join the firm of which his father was senior partner.

When his draft papers had arrived he had volunteered for the US Airborne, a decision he had made without consulting his parents, only informing them when he had been accepted for selection. After eighteen months in the Eighty-Second he had requested a secondment to the Berlin Brigade. The fact that his mother was German had never previously influenced his life, partly because she spoke English perfectly and partly because he did not view it as unusual – his ancestry on his father's side was Italian and many of his friends could trace their roots to Europe. All he had known was that his mother was from Berlin and that his father had met her there.

Only after he had written home about the Liesenstrasse cemetery escape had his mother asked for a photograph of the square, and even then she had not explained why.

He came to number twenty-eight. On the ground floor was a restaurant, double-fronted and obviously successful, the waiters inside white-coated and most of the tables already taken, even at seven in the evening. The entrance to the apartments above was to the right as he looked, the number on a small blue plaque, six steps leading to the door into the hallway. He stood back slightly and took two shots of the front of the building. Then he crossed to the grass opposite the restaurant, took another three photographs and walked back to the jeep.

Fats was waiting. 'Get what you want?'

Fats Walker had taken the nickname because of a slight resemblance to the singer. There, however, and except for the fact that both men were black, the similarity ended. Fats could neither sing nor play a note and, unlike the man from whom he took his name, every pound of his six-foot-two frame was muscle.

'The light was down, might have to come back some time.'

Fats started the engine, swung the jeep in a tight circle, and headed back for the lights of the Kurfurstendamm. The Mon Cher was off the eastern end; Fats parked the jeep and removed the HT lead from the distributor so that the vehicle could not be stolen.

Berlin was like a well-equipped whore. Rossini remembered the words of the sergeant at basic training – bold and brassy, and what she didn't have wasn't worth undoing your trousers for. He'd seen the West, done the standard tour of the East and come to what he assumed were the correct decisions about both without querying either, then settled down to the normal life of a member of the occupying forces. Eat and sleep in the barracks, American food in the mess and American programmes on the television. Supplies from the PX and the occasional trips to the bars and clubs off the K'Damm.

The street was alive with soldiers and hookers. Guess his father was here once, Rossini half thought. Not the old man, he rebuked himself, not the senior partner in the most blue-chip firm in town. The woman was looking at him. Nice eyes, he thought, too young and too attractive to be on the game. For one moment he hesitated, then he and Fats walked past and into the Mon Cher.

Six thirty in the evening and the beginning of the night patrol along the Wall. The sky to the west was pale pink and to the east purple black. A notice at the beginning of the bridge over the River Spree at Oberbaum carried the warning in English, German and French that beyond it lay the Russian sector, the floodlights already shining on the death strip to the north.

'Waiting for somebody, man?'

Fats was in the front seat, Buffalo and Axe in the back, Rossini driving. Constant radio contact with Brigade HQ – they knew the drill backwards – automatic rifles, empty mags in, loaded mags on webbing, Colts as side-arms, also unloaded, clips in combat jacket pockets. Standard procedure to prevent some madman starting the Third World War.

'If I was I wouldn't be telling you.'

Fats snorted and hung his right foot on the wing. In one of his quiet moments Fats had once confided that he wanted to be a doctor. Rossini knew he would make it, though he was not so sure about Buffalo and Axe. He crunched the jeep into gear and pulled away.

The area to which they were assigned that evening ran from the crossing over the River Spree at Oberbaumbruche to the position north of Checkpoint Charlie where the US sector gave way to the British. They drove north along the Wall, moving quickly, until they reached Potsdam Platz. Where the East German border lay to the west of the Wall, and where any street to the west of the Wall therefore lay within East German territory, they drove around rather than along it.

'Dollar for 'em, man.'

'Not worth it.'

The traffic at Checkpoint Charlie had stopped for the night, only an occasional pedestrian passing through, and then always walking west. On the western side the area to the right of the checkpoint had been cleared; to the left, however, the buildings were still intact, separated from the Wall by a cobbled pavement and half a cobbled street, the other half in the East. Most of the windows had been boarded up. The bar on the corner of Zimmer Strasse, however, had remained open, the view from its windows up Freidrichstrasse uninterrupted. Rossini parked the jeep outside the bar and switched off the engine.

The night was quiet. Perhaps that was the trouble, perhaps that was what had been troubling him. Berlin no longer mattered, even at the Wall, at places like Checkpoint Charlie. Of course the two sides stared at each other and of course there was the occasional incident. But the city was no longer at the centre of a crisis or the crisis itself. The action was elsewhere. The politicians still made their speeches, visitors to the Wall still felt a righteous anger and outrage at it, soldiers like him still felt the adrenaline when they patrolled it. But all everyone really wanted was for nothing to happen.

It was mid evening, creeping dark. He started the jeep and drove south. The Wall at Waldemarstrasse was being repaired, the concrete blocks being replaced in a section running some eighty metres, the barbed-wire strung across the gap and the guards spaced every few metres. They radioed the information to control and stood watching for twenty minutes, then continued south.

At two in the morning they pulled the jeep into the cluster of tall buildings around Luckauer Strasse and drank coffee laced with whiskey in Susie's Bar. At four, with the first grey in the sky, they drove back to Waldemarstrasse and checked the gap in the Wall. At six, with the city coming to life and the guards changing on both sides, they checked Waldemarstrasse again and returned to HQ.

The Humboldt Library was on Unter den Linden, halfway between Friedrichstrasse and Alexanderplatz, and almost opposite the Opera House. Although its walls were still flecked with bomb and machine-gun damage the building had survived remarkably intact. Wrought-iron gates led under its archway to a small and sheltered courtyard inside, an ornamental pond in the centre. A set of steps led from the courtyard to the hallway of the main building, the huge and elaborate marbled steps sweeping up the centre to the floors above.

Anja's section was on the first floor. Each day she arrived early and left late, not to impress her new employers but because she enjoyed both the place and the work, as well as the staff who worked there and the students from the university. In the warm days of early September she had eaten her lunch round the pond in the courtyard; now she usually went with either staff or students to the refectory. Twice, when she had been able to arrange it, she had attended lectures at the university. Sometimes, in the evenings, she would stay in the library and read, then go for a beer or a coffee.

Berlin itself fascinated her, partly because of what she liked about it and partly because of what she did not. Dialectic material-ism, she would have joked to Werner Langer, the synthesis of opposites. In the case of East Berlin the art and theatre of what she thought of as the old world and the military and political repression of the new. Sometimes, on her way to and from work, she looked at the Wall and barely noticed it, at other times even the thought of it made her shiver with an anger and fear she had not known before.

The day was sunny though with a chill. Instead of taking lunch she pulled on her coat and walked along Unter den Linden, stopping at the junction with Friedrichstrasse. Two hundred metres beyond stood the Brandenburg Gate, the guards around it and the Wall beyond. She turned left and walked the thousand metres to Checkpoint Charlie. If this is what Werner is guarding, she could not keep the thought away, if this is what he believes in, then it *was* better that they no longer wrote to each other, that they did not even know where the other was.

That evening she worked late, then went to the bar behind the university. Franz and Johan were in the corner where she knew she would find them. Franky and Johnny – they westernized their names in private, partly because it impressed the girls and partly they said, again in private, as a protest against the system. It was not much of a protest, Anja thought, and the claim was not private enough, though she remarked on neither and still felt grateful to them for befriending her.

Franz was tall, dark-haired, a postgraduate student in the physics department. Johan was shorter, blonder, in his final year of a chemistry degree. They saw her and waved to the waiter for another beer, asked her for the third time that day whether she could make it to the party the following evening.

The flat which they shared with two other students was in one of the back streets north of Unter den Linden which had never been properly repaired. The fronts of the houses bowed slightly and the roof lines were beginning to sag. Inside, however, the apartments were large, two on each floor and extending to the rear of the building.

Even as Anja climbed the stairs to the flat on the fourth floor she could hear the music. She left her coat in a bedroom off the hallway and went through to the lounge. The walls were painted yellow and the room was lit by candles, a fire roaring in the grate. The chairs and sofas were old but comfortable, and there were cushions on the floor. The room was crowded, most of the people students from the university. Franky waved at her and pushed his way through.

'Glad you made it.' He kissed her and took the beer she had brought. 'Let's introduce you.'

Something about Franky, she thought.

For the next two hours, she talked and danced, sometimes with Franky or Johnny, sometimes with others. Some of the records were rock and roll, brought in before the Wall had gone up, others bought from people visiting East Berlin from the West. This is crazy, she thought. I'm at a party in East Berlin. I'm half drunk. I'm dancing to the Beatles, and I'm having a great time. The sweat poured off her face and the fire crackled in the grate.

Not just something about Franky, something about them both.

The food was on a table in the kitchen. She helped herself and returned to the lounge, sitting on a cushion on the floor, her back against an armchair, and looking at the fire, the flames lighting her face.

'You're Anja. I've seen you in the library.' The student was slightly older than herself, longish brown hair and good-looking, his shirt open at the neck under his jacket. 'Actually I asked Franky your name.'

She moved over so that he could sit with her.

'Christian,' he introduced himself. 'I'm at the university.'

Isn't everyone? she suggested.

'You're from Berlin?'

'Leipzig. My mother and I moved this summer. You?' The fire was warm and she felt relaxed and secure.

'Berlin.'

He took her glass and fetched them each another drink. For the next half-hour they sat together, leaning against the armchair and talking. At one point she thought he was going to lean across and kiss her, and did not think she would have objected. Dylan's 'Tambourine Man' was playing. Like to dance? he asked. I'm fine here, she replied. The LP ended and someone put on the Who.

'Very decadent.'

'Depends on the party.' The ambiguity slipped in before she even thought about it.

'You're a member of the Party?'

'No. Yourself?'

He shook his head. 'Your parents?'

'I only have a mother. She isn't. Yours?'

'My father, yes.' He half shrugged. 'Not in any active way. Like most, I suppose.' They stared again at the fire. 'Come and meet some friends.'

He helped her up and they crossed the floor to the group in the corner beneath the window. Christian's hand was on her shoulder and she realized she had slipped her arm round his waist.

During the weekend the wind had died but the weather had become colder and sharper. When Michael Rossini began the day shift at six that morning the faces of the men he was replacing were pinched. He pulled his parka tight and began the check of the Wall.

Overnight there had been a minor incident on the eastern side of the Wall near Potsdam Platz, though the guards in the West had been unable to see the details. At Checkpoint Charlie everything was quiet. At Waldemarstrasse the workmen had almost finished their repairs to the Wall, only fifteen metres left now, border guards standing along the section which still needed work and others supervising the men themselves.

The city was slowly waking, the sounds of the first trams rattling in the chill air.

Typical Monday morning, Langer thought, two of the lads off with flu and the captain panicking. At the end of August he and his men had been moved south, from the section of the Wall including the cemetery at Liesenstrasse to a stretch ending just north of Heinrich-Heine Strasse. He parked the Grenztrabant, pulled up the collar of his coat, and went to check the patrols.

In the segment to the south the Wall was being rebuilt. To ensure that none of the workmen jumped the Wall while it was being repaired, the officer in charge of the section had withdrawn the guards from the watch-tower between his and Langer's section, and used them to supplement the guards on the ground and at the hole in the Wall itself.

The portable shed which the men used as a shelter and where they took their meal breaks was on the eastern edge of the strip. Langer watched as the men left the Wall and walked to the hut, some of the guards following them and three returning to the watch-tower. Then he returned to the jeep and went for breakfast.

Nine o'clock, the Wall quiet. At the site on Waldemarstrasse two West Berlin policemen stood watching the workmen. By the end of the day, Rossini calculated, the job would be finished. Fats started the jeep and they went for coffee.

Ten o'clock, the library was already busy. After the party on the Saturday Christian had walked Anja home; on the Sunday afternoon they had strolled in the Treptow Park, in the evening they had gone to friends of Christian's for coffee.

Franky and Johnny came at ten thirty. Normally they only came in the afternoon, Anja would think later. Franky was wearing a dark blue jacket and white shirt. No overcoat, she would remember. Johnny in a slightly lighter coat, a faint pattern on it, green shirt, no tie.

'Thanks for the party.'

'You enjoyed it?'

They were nervous, she thought. 'Great time.'

At eleven they packed their books and stood to leave. See you later, they normally said.

'Ciao, Anja.'

Twelve o'clock, the Wall at Waldemarstrasse was almost three metres high, too tall for the policemen in the West to look over it. One of them had borrowed a ladder and propped it against the wall of the houses so that he could see into the East. The bricklayers finished the row of blocks and cleaned their trowels. They would finish after lunch and be away by five, he heard the foreman say. The workmen put down their tools and began to walk in a group towards the shed on the far side of the death strip, the Grepos following them, always between them and the Wall, three of the guards moving towards the watch-tower.

One of the workmen seemed to be hanging back, allowing the others, as well as the guards, to pull ahead of him. The policeman sensed what was about to happen and felt the chill, stepped down the ladder a rung, still high enough to see but low enough to run to the Wall and throw the ladder against it and pull the man over, his colleague sensing the movement and understanding.

The guards returning to the watch-tower saw – not necessarily that the man was about to break, simply that there was no one between him and the Wall. Without even looking at them the

workman joined the others. The policeman on the ladder shook
his head and began to climb down. On the far side of the death
strip the workmen were at the door of the hut, most of the guards
by them and the other three at the foot of the watch-tower, going
inside.

The figures came out of the buildings on the far side. Two,
running for their lives. The policemen saw them, tried not to do
anything that would give them away. The workmen were still
gathered round the door to the hut, the guards still with them.
The figures were a third across the death strip, the guards still not
in position in the tower. The men were halfway. One tall, dark hair.
The second shorter, lighter hair. They had spotted the opening the
moment the repairs had been started, the policeman on the ladder
assumed, had waited for the precise moment. One of the workmen
looked up and saw, the expression on his face betraying them. The
first man was almost at the Wall, no breath in his lungs and the
fear and adrenaline on his face. The policeman dropped to the
ground, slung the ladder against the Wall and clambered up.

The shots were wide and inaccurate. The first man reached the
Wall, his momentum taking him half up it and his hands scrab-
bling for the top, the policeman pulling him over. The second man
was slowing, hands already out for help.

Langer heard and swung the Grenztrabant round and down
Heinrich-Heine Strasse.

Rossini heard and reached for the radio. The traffic lights were
red, three cars in front and a lorry coming in the opposite direction.
Fats crashed down a gear, horn blasting and headlamps suddenly
blazing, and pulled on to the wrong side of the road, his foot on
the floor. Incident at Waldemarstrasse: Rossini's voice was calm.
In the back seat Axe and Buffalo snapped out the empty mags
and loaded the full ones. Repeat: incident at Waldemarstrasse.
Fats squeezed between the lights and the lorry and accelerated up
Luckauer Strasse.

The ladder was broken where someone had slid down it. The
jeep screeched to a halt, each of the men automatically assessing
the situation. In front of them a policeman was helping a man
away. Young, short. Light jacket with slight pattern, green shirt.
There were five or six men and women already at the Wall, more
running. A second policeman unwrapped a bandage and threw it

over, the white trailing like a tail across the Wall and hanging from it.

'Two escapers.' He glanced at the Americans. 'One's the other side. They're still shooting at him.'

'He's alive?'

'Yes.'

There was another round of shots; they felt the thuds and heard the scream.

'Fuck that.'

Fats slammed the jeep into reverse, pulled back, smashed into first gear and drove forward, over the broken ladder and against the Wall, scattering the crowd. Rossini climbed on to the bonnet, Buffalo and Axe beside him.

The escaper was jerking with pain and crying for help, the shots splattering around him. The dark blue jacket was torn with bullet holes and the blood had already spread across the chest of the white shirt.

'Cover me,' Rossini shouted to make himself heard. 'For Chrissake don't hit anybody.'

Unarmed he stood a chance, he thought. To his left Axe and Buffalo began firing; Fats left the engine running, and joined them. Rossini grabbed the medi-pack, pulled the Colt from the holster, handed it to Fats, then climbed on to the Wall and dropped down the other side.

They're starting the bloody Third World War, Langer thought. He screamed the Grenztrabant off the tarmac and on to the death strip.

The shooting stopped. Michael Rossini heard the engine and glanced up, then down again. The face of the man on the ground was draining white, the eyes looking at him and the lips trying to move. He felt in the medi-pack and pressed the dressing lightly against the man's chest, knew there was no way he could stop the bleeding. The man's lips were moving again, trying to say something to him. His breathing was shallow, growing fainter; there was blood on his face now, smudged round his mouth. Rossini slid his hands under the man's body and lifted him up. The man tried to smile. Thank you, the words only just came out, the face creasing again in pain. A kid, thought Rossini, even younger than himself.

Langer swung the jeep in front of the border guards and jumped out.

They were a metre apart, facing each other.

Langer held out his arms. 'He's mine.'

Rossini felt the body of the boy in his arms relax, the hand no longer gripping his arm in pain, the sound no longer coming from the lungs. Felt the ice which descended upon him.

'He's dead anyway.'

'Time to get the hell outa here, man.'

Rossini heard Fats's voice. He turned, grabbed the man's hand, and pulled himself back into the West.

At four o'clock that afternoon East Germany lodged a formal complaint that its sovereign territory had been violated by members of the United States army; it also filed charges for damage to East German property, caused by American troops firing into the East. At five Michael Rossini was informed that an investigation was under way and that, until further notice, he was stood down from patrol duties. At six, on the assumption that it was better his parents heard the news of a probable court martial from him rather than from any other source, he placed two calls to the United States.

The first to be connected was to the family home. Hanni and Nick senior, pillars of the community, he thought. The successful law practice, the town house in the Beacon Hill neighbourhood of Boston and the cabin in the Green Mountains where they had taken their vacations ever since he could remember. His mother still a head-turner; his father quietly spoken and respected. His mother in particular, he could not shake off the feeling: as if life was effortless, as if everything had come easy.

He heard her voice and calculated what time it was, began to explain, saying that because of his father's position he wished them to know first, and wondering how they would both take it.

'So you went over the Wall?' He thought he heard a chuckle in his mother's voice, could not understand it, only knew it was not what he expected. 'I'm proud of you, Mike.' He heard the choke in her throat and knew she was wiping the tears from her eyes. 'You'll talk to your father?'

'I've booked a call to his office.'

'He's in conference, important people. I'll phone his secretary and tell her to put you through.'

What about the court martial? he had expected her to ask: do you need a lawyer? How will it affect your career?

'Why, Mike, why'd you do it?' The choke had gone from the voice and the chuckle was back.

'You know how it is. You know Berlin.'

'Sure we know, Mike. Sure we know Berlin.'

The Kurfurstendamm was hot and humid, even in the early evening, and she felt tired and irritable. Perhaps it was the mid August weather, perhaps Berlin.

The soldier was about her age, the beginnings of a smile even as he shook his head at someone else and drifted towards her. Not that it mattered, not that anything mattered as long as they paid for it. She caught his eye and confirmed the contact.

Sometimes they asked her to come to a bar, sometimes the price, sometimes just stated how much they were prepared to pay. Sometimes she was glad for a drink first, sometimes she just wanted to get it over with. He stopped in front of her.

'Buy you a drink?'

'Do you have a jeep or a truck?'

'No.'

'Two dollars.'

It was only sex, she had told herself the first time. You just lie there and let them do it. Either that or everyone went hungry.

'Okay.'

She led him to the waste ground behind the Zoo Gardens. God knows what it will be like in winter, she thought. God knows whether I'll be able to stand it in the wet and the cold.

He began to unbutton his trousers.

'Money first.'

He pulled out a wallet and gave her single bills. She lay down and unbuttoned her dress. Her muscles were tight; she licked her fingers with saliva and lubricated herself to reduce the pain as he penetrated her.

'What's your name?' The question took her by surprise. 'Your name,' he asked again.

'How many Berlin whores have you had?' The anger had been growing since the first day, since before the first time. 'How many joes do you think I've had?' Screw me if you want. But don't ask me to be nice to you. Don't even ask me my name.

He rolled over and came into her, ejaculated almost immediately, his shoulders sagging and the rawness of his fatigue maintaining his erection.

The tears were hidden by the hair across her face. 'You've only paid for one.'

He reached to his pocket and pushed a handful of bills into her palm, was moving again, longer, angry himself.

'Why?' she asked.

'Why what?'

'Why did you bastards stop at the Elbe? Why did you let the Russians take Berlin?'

He finished again and came out of her, rolled on to his back beside her. Hanni sat up and pulled on her pants, buttoned up her dress and scrabbled through the money.

'The change.'

'Keep it.'

'I don't want it.'

She rammed the bills into his pocket, aware now that she was crying, not disguising the fact, the sobs deep and shuddering. They were walking quickly, the lights of the Kurfurstendamm two hundred metres away. Her face was streaked with wet and her hair was dishevelled.

'I asked you if you wanted a drink.' He was striding, Hanni almost running.

'Yes.'

The bar was off Wittenbergplatz. The rubble had been cleared and the U-bahn station in the centre of the square had been reopened. He nodded at the two men at the door and led her down the stairs into the basement.

The room was large but poorly lit, tables crowding the floor and soldiers and the women they had brought with them seated at them, others standing between them. The bar was in the wall furthest from the door and the room hummed with music. The soldier took her arm and steered her through the mass of bodies to a table on the right side.

'I need to clean my face.'

The closet was small, the walls were dirty, the basin was cracked and the mirror was broken and covered with grease. At least there was water in the tap. She damped her handkerchief and wiped the stains from her eyes and cheeks, then brushed her hair and went back to the table.

'Bourbon?'

'What's that?'

'American whiskey.'

Anything to take away the taste in her mouth, anything to hide the disgust she felt with herself. 'Why not?'

He left the table and pushed his way towards the bar. For a moment Hanni lost sight of him and saw the way some of the men were looking at her now that she was alone. Christ, how she needed a drink. Next time she would have one before, anaesthetize herself, switch off her mind and her body. The shape was above her, lurching over her. She glanced up. The man fell into the chair opposite her, two others behind her.

'Looking for a good time?' The man was fat, the sweat pouring off his face and *the fingers which held the glass were thick and covered with hair.*

'I'm with someone.' She looked for the soldier and tried to get up, the two other men blocking her.

''Course you are. You're with me. Us.' He laughed at the two men behind her. 'A team job.' He pulled a wad of notes from his tunic pocket and unrolled it. 'Me and the boys always work as a team. How much?'

'She's with me.' The soldier put the glasses on the table. Who says, Hanni knew the fat man was going to say, saw the glance at the men still behind her. His eyes flicked up, at the soldier's face, switched to the insignia on his shoulder then back to his eyes.

'You're welcome.' He pushed the chair back hard, trying to save face, and disappeared into the crowd, taking the other two with him.

The soldier sat down. 'You all right?'

Of course I'm not all right, Hanni wanted to shout at him. She reached for the glass and realized how she was trembling. 'Yes.' The bourbon was hot and searing, making her feel better. She did not know how long the effect would last or how she would feel after. 'Why did he leave?' The glasses were empty, the burning gone from her throat and stomach, and her brain and body beginning to relax. Not relax, beginning to seep into numbness.

The soldier rose from the table. 'Another drink?'

Don't leave me, don't make me sit here by myself for them to come at me again.

'Don't worry. They won't be back.'

He left the table and walked to the bar. Even when he was buying the drinks, she saw, even when his back seemed to be towards her, he was looking. He returned to the table and sat down.

'What was it like?'

The anger flared again. What the hell do you think it was like? Just because you made it twice doesn't mean it was any better for me. It hurts my body and it eats away at my soul.

'Berlin during the bombing. During the fighting. What was it like?'

'I'm sorry.' It surprised her how the anger had led to an honesty. 'I thought you meant something else.' She played the glass round the table and tried to remember, began to tell him. What about you? she asked when she had finished, admonished herself immediately. The soldier was an enemy in her city and she was a whore. He had just screwed her twice, the second time simply to show her that her side had lost the war and his had won. And now she was asking him about the war and his part in it. Asking him about himself.

'On D-Day we dropped at Saint Marie-Eglise at five in the morning, got lucky. We were so dispersed most of us survived. Then Arnhem, the bridge at Nijmegen.

Thought we were the best. Lost a quarter of the guys in the first hour. Never seen anything like it, thought I never would again.'

He finished his whiskey and rose, looking at her to ask if she wanted another. She shook her head and waited. When he came back he placed the glass in front of him and continued.

'Same through Europe, really. Three-quarters of the guys dead or wounded. After a while you don't even miss them.' He picked up the glass and put it down again without drinking.

'What was it like?'

'What was what like? Killing people, being killed? Everybody killed, or thought they did.' Most times it was from a distance, he might have said, most times you couldn't even see the face of the man you were killing. 'How old are you?'

For the second time a question caught her off guard. 'Twenty-one. Why?'

'I'm twenty-two.' My old man broke his balls mending shoes in the North End so I could study to be a lawyer, now I'm Eighty-Second Airborne and I've forgotten how many times I've killed. Rifle, gun, knife. Bare hands. Even now it's difficult to come off the edge. Sometimes it shows, sometimes I can see it in my eyes in the morning, sometimes other people can see it. That's why the fat man left. 'How long have you been doing this?'

'Since the Americans came.'

'Why?'

Because the Americans pay; her head was thick with the bourbon. What the hell do you expect me to say? Because I like the nylon stockings, because after three years of nothing I wanted a good time. 'Two other women and their children, a man who is old before his time, and me. No food and only one way to get it.' She had faced sideways, so that she was not looking at him.

'Do the others know?'

'No.'

They sat without speaking.

'See you tomorrow?'

'Why not?'

The following evening Hanni selected a different dress. The soldier was waiting for her. They walked west along the Kurfurstendamm and found a table at a bar crowded, like all others, with servicemen and women, a pianist playing in the corner. When they left two and a half hours later it was raining. At least she was half drunk, she thought, at least she wouldn't feel much. Do it tonight and the dress will be muddy and dirty; her mind was confused, don't do it and there won't be any money.

'Walk you home?'

Have you got a room where we can go, she knew he meant. 'No.'

'*You'll get wet.*'

'*I'll get wet anyway.*'

'*Tomorrow?*'

She wanted to thank him and tell him she had misunderstood.

'*All right.*'

The soldier reached into his tunic pocket. She felt the disappointment that she had not misunderstood him and the anger with herself for ever thinking otherwise.

'*I thought the kids might like some chewing gum.*'

The next evening they went again to the bar on the Kurfurstendamm. Only as they left did the conversation become stilted and awkward.

'*I'm taking up your time, I should pay you.*'

The subject, or something like it, was bound to come up; she felt disappointed anyway. '*Do you want to do it?*' She knew she had to ask.

'*Yes and no.*'

There was some waste ground on their left.

'*Kids like the chewing gum?*'

'*Sort of.*'

'*No good for the black market?*'

'*No.*'

They walked past the waste ground.

'*Saturday. I'll get some cigarettes.*'

On the Saturday evening they met at the U-bahn station at Uhlandstrasse, then walked east along the Kurfurstendamm and through the Tiergarten towards the Brandenburg Gate.

'*Looked for you on the K'Damm last night and the night before. Didn't see you.*'

'*No.*'

'*Why not?*'

She was unsure what to say. '*My business.*' She knew how he would interpret it. They walked through the Gate, not talking, and stopped at the ice-cream stalls on the eastern side. '*Find someone else?*' The words came out before she realized what she had said.

'*My business.*'

They walked along Unter den Linden, destruction all round them, and turned right down Friedrichstrasse.

'*I've got some cigarettes for you; I can get some rations from the PX for the kids. But I don't know whether I should.*'

'*Why not?*' Sometimes the hardness in her voice frightened her.

'*Because if I do you'll accuse me of treating you like a whore.*'

'*But that's what I am.*'

He seized her arm and spun her round so that she was facing him. '*If that's what you are, fine; if it's not, then fine as well. The decision's yours. Just stop feeling sorry for yourself.'*

He took the cigarettes from his overcoat pocket and stuffed them into her hand, some of the packets falling on to the pavement. She bent down and picked them up, put them into the shopping bag she always carried in her coat.

'You want to do it now or later?'

'Neither.'

'Why not? You've paid for it.'

'I haven't. The cigarettes are for the kids and the others.'

He left her and strode down Friedrichstrasse, the anger boiling in him. She ran after him, caught him up.

'Hanni.'

He stopped and looked at her.

'The first night. You asked my name. It's Hanni.'

'Nick.' He held out his hand. 'Nick Rossini.'

The clients were corporate, and had flown in from New York, Chicago and LA. The conference room was on the fourth floor, the windows shaded and the table leather-topped, the case summaries in front of them and Nicholas Rossini facing them.

The telephone rang. At the beginning of the meeting Rossini had made a point of instructing his secretary that he would take no calls; it was no more than they expected. He ignored it and continued. The telephone rang again. He apologized to them and began to remind his secretary of his instructions, then listened for ten seconds and informed her that he would take the call when it came. Fifteen minutes later the telephone rang again.

'Excuse me.' He half turned from them. 'Mike, good to speak to you.' He listened for two minutes, grunting occasionally, the clients looking at him. In Berlin Michael Rossini finished speaking and wondered how his father would react.

'And what did your mother say?'

The clients could not hear the reply, only heard Nicholas Rossini laugh.

'She did, did she?'

Rossini's son, they understood, probably a Harvard man, phoning with some good news, first in his class or editorship of his college law review.

They talked for thirty seconds more, then Rossini put the telephone down and turned back to his clients. They watched as he glanced again at the case summary in front of him then up at them.

'My son.' Just landed a big one, they knew again. Ivy League past and blue-chip future. 'Eighty-Second Airborne, the Screaming Eagles.' There was the slightest smile in the eyes and the slightest steel in the smile. 'Kicked ass in Berlin this morning.'

The concluding meeting of the enquiry into the incident at Waldemarstrasse took place at the US Mission on Clay Allee. Present, in addition to Michael Rossini, were a colonel and the Brigadier-General commanding the US garrison in Berlin.

'There has been a varied response to your action. The Russians and East Germans have objected, the mayor of Berlin wishes to present you with a certificate. I have ignored the first and, on your behalf, have declined the second.'

A portrait of the President hung from the wall behind the general's desk, next to the Stars and Stripes.

'The response in Washington has also been ambiguous. Part of the establishment there wishes to bring charges against you. I have protected you from this on the grounds that you crossed the Wall unarmed, as an act of humanity rather than of belligerence, and that no shots were fired. You do, of course, have certain support in the Senate.'

The general pursed his lips. 'There remains, however, one last problem which I have difficulty in resolving.' He took a single sheet of paper from the file. 'According to Stores, there's a discrepancy in the records relating to the amount of ammunition issued to your patrol, and the amount returned at the end.'

He pushed a cigar into his mouth, came round the desk and shook Rossini by the hand. 'While they're sorting that out, what'll you have to drink?'

The disciplinary meeting following the incident at Waldemarstrasse took place in the GMK headquarters off Unter den Linden. Present, in addition to Werner Langer, were the colonel of the border guards in the East Berlin military region and a civilian whom he recognized but whose name he did not know.

'The reaction to your conduct at Waldemarstrasse has been twofold. There are those who consider that the main item under consideration should be the security flaw which allowed the situation in the first place, and who wish to see you court-martialled because of this.

'I have explained that the sector in question was not your responsibility and that your presence there was not dereliction of duty, but an example of your devotion to it. I am pleased to inform you that this has been accepted.'

A photograph of General Secretary Ulbricht hung on the wall behind the colonel's desk, the Party flag next to it.

'There is also a group which feels that your conduct at Waldemarstrasse should be rewarded, and have recommended that you be offered a commission in the People's Army. This position enjoyed my full support.'

Langer picked up the past tense, the word *enjoyed*.

'I regret to inform you, however, that it has not been accepted.'

The colonel closed the file and looked at the man to his left. The civilian nodded his thanks, the colonel left the room, and the man took his place behind the desk.

'You don't smoke, of course.' Dieter Lindner took a cigarette from the silver case.

'No, thank you anyway.'

'Werner Langer.' He gestured for Langer to sit, not taking his eyes from him. 'Born Leipzig, domicile with grandparents. Father Werner Langer, 195th regiment of the 78th Infantry division, killed in action. Mother Eva, a member of the Party and highly regarded employee. You yourself attended local school, highest grade in each subject in each class. Member of the Free German Youth and the GST, in which you rose to senior rank. You joined the Party as soon as you became eligible.

'Top of course at GMK training school, including highest marks ever obtained in mathematics, political history and Marxism-Leninism. Service with distinction, including three recommendations, in Berlin.'

His voice changed, as if he had closed a file. 'It seems to me, Corporal, that however well intended it may have been, you would not find a commission in the People's Army or the Frontier Troop entirely satisfying.'

He leaned forward, elbows on desk. 'Your military service ends with this meeting. When it is over you return to your barracks and collect your personal possessions. You take one week's leave then report back to me. Your first course begins five days after that.'

'I'd like a last drink with the lads.'

'Already arranged. They have tonight off.'

'What do I tell them?'

'That you've been promoted and posted to the officer school at Koblenz.'

'And where have I been posted?'

He already knew, he would think in retrospect.

'State Security.'

CHAPTER SIX

HANS-JOACHIM SCHILLER and Max Steiner had discussed the possibility of a tunnel during the last stages of the Liesenstrasse cemetery escape and worked on the details over the summer when they had spent a month in France.

Item one, the start point in the West. The cellar should be large enough to store the earth.

Item two, the finish point in the East. The cellar should not be in use. In winter, for example, they should avoid cellars where coal was stored.

Item three, organization. The team would be divided into tunnellers and couriers, the tunnellers themselves divided into shifts and the couriers only brought in at the last moment.

Item four, security. Tunnellers would not know of the existence of the courier system, and couriers would not know the method of escape. All identities would be carefully concealed; escapers in the East would not be told who had nominated them.

Item five, technical assistance. They had recruited an engineering student, explained to him what they wanted and listened while he detailed the skills they would need, thanked him when he offered to help.

Item six, finance. Although labour was voluntary there would still be considerable costs. The hire or lease, even the purchase, of the cellar and the apartment above it. Equipment, radios for communication both within the West and between the West and the East. Weapons for the guards at the tunnel entrance in the East.

After the Liesenstrasse escape Kurt Meixner had moved to a flat with his brother, Conrad Wismar had left West Berlin for a job in

Stuttgart and Rolf Hanniman had moved in with a girlfriend. It had been logical that Max should take their place, and equally logical for reasons of security that although it meant the flat was not full, the two men kept it to themselves.

That evening they sat in the lounge and finalized their plans. Originally they had identified eight possible start points in the West, only four of which – when they checked – had empty cellars opposite them in the East. When they inspected each again, however, they had discovered that the cellars of one pair were not exactly opposite, which would have meant tunnelling diagonally, and had therefore further reduced the list to three.

Max went to the kitchen and fetched them each a beer. 'I suggest we assume that we can use the tunnel for two nights, no more. After that its security will be blown.' The game had changed, was no longer a game. Mass escapes, security measures, guns to protect themselves. 'Given the problems in the East, the maximum number we can bring out each night is probably ten to twelve. Assuming that most of the people who have approached us only want one person out, that gives a total of, say, twenty helpers. We'll need three or four couriers, which leaves sixteen to tunnel, plus you and me. Rolf still wants to help. Which gives two shifts of eight or nine per shift.'

They had calculated they would be able to dig a metre a day. The tunnel would therefore take between thirty and forty days, depending on the location and the soil conditions.

'Who?'

There were more than forty names on the list. They went through them, balancing the contribution which those in the West could make to the escape against the needs of those in the East to escape. The name which they agreed without hesitation or discussion should be at the top of the list was that of Michael Madetski.

The next morning they went into the East, travelling separately and using false West German identity cards, meeting below the bridge over Friedrichstrasse next to the station, then walking to the first location to be checked, opposite the lower end of Bernauer Strasse.

The blocks along the street were almost identical to those opposite them in the West, grey-faced with unattractive rectangular metal-framed windows, four or five storeys high and built round a central courtyard. The section in which the cellar was situated was halfway down, one side fronting the street and the other facing the death strip. They walked down the street as if they lived on it, saw the moment the man in the doorway to the courtyard picked them up. His face was lined and friendly and the elbows of his coat were neatly patched. Stasi, they knew immediately, typical local informant employed to report on anything suspicious near the Wall. They walked past without slowing and went to the next location.

The cellar was perfect, few police in the area and, because of a bend in the Wall, little more than thirty metres from the start point in the West. They smiled at a woman outside and went down the stairs. The sacks of coal had been dragged in since they had last inspected the block.

The street in which the third cellar was positioned was similar to the others, divided into sections with each section built round a cobbled courtyard, the washing hanging from the windows like flags. The door to the cellar was in the right-hand corner and unlocked. They opened it and went down: twenty steps, bending at a right angle in the middle, then another door. They pushed it open and went in, smelling the dust. The cellar was empty, the naked light bulb hanging from the ceiling by the thinnest of wires and the floor made of earth.

'Superstitious?'

The Wall opposite was where they had bundled Rudi Fischer and his wife and children over.

'Made it last time.'

The next day, using a bank account in the company name of Wannsee Caterers and a West German identity confirmed by a forged ID card, Hans-Joachim Schiller took out a three-month lease on the empty baker's shop on Heidelbergerstrasse. That afternoon he and Max sought out Michael Madetski.

The man had aged since he had first approached them for help, his face was leaner and his hair was thinning slightly. They found him where they knew they would, snatching a rest between lectures.

'There's some work.' Hans-Joachim joined him while Max bought three coffees. 'Thought you might like to help.'

'Anything I can do.' Mike Madetski was tired, the crescents blacking under his eyes.

'Bit of digging.' There was no one near them.

The other man nodded again, not realizing.

'Women and children as well this time, Mike.'

Madetski understood and looked away, tried not to let Hans-Joachim see the wet in his eyes. 'Thanks.'

Max put the coffees on the table and sat down.

'Thanks,' Madetski said again.

The following Monday morning, dressed in workmen's overalls, Hans-Joachim Schiller and Max Steiner drove to Heidelbergerstrasse and parked the VW outside the door leading to the hallway into the courtyard. The window on the third level of the watch-tower closest to them opened and the Grepo focused his binoculars on them. They unloaded the dust-sheets and cans of paint from the back of the van, stacked some on the pavement, and carried the rest through the courtyard to the baker's shop. The rear room was the former bakery, the ovens and equipment removed long ago, and the front the shop, the windows blocked in. The trap-door to the cellar was in the corner of the back room. They left the first tins in the room and went back to the van.

The guard in the watch-tower was still looking at them. Max lit himself a cigarette and offered one to Hans-Joachim. The window in the watch-tower shut. Casually, the cigarettes hanging from their mouths, the two men unloaded the lengths of wood from the van and carried them through, followed by the boxes marked catering equipment. Except for a woman coming through the hallway the street and courtyard remained empty. Half an hour later they locked the door of the bakery and drove away.

For the following seven days, until he was satisfied that no one's suspicions had been roused, Hans-Joachim kept the block under surveillance. On the eighth day he unlocked the bakery and went inside. It was three in the afternoon. At four the first tunneller on the first shift arrived, the others following at irregular intervals over the next five hours. Once inside they changed into their working clothes, packing their street clothes in bags to keep them clean.

The shift itself was divided into three-man teams. Within each team one man would dig, a second would pull the bucket of soil out of the tunnel and up the shaft, and a third would pack the waste in the corner of the cellar, changing at regular intervals.

The cellar felt cold but dry, its walls were red-brown brick, the remains of flour giving it a slightly ghostly appearance, and the earth on the floor had been trodden hard. The room itself extended to the front line of the building and was illuminated by a single electric light hanging from a beam, the wiring worn and unsafe. Hans-Joachim took the electrical wiring, fuses and bulbs from one of the boxes and ran extra lighting into the cellar while the others unpacked the food and equipment from the others and shifted the wood.

The cellars which were to be connected were exactly opposite each other and the two streets parallel. They watched while the mining engineer made his calculations, then drew a line on the front wall of the basement.

'We go down four metres. That way we clear the cellars of the houses which have been demolished and which are between us and the finish point.' He drew a mark down the front wall of the cellar. 'This is our line.' He measured two metres in from the wall and drew the outline of the shaft on the ground with his foot. 'Forty-seven metres from here and we're under the cellar in Karl-Issing Strasse.'

They stood back. Hans-Joachim picked up a shovel and began to dig. They had calculated it would take them six hours to dig the shaft; in the end it took them almost twenty and was an indication of what lay ahead. In order to reduce the amount of waste which would need to be stored, they had planned that the shaft should be little more than a metre square. In the first metre of depth this was feasible, but between one and two metres there was insufficient room for a man to dig and throw the waste out. The shaft was therefore widened to one and a half metres. Even so there was little room to dig, so that instead of being thrown up the waste was loaded into a bucket and hauled to the surface. Even before they reached the bottom of the shaft the temperature in the cellar had risen and they were working stripped to the waist, the sweat pouring off them and their hands were red and blistered, their muscles tight with pain.

In the early hours of the second evening they began the tunnel itself. Again it was Hans-Joachim who made the first cuts. The walls of the shaft loomed over him, frightening him. If this is only the shaft, the thought thudded through his mind, what will it be like twenty-five metres into the tunnel when there's no one around me and so much earth above me? He forced the fear from him, swung the pickaxe and tore away the first soil.

Within ten minutes his muscles were seized with cramp and his head thudded with claustrophobia and exertion. He tried to look round and saw how little soil he had moved. Another five minutes, he told himself, then he would take a break. Max Steiner climbed down the ladder and took the shovel.

'Early days. We'll get used to it.'

Twelve hours later he returned to the tunnel. The men they were replacing were tired, faces streaked with strain. Hans-Joachim climbed down the ladder to the shaft bottom; the man edged backwards from the tunnel and stood up, barely enough room for them both. His body was brown-black and his shoulders and elbows were chaffed. Half a day, Hans-Joachim thought, and so little progress.

'Doing well.'

He ducked into the tunnel and felt the fear. Christ, it's small. I'll never get in there, never get out. He made himself pick up the chisel and began to pick at the face.

In the far corner the men were trying to sleep, the blankets pulled over them. Max was sitting beside him munching a loaf of bread. They stood up and went to the cellar. In the past two days they had built a pulley system over the shaft to haul the buckets of earth from the bottom. In addition to the electric cable into the cellar a second now looped down the stairs, across the floor, down the side of the shaft and into the tunnel. In the far corner the earth was stacked tight.

The boots were half a metre into the tunnel. There was a roof support made of wood at the entrance and a second a metre and a half in. A rope ran alongside the body of the man working at the face, a canvas sheet on the other end on to which the man loaded the sand and soil he worked free from the face.

Hans-Joachim tapped the legs and waited. Rolf wriggled out and stood up, stretching his back and straightening his shoulders. Hans-Joachim stood back as he climbed the ladder, then knelt down and entered the tunnel. The sound changed. The feel, the sense, the popping in his ears. God, may it not cave in; he tried to stop himself but prayed anyway. Don't touch the ceiling. Don't knock the roof supports with your shoulders. He froze, only half in, and tried to make himself go on, could not move. The sides and roof were rough but straight and the floor was worn smooth by the men who had gone before him. He made himself go forward and reached the face. Take your time, he told himself; calm down and let yourself get used to it. He was breathing deeply, drawing in lungfuls of air. The canvas sheet was on his right, the trowel, hammer and chisel beside it. He lay on his left side and tried to hold the chisel against the face with his left hand and the hammer in his right, changed position, tried to crouch so that he could strike the chisel. Knocked the roof support and almost panicked. All right, he tried to calm himself, nothing's going to happen. He half twisted and began to chip at the soil. Two metres, he began to think, almost three; the boys had done well. Max tapped on his leg and he stopped.

'You've been in thirty minutes.'

The canvas sheet was covered with soil; Hans-Joachim leaned to one side so that Max could pull it out then shuffled backwards. Only when he was standing upright in the shaft and the next man had gone in did he begin to shiver.

Even in the years to come Hans-Joachim would remember the moment. At some point in the early hours of the next morning, perhaps the morning after – time lost its significance no matter whether one was resting or working – he crawled again into the tunnel. Suddenly he felt easier, more confident to turn his body without the fear that all would collapse around him and therefore more able to throw more strength and power against the tight-packed soil of the tunnel face. Eight hours later he entered the tunnel again. It was only when the man taking his place tapped him on the leg to come out that Hans-Joachim Schiller realized he was singing to himself.

The shifts changed that evening, the men leaving and entering the bakery over a six-hour period. Before he left each man washed and shaved, and changed out of his working clothes.

The first man of the new shift to begin working in the tunnel was Michael Madetski. With the others the sound of tunnelling was varied and intermittent, as the men grew tired or changed position to ease the strain on muscles and bones. With Madetski, however, there was never any change, simply the steady chipping sound, relentless and unremitting. With the others it was only after their third or fourth session at the work face that they began to sing. With Madetski, however, he began to sing within minutes of entering the tunnel for the first time. Even when he was resting, and especially in the minutes before he went back to work, Mike Madetski never stopped singing.

The informants' reports from West Berlin were updated daily. Werner Langer left the communications room and leafed through them.

The grey-slabbed building on Lenin-Allee which housed the headquarters of the Berlin region of State Security was large and anonymous, the atmosphere of fear permeating the streets around it. In 1961 it had been the then Minister of State Security in the politburo, Erich Honecker, who had supervised the building of the Berlin Wall, and the general who headed the MfS, Erich Mielke, who had assisted him.

The organization's contacts with the security services of the other Warsaw Pact nations were strong, although – except for its relationship with the Soviet Union – the MfS retained an element of distrust even with those it called its allies. Its contact with Moscow, however, was firm and unbreakable, served by its constant liaison with those it called the Friends, the East Berlin station of the KGB based in the huge and sprawling Soviet embassy on Unter den Linden, just east of the Brandenburg Gate.

In the Democratic Republic its ever-widening network of informants covered all occupations and professions. In the Federal Republic it included politicians and industrialists, many of its agents having been infiltrated during the massive exodus in the late fifties and early sixties which had culminated in the erection of the Wall. In West Berlin its information came from a range of informants, even the various commercial escape organizations which had suddenly sprung up, as well as from the thriving black market and criminal underworld of the city.

It was late afternoon, the sky outside a leaden grey. He returned to the office on the second floor and leafed through the intelligence bulletins from West Berlin, then turned his attention to the minutes of the meeting that evening.

*

The appointment had been arranged three days before. Hans-Joachim Schiller left Heidelbergerstrasse, returned to the flat on Vorbergstrasse, showered and changed. By the time he reached the Berlin offices of the magazine the first flakes of snow were settling on the cars parked outside.

The editor was one of the new breed: mid thirties, immaculately ironed white shirt, tie loose and sleeves rolled to just below the elbow. His desk was strewn with photographs and page paste-ups from the editorial he had just held.

'What is it?'

'No details.'

'But the story is guaranteed and exclusive?'

'Yes.'

The first instincts of both Hans-Joachim and Max had been to avoid allowing any details of the tunnel to be made public, even after the event. They had changed their minds for three reasons. The first was the certain knowledge that the tunnel would only cease to be operational because the East, and by the East they meant the Stasi, knew of it. The second was the equally certain understanding that as soon as the first escapers came out news of the tunnel would leak anyway. And the third was that, in order to finish the tunnel, they needed the money.

'We'll need interviews and pictures.'

'We'll provide you with both. Some of the faces on the pictures will have to be blackened out.'

'Agreed. How much do you want?'

The list seemed endless: the rental of the premises for three months, the purchase of the night binoculars, guns and radios, the cost of running the van, forged identity cards for the couriers plus their expenses, food and other equipment used for digging, plus a contingency fund for the items they had not even thought of yet.

'Twenty-five thousand Deutschmarks.'

'Sounds a lot.'

'It isn't.'

'A big one?' The editor's eyes began to shine.

'No details.'

'Fifteen up front, the rest when we publish.'

'Agreed.'

By the time he returned to Heidelbergerstrasse the street was deserted, a solitary set of footprints in front of him and the Wall and the watch-towers on his left. Schiller could not come close to the Wall without feeling its presence, almost without being aware of the fear it cast. He turned through the hallway and into the courtyard, making sure he kept to the clear strip of ground protected by the overhang of the roof so that he would leave no footprints to the baker's.

The atmosphere hit him the moment he went inside. He changed quickly and went to the cellar. The entire left half of the floor was packed with soil and the room was hot. No one was sleeping, everyone waiting. The man at the top of the shaft waiting his turn to go into the tunnel was Michael Madetski; when he saw Hans-Joachim he stood aside and let him down the ladder. Kurt Meixner pulled himself out of the tunnel and Hans-Joachim took his place. Have to clean up the escapers when they come out, he thought; the women should take off their nylons or stockings or they would tear, the men should roll up their trousers to avoid getting the knees muddy or they would be a giveaway once they stepped outside. He came to the fourth roof support and saw the notice.

WARNING.

YOU ARE NOW LEAVING

THE AMERICAN SECTOR.

He crawled past and looked back, saw the words on the other side.

The meeting began at seven thirty. It had been a routine day; Langer worked till seven, took a quick coffee, then went to the hall. By the time he arrived the room was crowded, the two hundred or so men sitting in rows and the committee positioned behind a long table on a dais at the front.

The chairman shuffled the block of papers in front of him and brought the meeting to order. Not just any meeting of any branch within any political party, they were all aware: the delegates' meeting of the Central Berlin branch of the State Security division of the Party.

They dealt quickly with the first two items and came to the third: election of officers. The chairman was fifty years old and one of the old-timers. Like all the committee, Langer thought – no room yet for the new generation. The chairman handed the chair to the secretary, left the platform and sat in the single empty chair in the front row of the meeting. The secretary asked for nominations and the treasurer nominated the outgoing chairman, the nomination seconded immediately from the floor. The politicking already done and the decisions already taken, Langer reflected. Just like the Party. The meeting voted, the decision unanimous, and the chairman resumed his position on the platform.

They came to the position of secretary. Bergner was an ill man, everyone knew it, could see it in the way he held his body and his face. Slowly he left the platform and sat in the empty chair in the front row. The chairman asked for nominations.

'Major Bergner.'

It was seconded immediately and the chairman went through the formality of waiting for other nominations. There would be none, Langer knew, the committee already firm in its decision.

'Captain Meyer.'

The second nomination caught both the meeting and the committee by surprise. Gerhard Meyer: Langer remembered their first meeting at the crossing at Invalidenstrasse. Slightly older than himself, university educated. One of Heinz Moessner's protégés just as he himself was now one of Dieter Lindner's. It was an interesting move, he thought. Meyer had no hope of winning, no hope of attracting votes outside his immediate group of supporters, but was laying down his mark, making his first play for the future. The vote was taken, all but ten voting for the outgoing secretary. The man returned to the platform and the chairman prepared to move to the vote for branch treasurer. Meyer stood and the chairman turned to him.

'Chairman. I realize this may be out of order, but I would like to offer my congratulations to Major Bergner.'

The meeting ended at ten thirty, the hall clearing quickly. As Meyer left he made a point of looking round, making sure he was noticed. On the platform the committee packed their documents and prepared to leave, the chairman, treasurer and all but one of the other members of the committee talking together. At their side the branch secretary was still seated, shuffling his papers and taking his time as he placed them in the briefcase. Langer turned from the door and weaved his way back into the hall.

'Major Bergner.'

The branch secretary looked up at him. Even during the evening his eyes had sunk a little, and the hollows in which they were set had darkened. 'Yes.'

'If the committee is ever in need of clerical or other assistance, I would be only too pleased to help.'

The chairman overheard and understood. Not the committee, but you as branch secretary.

The following day Langer began work at seven, his timetable already full. Surveillance of political suspects, investigations into a black market with possible links to the West which he might be able to develop and exploit, a meeting with an informant at the university. At eleven the branch chairman telephoned Lindner and asked for a private meeting. Half an hour later Lindner welcomed the chairman and the branch treasurer to his office and offered them chairs.

'As you are aware, last night Major Bergner was re-elected branch secretary.' It was the branch chairman who opened the conversation. 'As you are also aware, Major Bergner is ill and retires in six months. His re-election last night was in consideration of his services to the Party, rather than meeting an administrative requirement in the Party itself.'

Lindner nodded his understanding.

'Which means that in six months the position of branch secretary will become vacant.'

The implication was clear: branch secretary in the Berlin branch of the MfS, with the acceleration through the Party ranks which the position ensured. Ipso facto, guaranteed and rapid advancement in State Security.

'Last night one of Colonel Moessner's officers stood against Herr Bergner. He was, of course, defeated. Afterwards one of your men offered to help.'

'What was his name?'

'Captain Langer.'

'So why have you come to see me?'

'Both the offer and the manner in which it was made were greatly appreciated.'

Lindner lit himself a cigarette and telephoned for coffee.

Hans-Joachim was asleep on the floor. It could have been night or day, he would not have known, lived only by the shifts in the tunnel. It was almost two months since they had begun, the days marked on the calendar on the wall. The hand gripped his shoulder and shook him. He rolled over, blinking, and saw Rolf Hanniman.

'We're there.'

He followed Rolf down the stairs and into the cellar. The men were standing round the shaft waiting for him; Rolf hands on hips, panting, and Madetski beside him. Hans-Joachim crawled into the tunnel and checked the measurement as he knew they wanted him to.

'Forty-seven metres.' He wished he'd thought of beer to celebrate and saw that Michael Madetski was waiting to go back into the tunnel. 'Widen it slightly on each side to match the shaft in the West, then straight up.'

Madetski nodded. As he disappeared down the tunnel they heard him begin to sing.

That night Max Steiner left the bakery; that night he felt the other fear again. When he had been tunnelling he had forgotten it, perhaps not forgotten it but pushed it aside. The following day he began the contacts with the two men and one woman he had selected as couriers, starting with the woman.

Ellen Scheering was twenty-three years old, short with dark hair.

'Some time ago you offered to help.' Max sat opposite her at the kitchen table.

'Yes.' She understood why he had called.

'From now on you're on stand-by. You arrange your timetable as a matter of priority, building in reasons for any sudden and unexpected absence.'

Even now he only gave her as much information as was necessary. 'When activated you will be given three names; that day you will cross the Wall, make contact and arrange to meet each the following evening. The next day you rendezvous with them and escort them to the start point of the escape. You'll be given further details, including certain codes, immediately prior to your crossing on the second day. That day you will also be given a second list whom you will contact for an escape on the third day.'

Ellen's eyes were excited, glowing.

'Any questions?'

'What about my people?'

'Arranged.'

Each courier would bring out someone else's friends or relatives and someone else would bring out theirs – the security measure was deliberate though unspoken. The only people not on any of the lists given to the couriers were the wife and children of Michael Madetski.

When the briefing was over Max took a photograph of each courier; that evening he developed and printed them and prepared the false West German identity card which each would carry. By the time he finished it was almost midnight.

Two hours earlier Hans-Joachim and Rolf Hanniman had washed and changed, then left the bakery and climbed the stairs to the top landing of the apartment block on the side overlooking the Wall. With them they carried a step-ladder and a torch. The trap-door fitted neatly into the ceiling. Hans-Joachim opened it, pulled himself into the roof space, closed the door after him and shone the torch round him.

The beams were old but strong and the cobwebs hung like shrouds from the rafters. He and Max had checked the roof space when they were first considering the bakery as an escape location. A month before, when the tunnel was under way, he had brought up floorboards and laid them across the beams. He checked that no one else had been in the roof space, then removed a tile from the roof, confirmed that the line of vision to the key points in the East remained unobstructed, replaced the tile and climbed back down. The following morning he left the bakery and returned three hours later with a sports bag containing Walther hand-guns – purchased on the black market and, unknown to them, stolen from the BGS, the West German border guards – plus ammunition and VHF radios.

Two afternoons later, twenty-four hours before they had anticipated, Rolf Hanniman again woke Hans-Joachim Schiller.

'We're ready to break through.'

'How much more to go?' He was wide awake.

'Half a metre from the floor of the cellar in Karl-Issing Strasse.'

'Clear the tunnel.'

At eight that evening, when they presumed that the cellar would be empty, Hans-Joachim and Max crawled back down the tunnel. The line of lights ran along the wall and up the side of the shaft; a ladder, built in sections and now bolted together, was against the wall. Hans-Joachim climbed up and Max passed him a length of broomstick, its end sharpened to a point. Hans-Joachim placed the end against the centre of the ceiling and began to push. The soil was packed tight, Max handed him a mallet and Hans-Joachim tapped the bottom end of the wood carefully but firmly. Slowly the broomstick disappeared into the ceiling, the soil trickling on to his face. It was the first danger point, they were aware. The first time they might know if the Stasi was waiting for them.

Without warning the broomstick slid easily through the soil and broke through to the East. Hans-Joachim reached down for a trowel and scraped carefully away at the remainder of the ceiling. After twenty minutes Max took his place, after another twenty Rolf, then Michael Madetski. An hour after the broomstick had broken through there was an area of ceiling a mere four centimetres thick and wide enough for a man to push his head and shoulders through.

They pulled back to the cellar and waited, drinking coffee and listening for even the slightest indication that all was not well. After half an hour Hans-Joachim, Max, Rolf and Mike went upstairs, selected a hand-gun each and crawled back down the tunnel. Carefully Hans-Joachim chipped away at the remaining earth, Max immediately below him at the foot of the ladder, Rolf at the east end and Madetski at the shaft bottom in the West.

The darkness was above them. No one speaking – in the tunnel, the shaft, the cellar. No noise except the scraping of the trowel. Hans-Joachim handed down the trowel and the tailor's dummy was passed up to him. It was life-size, sawn off just below the chest, with the neck modified so that the head could be moved sideways, as if it was looking round. A wig had been glued on and the torso was dressed in a sweatshirt, both the cloth and the face made up and streaked with earth.

Hans-Joachim pushed the head and shoulders through the hole and waited for the shots. His heart was thumping and the blood was pounding in his ears. Carefully he eased the dummy to one side and pushed his head and shoulders through. The cellar was empty.

Half an hour later Max Steiner left the bakery. The last thing he saw was the face of Michael Madetski, streaked in sweat and anxiety, the eyes white and staring at him. At nine he went to the flat where Ellen Scheering lived. It was strange how he felt, he would think later, strange how he could feel so calm and detached, yet so full of adrenaline. The nerves biting through his stomach yet no nerves at all. He knocked on the door and waited. The door opened and he saw Ellen's face, the look on it the moment she realized.

The following morning, beginning at nine, he sent his couriers across the border. At eleven he made his way to the U-bahn station at Nollendorfplatz and began his own journey to the East. Gleisdreieck. He began to feel the fear, see the Wall in front of him. Möckernbrüche. The fear was growing, the nerves so tight that he felt he was going to vomit. Hallesches Tor. He realized he was tapping his feet and tried to control it, rehearsed his cover story. Changed trains.

Kochstrasse. He left the station and walked to Checkpoint Charlie, one of the East Germans already raising his binoculars and picking him out. You know they do it to everyone, he told himself, part of the process of making you give yourself away. Part of the Wall itself. He passed the Allied line and stepped into the East German control box.

'Reason for entry.' The guards were officious, their voices and mannerisms threatening.

The nerves disappeared, ice in their place. 'I'm attending the machine tool trade fair.' He had checked the details, even knew the names of the exhibitors he wanted to visit. The official stamped his entry visa, changed his Deutschmarks and issued him with his currency exchange form.

The train ride should have taken forty minutes. Max Steiner caught the one thirty train, arriving an hour and twenty minutes later, the train delayed just outside Berlin. The day was bright but cold, the snow swept clear from the streets but lying frozen on the hills under which the town nestled, the yellow-green smoke from the chemical factory hanging like a mantle over the roofs.

He left the station and hurried to the school, not wanting to be late. The parents were already gathering. It was just like before: he could not shake the thought from his mind, wondered how Madetski's wife had coped with the waiting and how she would react. There were no Vopos or Stasi in sight, no reason to be. Stasi informants everywhere, even here. He stood fifty metres away, hands in pockets to keep them warm, and waited. The woman came down the road with the child. Since he had last seen her she was thinner, he thought, her hair hanging loose and her black coat tied tight around her.

'Hello, Gisela.'

She was startled, tried not to show it. 'Hello, Harry.'

The girl left them and joined her friends.

Fresh news of Mike, he saw the hope flicker on her face.

'It's tomorrow.'

'What's tomorrow?' She did not understand, tried to hide the expression on her face as she began to realize.

'Tomorrow afternoon you and the girls go to Berlin. Make sure you arrive by four.' It would mean she would have three hours to wait but would give her time if the train was delayed. 'I'll meet you at the ticket office at Alexanderplatz at seven.' It would be dark by five, the streets would be empty by six and the first escapers would come through at seven thirty, but he wanted to allow someone else to test the system before he brought Madetski's family through. 'Leave everything, even photographs. You mustn't carry anything which might suggest that you're not coming back.'

Gisela was nodding, her face tight.

'You have enough money for the train fare?'

'Yes.'

When Max Steiner crossed back into West Berlin that evening the night was cold and the searchlights on the Wall hung like haloes in the black. By nine he had contacted the men on the other shift and ordered them to report to the bakery, allocating times they should arrive and instructing them to bring food with them. From this point on, he and Hans-Joachim had agreed, no one – tunnellers or escapers – would enter or leave the bakery until the escape was over.

That evening Hans-Joachim Schiller lay on the blanket on the floor of the baker's shop in Heidelbergerstrasse and listened to the men trying to sleep around him, waited for the news from Max that something had gone wrong in the East and the tunnel had been in vain. Once, he thought at three in the morning, he heard Michael Madetski talking in what passed that night for sleep. Or perhaps, Hans-Joachim would think later, the man was praying.

The cut-off point was at midday; at twelve fifteen Max Steiner left the flat, at one he met Ellen.

'You collect your parcels at the times and places specified. The start point is the corner of Schmollar Platz.' He drew a map, though he did not write the street names on it. 'You bring the first there at seven thirty, the second at eight thirty and the third at nine thirty. The timing must be precise, no more than one minute early or late.' Even now he gave no indication of what would happen to the escapers after they left the courier, no sign that a tunnel was involved.

'You only bring them to that point if you are totally satisfied that neither your security nor theirs has been breached. From there they go left across Karl-Issing Strasse to number sixty-seven.' He indicated the address on the map. 'Number sixty-seven is the third door along, on the opposite side of the road. Someone will be waiting for them. There's a code word. You give it to them just before they leave you and not before. They'll be asked it when they reach the door. Everything clear?'

The courier nodded.

'The code is an expression.' The codes would always be simple and topical, easy to remember, 'Happy New Year. Remember, you only tell them at the last moment.' The following day, he did not tell her, the code would be changed.

'Today, you also contact three other people, make the same arrangements for them for tomorrow.' He gave her the names and addresses. 'When you finish tonight you cross back to the West and go straight home. You talk to no one. When you finish tomorrow you do the same.'

What about my sister, he knew the woman was going to ask, when will I see her?

'You wait in your flat until we come to you. Any questions?'

'No.'

'Good luck.' He burned the paper on which he had drawn the map, even though there were no street names on it, crumpled it into dust, and went to the next meeting.

The last contact ended at two thirty; within half an hour all his couriers were in East Berlin. Max Steiner himself crossed at three fifteen; by twenty minutes to four he was in position. The woman and two children arrived ten minutes later. He saw them the moment they stepped from the train, making sure they did not see him. Gisela was wearing the same coat, a beret on her head. The older child clutched a teddy bear and the other was in her mother's arms. No tail. He watched them as they left the station. No need for a tail until the moment he made contact with them.

'We go in an hour.'

The men were seated on the floor of the baker's shop, only one absent – on lookout in the cellar below them. Their faces were tight and the stubble was black on their chins, their trousers were dirty and their vests caked with sweat.

'I'll be in the roof space, equipped with night binoculars and radio.' Hans-Joachim directed their attention to the plan on the first of the two sheets of paper pinned to the wall. The diagram was a cross-section of the tunnel. In the West the roof space, the baker's shop, the cellar and the shaft; in the East the shaft, the cellar, the steps to the courtyard above it, the courtyard itself and the entrance to it from the street.

'Section A colour-code White covers the West cellar, shaft and tunnel exit; they will help people as they come out and supervise arrangements upstairs. Section B colour-code Green is responsible for the tunnel entrance, shaft and cellar in the East. Section C colour-code Blue will deal with the door to the address in the East, as well as the security of the courtyard and the entrance to the cellar. My colour-code is Red.

'We've got four radio points: me in the roof space; the entry point to the building in the East, and the tunnel entrance and exit.' He indicated each of the positions on the diagram, then referred them to the second wall chart and the street plan of East Berlin. 'At this moment the people coming out tonight are being picked up by couriers.' He felt the surge of excitement and allowed it to settle. 'The start point is on the corner diagonally opposite the entrance to number sixty-seven. The escapers will be brought there at intervals, with enough time between each to allow the escaper in front to be out of the tunnel before the next arrives.'

He could almost hear the fingers tapping, feel the nails digging into the soft flesh of the palm. 'As soon as the courier brings the escaper to the start point, I inform the men on the doorway. The radio channel is open so everyone will know what's happening, but only those who need to speak will do so. I also inform the door party once the escaper leaves the corner. When the escaper arrives at the door and the men there have checked the code, two of them will take him or her to the cellar. The moment he or she enters the tunnel the cellar party in the East will inform the party in the West that someone is coming through. The West party will inform us immediately the escaper is safe and out.'

He looked at them for questions.

'How many nights?'

'Two. Half your people come out tonight, the rest tomorrow. No one, helper or escaper, leaves until the operation is complete and everyone is out.'

He looked around him again. 'Good luck.'

They tested the radios. As the men began to leave Hans-Joachim took Rolf aside. 'You're the one at the door. All your people are armed. If the Stasi or the Vopos arrive try to shoot over their heads but don't take any chances.'

The last of the light had seeped from the sky two hours before. Hans-Joachim settled in the roof space and concentrated on the pavement at the corner of Schmollar Platz. The figures appeared suddenly, their images grey-green in the night glasses. Two, female courier and male escaper. He checked the number and pressed the send button of the radio. 'Red. Parcel in position.'

The man left the corner and walked diagonally across the road. 'On way.'

The figure passed from his view and he waited.

'Blue. Parcel intact.'

He could imagine the team at the door, hurrying the man round the side of the courtyard, through the second door then down the steps to the cellar.

'Green. Coming in.'

Hans-Joachim did not even try to imagine what the man must be thinking, feeling, as he crawled along the tunnel. Concentrated instead on the corner and the streets around it.

'White. Received.'

At the bottom of the shaft in the cellar below him the escaper looked up and saw his own brother, stripped to the waist and lathered in sweat. 'You,' he managed to say. 'I never knew.'

On the corner of Schmollar Platz Hans-Joachim saw the next figures. 'Red. Parcel in position. On way.'

'Blue. Parcel intact.'

He focused the binoculars on the corner and waited for Max Steiner.

The night before Gisela had mentioned to the woman on the next floor that the girls' grandmother was sick; that morning, when the woman took her own children to school, Gisela had asked her to explain to Monika's teacher that she was taking her to visit the old lady. To the children she said merely that the teacher had given Monika the day off.

The morning had been long; she had fretted, tried to keep the girls amused. When she had finally made her way to the station there had been a Vopo car parked outside; she had tried to ignore it but felt instinctively that it must be for her and was still looking behind her when she arrived in East Berlin.

Four o'clock, the man called Harry had said. She had allowed plenty of time but the train had been late and she had made it with only ten minutes to spare. She could not believe it was happening, still could not understand how they could get her and the girls out. At half past six they caught a tram along Unter den Linden, the Brandenburg Gate behind them to the West, and got off at Alexanderplatz. The square was empty and windswept. What do I do if Harry's not here? she suddenly thought. She held the girls' hands and led them into the vast draughty hall. It was ten minutes to seven.

'Hello, Gisela.'

She turned and saw Max. 'Hello, Harry.'

They left Alexanderplatz and began walking, Gisela sometimes holding one of the girls. In front of her she saw the light, almost like a fog, which hung over the Wall. If they catch us as we climb over they'll shoot us, she suddenly thought; if they see us as we cross the death strip the dogs will tear us to pieces. They reached the corner of Schmollar Platz.

'Red. Parcel in position.'

'Almost there.' Max's voice was calm and reassuring. 'Just walk across the street to number sixty-seven on the other side, third door along. There's a man waiting for you. He'll ask you for a code and you tell him Happy New Year. Got that, Happy New Year. Then he'll take you to the West.'

'What about you,' Gisela asked, 'aren't you coming with us?'

'No,' he answered, 'from here you have to go by yourself. What's the code? You must remember the code.'

What's happening, she wanted to ask, how will you get us out? Happy New Year.

'Good luck, Gisela.'

She was almost too frightened to leave him.

'Red. On way.'

The street was dark and full of shadows. Monika clutched her hand, teddy bear held tight. Where are we going, Mummy, what are we doing? Brigita was cold, beginning to cry. First door, second, third. The man was waiting just inside.

Happy New Year.

'Blue. Parcel intact.'

There were more men inside, all young. Carrying guns. The first stayed at the door and two others led her through the hallway and into a courtyard, then through another door and down some stairs. Gisela still did not understand.

The cellar was lit by torches, three more men, a hole in the floor. Almost there, one of the men told her, the girls clinging to her in fright. Take off your stockings or nylons and go down the ladder, someone is waiting there to help you. She climbed down the ladder and saw the tunnel. I can't, she almost cried out, the girls are afraid of the dark. Gently now, the man told her. It's not far and there's plenty of time. She tried again to be brave, to smile at Monika and Brigita, tell them what to do.

'Green. Coming in.'

Hans-Joachim broke the rules he himself had set down. 'Where's Mike?'

'Above.'

'Shaft bottom now.'

The tunnel was long, more frightening than anything Gisela could have imagined. The death strip is above us: she tried not to think of it, the guards and the guns and the dogs. The ceiling and walls closed in on her, Monika and Brigita were beginning to slow down, to cry again. Somebody built this, she suddenly thought, somebody sweated and bled to dig this so you and the girls could see Mike again. Her fear was gone, the tunnel higher, wider. Almost there, she whispered, coaxed the girls. Tonight we'll go to sleep and tomorrow we'll see someone special. She looked up and saw the notice.

YOU ARE NOW LEAVING
THE SOVIET SECTOR.
WELCOME TO WEST BERLIN.

Michael Madetski received the message and clambered down the ladder. Someone in trouble in the tunnel, he knew, someone who couldn't make it through. He bent down and looked in, saw the figures, shuffling slowly, could only see the vaguest outlines in the shadows of the light bulbs. Come on, he whispered, almost there, almost made it. He climbed in and reached out his arms to help, saw the face.

'Daddy.'

The information was on page two of the informants' reports from West Berlin. Rumours were beginning of a mass escape three nights before. Twenty people, possibly more, through a tunnel under the Wall, though there was no information to date on the location of the alleged tunnel or the identities of those responsible.

Langer lifted the telephone. 'Immediate search of all cellars in streets bordering the Anti-Fascist Wall.'

'The Wall's a long place.' There was an element of challenge in the response. 'Any suggestions where we start?'

'Begin with the streets opposite Kommandante Allee.' He thought back through the other escape reports. 'Then Liesenstrasse and Heidelbergerstrasse.'

CHAPTER SEVEN

ANJA WAS happy. With Berlin, despite the Wall. With her job. Particularly with Christian, partly because of who and what he was, but also because of the new life and friends to whom he had introduced her. Sometimes they went to the opera – at least the system made such things cheap – sometimes they just sat in each other's flats, everyone bringing food and drink, and talked. About music, philosophy, history. About politics.

Occasionally, however, she would lie awake, either after she and Christian had made love or when she was alone in the flat, and wonder whether merely talking about one's opposition to the system was enough. Occasionally, though she never admitted it to anyone, she would lie staring at the ceiling in the early hours of the morning and remember the girl in Leipzig whose beliefs had been so passionate.

The tanks were from the Russian barracks outside the city; Eva passed them as she returned from work. It was the beginning of the third week in June, the weather warm and the blossom hanging from the trees. The children had just left school, the boys kicking a ball in the square near the Nicholaikirche and the girls clustered in groups. Anja and Werner were sitting on the steps of the fountain in the corner.

It was six years since they had become friends, Eva could barely remember how they had been then and how much they had grown since. Werner more like his father every day and Anja growing prettier, her hair blonde and long and her eyes sharp blue and piercing, her body beginning to change shape.

She waved at them and laughed at the way they looked up from their conversation. Sometimes they were so serious, sometimes the way they talked together seemed so full of fire, their eyes flashing like coals, that it frightened her. They saw her and waved back.

'Committee meeting tonight?' Anja was on the right, her skirt pulled over her knees.

'Wednesday's always committee meeting.' Werner watched as Eva disappeared. 'Why doesn't your mum join the Party?'

'Doesn't want to.'

'Why not?' It would help her, he meant, help her get a better job. Help her not to look so tired and worn when she came home from the factory each evening.

'Because the Party's no good. Because it's full of ex-Nazis or people who are as bad as the Nazis.' Her eyes were beginning to blaze.

'But my mum isn't an ex-Nazi, my mum doesn't like the Russians either.' It was the way some of their conversations went, fire replying to fire.

'Your mum's different.'

'But Ulbricht isn't a Nazi either.' The boy knew the fullest details of the leadership. 'Ulbricht fought on the Leipzig barricades in 1919, organized the Party against the Nazis when Hitler came to power.'

'Magraff was a Nazi before the Russians made him police chief in Berlin.'

'Honecker was put in prison by the Nazis.'

It was as if they were no longer children, as if they were a generation apart from those playing in the square.

'Ulbricht spent the war in Moscow. Stalin supported him, selected him as Party chief for Germany. Gave him rooms at the Hotel Luz at the same time that it was used by his secret police.' It was what she had learned from her mother. 'It was Stalin who allowed him to go to Krasnogorsk' – she mispronounced the name of the prison camp outside Moscow – 'Stalin who allowed him to tell the prisoners there about his plans for a communist Germany. Stalin who sent him to organize Berlin when the war ended, before the Americans and British reached the city.' Her voice was louder, almost harsh. 'Ulbricht is like Stalin. Ulbricht is using us as Stalin is using him.'

'Be careful, Anja Lehnartz.' The boy's voice was lower, softer, in a way that almost frightened her. 'Or one day what you say will get you into trouble.'

The morning was warm, June going into July. Anja kissed her mother and aunt goodbye and left for work. If she really did believe in what she called her political beliefs, she had thought the night before, then she should do something about it. Politics were all about her, about them all, but somehow they had given up. Perhaps because Christian and their friends were so wrapped up with their studies and examinations, perhaps because it was summer and in the little free time available to them they all preferred to relax and enjoy themselves. Perhaps because in summer everyone and everything took a break. She stood on the street corner and waited for the tram.

Yet the state was not taking a break. Everywhere around her there was change, the process of what the authorities called de-Stalinization – the purging from public sight of everything connected with the former Soviet leader, as well as the rewriting of his role in history. The new guard apparently sweeping in, yet one thing always the same: everything controlled by Moscow, everything dictated by the Kremlin.

She left the tram at Alexanderplatz, walked along Unter den Linden and turned under the archway into the library. The court-yard inside was quiet, the water sprinkling from the fountain. It was almost too good a morning to be burdening herself with politics, too fine a summer not to enjoy herself with Christian. She dragged her fingers across the water, watching the ripples, then went inside and up the wide marble stairs which swept to the sections on the first floor. The library was quiet; it was too early for the students. The light trickled through the windows and settled on her. She sat at her desk and breathed in the smell; she loved it here, loved the smell of the books and what they stood for. There were so many books dictated by the Party line, of course; yet so many others, so many different and varied thoughts bound in their pages.

There was a roneo machine in the basement and another at the university – her thoughts had an independent logic, as if they ignored the warnings she threw at them. The roneo machines were no good; the Stasi would trace anything done in such a way – not the specific place or machine, but they would know where there were such machines and therefore where to start looking.

In a way she had always known that one day she would do it. She took a sheet of paper and began to write, quickly, as if she was suddenly cut off from the world, glancing up only occasionally to make sure she was still alone, not even glancing up any more. She would not tell Christian and the others, not until their exams were over, perhaps not even tell them. She was writing more quickly, body bent over the desk and mind totally absorbed. It was just like the old days – she was not conscious of the thought – just like when she and Werner had been young and cared so much for everything. She knew what she would do and how she would do it, was writing even quicker, the fire consuming her as he had warned her it would.

Two mornings later she bought the printing kit from one of the stores off Friedrichstrasse, making sure it was only one of a number of items so that they would not remember the purchase, and buying the paper at a different store.

That evening she began to print the document. Her hands were smudged with black and there was ink on her cheek where she had brushed her hair back. Anja concentrated on the paper, making sure that the block was correctly positioned, and pressed down firmly on it. She finished the last paragraph of the last sheet, washed the ink from her hands and face, folded each of the sheets three times and put them in the carrier bag, then hid it in the suitcase under her bed.

Tonight was the easy part. She tried to ignore the sickness in her stomach. Tomorrow she would distribute them, tomorrow she would know if the Stasi was waiting for her.

The courtyard between the main library building and the gate on to Unter den Linden was cool, refreshing. Anja sat on the edge of the fountain and opened the sandwiches. The others were talking about their holidays. She smiled as if she was listening and felt the nausea rising again in her throat, the nerves eating their way through her body. The afternoon seemed to last for ever. At five Anja cleared her desk and left the library. At six she sat down to eat with her mother and aunt, picking at the food. At seven she collected the carrier bag and left the flat. The evening was sunny and warm, people walking in the streets. She took a tram to Alexanderplatz and walked down Karl Marx Allee. It had been here that the workers had risen in 1953; it was here, therefore, that she would begin her act of protest.

The blocks were monolithic and unattractive, not even the curtains bringing colour to them, the children playing between them and their parents and grandparents sitting watching. Her heart was thumping and the nerves were biting into her. She laughed at the children and ran up the steps as if she belonged.

The entrance hall was cold, the metal post-boxes built into the wall on the right. She glanced back and felt the fear. There was no one in sight, other than the children. She opened the bag, took out a sheaf of folded sheets, and began sliding them through the slots in the boxes. Her nerves were tight and she felt she could sense or hear anything, anybody. Not too many here, she told herself, one family will show the leaflet to another. Save some for another block. She finished the batch and began to leave. A woman with a pram came up the steps and into the door. Not just men amongst the ranks of Stasi informants, Anja knew. She smiled at the woman and went to the next block.

The feeling was as nothing she had ever experienced, more exhilarating than she could ever have imagined. Anja lay on her bed, watching the moonlight playing through the window, and reliving the moments of the evening before. At five she made herself coffee; at six she went back to bed, the curtains and windows open so she could breathe in the freedom. The excitement was intoxicating, making her head spin. I took on the system and beat it. I outfoxed the Stasi. In her mind she was already writing the next leaflet.

The reception at the Soviet embassy was informal, Langer had been told. The ambassador might drop in but other than that it was a friendly get-together of intelligence and security colleagues from Moscow and East Berlin, drinks between the Friends and the Stasi officers with whom they were in daily contact.

Nothing with the Russians was ever informal, he knew, no meeting was ever just a friendly get-together.

He showered and dressed, then drove to the complex on Unter den Linden, the ornate façade of the embassy at the front concealing the machinery of power in the mass of departments behind. The evening was light and warm and the streets filled with people walking. Even at a distance he could spot the security, some men and cars positioned discreetly, others openly as a deterrent. He slowed at the gate and showed his pass, waiting while his name was checked against the list, then drove in.

The windows of the reception room were tall, from the floor to the ceiling, the ornamental pillars marbled and the walls and ceiling immaculately decorated. He accepted a vodka and looked round. The men in the room stood in groups, the voices low. Arrangements being hinted at and deals struck, he assumed, a new alliance suggested or an old partnership cemented. The older officers laughing and joking and never stopping working, the younger ones who were being introduced to the circuit for the first time always looking over their shoulders.

In one corner Erich Honecker was sharing a reference to the old days with the steel-grey men from Moscow, Mielke close by him. Honecker, short and slim, immaculate dark blue suit, light shining off his spectacles and eyes glinting through them. Honecker, the man trusted by head of state Ulbricht to put up the Wall, now tipped as his successor. Mielke, his confidant, running State Security from his office on the first floor of what was known as House One at the centre of the massive complex on Normannenstrasse.

Others he knew – Dieter Lindner and Heinz Moessner. And the rest whose names he might not yet be told but whose faces he would remember. Plus himself and Gerhard Meyer. In the centre of the room Moessner was introducing Meyer to one of the Russians. It was the first time Langer had attended such a reception; he and Meyer were the youngest and most junior to be invited, both aware of the significance of the invitation. In the far corner both Honecker and Mielke registered his presence.

The meeting of the branch committee was the following lunchtime. The chairman had been at the Soviet reception, though none of the others. He called them to order, even though the meeting was informal, and took them through the evening's agenda. The committee met at least once a week, normally in the evening, as well as over the lunchtime before a branch meeting, and always over sandwiches and coffee. Like committee like branch like Party, Langer always thought: the deals done and the decisions made in advance. They came to the second item on the agenda: the chairman's vote of thanks to the retiring branch secretary and the election of his successor.

'There will be one other nomination.' The chairman had the details at his fingertips. 'Gerhard Meyer. He will be outvoted. I suggest that you include in your acceptance a word or two for his backers.'

The Party within the Stasi and the Stasi within the Party, Langer thought, the eyes always to the future. 'Of course.'

'Any tricks up their sleeves?' The treasurer was a good man to have on his side for the future. 'I would have if I were them.'

The branch meeting began at seven, at seven fifteen they came to the resignation due to ill health of the incumbent secretary and the election of his successor. After formally announcing Bergner's resignation the chairman presented the man with a set of leather-bound books, paid by donation by the branch members, then called upon the secretary to say a few words. When the speech was over the chairman referred the branch back to the agenda and asked for nominations for the post.

The contest was between Meyer and Langer, they all understood; but Langer had the support of the committee and the grouping behind Meyer knew they would be outvoted.

Meyer stood up and waited for silence. 'I propose Captain Langer as branch secretary.'

The day had degenerated into the sort he disliked: meetings and administration, and no real work. By the time he returned to his office it was gone two. Langer flopped into his chair and flicked through the intelligence summaries which had arrived over lunch. Local and therefore not worth bothering about; the important items came in overnight. He pushed the file aside and reached for the reports from agents and informants in West Berlin: the first suggestion of corruption involving a Social Democrat politician that he might be able to use, a bent policeman, rumours of another tunnel under way somewhere in the city.

There was always the chance of something in the local reports, he reminded himself, even tucked away amongst the small print which everyone else ignored. He retrieved the file, read through it again and reached for the telephone. 'The Vopo report on the pamphlets on Karl Marx Allee.'

The police and the collator's office would be right, the propaganda sheets pushed into the post-boxes in the blocks on Karl Marx Allee the night before would be the work of an amateur. Always the chance of something else, the feeling hung in the air, always the outside chance of a Western connection or the more realistic possibility of turning an enemy into an informant.

'I want an original this afternoon.'

The document, plus copies of first statements by local residents, was delivered at four. That the report was correct and the document the work of an amateur was obvious immediately: the paper was cheap and the printing had been done using a set available from one of several shops in the city. Why take the trouble to print it, why not simply type it out and duplicate it on a roneo machine? Because that would imply access to such facilities, and that would give a clue to the identity of the writer. He leaned back in his chair, his feet on his desk, and read the leaflet again.

NEWS SHEET ONE
The Party says that socialism is the result of
countless good deeds by millions of people.
It says it is the transition into the realm of true humanity,
equality and fraternity, of peace and freedom.

He recognized the quote immediately, the new programme published the year before, and read on.

The Party talks of peace.
But what is peace without freedom?

The Party talks of freedom.
But what is freedom with the Wall?

The Party talks of equality and fraternity.
But what is equality when we are governed by Moscow?
What is fraternity when our country exists
only to defend the Soviet Union?

In his mind he saw the boy and girl in the street beside the Nicholaikirche in Leipzig, her hair blonde and her face almost translucent in the summer light, saw the young man and woman in the yellow of the cornfield the day before he had left home.

'Two of you check it out.' He tossed the sheet on to the next desk. 'Sounds as if it should be someone from the university but they're doing exams.'

The end-of-exams party was held in the flat where she and Christian had met. It was a long time since Franky and Johnny had thrown their Last Supper, Anja thought. She sat on the floor, Christian's arm round her shoulders. I want to tell you what I've done, but I don't want to spoil tonight for you – she smiled at him and played with his fingers – don't want to take away from the fact that the exams are over and that you've all passed.

'What are you thinking?' Christian bent down and kissed her.

'Nothing that matters. I'll tell you when you're all back in September.'

The next morning Christian and the others left Berlin for the summer vacation; in two weeks, when her own holidays began, Anja would join him. That afternoon she bought more paper; that evening she began printing Newsletter Two. Five evenings later she distributed it in the housing blocks near Nordbahnhof, on the opposite side of the city from Karl Marx Allee.

The first copy was delivered to Langer the following afternoon. Just when he didn't need it, he thought: more rumours about a fresh tunnel in the West and suggestions that the politicians were up to something. He leaned back in the chair and read the newsletter. Same person or persons, same style, different location. A week into the summer vacation, so probably not students. Either that or students who lived in East Berlin. He finished reading the sheet and passed it to the team. More reports from West Berlin on a new tunnel, he thought again, wondered how he could get to it. More specifically, how he could get to it before Gerhard Meyer.

The tunnel was fifteen metres in. The soil was more sandy than in the previous two and therefore more prone to subsidence; for this reason they already lived in fear of the first trickle on their neck, and for this reason had built in more props. Hans-Joachim crawled out and Rolf Hanniman took his place.

The tunnels themselves had become known by the number of people brought out in each rather than by chronological sequence; the first, therefore, was referred to as Tunnel Twenty-Three and the second Tunnel Nineteen. The third was on Sebastian Strasse, which they had considered once before but rejected because the cellar opposite was being used for storage. Three weeks before, however, the authorities in the East had moved the occupants out of the houses but had not yet demolished the buildings or filled them with Party members or other people they knew they could trust.

Hans-Joachim climbed the stairs, went to the room above and made himself a coffee. The drink was piping hot and the tinned milk thick and sweet. He slumped against the wall and tried to ease the ache in his shoulders. That morning he had been informed by the businessman financing the tunnel that he was withdrawing his support. The meeting had been short and abrupt, and the decision announced without explanation.

'So what do we do?' Max sat beside him.

'No option.' It was too soon after the story and pictures of the first tunnel to seek finance from a magazine, they both understood. 'I'll make the call this afternoon.'

The next shift were already working in the tunnel. He washed and changed, then left the building and telephoned the politician who had helped fund some of the earlier escapes. To his surprise the man's secretary asked him to wait, checked the diary and suggested two the following afternoon. He thanked her and returned to Sebastian Strasse. Everything in order on the surface – the thought was like an itch down his back – the problems created by the businessman's withdrawal covered by the possibility of further help from the politician. Except that he was a Berliner. And if you were a Berliner you smelt instinctively when something was not quite as it appeared.

The meeting the next afternoon was in the Christian Democrat headquarters. The politician was late, his face red with the wine and the smell of an after-lunch cigar hung on his clothes.

'What can we do for you this time?' He fitted his girth behind the desk and made a show of busying himself with a file.

'Same as before.' Hans-Joachim reminded himself that the man was useful, not merely because of his access to money but also because of his contacts. 'I'm about to start another project and I need money for it.'

'Details?'

'Sorry. You know the score. No details.'

The politician grimaced. 'Bit difficult, old man. Easier before but things have got tighter since. Especially if I can't say what it's about.' He spoke in short bursts, as if to save breath.

'I'm sure there's something you can do.' The cemetery escape had brought the man's party votes, and the votes had brought the man's name to the attention of the party's hierarchy in Bonn. 'Might be more than one this time, might be rather spectacular.'

'Know anyone in the BfV?'

Hans-Joachim wondered how he might know anyone in counter-intelligence. 'No.'

The politician scribbled a name and telephone number on a sheet of paper and passed it to him. 'I'll give him a ring, tell him you'll be contacting him.'

'Thanks.'

The telephone kiosk was on the corner opposite. Half Berlin were spies, he remembered the old joke, and the other half were spying on them. He dialled the number and asked for Herr Riese.

'Who wants him?'

It was too simple, too few pieces falling too easily into place. 'Walter Thomaschett told me to call.'

'Three o'clock tomorrow afternoon.'

The woman gave him the address. He thanked her, telephoned the politician and spoke to his secretary. Herr Thomaschett, he was informed, was in a meeting and could not be disturbed.

'He was going to make a telephone call for me.'

'Sorry. He went straight in the moment you left, wouldn't have had the time. I'll remind him when he comes out.'

'Don't worry.'

The city seemed strange, almost as if he did not know it. He should go to the cellar in Sebastian Strasse, they would need help with the digging. He should sort out in his mind whether finance from counter-intelligence would jeopardize the integrity of the organization. He should sort out what the hell the politician and the security people were playing at. That evening he ate in the rear bar of the Moritz, picturing the men stripped to the waist and sweating like pigs in the tunnel or wrapped in blankets and trying to rest on the hard wooden floor above. That was part of what was disorientating him, he admitted: that there was an escape on and at that moment he was not active in it. He pushed the images aside, bought another beer and thought about the meeting the next afternoon. Thought about Berlin.

The old days, when he was a child and the city was in ruins, he and the others playing in the bomb damage. So long ago now that he had almost forgotten, could barely remember anything other than vague memories, activated by the occasional and unexpected noise or smell. The reconstruction, the city rising from the ruins, again so much part of his own life that he barely noticed it. The same with the people: the refugees, with their different faces and clothes; the soldiers and airmen, the jeeps and trucks and tanks. The grim-faced men along the border. Even the border itself, at first existing only in theory, then the blockade and the airlift, finally the Wall.

And the spooks, above all the spooks. Berlin was not only a city of spies, Berlin was so much a city of spies that no one took any notice any more. Yet still the grey-macked men crossed the Wall, still the men with the trilbies waited for the grey-macked men from the other side. Still people disappeared in the night and reappeared floating face down on the greasy surface of the Teltow Canal the next day. And somewhere in the corner, like a pinprick that no one noticed, Max and himself, their game so small that they had never seen it that way, yet part of the game nevertheless. He finished the beer and waved for another.

The address of the meeting with the BfV was a travel agency off Adenauerplatz. The office was smart and well equipped, two desks with comfortable chairs facing them, and the walls lined with posters, mainly of European holiday resorts. The younger of the two assistants was dealing with another customer; Hans-Joachim waited till the other looked up at him and informed her that he was expected. The woman lifted the telephone, dialled a three-digit extension and said simply that the client had arrived.

'Third floor.'

The door was at the rear. 'Thank you.'

The stairs were narrow, the man waiting for him on the landing. He was in his mid thirties, short with a square face and dark suit. 'This way.'

The room was almost bare, one metal desk and three chairs, the first behind it, the second in front and the third to the side. The only items on the desk were a telephone and a glass ashtray; in the corner on the right of the door was a hatstand.

'Thanks for coming.' The man behind the desk indicated with his hand that Hans-Joachim should sit down. He was older than the other, thinning hair swept back, and grey suit slightly shiny at the elbows. 'We all know why we're here.' He moved the ashtray to one side, as if clearing any obstacles to the conversation. 'Tell me about it.'

'A project to bring a number of people out, I need the money for certain equipment.'

How much money, he expected them to ask, what sort of project, how many people?

'Let's start at the beginning.' It was as if the man was settling into a routine. 'How did it start?'

When the Wall went up some students had family and friends in the East who needed help to get out, he began to say. Changed the word *students* to *people*. Of course Walter Thomaschett knew he was a student, he reminded himself, of course the politician would have told them all he knew about them.

'How did the people in the East know where to go.'

'We told them.'

'And how many people came out that way?'

'Eighteen, possibly twenty, sometimes more turned up than we expected or someone saw what was happening and joined in.'

The interrogator shook his head in apparent admiration, offered Hans-Joachim a cigarette and lit one for himself. 'What about after that?'

The man had not asked the obvious question, Hans-Joachim thought: how he communicated with those in the East. 'When they tightened security round the wire, and before they introduced the currency exchange certificates, we brought people out using false IDs.'

Again the man laughed. 'After that?'

'Over the Wall. The Liesenstrasse cemetery escape, for example.' Only where the politician knew names and locations did he give details.

'How did you manage that?'

The details were already public, but once he had talked about one case in detail the interrogator would take him back through the others. Not ask for names and personal details immediately, of course. First he would establish a general framework, then he would fill in the flesh and the muscle. Then he would ask the names.

He told the man what had been published about the Liesenstrasse escape.

'Going back to the early days. How did you get in touch with the people in the East?'

'Someone made contact with them, confirmed their identities and told them where to go and what to do.'

'How did they know who were the other escapers?'

'Simple code system.'

'Of course. Fancy a coffee?'

'Thanks.'

The second man left the room.

Everything calculated, Hans-Joachim thought. Even the timing of the interruption, designed to throw him off guard. As if – with only the other man in the room – the conversation would seem less important and he would relax.

'West German, of course.'

'Sorry?'

'West German who made the contacts in the East. West Berliners aren't allowed over.'

'Of course.' He sensed the flicker of first triumph in the other man, the elation at the withdrawing of first real information. 'Of course West Berliners aren't allowed over.'

'So he had to be West German?'

'West German ID cards. Everyone who went over used them because they were easy to forge.'

The second man returned with the coffee.

'What about the money?' Hans-Joachim cut the interrogation short.

'What money?'

'The money to finance another escape.'

'How many people?' It was the first time the second man had spoken, other than at the top of the stairs.

'Four or five.' Any more and the escape would have to be by tunnel. Unless it was by bus. In other circumstances he might have laughed. 'If it worked it might be possible to bring the same number over a second time.' There was a way he used the word *over* that they picked up – the suggestion that he was bringing escapers over the Wall in the specific sense rather than over from the East in general.

'Details?'

'No details.'

'No details no money.'

It was interesting how he had assumed that the man asking the questions was the one with the power, whereas it was the second man, the one who had fetched the coffee, who now confronted him.

'That was always the arrangement with Walter Thomaschett.'

'We're not Thomaschett.'

A set-up, he remembered he had sensed from the beginning. Something to do with the bloody politicians. He pushed back his chair and left.

The end of August was wet and stormy, clearing the air; the first day of September, a Sunday, was warm but fresh. Anja had returned to Berlin two weeks before, hated its sudden oppression. That afternoon she met Christian at the station and took the tram with him to his flat. That evening they ate the sauerkraut which she cooked and drank the red wine which he had brought back with him.

'Before you left for the vacation there was something I said I would tell you.'

'I remember.'

Christian lit a candle, the shadows dancing on the wall. Anja told him what she had done and studied his face for its reaction.

'I'm proud of you.' He knelt in front of her and cupped her face in his hands. 'You can't imagine how proud.'

'What about the others?'

'When they know they'll want to help.'

The Isetta bubble car was three years old and well maintained; its bodywork was red and unmarked, though it had not been polished recently. The driver was in his mid twenties, hair neatly cut, with spectacles; he wore an open-necked shirt and sports jacket and showed neither more nor fewer signs of nerves as he waited to leave the East at Checkpoint Charlie than any of those in front or behind him.

It was seven in the evening. Although it was still light the spotlights had been turned on for over an hour and there were border guards at every point in the complex as well as in the road leading to it. One guard in front and slightly to his right concentrating on him, the driver was aware, another behind also concentrating on him. He edged forward, pulled on the handbrake and switched off the engine. The Grepo in front was still looking at him, the other seeming to look at something else, no longer at him. He felt the relief and pushed open the front of the car.

Hardly any room for passengers let alone escapers, the Grepo at the rear thought. He shouldered the machine-pistol and waited. Standard procedure, two guards for every vehicle, partly psychological but partly to spot the telltale sign that one man might miss. The driver stepped from the car and walked towards the control station. The Grepo at the rear waited till he was inside then nodded at the guard in front. Even when it was apparently empty the car was still hard down on its suspension.

The telephone rang at ten.

'Detainees at Checkpoint Charlie.'

'One moment.' Langer switched off the record-player. 'How many?'

'Two.'

'We have them?'

'Yes.'

'Complications?'

'No.'

'Vehicle?'

'Cold storage.'

'You're carrying on?'

'Yes.'

When he arrived at work the following morning the initial reports were on his desk. It was not quite seven. Langer read them then drove to the detention and interrogation centre at Hohen-schoenhausen.

The room was six metres long and five wide, the interrogator seated behind a desk under the wall opposite the door, and the prisoner sitting on a chair in the centre of the floor and facing him, back to the door. The walls were white, although the suspect would not have noticed because of the arrangement of the lights, and the sound in the room was deadened, as if it was cut off even from the passage outside.

Langer entered the room and sat in the shadows. The prisoner's face was white with tiredness and his eyes were red, the stubble on his chin. He sat slightly forward, on the edge of the seat, his hands clasped in front of him between his knees, and his left eyebrow beginning to twitch. Without explanation the interrogator rose and left the room, Langer with him, and another took his place.

'How's it going?'

'I'm not sure.' The man's shirt was creased and he needed a shave. 'Something I can't put my finger on.'

Langer nodded then went into the second room. The woman seemed small, almost curled on the chair, as if she had not unwound from the position she had occupied in the concealed compartment of the Isetta. Her eyes were frightened and ringed in black, and the exhaustion was gravelled into her face.

'Stand up.'

She had barely noticed him yet had been terrified by his entry, had tried to ignore his presence. Slowly she rose from the chair, her body still curled as if she was protecting herself, as if she had received one beating and expected another. Langer left the room, the interrogator with him.

'Has she been like that all night?'

'Ever since she was brought in.'

'And nobody's touched her?'

'No one. First thing I checked when I saw her.'

The conference began at eight and was attended by the four men responsible for the interrogations overnight. Willhelm Schultz, aged twenty-five. Nationality West German. Marga Klein, aged twenty-three. Nationality East German. The details had been on the documents the couple had carried, everything apparently straightforward.

'What's wrong?' Langer came straight to the point.

'Him, her. We've talked about the details of the escape, but there's something about both of them.'

'Professional job?' Langer poured himself a second coffee. 'Money involved?'

'No. Personal.'

'How do they know each other?'

'He's at the Free University. We think she was a student there before the Wall went up, but neither have admitted that yet.' The men round the table contributed as they saw fit.

'What else?'

'The car. Neat job, heater removed and fuel tank reduced in size to create space, just enough petrol to get in and out.'

'But?'

'It's an old trick, they must have known we'd be looking for it.'

'So why did they try it?'

'Perhaps they had no alternative.'

'They would have.' He remembered the rumours of the tunnel.

'But if he had a better alternative then why didn't he wait for it?' It was the agent who had conducted the main interrogation with the woman.

'Perhaps he couldn't.'

'Why not?'

There were no suggestions.

One possible reason why not, he suddenly thought. Unlikely but worth a try. 'Break for ten minutes.'

The woman was curled on the chair, as if she had not moved. Langer nodded to the other man to leave and walked with him to the door so that the woman was aware the two of them were alone.

'Black or white coffee?' He moved the chair to the side of the desk, his features in the pool of light, and sat facing her.

She shook her head, arms wrapped in front of her, not looking at him.

'The doctor will be here in an hour.'

The woman glared at him and tightened her arms round her stomach.

'We're not monsters, Marga, we don't want any harm to come to the baby.' Find the weak link, they had taught him at the training school. Fear or friendship, it didn't matter. Then exploit it. 'When the doctor comes she'll take you both to hospital.'

'She?'

'Of course.'

'Thank you.'

'Black or white?' The repetition of the question and the omission of the word coffee cemented the relationship.

'White.'

'Sugar?' He led her to the beginning of the path.

She nodded.

'When did you last eat?' Helped her take her first steps along it.

'Yesterday morning. I was too worried to hold anything down after that.'

He rose, patted her on the shoulder and spoke to the guard

outside. 'A pot of coffee, please. Hot milk and sugar, and a plate of sandwiches.' Even the *please* was calculated and deliberate. When he sat down again she was wiping her face.

'How many months are you?'

'Five.'

'Doesn't show.'

'Thank God.'

He laughed with her. 'Parents not know?'

About the baby, she knew he meant, not about the escape. 'No.'

'You must have been worried curled up in the car like that, must have been frightened for him last night.'

'I was.'

'So why the car?'

'Why not the tunnel?' She was already so far down the path that she was not even aware what she had said.

He nodded as if he had known from the beginning. If only they were all so easy, he thought.

'Too many people on the list by the time we knew. This one's full up and I'd be too big to get through the next.'

He laughed again and went to the door. 'When the doctor comes Marga will be going to hospital. Can we find somewhere for her to lie down till her breakfast arrives?' He smiled at her the last time and went to the other interrogation room, again indicating that the agent questioning the prisoner should leave and taking his place behind the desk.

'Marga's going to hospital.' He was in the shadows, voice hard; he saw the new fear on the prisoner's face and the realization that Langer knew.

'How long will we get?' Willhelm Schultz was beginning to shake.

'A long time.'

'Months?' There was a desperation in the question.

'Marga's all right, the child's fine.' He did not answer the question. 'Hospital's just a precaution after all they've been through.' The voice may have been less harsh. Give a little, they had trained him, then threaten that it might be taken back. 'The child will be adopted at birth of course.' The voice was hard and bleak again. 'Don't worry, he'll be brought up by a good family.' The last edge of harshness was wrapped in apparent humanity and the more cutting for it. He moved into the light slightly. 'It's a long shot, but there may be an option.'

The prisoner straightened slightly.

'Marga keeps the child, I'll keep her out of a prison sentence on compassionate grounds.'

The man on the chair began to nod.

'You're lucky you tried the car.' Langer leaned forward slightly, face edged between light and dark, and gave Schultz the way out before the man even had the need to look for it. 'We've known about the tunnel for months.'

The prisoner relaxed, partly because he believed it, mainly because he wanted to.

'Who's involved?'

'I don't know.'

'Of course you know.' The hardness again, an astonishment that Schultz would expect him to believe that the prisoner did not know. 'Someone had to tell you that this list was closed; someone had to put Marga on the next.'

Schultz was turning, glancing from side to side. 'I mean I don't know their names.'

'But you could find out.' Nobody would know it was you, it did not need to be said. 'You'd have to be sentenced, of course.' Langer gave him no time to think. How long, Schultz had asked, still wanted to know. 'Nobody's denying that prison will be hard.' But if he went to prison, Langer reached inside the man's soul, manipulated the currents and cross-currents there, then he would have been punished for his act of betrayal *and* saved his son. Especially if prison was hard, especially if he suffered. 'Sometimes it will be bloody hell.'

'How long?'

'I'd get you out as soon as I could, then you could all leave the country.' He rose as if to leave, as if his leaving would close the option.

'How?' Schultz looked up in panic.

Langer knew he had won. 'Anyone waiting for you last night?'

'No.'

'In that case you return to West Berlin today. If anyone asks you tell them that Marga was sick and couldn't make the trip. One of my people will be on call for you to pass the names to. When we tell you, you come back again. Then we'll announce that you and Marga have been captured trying to escape.'

'You promise that Marga can keep the child?'

'I promise.'

Two hours later Marga Klein was admitted to hospital for observation. Shortly before midday she was visited by Willhelm Schultz, although she was given no time with him by herself. At one thirty Schultz was assigned the code name October and drove back across Checkpoint Charlie. On instructions from Langer, and in case the crossing was under observation from the West, his car was pulled aside and subjected to a search. The moment he drove out of the checkpoint and turned left into Kochstrasse the tails from State Security closed on him.

Anja left the library at six and went straight to Christian's flat. She was nervous, uncertain how the others would react. When he had first talked to them about the political leaflets, Christian had not told them that she had been involved. Only when he had been sure of them had he disclosed who had written and distributed the newsletters.

Christian arrived at six thirty, the first of the others at seven. Heinrich Gossmann was a postgraduate student in the philosophy department, almost Leninist in appearance Anja had often thought, but thinner and taller. She also considered him the most intellectual and therefore, she assumed, the most critical of the group. Christian opened the door and let him in.

'Brilliant.' Gossmann took her shoulders and kissed her. 'Absolutely brilliant.'

She began to smile, began to laugh, knew that after Christian's, his was the judgment she had most waited to hear.

'You mean it?'

He let her go and stood back, still looking at her. 'I wouldn't have said it unless I did.'

As each of the others arrived they reacted in the same way. When they had eaten the bread and cheese Christian had brought they sat round the kitchen table and pored over the first two newsletters, analysing their style and content, questioning Anja on her selection of subject matter and references to Party documents. At nine they began to write Newsletter Three.

*

The tunnel was close around him though Hans-Joachim Schiller hardly noticed. Forty-six metres, he checked the measurement. Another six and they would break through in the East. Four days at the present rate, he calculated, perhaps five, then the people would be coming through. It was mid evening, the men from one shift leaving and the first of the other beginning to arrive. He left the cellar and went upstairs to welcome them.

'The good news or the bad?'

It was two days since Langer had allowed Willhelm Schultz back into West Berlin. Present at the briefing were the agent who had been the contact point for him and the supervisor in charge of the surveillance team.

'The good.' Langer always believed in a positive attitude.

'We were lucky. October made his identification just before a shift change.'

'Address?'

'Sebastian Strasse. Two entrances, back and front, they use the back.'

'What's it opposite?'

'Dresdener Strasse.'

'You've checked it?'

'Not until you say so.'

Langer nodded. 'And the bad news?'

'Somebody got there before us.'

'What the hell do you mean?'

'The place is already staked out.'

Meyer, Langer knew. 'How?'

The supervisor drew a map and indicated the positions of the watchers and the back-up cars.

'But we're secure?'

'We're secure, the silly sods were too busy looking the other way.'

'I'll check, see if they're ours.' Bloody Meyer on to the tunnel after all the strings he had pulled to get Willi Schultz and Marga Klein their deal. 'Anything else?'

'October thinks it's about to happen.' Once Schultz had agreed to co-operate there had been a pride in the way he passed on the information about his friends. 'He identified some of the men coming off shift. Apparently they were elated. They wouldn't say anything but he reckons the tunnel's almost finished.'

The following morning, dressed as a tourist and carrying an FDR identification card, Langer crossed to the West and passed along Sebastian Strasse; three hours later and dressed as a workman, he entered Dresdener Strasse and made his way to the empty building where he assumed the tunnel from the West would be breaking through. The area was quiet, the steps to the cellar on the right, a door at the top. No point in checking, he knew, every reason not to. He left the area and returned to Lenin-Allee.

The telephone call came at seven on the direct line which his informants used.

'The leafletting at Karl Marx Allee and Nordbahnhof.' The informant always spoke quickly, almost in bursts. 'Someone from the university is involved.'

'Names?'

'None yet. There was a meeting last night.'

If the informant knew of the meeting then he would know at least some of those present, Langer thought. Small stuff, he was aware, the informant needing to play his game in his way. At another time, perhaps, he would have pushed the man. Tonight, however, his concern was the tunnel on Sebastian Strasse and the other team staking it out.

'Well done. Let me know as soon as you hear anything.'

The group met at eight in Christian's flat, at eight thirty they began the printing. By midnight the copies of Newsletter Three were folded neatly in the space Christian had prepared for them beneath the floorboards. That night, after she and Christian had made love, Anja lay looking at the ceiling and feeling the excitement running through her.

The breakthrough came ten hours earlier than anyone had anticipated. One moment the tunnel face was solid and the next the trowel had gone through. At ten that evening, after they had confirmed that the cellar in the East was secure, Max Steiner left to contact his couriers and Hans-Joachim Schiller to recall the men of the other shift.

Eleven hours later Langer was informed that men identified as tunnellers had entered the target location on Sebastian Strasse but that no one had left. At midday he received confirmation that, officially at least, no other Stasi team was operating in the relevant area of West Berlin. It could still be Gerhard Meyer, he knew; that was how Meyer would operate. One hour later he briefed his team leaders.

'The exit point of the tunnel is on Sebastain Strasse, entrance in Dresdener Strasse.' The locations were marked on the street map. 'Our teams will be in empty rooms round the courtyard in Dresdener Street, their job will be to apprehend anyone at the door, in the yard or in the cellar. They act only on my radio orders. Once they move other teams seal off the area. Operational headquarters will be here.' He indicated a building two blocks from Dresdener Strasse. 'I'll be there, in radio contact with the teams and telephone contact with Lenin-Allee. Any questions?'

'When do we think it goes down?'

'Tomorrow evening.'

The teams moved into position in the grey of morning. At two Langer gave his final briefing, at three he took position in the premises he had made his operational headquarters and from where he could observe the relevant buildings in both the East and the West. At four he confirmed communication links. At five he ordered radio silence.

The first courier crossed Checkpoint Charlie at eleven, the others following at half-hour intervals. At three thirty Max Steiner himself crossed. The afternoon was warm, slightly sticky, more like August than September. The minutes dragging, then the hours suddenly gone.

First dusk, the sky to the west a blaze of red turning purple. Anja stood looking at it from the window then left the library and took the tram to the café named after Unter den Linden, at the side of the university.

'Red. Parcel in position.' Even through the binoculars the figures on the corner seemed small, almost pathetic. 'On way.' Hans-Joachim watched the figure cross the street.

Corner of Dresdener Strasse, Langer noted, the intelligence he had received and the plans he had made based on that intelligence both correct, and his men perfectly positioned.

Package received, the words crackled on the radio. Two sets through, another eight to come that night. Hans-Joachim laid the walkie-talkie on the floorboards and focused the binoculars on the start point on the other side of the Wall.

Not yet, thought Langer. Let them relax – if that was the word – let them get a little more confident. The telephone from Lenin-Allee rang; he concentrated on the corner of Dresdener Strasse and waved to a lieutenant to take it.

'Headquarters. For you.'

The next escapers would be appearing at any moment. He held the telephone in one hand and the binoculars with the other.

'Duty officer. Someone giving the name of Otto Bruske called. Said it was urgent.'

The leafletting on Karl Marx Allee and Nordbahnhof, Langer knew, saw the figures. 'What did he say?'

'That they're meeting in the Unter den Linden in half an hour and putting out the pamphlets tonight.'

'Thanks.'

Tonight was the tunnel, the leafletting was a bonus. If the informant knew of the meeting then he now knew the names. And if he knew the names they could pick the bastards up in the morning.

'Red. Parcel in position.'

The next group through, he decided, and broke radio silence for the first time.

Langer was up to something, Meyer knew. All his team were out and the tension hung in the department like a tightrope. He left his office and walked to the operations room. 'Anything happening?' He looked over the man's shoulder at the duty log.

'Not much.'

Leaflets, Meyer picked out the words against Langer's name. Reference Karl Marx Allee and Nordbahnhof. Café Unter den Linden. 'Major Langer get the message?'

'Passed to him ten minutes ago.'

Langer doing the legwork but delaying the kill. Perhaps not making the kill at all.

*

They were all nervous, excited. Even Heinrich Gossmann, the philosopher. Anja had arrived at seven fifteen, Christian with the pamphlets minutes later, the others shortly after. Franz-Holger was the last to arrive, just before seven thirty, slightly out of breath from running. One more drink before they left: she would always remember it was Franz-Holger who suggested it.

'To us.' Christian raised his glass and smiled at her.

Everything was quiet, not even any Vopos around. Hans-Joachim watched the courier bring the escaper to the start point. Third set this evening and everything going to plan.

Let this one go half through, Langer decided. Wait until the attention was on the tunnel and the courier had left the corner, then he would move. Take out the men and escapers in the court-yard and cellar at the East end of the tunnel, then pick up the couriers as they arrived with the rest of the escapers. Only drop the charge down the shaft to seal the tunnel itself when he was sure he had everyone possible.

'Red. Package on way.'

'To us.' Anja smiled back and raised her glass to all of them. The café door opened and she glanced round. Stasi, the fear shrieked through her, mind racing and heart thumping. Not for us, can't be for us, nobody knows we're here. It was happening so quickly, no shouting or screaming, no one fighting back or trying to escape. The men leading them quickly and quietly from the café, two Stasi to each of them. She was looking for Christian, already separated. What will I say about him, what he will say about me? The first car drew up at the pavement and she was bundled into the rear seat, the two men still on either side of her. Mamma, what will happen to Mamma because of what I've done?

'Green. Coming through.'

In the cellar in the West Rolf crouched in the mouth of the tunnel and saw the shape of the escaper crawling through the shadows. 'White. Received.' He heard the crash on the door and looked up. The sledgehammers smashing against it and the men outside shouting. 'Stasi. Coming in the door now.'

Hans-Joachim heard the shout on the radio and misunderstood, assumed it must be the teams in the East.

'Red to all units. Stasi attacking cellar in East. Repeat, Stasi attacking cellar in East. Cellar in West get out now.'

'No.' He recognized Rolf's voice through the static. 'Stasi in West.'

What's happening, what the hell's happening? He swept the binoculars along the street in the East. Nothing. All quiet. 'Everyone, this is Red. Disturbance in West, all clear in East. On my way down. Stand by.' He dropped out of the roof space and ran down the stairs, radio in pocket and gun in hand.

Blue police lights: Langer saw the first flash across the Wall, what the hell was going on?

Hans-Joachim turned into the hallway and saw the policemen. West German. Thank Christ, he thought. 'Stasi,' he shouted at them. 'There's an escape going on, the Stasi are trying to stop it.'

'This is White.' He heard Rolf Hanniman's voice on the radio. 'We're ready.'

Six Walthers, Hans-Joachim thought; he had one, three in the East, two in the West. He raced into the yard and saw the uniforms of the policemen sledgehammering the door to the cellar. 'Stop.' Someone tried to stop him, he bulldozed through and came to the door. 'What the hell are you doing?'

The inspector at the door half turned and nodded to a sergeant to get him out of the way.

'The men inside are armed, they think you're Stasi.'

The inspector stopped the man with the sledgehammer. 'Who are you?'

'I'm in charge.' Hans-Joachim pulled the radio from his pocket. 'This is Red to White. It's our own police. Repeat. It's our own police. Open the door and let me in.' He faced the inspector. 'Pull your men back, I'll go first.' He heard the bolts being drawn and saw the door open. Rolf was crouched inside, the Walther pointing out.

Risk leaving the men in the East in position and give the couriers and remaining escapers a chance – Hans-Joachim's mind spun with the dilemma – or bring out the men round the tunnel now while they at least were safe. Max Steiner amongst the couriers in the East.

'Red to Blue and Green. Come out now.' Max would know when there was no one at the door, Max would be all right. The Grepos would soon be clambering over the place, alerted by the sirens and flashing lights in the West, Stasi as well. 'Repeat. Abandon everything and come out now.' No option, he knew. Good luck, Max.

Salvage what you can, Langer's calculations were fast and analytical. 'Abort operation.' The contact was still in place in the West. He would have to put more pressure on him, but there was no point revealing his knowledge of the tunnel and therefore his access to the tunnellers. 'All units maintain positions and observe but do not move.'

The police stood in a semicircle, guns trained on the mouth of the tunnel, and watched the last man crawl from the darkness.

'Why?' Hans-Joachim confronted the inspector.

'Reasons of state.'

They filed out of the cellar and into the vans parked outside, the police still around them and the guns still trained on them. Hans-Joachim saw the way the sergeant was looking at him and knew what he was going to say.

'Don't tell me that you're just obeying orders.' He stared hard at the man's eyes. 'That's what the guards said at Auschwitz and Dachau.'

The street was empty. It was ten minutes past eight, five minutes until he and the escaper were due at the start point, three blocks from the street on which the start point was situated. He had heard the police sirens earlier, coming from the West, but the evening was quiet again now. Max led the man round the corner and saw the courier. She shouldn't be here, he thought, she should be in Alexanderplatz picking up her next package. Meet me here in five minutes, he told the escaper. The courier saw him and turned right. Max Steiner crossed the road after her.

'Something's happened.' She was fighting to control herself. 'Everything seemed normal, I took my package to the start point and watched him cross the road. There was no one waiting for him, in the doorway or the courtyard.'

'You're sure he had the right door?'

'Positive. I watched him.'

'You didn't check yourself?'

'No.'

'You did the right thing.' Stasi, he knew. And if the Stasi knew about the tunnel then they would have the checkpoints covered, would know there would be couriers trying to get out and pick up anyone leaving East Berlin that night. But anyone staying till tomorrow would rouse suspicion anyway. Wait for the other couriers and send the rest of the escapers home, he made his decision. Risk Checkpoint Charlie tonight. He told the woman what to do and returned to the escaper.

The police station was busy. Hans-Joachim and the others were held for twenty minutes then released without charges or explanations. Why? Hans-Joachim wanted to ask again, knew there would be no answer. He told the others he would see them in the morning and went to Checkpoint Charlie.

The crossing was a blaze of searchlamps. Under normal circumstances Max would not have gone through so late. Not normal circumstances, he reminded himself. He opened the bottle of cheap schnapps, took a mouthful then spat it out and sprinkled the rest over his jacket, pulled at his shirt so that it was hanging outside his trousers, and walked unsteadily down Friedrichstrasse.

The doorway was behind the U-bahn station at Kochstrasse, a hundred metres from the crossing. Hans-Joachim stood back in it and watched the drunk lurch out of the control box, turn as if to offer the bottle to the guards, then stumble along the pedestrian walkway. A jeep was parked at the Allied post thirty metres west of the crossing. The drunk passed it, the soldiers not even looking, and walked up the road, saw the shadow in the doorway.

'The others are coming out at fifteen-minute intervals.' Max bent to tie a shoelace. 'I'll see you round the corner.'

The world outside the circle of light was dark and featureless. Anja saw the faces of the men only occasionally and then she wished she had not. Like the Nazis, she thought, like the Gestapo. She no longer knew how many hours, days, weeks it was since she had been taken, still trembled with every muscle of her body and every fibre of her soul when they brought her to the room and interrogated her. There had been no physical violence, but the fear they instilled in her had been worse. She was tired and hungry, and would give anything for a sip of water. The questioning began again.

Who helped you? Who gave you the words? Who told you to do it? Let's start from the beginning. Tell us about the leaflets on Karl Marx Allee.

These men rule the world, she thought, these men know everything and everybody and can do whatever they wish. I have been betrayed: the realization was almost as bad as the fact of her arrest and suffering, part of the weaponry they used against her. I have been betrayed by someone I called a friend.

'I did it by myself.' She reminded herself it was the truth, had begun to doubt whether it was. 'The last time was the first occasion on which the others were involved. My mother and my aunt knew nothing.' She repeated the line endlessly, even when they did not ask her, knew that if her mother was sent to prison she would not survive. 'My mother and my aunt knew nothing of what I was doing.'

The shadow left the room. Anja stared straight ahead and felt the terror as the other ghost stood behind her. Close enough to her to touch her.

'There *is* another way, Anja.'

The words recorded on the tape by the microphones in the ceiling conveyed the first sense of an offer, the first indication of a suggestion that if she herself became an informant things would be better for her.

'There *is* something you could do which might make things easier for you.' His fingers ran across her shoulders and down her back. 'No guarantee, of course, but there's always a chance.' Meyer's fingers ran up her sides and across her shoulders again, stroked her neck. 'The matter would only be between the two of us, of course. Nobody else would know.' The fingers were strong and thick, the hair on them black. Running across her face and down her throat, inside the first button. 'But if you did something for me then I might do something for you.' Meyer's hands were round her breasts, fondling them, his body hard against her back.

'No one else was involved. My mother and my aunt knew nothing of what I was doing.' She felt the trickle down her chin and on to her blouse, and realized it was the blood where she had bitten through her lip.

Langer was unsure how or when the idea had crept into his mind. Perhaps, he thought, it had been there for some time, feeling its way through the maze of games they all played, working out its own logic before becoming a conscious thought. It was six in the morning. He had woken at two and been in the office on Lenin-Allee by five, sitting at his desk and working out the details.

The incident at Sebastian Strasse had been a farce. In the long term, however, he had lost nothing – the informant Willi Schultz was still in place, still delivering details of the escape organization involved, even the first suggestion that another tunnel was already under way.

He sat back in his chair and looked again at the two options. Either he could play safe and go for the next tunnel, or he could take the risk and aim for something bigger, more ambitious. Something that would pay dividends in ten, twenty years' time. He cupped his chin in his hands and considered the second. If it did not come off he could still minimize his losses, might still be able to arrange things so that he got the next tunnel. But if it did then even the incident at Sebastian Strasse would contribute to it, help cover it.

He swung in his chair and looked at the names Schultz had provided: Schiller and Steiner, planners and original organizers; Conrad Wismar, one of the originals, now working in Stuttgart but still worth considering; Kurt Meixner and Rolf Hanniman, the other two originals and both still involved. Schiller and Steiner were non-runners, he already had the gut reaction; therefore he should target Wismar, Meixner and Hanniman. Find out more about all of them, he told himself, look for the weak link and the way in to it, then decide.

He turned his attention to the other problem. The case report and the interrogation transcripts lay in front of him. He had confronted Meyer, complained to Lindner that another officer had intervened in his case. Yet perhaps he owed Meyer, perhaps it was lucky that Meyer had acted the way he had done. For three nights now he had sat in his flat, drinking till the dawn came, and asking himself the same questions. What would he have done if it *had* been him who had gone to the bar? What would he have done when he saw Anja sitting there? What would he do now that he knew?

His own name was not in the description she had given of her background; as far as Meyer was concerned her political attitudes had only begun when Anja and her mother had come to Berlin. Langer had checked the transcripts of her interrogations himself. Covered his action a first time by saying he needed to protect his informant, and a second by asking for the transcripts of all the interrogations of those arrested.

Of course it was better to stay quiet, he decided. Not quiet, simply in the background. Of course it was better to wait till the moment when he really *could* help her.

The trial of Anja Lehnartz took place in room two of the People's Court in the centre of East Berlin. It lasted five minutes less than two hours and consisted of three items. The case against her, presented by a lawyer from the Prosecutor's Office; the Stasi evidence and samples of the material she had written and distributed; and a statement in her defence made by a lawyer who was also from the Prosecutor's Office. When the final submissions had been made the judge ordered her to stand.

'You have been found guilty of the most heinous act of treachery against the state.'

Anja stood straight, hands gripping the bar in front of her and a guard on either side. She could survive a year in prison, she thought, eighteen months, even two years.

'Not only were you the perpetrator of that act, but you have consistently refused to co-operate with the officers of State Security on the matter. Quite rightly, I am obliged to take this into consideration when passing sentence.'

She should have let the bastard in the shadows have her, the fear suddenly gripped her. Should have allowed him to do whatever he wanted.

'I therefore sentence you to seven years' imprisonment.'

*

The information had come from a range of sources, none of those supplying it knowing how it might be used. Each evening Langer sat alone and pulled the pieces together, tried to see where they were taking him. His original assessment had been confirmed: Schiller and Steiner were non-starters. Conrad Wismar was too comfortable in his job in Stuttgart. Rolf Hanniman was always at the front of everything and too close to Schiller and Steiner to turn against them, therefore also a non-runner. Kurt Meixner, he knew that logic dictated: family in the East – therefore both he and they exposed to blackmail and other pressures. Kurt Meixner, the logic was infallible.

The Kurfurstendamm was busy, the pavements packed with people and the shop windows filled with decorations and presents. In the square at the foot of the Kaiser Wilhelm Church someone was dressed as Santa Klaus, close to him a monkey danced on a barrel organ, children clustered round. Further away a band was playing carols.

The announcement was made simultaneously in the two halves of the city. *Realpolitik*. The new word in Berlin and Bonn. The Wall still standing and people still being shot when they tried to escape, but the East and West coming to the first understandings. Why the businessman had been persuaded to withdraw his funding, why the politician had passed Hans-Joachim to the BfV. The reason for the BfV interrogation and the police attack on the tunnel at Sebastian. The authorities in the East wanting the deal and those in the West cracking down on anything which might jeopardize it.

> *Following discussions between the German Democratic Republic and the German Federal Republic, special passes would be available to citizens of West Berlin to visit their relatives in the East of the city that Christmas.*

The detail was almost lost in the mass of information he had compiled. Langer directed the light from the desk lamp on to the page and wondered how many times he had missed it. Not missed it, failed to see how he could use it. The first run, Schiller waiting at the wire on Kommandante Allee and Steiner at the pick-up points along Karl-Liebknecht Strasse: Conrad Wismar's girlfriend, Kurt Meixner's brother, Rolf Hanniman's girlfriend. Three contacts, only two turning up.

Thank God people were less security-conscious about the past, he thought; thank God that even though those who helped with the escapes seldom talked about them, the escapers themselves did. He already knew how he would ensnare then turn her, how he would persuade her to run against her former boyfriend.

Of course I was there. Of course I waited. He could imagine the moment Rolf Hanniman's girlfriend confronted him. It was Max Steiner who didn't show. Max Steiner who let me down and Hans-Joachim who covered for him and lied to you about it.

I don't want you to do anything against those you thought were your friends, even though they betrayed you. He was already planning his own meeting with Rolf Hanniman, what he would say and how he would say it. I don't even want you to stay in Berlin. I want you to go West, screw the bastards who screwed you when you were the one inside the door at Sebastian Strasse. There would be risks of course, he would concede that at the right point, but that was all part of it, one of the reasons Hanniman might agree to it. Plus the details of the bank account in Switzerland if he saw that Rolf Hanniman was beginning to turn.

CHAPTER EIGHT

EXACTLY TWO weeks following the Christmas Day which had caused the débâcle on Sebastian Strasse, Tunnel Twenty-Eight broke through; the following morning the couriers went into East Berlin. Max Steiner crossed shortly after ten through Gartenstrasse, driving the light blue second-hand Opel he and Hans-Joachim had bought. He wore a suit and his hair was neatly cut, as if he was a businessman or a company rep. When questioned by border officials he stated he was attending a trade fair being held in the city. At nine that evening he waited for word that the escape had been cancelled, by ten he knew it was confirmed, at eleven he went to bed. At three, almost four, he finally managed to sleep.

It was three minutes past seven, the evening wet outside and the first escaper about to enter the tunnel in the East. The cellar was stacked high with soil and the electric lights were draped along the wall.

'Green. Coming through.'

Rolf Hanniman looked across at Hans-Joachim Schiller. 'This is my last time, Hans.'

They heard the breathing in the tunnel as the woman shuffled through.

'I've got a job in West Germany. This is my last run.'

The woman reached the end of the tunnel; they saw her head suddenly appear and the disbelief on her face. One of the others began to help her up but Hans-Joachim held him back.

'This one's Rolf's.'

Two Saturdays later they held a party for Rolf Hanniman in the flat on Vorbergstrasse. When the last guests left Hans-Joachim, Max and Rolf sat on the floor, drinking beer and remembering the escapes in which the three of them had worked together. Six hours later they drove to Tegel airport.

So many people with the one simple reason to thank Rolf, Hans-Joachim thought.

'Good luck.'

The airport was quiet, only a handful of people checking in for the flight.

'You too.'

The May Day parade along Unter den Linden began at ten and finished in the early afternoon. When it was over Werner Langer spent thirty minutes confirming the success of that section of the security arrangements which had been his responsibility, then was driven to the reception which customarily ended the day.

The banqueting hall was full. The old guard and the new, he looked around: the men who held power now and those who wished to inherit it from them. Party leader Ulbricht talking to Honecker; Mielke, head of State Security and Honecker's man, always close by. The politburo in attendance and the general council waiting upon them. Dieter Lindner was in a group on the far side of the room; in the opposite corner Heinz Moessner was talking with Gerhard Meyer. When Ulbricht went and if Honecker took his place, Langer thought, both Lindner and Moessner were certain of places on the Collegiate of State Security. Both too old to be Mielke's successor, but both would be close enough then to help determine who it might be. Twenty-five years into the future.

'Someone was asking about the escape attempt at Sebastian Strasse.' Lindner lit himself a cigarette. 'It was noted that you had advance intelligence on the plan and that your teams were in position but were thwarted by the West police.'

Langer wondered what he was being told.

'It was also noted, however, that even after the West intervened you could still have arrested a number of the escapers and helpers.'

'Why is that important?'

'Of this year's promotions, people were looking at two in particular. Meyer's is one, yours was the other.'

'Why *was*?'

'Some consider that you showed a lack of judgement in not arresting those you could on Sebastian Strasse.' Lindner waved to a waiter for fresh drinks. 'I assume there was a reason.'

Why now? Langer thought. What was happening that Lindner had chosen to warn him today?

'Of course.'

Lindner waited. Langer took a drink from the tray and allowed the waiter to drift away.

'The escape organization in question is run by two men, Hans-Joachim Schiller and Max Steiner, both officially students at the Free University. There was a third, Rolf Hanniman, but he left Berlin three weeks ago.'

'How long have you known?'

Langer shrugged.

'So the next tunnel and you take them?' Lindner lit himself another cigarette.

'Not the next, the one after.'

'I assume you have a reason.'

Langer told him.

Mielke was walking towards them.

'Excellent.'

Even through the cell window Anja could sense the change in the season. She had been in the prison at Brandenburg almost a year, autumn into winter into spring into summer. Now summer into the first stages of autumn. Another six such cycles and she would be free. Another six years and she would be old and worn before her time. It was five in the morning. The cell was cold and damp, with faded lime green walls and concrete floor, and the four women crammed into it.

Once a month she received a letter from her mother, carefully written and closely censored. Once a month she sent her mother a letter, even more carefully composed, always happy and full of confidence. At no point had either mentioned Christian or the others in the group. It was the way she conducted her life now. Making contacts but few friends, making friends but trusting hardly any of them, even though they were her age and political prisoners like herself. Ursula from Dessau. Isolade, who they called Isa, from Magdeburg. Heidi from Dresden.

At five thirty she pushed back the blanket and rolled off the bunk. Fifteen minutes later she was let out of the cell and escorted to her job in the kitchens. The day was long and the work hard, the kitchen supplying food for both the women and the men held separately on another floor. By the time she returned to her cell Anja was exhausted.

The evening was drawing in; through the window she could smell the autumn. Only six more years, she told herself. She pulled the blanket over her and tried to sleep.

Langer received Lindner's call shortly before five. That evening he had tickets for the Distel cabaret. He hoped the meeting wouldn't take long and took the lift to the third floor.

Lindner's desk was across the top of the room, in the centre, the other desk running from it. The longer the conference desk, they all joked, the greater the power. The walls were sparsely furnished, each item carrying a political significance for Lindner: a photograph of the Kremlin, a meeting with Ulbricht, a third showing Khrushchev arriving at East Berlin's Schönefeld airfield, another with Honecker and Mielke. Langer had seen them before, studied the detail in them. One photograph was missing.

'Khrushchev.' Lindner poured them each a coffee.

The Soviet leader was holidaying on the Black Sea, Langer knew. He took the cup and poured a little milk into it.

'The old guard kicked him out this morning.' Lindner's voice was matter of fact. 'Not like a Russian to be away when someone might stab him in the back. Brezhnev's the new General Secretary.'

There would be repercussions down the line, they both understood, the changes in Moscow bringing changes throughout the Soviet empire and the countries of the Warsaw Pact. In the office on the other side of the building, Langer was aware, Moessner would be briefing Meyer.

'We talked of promotions.' Lindner placed his cup on the desk. 'If you have anything interesting, now might be the time to bring it together.'

The tunnel on Bernauer Strasse was one hundred and fifty metres long – it had been necessary to clear not only the Wall but the area stripped of houses on the eastern side – and cost one hundred thousand Deutschmarks. Its start point, like the start point for the first tunnel at Heidelbergerstrasse, was a disused bakery but larger, the massive cellar and ground floor packed with the earth they had removed, and the finish was in Schönholzer Strasse, a nondescript street directly opposite. Its floor was rutted by the iron wheels of the trolleys they had used to remove the earth from the tunnel face, and ventilation pumps ran along its length to provide at least some air to the men digging.

In a way they had known for some time that the tunnel on Bernauer Strasse would be the last. The Wall had changed: the death strip had been widened, security within it increased, and the last of the houses close to it demolished. In addition to the main wall in the West, a second wall had been built in the East, partly to deter escapers but also to obstruct the view of the death strip from the East. Two weeks before the rumour had started that the authorities were considering a prohibited zone adjacent to the strip to which only those with special passes would be admitted.

Hans-Joachim felt the hand on his shoulder and jerked awake. The wood was creaking; he was unsure whether it was the roofing props in the tunnel or the floorboards in the shop, one straining under the weight of soil above it and the other from the mass of excavated material.

'We're ready to break through.'

Eleven thirty-seven, Tuesday evening. He pulled on his shoes, went to the cellar and climbed into the tunnel. Three minutes later he reached the shaft in the East.

The dummy had already been brought through. Hans-Joachim climbed the ladder, Max just below him, and pushed the broom handle against the crust of soil. He felt the handle break through, the crust only two centimetres thick, and withdrew it, transferred the gun to his right hand.

The eye looked at them. Green, the light dazzling like crystals from the dark of the pupil. The eye moved fractionally, the patterns of light in it changing, then disappeared. Now, he knew. The paw of the cat came through the hole, the pads black and the claws feeling for the creatures below.

The crossing at Heinrich-Heine Strasse was on what had once been a major road, the concrete either side, the barrier across the entrance and zigzags inside to prevent anyone crashing through.

The control box itself was on the right, guards searching each of the vehicles leaving the East and examining beneath them with mirrors. The driver in front stepped into the box; five minutes later he came out and Max Steiner took his place. The room was ten metres by eight, an official seated at a desk, what appeared to be a window of smoked glass behind him, and guards all round.

'Reason for entering the GDR?' The official was short and did not seem to have shaved properly, his suit was cheap grey and the collars of his shirt turned up at the edges.

'Business. I'm visiting the engineering fair.'

The official stamped his entry visa, exchanged his Deutschmarks for Ostmarks and nodded him through.

The man behind the one-way mirror was younger and better dressed. Only after Max Steiner had left and the official at the front desk had turned his attention to the next motorist did he lift the telephone and dial the direct number into the office on Lenin-Allee. Langer was informed immediately. His first action was to telephone the Stasi officer at the Henrich-Heine crossing and congratulate him on his observation and his second was to notify Lindner.

The brigadier, he was told, was not available. Langer could imagine where he was. After the fall of Khrushchev in Moscow, the first reaction of Party chief Ulbricht would be to speak to the Soviet ambassador in Berlin, and the second to liaise with his favoured son. Honecker, in turn, would consult with Mielke and Mielke would summon his cabal. Throughout the country over the next days each branch of each section of the Party would be discussing the future, faction lobbying faction, but none so important as the Party within State Security.

He thanked Lindner's secretary and called a meeting of his team leaders.

Lindner returned at seven and Langer was summoned at eight. The meeting with Mielke had gone well, he sensed immediately, the mere fact of Lindner's presence at it a guarantee of the future.

'Everything's in order.' Lindner poured two glasses of Moscow Sky. 'Better than that.' He pushed a glass across the desk top. 'Honecker built the Wall, Brezhnev likes it, so Honecker's in favour in Moscow. It gives the old guard a strong hand here, of course. The Central Committee will be split for the next ten years.' He savoured the vodka. 'You have something for me.'

'Steiner came East today, which means they broke through last night. If the routine is the same as on previous tunnels the first escapers will go out tomorrow night.'

'How can you be sure?'

'He only comes East when he's sending his couriers over.'

'Where is he now?'

'He went back at six.'

'So what do you intend?' Lindner's eyes were sharp, his mind planning ahead.

'Pick him up as he comes over tomorrow and try to get the location of the tunnel from him.'

'And if we don't?'

'Then we saturate the area close to the Wall, identify the couriers and their escapers, and let them run until they lead us to the tunnel.'

'And pick them up when?'

'When we know where the tunnel is, sometime tomorrow night.'

'They normally take people out over two nights?'

'Normally, yes.'

'In that case leave it till the second.'

'Why?'

'There's a meeting that night. Honecker and Mielke, plus others, as well as some of the Friends. It would help if you could report in with an arrest while the meeting was in progress.'

'A gamble.'

'Worth taking.'

'A compromise. Go for the tunnel on the night of your meeting but pick up Steiner tomorrow.' There was no protest at the assumption that Lindner would attend the Honecker meeting. 'There's a chance they might abandon the tunnel when he goes missing but at least you're guaranteed a body.'

'Agreed, just make sure that whatever you do is spectacular.'

The crossing at Heinrich-Heine Strasse was busy, three cars pulled in front of him and two behind. It was ten in the morning, the day cold but dry. Max Steiner switched off the engine and went into the control box. The same officials as yesterday, he thought, and handed his identity card over the desk.

'Reason for entering the GDR?'

Sometimes the procedure took only minutes, sometimes the guards were under instructions to inconvenience travellers and it took two hours.

'Business, I'm attending a trade fair.'

'You attend an awful lot of trade fairs, Herr Steiner.' The two men were in their thirties, neat dark suits, not crumpled like that of the official at the desk, white shirts and blue ties.

'I'm sorry, I don't know what you mean.' He knew who they were and why they were there. Thank God he'd brought some samples, collected some brochures from yesterday. Thank God he'd built up his cover.

Eighteen years; the blood suddenly pounded through his brain. He walked between them into the small office at the rear. There were more Stasi there, also wearing suits. Quickly they searched him, placed the contents of his pockets in brown paper envelopes and the envelopes in a briefcase. The handcuffs were slipped on him then the dark glasses, and he was led quickly from the room. Everything designed to induce fear if it did not yet exist, increase it the moment it began. The rear of each lens of the glasses was lined with a layer of cork, so that he could not see where he was going. The engine of the car was already running. He was half pulled half pushed into the rear seat, the doors shut and the driver accelerated out of the compound and into the traffic of East Berlin.

The rest of the world sees me and thinks I am still part of it, he suddenly thought. Only I know that I am not.

The room outside the circle of light was like a void, nothing except the vaguest outlines of the men and the razor sharpness of their questions.

'Your visits to East Berlin last September?'

'The book trade fair.'

'In April?'

'The printing exhibition.' He had lost count of time, no longer knew whether it was night or day.

'What about yesterday?'

His mind and body were already weakening, the interrogators changing, always seeming to be fresh and alert.

'Forget the fairs, Max, let's just look at the dates. The first tunnel. That was on Heidelbergerstrasse, wasn't it?'

Don't think of the tunnel on Bernauer Strasse, Max.

'Then the little problem at Sebastian Strasse. After that Tunnel Twenty-Eight.'

You're already thinking about it, and once they've got you thinking about it they'll soon have you telling them where it is.

'Then April and Tunnel Thirty-Three.'

How do they know so much, how do they know everything? How do they even know what we call the tunnels? Same reason they knew about you, Max, same reason they were waiting for you.

'Red. Package in position.'

It had been dark an hour and a half.

'On way.'

The second courier of the night. Hans-Joachim watched as the escapers walked diagonally across Schönholzer Strasse. One of the lights on the death strip blinked out then came on again.

'Blue. Received.'

'Green. Coming in.'

The twin headlamps of the Grenztrabant bumped along the patrol road inside the Wall and stopped at a watch-tower. He smiled. Right over the tunnel, the escapers probably directly beneath it.

'White. Through.'

Two minutes to eight, time for Max. Hans-Joachim forgot about the elation in the cellar and concentrated on the corner. Eight o'clock. No problem, a minute either side, they normally agreed, two minutes tonight but then they would be pushing it, in danger of a traffic jam in the tunnel. Three minutes past.

'Red, no contact.' Max being careful, he told himself, it had happened before: an escaper slightly late, a Vopo patrol in the wrong place at the wrong time. 'Everything quiet,' he reassured everyone. 'Looking good.' He focused the binoculars on the corner and waited for the next escapers.

Blocks one, five and nine were clean, no activity in any one of them. Langer had divided the streets to the east of the Wall into sections then subdivided the sections into blocks and assigned men to each, beginning with those closest to streets in the West. The teams moved on to the next; he left his office and returned to the interrogation room.

Nine thirty-three. No Max for the second time.

'Red. No contact. Everything fine.'

What must the men in the doorway and the cellar in Schönholzer Strasse be thinking, how must the escapers Max was supposed to be escorting out be feeling? What's up, Max? Where the hell are you?

Blocks two, six and ten were clean, Langer was informed, the teams were moving on to three, seven and eleven. He had planned the blocks logically beginning with the locations where a tunnel would be shortest. Perhaps he was wrong, he began to think, perhaps he had been too logical. He lifted the telephone and changed his orders.

Hans-Joachim watched the last escapers leave the corner and cross Rheinsberger Strasse. All quiet and everything like clockwork, except for Max. He waited till the men at the bottom of the shaft in the East had radioed that the escapers were in the tunnel and that the cellar had been cleared, then came down from the roof space.

Max was in trouble, he knew; either someone he was picking up that night had betrayed him or the Stasi had infiltrated them. The other runs had gone well, so it was more likely to be the first. But if Max had been betrayed, he argued, he would not have been arrested, would have been allowed through so that he could lead the Stasi to the tunnel. Therefore something minor, he tried to tell himself; Max was safe, probably waiting at the flat.

The courtyard behind Bernauer Strasse was empty. He checked that the bakery was not under surveillance, let himself in and went to the cellar. The last escapers had just crawled from the tunnel. The girl being hauled up on the hoist on the rough wooden seat was seven, perhaps eight, wearing only a black vest and white underpants; her hands were clutching the rope and the bandages

which the men in the East shaft had wrapped round her knees
were brown with soil. At the top her mother held a bag containing
her coat, trousers, shoes and socks. In the room upstairs some of
the escapers were sipping soup, others sitting quietly and staring,
beginning to shake at the realization of what they had just done.

'There might be a problem.' Hans-Joachim cleared the cellar of
escapers and addressed the tunnellers. 'Max didn't show tonight.
It could be that there's a simple reason, it could be he's been
captured. We have no idea at all about the escapers he was
escorting.'

The men around him were still stripped to the waist, their
trousers and bodies dirty and their faces etched with fatigue and
sudden anxiety.

'I'll leave now and see if Max is back. If he's not we have to
decide whether to abandon the tunnel or to risk bringing the rest
of the people out tomorrow night.' He was aware that whilst some
of the men had seen their friends and families come through that
night others were still waiting. 'I suggest that none of us here has
a right to make that decision; the only people with that right are
the couriers who go over again tomorrow.' The men nodded and
he came to the last point. 'If we do go ahead there'll be a minor
change of plan. I'll be in charge of the party in the East.'

'Schönholzer Strasse, number twenty-two. Same routine as before.'
It was two in the morning, the last teams had arrived fifty minutes
before, the table littered with coffee cups and sandwich plates.
'The start point is on the corner with Ruppiner Strasse.'

Nobody except the interrogators knew of the presence of Max
Steiner in the room below.

The other end of the tunnel in Bernauer Strasse, over a hundred
and fifty metres across the Wall. Langer felt the frisson of admiration for the opposition and pushed on with the briefing for the
following evening.

'Number twenty-two is sacrosanct, nobody goes near it. Teams
in position in surrounding streets ready to close in, but not in the
approach road which the couriers use. I'll be in Schönholzer
Strasse, as close as I can to number twenty-two; I'll try to find
out what's happening inside then call you in.'

It was past three. He asked the chief interrogator and team

leader to stay, congratulated the squads on the night's work and told them to go home. 'I'll be down in ten minutes. Don't mention Schönholzer Strasse till I do.'

The interrogator left, only the section leader and Langer remaining.

'Tomorrow's important. When we find the tunnel we blow it up, even if there's no escape going on.'

'What if we don't find it?' The section leader sat on the edge of the desk, the cups and plates scattered behind him and his eyes tinged pink with tiredness.

'We blow it up anyway.' He drained the coffee and went to the interrogation room.

All Max Steiner wanted to do was sleep; all he could do was to keep awake, he told himself, remain alert to their questions. Once he relaxed he would be off his guard, and once he was off his guard they would have him. The door behind him opened and another man came in and sat in the dark to the right of the interrogator.

'Shame about Hans-Joachim. Shame about Bernauer Strasse.'

Langer leaned forward and Max saw his face, recognized him.

'Schönholzer Strasse, number twenty-two. Escapers every thirty minutes just as you said.'

Max was not at the flat; Hans-Joachim had spent the hours till first light between Checkpoint Charlie and the crossing at Heinrich-Heine Strasse. At seven he drove to the apartment block on Reuterstrasse; the courier's flat was on the third floor and the man was already awake.

'There's a problem.' The kitchen was at the rear of the apartment; Hans-Joachim sat at the table and wrapped his hands round the mug of coffee. 'Max is missing, the Stasi might know about the escape.'

'Why are you telling me?'

'Because you and the others who are supposed to go in to the East today are the only ones with the right to decide whether or not you do.'

'Are my parents out?'

Hans-Joachim knew why the man asked. 'They came through last night.'

'Who brought them out?'

'It doesn't matter.'

'Are his or her people out?'

'No.' He had known all along how the courier would react but felt a duty to ask. 'You were going to bring them out tonight.'

The courier nodded. 'I didn't sleep much last night, not at all in fact. I'm due to cross again at twelve. I really should get some rest before then.'

The night was dark, the thinnest crescent of a moon. In the green of the night binoculars the figures on the corner seemed smaller and even more pathetic than usual.

'Red. Package in position.'

Hans-Joachim heard the message on the radio. Three groups through so far. He opened the door and looked up and down the street.

'On way.'

The Walther hung heavily in his right jacket pocket. He glanced up and down the street again and saw the four people hurrying from the corner with Ruppiner Strasse.

'Tokyo.' The code was different tonight, not because of Max's disappearance but as standard security.

Hans-Joachim led them through the archway, around the court-yard and into the cellar, a lookout taking his place at the door. Nobody was due for another twenty minutes but there was no point in taking risks. He handed the family to the men at the shaft and watched as the first was lowered on the hoist.

'Tokyo.' The surveillance technician pulled the headset off. Directional microphone at thirty-five metres.

Langer crossed Schönholzer Strasse and knocked on number twenty-two.

The guard opened the door fractionally, the security chain still in place, and saw the man outside: twenties, slightly frightened, coat threadbare and trousers bagging at the knees.

'A friend told me to come here.' Langer glanced over his shoulder.

'Who?' The guard saw the way the man looked round him again, saw how terrified he was.

'He said you would help me. He said to tell you Tokyo.'

The guard slid off the security chain and let him in. 'This way.'

Hans-Joachim left the shaft, closed the door of the cellar and began to skirt round the courtyard. In the shadows he saw the two figures, faces lost in the dark inside the door to the street. He recognized the man he had left on the front door but not the other, stayed in the shadow and watched.

'What did you say your friend was called?'

Hans-Joachim heard the whisper of the question across the yard.

'Helmut, he's at the university.'

Hans-Joachim tried to remember the list of escapers.

'Okay.' He heard the guard again. 'Come on.'

'There's another friend, he was too scared to come. Can I get him?'

'Where is he?'

'Two streets away.'

'Ten minutes.' The guard opened the door and Langer slipped back across the street.

'Who was that?' Hans-Joachim ran across the yard.

'Friend of Helmut's, he's gone to get another friend. It's okay, he knew the code word.'

No way the man could have the night's code. There had been nothing on the radio to suggest that a courier had brought an escaper to the start point and no way an escaper could know the code or the location without a courier telling him.

'Stasi,' Hans-Joachim whispered in the radio. 'Everyone in East get out now. Repeat out now. West clear shaft and cellar.' One way the Stasi would know the code, the suspicion hung in his brain.

The other man was already running, across the courtyard and into the cellar. Hans-Joachim locked and bolted the door from the street into the archway and pulled the security chain into place, then closed and locked the door from the archway into the court-yard. It couldn't have been Max who had betrayed them, Max didn't know the code for tonight.

Two minutes gone – his mind was cold, analytical – eight minutes before the Stasi came back. The men in the East shaft would be three-quarters of the way through the tunnel now, the man who had guarded the door almost half. What about the couriers, what about the poor bastards they were bringing in?

It was six minutes before he was due back. Langer slipped the machine pistol under his coat. All units stand by, he whispered on the radio. The first team round the corner as soon as the front door was opened, no more than five seconds behind him. Standing by, he heard the crackling on the radio. The gunfire shattered the silence and carried across the city. Small arms in a confined space – the thought was automatic.

'Go.' Langer knew what it was and screamed down the radio.

'What the hell is it?' The man beside him was still reacting.

'Schiller warning his couriers.'

Hans-Joachim locked the door behind him, locked the second door into the cellar. No time for the ladder, hope to Christ the lights stay on. He grabbed the rope of the hoist and slid down, skin burning and ankle twisting as he struck the bottom. Two and a half minutes to the end of the tunnel, two if he was lucky. One and a half before the bastards got through the doors into the cellar. Everybody out; he was almost talking to himself, scurrying on his hands and knees, for Chrissake everybody out. Thirty seconds, forty. A quarter way through the tunnel, almost a third. He bumped into a prop and felt it give slightly. There was little oxygen in the tunnel and his lungs were on fire. A minute gone, minute to go. Langer was in the cellar and down the ladder. Hans-Joachim knew what the bastard was going to do and saw someone at the end of the tunnel. Get out the way, he shouted. Langer took the hand-grenade from his pocket, pulled the pin, lobbed it into the mouth of the tunnel and ran from the cellar. F1 anti-personnel hand-grenade, six-hundred-gram weight filled with TNT, fuse delay four and a quarter seconds, fragmentation radius above ground twenty metres. Almost there, Hans-Joachim thought, the face gone from the end. Back racked and muscles seizing. He reached the bottom of the shaft and began to pull himself up the ladder, hands reaching down and hauling him up. Get out of the cellar, he was shouting, get upstairs. The night erupted, the shock waves pounding down the tunnel and bursting into the shaft. Out, Hans-Joachim could hear his own voice. No point in secrecy now. His head was bursting and his ears almost rupturing. Get everyone outside.

The meeting began at eight and was chaired by Erich Honecker, refreshments being served at nine thirty. At five minutes past ten, as the food was being cleared, an official entered the room and handed a typewritten note to Mielke. The head of State Security read it, folded it again and passed it across the table to Honecker.

'There's been a shooting incident on Schönholzer Strasse.' Honecker rubbed his forehead with his fingers, as if he had a sudden headache. 'It was followed by an explosion.' They all knew what he was thinking. Not a report about an explosion in the heart of the capital relayed to him in the presence of senior security officials from Moscow. Not so soon after the Brezhnev coup.

There was a second knock on the door, the same official entered and handed Lindner a single sheet of paper. He read it and looked up.

'The incident on Schönholzer Strasse. It seems there was a tunnel under the Wall. The explosion was my men blowing it up. The ringleader is already being interrogated.' He did not see fit to add that Max Steiner had already been in custody for thirty-six hours.

'Excellent.' Both Honecker and Mielke noted the agreement from the officials from Moscow. 'Who was in charge?'

'Major Langer.'

CHAPTER NINE

THE WINDOW was less than half a metre high and barely a quarter of a metre wide, tucked into the folds of the roof so that from below it was barely visible. The attic, if it was large enough to be called that, was entered by a set of rickety wooden stairs leading off a landing packed with discarded chairs and boxes of food for the shop below. The plaster was falling from the walls and there was no heating or ventilation, so that in winter it was painfully cold and in summer stifling hot. Hans-Joachim had rented it for cash, no receipt asked for or given, and it overlooked the crossing into East Berlin at Checkpoint Charlie. The only furniture was a chair, placed half a metre back from the window. Now he sat, binoculars in hand and flask of coffee laced with whiskey on the floor, and waited.

Fifty-seven people had crawled from the tunnel in Bernauer Strasse. In the weeks after, Hans-Joachim had pored over the details, tried to work out how Max Steiner had been taken, come to the inevitable conclusion. Because of this, and because there was no way he could identify the traitor, he had wrapped up the organization and apparently shut himself off from the world.

It was eight in the evening, exactly on time: he saw the taxi and focused the binoculars. There had been eleven vehicles or individuals in which he had been interested, reduced to three and now to one. The cab stopped and the man left it and walked into the control box by the vehicle lane reserved for those with diplomatic clearance. Less than a minute later he left the box and walked briskly through the checkpoint to the cab waiting for him in the West.

The routine was clockwork – Tuesdays, Fridays and Saturdays. Hans-Joachim had seen it after four weeks and confirmed it over another two. Low-ranking diplomat from one of the Middle East embassies, not much older than himself, probably a student who somehow engineered his way to a diplomatic posting and found himself grounded in the frugality of East Berlin. Diplomatic status but not enough money to buy the CD plates to which he was entitled and which would have guaranteed him unfettered access through the borders of any country, let alone a car on which to put them.

He locked the attic and left.

The magazine meeting was at ten the following morning.

'Good to see you again. What do you want?' The editor offered coffee and came straight to the point.

'As you know, Max Steiner has been sentenced to eighteen years. I want to get him out.'

The magazine, like all other publications both in West Berlin and West Germany, had carried photographs of the remnants of Tunnel Fifty-Seven. Unlike the others, however, it had carried exclusive photographs of the escapers emerging from the tunnel itself the night before, a girl on the hoist and the moments of triumph and reunion.

'So what do you want from me?'

'A contact in the mayor's office.'

You're *persona non grata*. The journalist's expression said it all. You make trouble on both sides of the Wall. He leaned forward, picked up the telephone and dialled a number.

'Tomas, it's Wolfgang. Good to speak to you again; how's business?' It was the way he started each conversation. 'Look, I've got someone with me who'd appreciate a meeting; I'm not sure what it's about but I think it could be important.' Who, Hans-Joachim heard the question. 'Hans-Joachim Schiller.' He sensed the way the other man prevaricated. 'Good photo of the mayor last week, I thought. Wouldn't mind another like it some time. Excellent. Speak to you soon.'

He put down the telephone. 'Tomas Schubert next Tuesday at four o'clock. He says he's busy, you've got ten minutes. If you get him on-side, he's your man.'

'But?'

'He's slippery. He'll probably ask if you take coffee and by the time he's given you the milk your time's up and you're out.'

'Thanks.'

'If anything happens I want in.'

'Of course.'

The meeting the following Tuesday took place at the Senate

House. Hans-Joachim Schiller wore a suit, collar and tie and arrived earlier. At four exactly he was shown into the office of the mayor's political secretary. The man was in his early thirties, well dressed, with the photogenic features and diplomatic calm which had already marked him for advancement. The coffee was on the table at the side. The politician poured them each a cup, taking his time, and asked whether Hans-Joachim preferred milk or cream.

'Milk.' He leaned forward and accepted the cup, did not need to look at the clock.

'Sugar?'

'No.'

'How do you know Wolfgang?' The politician settled behind his desk, laid his own coffee on a mat and adjusted a cuff-link.

Hans-Joachim ignored the pleasantries and came to the point. 'As you know, I organize escapes from East Berlin. As you also know a colleague has been arrested in the East and is now serving an eighteen-year prison sentence. I would like your help in getting him out.'

'Difficult.' The composure was unruffled, the hand still playing with the cuff-links.

Any moment now he'll look at his watch, Hans-Joachim thought, any moment now his personal assistant will telephone and inform him that his next appointment was waiting. '*Realpolitik*,' he suggested.

'Exactly.' Tomas Schubert looked at his watch.

'Let me tell you what I intend to do if you don't help me.' Hans-Joachim stirred the coffee and sat back in his chair as if he had all the time in the world. 'I intend to kidnap an East German politician and hold him to ransom. If you, or your counterpart in the East, still refuse to help, I intend to kill him.' For the first time the politician began to react. 'Not only that. I also intend posting up parts of his body around the city and letting everyone know why I'm doing it.'

'You're serious.' The colour drained from the face and the hands no longer played with the cuff-links.

'Perfectly.'

The telephone rang. 'Busy,' the politician snapped and put it down again. He played with his cup, thinking. 'It's just possible that there might be a way.'

'How?'

'Difficult.' Bonn is involved, the implication was clear. 'I'll contact you when I know anything.'

'Be careful, the telephone at the flat is tapped.'

'Of course.'

Hans-Joachim was uncertain whether the politician meant that of course he would be careful or that of course the telephone was tapped.

In the Empress Bar the diplomat sat at a table close to the piano, in the Hawaii near the window. In the Brasserie, however, he sat at the bar itself, never more than four stools from the right, close to the till where the two barmaids stood when they weren't serving or talking to other customers.

The Brasserie was a comfortable size. Its decoration was classic thirties, dark red wallpaper and elaborate large lampshades hanging from the ceiling.

Hans-Joachim arrived at seven thirty, chose a seat two stools from where the diplomat always sat and ordered a beer. Three evenings every week now, ever since he had identified the diplomat's routine, he came to the bar and talked to the women behind it, sometimes early sometimes late, but never when the diplomat was there. Outside there was snow on the pavement, inside the bar was warm and friendly, people sitting at the tables behind him and regulars drifting in and out. He ordered a second beer, bought a wine for the barmaid, and waited.

They all felt the gust of air as the door opened and the diplomat came in. He was wearing an overcoat over a suit, white flakes of snow in his dark hair. In the street outside Hans-Joachim saw the cab pull away. The diplomat took off the outer coat and hung it on the rack near the door. Already the barmaid had begun to pull him a beer.

'Ciao, Assad.'

'Ciao, Ilsa.' He sat on the stool opposite the till and she gave him the menu.

'How's the other side?'

'Cold.'

Hans-Joachim finished the beer, put the money on the bar and stood up. 'Ciao, Ilsa.'

The barmaid saw that he was leaving. 'Ciao, Hans.'

Automatically the diplomat looked at him. Hans-Joachim nodded good evening to him and the man nodded back. First contact was made.

The American Mission was on Clay Allee, the Stars and Stripes hanging above the front door of the main building and military jeeps and other vehicles parked outside, Marine guards at the foot of the steps to the door as well as inside. The reception area was large, marble floor and high walls and ceiling. Another Stars and Stripes hung at the side of the reception desk, a Marine corporal manning the desk itself. Hans-Joachim crossed the floor to the desk and waited until the Marine looked up at him.

'Good morning. My name's Schiller. I'd like to talk to someone from Intelligence.'

'Your name again, sir.' The corporal's manner was firm and the politeness a formality.

'Hans-Joachim Schiller.' Everyone knew the CIA ran from Clay Allee and everyone in the business knew that the CIA was not averse to sponsoring escapes, especially if it suited them.

'Address.'

Hans-Joachim told him.

'Take a seat.'

The chairs were along the wall to the right of the door. Hans-Joachim sat patiently and watched the assortment of men and women coming and going. Somewhere, he correctly assumed, someone was checking his name and address, as well as his personal and political details. At some point he assumed, also correctly, someone checked his face against the photograph held on file. After ninety minutes he was collected by two Marine guards, one a corporal, and escorted out of the reception area, through a set of security doors, to the second floor.

The room was clinically white and windowless, eight metres long and four wide. The table which ran down the centre was plain wood, nothing on it. The only other contents were three straight-backed chairs, two opposite each other on either side of the table and one at the head. The Marine corporal indicated without speaking that Hans-Joachim should sit in the chair with its back to the door. Two men entered and took their seats and the guards left.

The man opposite him was in his mid forties, thick-set and short crew-cut, wearing a short-sleeved shirt; the one to his left, at the head of the table, was younger, long-sleeved shirt and tie.

'Let's start at the beginning. The first escapes.' The man opposite placed the file on the table. There was no introduction, and no confirmation of who they were.

'You know who I am and why I'm here.'

'The first escapes.' The man opposite was adamant.

'My name is Hans-Joachim Schiller. Since the Berlin Wall went up I and my organization have brought out some three hundred people from the East. I need your money to continue.'

'As I said, let's start at the beginning.'

It was just like the interview with the BfV, Hans-Joachim thought. 'As long as you know why I'm here.'

For the next two hours the man opposite took him through the details of the escapes, the stages and development of his organization and the financial arrangements by which he had kept going. At no time did he open or consult the file in front of him, and at no time did the man on Hans-Joachim's left say anything.

Without warning the man opposite picked up the file and stood up. 'We cannot assist you, Herr Schiller. You'll get no money or other help from this organization.' He pressed a buzzer concealed beneath his side of the table and the Marine guards appeared. 'Escort this gentleman from the building.'

Hans-Joachim shook the guard's hand from his arm and walked between the two Marines to the front door and on to the pavement outside.

In the room on the second floor the man who had sat opposite him tucked in his shirt.

'Why not?' Michael Rossini spoke for the first time.

'Stasi,' his superior snorted. 'Smell it a mile off.'

'Who says so?'

'West German security.' They left the room and went to collect the interview tape. 'The Stasi let him run, bring a few people across to make us think he was on-side.' They locked the tape in one of the security cabinets and went for lunch.

The afternoon was routine, standard material from standard sources. A minor scare at three over a black marketeer they were trying to run in the East and quiet again by six. At six thirty the office emptied. At seven Michael Rossini removed the file on Hans-

Joachim Schiller, poured himself a coffee from the percolator still bubbling in the corner, and settled down to read it. Outside it was dark and cold. Plenty of time, he thought, he was not due at the bar till nine thirty.

The file was thirty pages thick, the details in it based on the West German BfV report submitted after Hans-Joachim's meeting with them. Some of the details Rossini already knew, partly from the magazine reports which had appeared after the escapes. He came to the report on the tunnel on Sebastian Strasse and the details of the West German police operation against it, the BfV conclusions about Schiller both before and after the incident. Schiller was a Stasi plant: the counter-intelligence report was specific. East German State Security had allowed the escapes he had appeared to organize in order to establish his credibility.

The assumption might have been valid when Schiller was only bringing out escapers in twos and threes, Rossini thought. But not valid once he started the tunnels, not when he was bringing out twenty or thirty at a time. Not even the bastards in State Security could swing that one over their political bosses. He remembered the political background to the tunnel on Sebastian Strasse and checked the file. There was no reference to it in the report. It was almost nine o'clock; he returned the file to the cabinet and went to the Hilton.

Eddie Daley was waiting for him. Ever since he had been seconded to the Military Mission, and from the Mission on temporary assignment to Intelligence, Rossini had made it his practice to drink at least once a week with those correspondents of American newspapers, radio or television stations based in Berlin, and especially with those whom he might help or who might, at some time, be able to help him. There were few he trusted; even fewer, he supposed, who trusted him. Eddie Daley was one of them. He was forty-one years old, had first come to Berlin to cover the airlift for the *LA Times* and had somehow persuaded his editor that he could afford to allow him to stay by syndicating his material.

When Rossini arrived he was sitting in the Golden City Bar, a Lucky Strike smouldering in the ashtray and a Jack Daniels half finished. Rossini sat beside him and ordered two more Black Labels.

Daley raised his glass. 'King and country.'

For ten minutes they talked generally.

'You know Hans-Joachim Schiller?' Rossini nodded to the barmaid to refill the glasses.

'I've met him once or twice.'

'He's looking for money.'

'Poor bastard's always looking for money. Plenty of people willing to pay him when he's delivered, not so many willing to help
when he needs it.' Rossini had heard that the reporter had dug
into his own pocket on occasions, come up with number plates
when they were needed, other items that nobody wanted to talk
about. 'So he's finally come to your lot.'

'Finally.'

'Must be desperate.' Daley raised his glass.

'We turned him down.'

'Why?'

'Because the file says the Stasi are running him.'

'Of course the Stasi are running him.' Daley downed the bourbon and pushed the glass across the bar for another. 'That's why
they dropped a bomb on him in Bernauer Strasse.' He lit another
Lucky. 'So what do you want?'

'Find out how much he needs. Let me know.'

'What's the catch?'

'None.'

'Official?'

'Unofficial.'

The Brasserie was quiet. The Lebanese and the West Berliner sat
together on the stools opposite the till. First-name terms, Assad
and Hans-Joachim, normally abbreviated to Hans. There had been
no formal introductions, just the informal conversations with Ilsa
and the other regulars, the picking up of the other's name and the
natural conversation when they next met. The evenings were
lighter, with the first hint of warmth in the air.

'So what's East Berlin like nowadays?'

Assad Hussein laughed. 'Why do you think I come to the West
whenever I can?' He drained his glass and wiped the froth from
his moustache. Assad Hussein was always neat and meticulous.
'What was it like before the Wall? You must have known it quite
well?'

Sometime he would have to commit himself, Hans-Joachim

knew, sometime he would have to know whether he was wasting his time with the diplomat. 'I still do.'

The telephone call from Edward Daley came the following afternoon and they met that evening at the Hofbrauhaus, near the Hilton.

There was a possibility, Daley said, that some finance might be available – whether from his newspaper, from readers who had read the article on the Bernauer Strasse tunnel and wished to help, or from other sources, he did not say. He was not saying that Hans-Joachim was still in business, but if he was and ever needed money he should bear the offer in mind.

'How much had you in mind?'

'How much might you need?'

A good second-hand Mercedes he would probably have to get from the West, plus other expenses. 'Ten thousand D'marks.'

The day had been busy, briefing papers for a group of visiting Congressmen and the normal problems associated with politicians. Everyone on their best behaviour and saying nothing that mattered. Rossini sat back in his chair and put his feet on the desk. The last secretary left, joking at him not to work too late. He waited another twenty minutes, unlocked the security cabinet and removed a file relating to an operation that was just closing. So much money being spent on second-grade sources; he flicked through the pages of expenses: pimps and hookers, local mafia, crooks who claimed they could run people into and out of the East.

From the drawer of his desk he took three expenses sheets, and filled them in with names and details from the file in front of him. The authorization on the bottom of each genuine sheet had been signed in a hurry and was practically illegible. He practised it twice then signed the counterfeit sheets he had prepared. The total of the three pages was a fraction of the monies being wasted elsewhere; it would pass through the system unnoticed and came to fifty-seven Deutschmarks over ten thousand.

It was raining. Spring rain but drenching nevertheless. Hans-Joachim Schiller and Assad Hussein hurried along the Kurfurstendamm; the water soaked through their shoes and their jackets and trousers were flattened with wet.

'You're a diplomat, Assad. You should have a car. Good for the girls as well.'

They pushed across Wittenbergplatz into the Brasserie.

'On my salary you have to be joking. Get me one and I owe you.'

The telephone rang three times before Hans-Joachim answered it.

'I might be able to help. I suggest a meeting tomorrow after-noon.'

He recognized the voice of the mayor's political secretary. 'What time?'

'Three thirty.'

Hans-Joachim was fifteen minutes early. Even though the coffee was ready on the side table he sensed there was no time limit on the meeting. He accepted a cup and settled in the chair.

'Something's under way; it's possible we can use it to bring Max out.'

'How long?'

'We'll have to be careful, not rush it. A year, perhaps eighteen months.'

A long time, thought Hans-Joachim, but better than eighteen years. 'What is it?'

The mayor's political secretary shook his head. 'Something between Bonn and the East. Not even I know the details.'

'But?'

'But Max's name has already been mentioned. Someone will make the first approach on his behalf next week.'

The fifth congress of the Social Unity Party of the German Demo-cratic Republic was held in the Palace of the Republic in East Berlin and lasted three days. It was the first such gathering since the removal of Khrushchev in Moscow and was therefore expected to provide the first formal battlefield for the new and old guard. In the event the expectations proved well founded, not only in the main proceedings in the massive hall itself but in the plethora of discussions, arguments and lobbying sessions which took place round its fringes.

On the third and final day Werner Langer attended, ostensibly as an elected officer of his local Party branch. When the congress broke at midday he joined Lindner in the foyer. The area was full of delegates, most of them intent on putting their comments on the morning session to anyone who would listen.

'There's someone you should meet.' Lindner steered him to the other side of the room. The men in the corner were in their forties and fifties, with an air of quiet authority about them and noticeably better dressed than the majority of those around them.

'Ernst Vöckel, Werner Langer.'

The man was in his late forties, dark-haired and spectacles; his suit, Langer guessed, was from the West.

'Colonel Langer, congratulations on your promotion.'

'Luck, the right place at the right time.'

They shook hands.

'Ten per cent luck, ninety per cent planning.'

'Forty, sixty.'

The other man shook his head. 'Let's settle for twenty-five, seventy-five.'

The conversation appeared informal, the edge of seriousness distinguishable only to those who wished to identify it. He wondered who the man was and why Lindner had introduced them.

'I'm a lawyer.'

'Not the Prosecutor's Office?' Not with the authority and suit he wore with equal ease, Langer thought. He saw the woman for the first time, saw her glance at him.

'Once, no longer.'

The woman was attractive, the scarf round her neck adding a dash of colour, slim face and dark hair curling round her cheeks.

One of the others reminded the lawyer that they were late for lunch. Vöckel took his wallet from his jacket and gave Langer a Western-style visiting card. 'There's a small party on Sunday, interesting people. Perhaps you'd like to come.' The private address was already handwritten on the back.

'It would be a pleasure.'

'Three thirty.'

The woman was facing the other way, listening to a group of

delegates. Langer crossed to where she was standing and she moved slightly to make room for him.

'Interesting debate this morning.'

The others continued their discussion.

'Which one?' She laughed, caught him out. 'Which branch are you representing?'

'I'm not, I'm here as an observer.'

'So what are you?'

'I'm an economist. And you?'

'Economist as well, Finance Ministry.'

The group she was with began to move away, some of them looking back and waiting for her.

'I was wondering whether you'd like to go to the opera on Wednesday. I could get some tickets.'

Nobody could get tickets for the opera at such short notice, she thought; even her father would find it difficult. 'Love to.'

'The foyer, seven o'clock.'

They shook hands.

'Gabi Ullman,' she told him.

Horst Ullman, the connection was automatic, confidant of Ulbricht during the heady days of the late forties and Council of Ministers for most of the fifties, might have been in the politburo except for severe ill-health.

'Werner Langer.'

Ernst Vöckel's house was in what was known as the Colony. The garden around it was neat, the lawn had received its first mowing and the spring bulbs were showing. Langer parked the Lada with the other cars and went inside. The guests had filled the ground floor and spilled through the open doors on to the lawn at the rear. Vöckel excused himself, crossed the room and greeted him.

'Glad you could make it. What would you like?'

'White wine, dry, thank you.'

Ernst Vöckel: close to the régime, good connections at the highest levels of the Party. It was the first thing Langer had checked.

'Perhaps we could talk later.'

'Of course.'

In the far corner of the room he saw Erich Honecker, Horst Ullman by the window. In his youth he had been a steelworker;

his face was still like pickled cabbage and his hands hard and calloused. Langer accepted the glass and walked on to the lawn. If Honecker was here, he thought, then Vöckel was a friend of Honecker. If Ullman was here, he also thought, then his daughter might also be. He smiled at someone he did not know and went back into the house.

Gabi was in the lounge. Her dress was light blue and well cut and her high-heeled shoes showed off her legs.

'You look too attractive to be an economist.' He crossed the room and shook hands, his words polite enough to be formal.

'I didn't expect to see you here today.' It was half flirting, half asking the reason for his being there.

'I was introduced to Dr Vöckel at the congress.'

They walked to the bar and he refilled their glasses. 'You're still okay for Wednesday?'

'I still can't believe you'll manage to get the tickets.'

'Dress circle. I collected them yesterday.'

'Who do you know, the President?'

'Sometimes the person to know is not at the top.'

The doorman at the Opera House had been a Party member for twenty years. In that time he remembered three things. The first was the night of the birth of his only child and the second was the morning he and his wife had been taken to the State Security building on Lenin-Allee and informed that the night before their son had tried to escape to the West. The third was the lunchtime of the same day when the Stasi captain had sat with them and told them that they should still be proud of themselves and that although their son would have to go to prison he would take personal care of him. Two days before, therefore, when Langer had asked him for tickets, it had been a matter of honour that he should not only secure two for him but that they should be the best in the house.

'You're amazing.'

'So are you.'

Vöckel was waiting for him.

'You have to go?'

'I have to talk to someone.'

'You'll be back.'

'Of course.'

The lawyer was talking to a colleague; as soon as Langer joined

them he excused himself and took him to the rear of the house
and down a narrow stairway. The cellar below had been converted
into a small bar. The walls were a pale but warm pastel, the bar
itself and bookcase on the wall opposite were made of wood, the
craftsmanship in each flawless. A Persian rug covered the floor
and the armchairs were finished in leather.

Vöckel closed the door and poured them each a wine. 'Thank
you for coming today.'

'Thank you for the invitation.'

The lawyer waved the politeness aside. 'Perhaps next time it
can be purely social: this time, I have to confess, there is an
element of business.'

He sat back in the chair and balanced the glass on the left arm.
'This room is rather special to me. I call it the orange room.' His
chin was dipped into his right hand, forefinger playing subconsciously against his lips and cheek as if he was working out what
to say. 'You were the case officer for Max Steiner?'

'Yes.'

'I'm now his lawyer.'

Impossible, Langer thought. Vöckel was too well connected, too
important. The lawyer who had defended the tunneller in court
had been a junior from the Prosecutor's Office. 'How? The case is
closed.'

'Two Christmases ago East and West Germany did a deal,
special passes for West Berliners to visit their relatives in the East.
Last Christmas there was another.' Last Christmas there had been
snow in the streets and oranges in the shops, Langer remembered.
'Last Christmas East Germany released a number of political
prisoners to the West. Exchanged them, sold them, bartered them,
call it what you will, it doesn't matter. West Germany paid for
them in oranges.'

'You were involved?'

'I was what the Americans would call the go-between.'

'So why are you now representing Steiner?'

'I'm about to become the go-between again.'

'How?'

'East Germany is about to announce another amnesty; those
released will be allowed to go to the West. Bonn, in turn, will pay.
The arrangement itself is secret, its terms even more so.'

'Not oranges?'

'Forty thousand Deutschmarks a head.'

'And Steiner is on the list?'

'Only if you say so.'

'Why only if I say so?'

Vöckel did not answer.

'Are other case officers being consulted?'

'No.'

Their glasses were empty.

'Isn't your position a strange one for a lawyer?'

'Why? The East gets the hard currency it wants, the West its bodies and its conscience, and the men and women concerned get their freedom. Everyone is satisfied. What more could a lawyer want for his clients?' He poured them each another drink.

'Steiner.' Langer returned them to their original subject. 'I have no objections, but I can see a problem.'

'What?' Vöckel sat down again.

'His case was important, not the court case, which was a formality, but the timing of his arrest and the blowing up of the tunnel on Schönholzer Strasse. They came just as people were discussing the changes in Moscow after the removal of Khrushchev. And the Soviets were involved. They were at the meeting when the news of the tunnel and Steiner's arrest was first reported. People will therefore remember the case.'

'So why is this a problem?'

'He was given an eighteen-year sentence. Some might feel he's not served enough of it.'

'And the other problem?'

Langer had not mentioned another. 'That I get nothing out of it.'

'So what do you propose?'

'You represent prisoners in the East, you also act for our people in the West.'

'Yes.'

'Steiner for one of mine when I want someone back.'

'There'll need to be a time limit.'

'Why?'

'Because certain threats have been made in the West if Max Steiner is not released.'

'Eighteen months should be long enough. If we can't do an exchange after that he goes on the list.'

'Agreed.' Ernst Vöckel refilled their glasses a second time.

'The list,' said Werner Langer. 'Out of interest, how is it drawn up?'

The meeting was at eleven, on the corner of Adenauerplatz. By the time Langer reached the café the tables were already laid for lunch.

'So, Fritz, what do you have for me?' Karl-Heinz Schneider had been a reporter on the *Berliner der Tagesspiegel* for eight years. He was tall, well dressed, drove a Porsche – which he had paid for with the articles he had sold to West German magazines such as *Stern* and *Spiegel* – and made no pretence of hiding his ambition. The man he was meeting he assumed was West German and therefore – unlike Schneider – able to travel regularly into East Berlin.

'There's going to be another amnesty. The East have agreed to release some political prisoners – my contacts aren't sure how many – and the West are drawing up a list of those they are prepared to accept.'

Sometimes, though not often, Schneider envied Fritz Wordel: his contacts and his freedom of travel. Usually, however, he despised him: his manners, his insistence that he was a member of what he constantly referred to as the big league whereas all he dealt in was the occasional consignment of nylon stockings into the East and a few snippets of gossip out. The farce which surrounded their meetings and the charade that Wordel insisted on when contacting him, explained that his life would be in danger if he even gave Schneider a telephone number. The fact that he could always take Fritz Wordel for the proverbial ride.

'So what's in it for me?' A second amnesty wasn't news, he meant; in his business only the first of anything counted.

'People with good stories to tell about life in prison in the East.'

Karl-Heinz Schneider began to take notice. 'What sort of stories?'

The envelope was brown and crumpled. The man he called Fritz Wordel pulled it from his pocket, glanced sideways, and took out the list of names. 'This one.' His finger searched down the list. 'Apparently she was raped by the Stasi. When she was in prison she had to attend parties for the guards.' He stabbed at another name. 'She was beaten up, still can't walk.'

'And these are on the list for the amnesty?'

'No way.' Fritz Wordel sniffed in the manner which always disgusted Schneider. 'The East wouldn't put them on any list.'

'But . . .' Karl-Heinz Schneider began to object then realized.

'Exactly.' Fritz Wordel winked. 'Your political contacts, get them to slip the names on when the West is drawing up the list so nobody notices.'

'How much?' His contacts were good enough, Schneider knew. One story for his paper, he was already calculating, the second for *Stern* or *Spiegel*.

'Five thousand.'

Stern or *Spiegel* would pay twice that, more if he could get pictures. 'You must be joking.'

'Three.'

'I'd never get it through.'

'Two.'

'Five hundred.'

Bastard, he thought he heard Fritz Wordel whisper.

It was the least he could do, Langer thought. Of the fourteen names on the list, two – the women he had singled out to Karl-Heinz Schneider – were false. Of those remaining, eleven of the names were genuine but of no consequence and the twelfth was that of Anja Lehnartz.

'A thousand.'

'Done.'

The performance was due to start at seven thirty. At five to seven when he entered the Opera House on Unter den Linden, the foyer was already filling, the excitement in the air. At seven exactly Gabi Ullman arrived. She wore a red dress, close-fitting and well styled, a shawl round her shoulders.

'I can't believe anyone could look so beautiful.'

She kissed him on the cheek. 'I can't believe you really do have the tickets.'

The bell sounded and they went through to the auditorium.

*

Max Steiner woke at four. Each morning he woke at the same time and thought about the moment at the crossing at Heinrich-Heine Strasse, the person in the organization who had betrayed him. Each morning he told himself that at least the other members of the organization were safe, that at least he had told the Stasi nothing.

The light streamed through the bars of the window, the cell small and cramped and the bunks packed together. The East Germans were efficient and ran the prison as he supposed they ran their economy. Starting the day he had arrived in the prison at Brandenburg he had been trained as a mechanic; each day now he made parts for Trabant motor cars.

It was already six. He rolled off the bunk, washed his hands and face in the bucket of water in the corner, and waited for the breakfast which the women prisoners in the kitchens downstairs prepared.

Anja's hands were red and hardened with the work. The sun streamed through the windows and the steam rose in clouds to the ceiling. The day before one of the other women had been badly scalded. Nearly summer. She finished peeling the potatoes and tipped them into the massive blackened pot. After summer autumn and she would have been in Brandenburg two years. Only another five years to go, only another one thousand eight hundred and twenty-five days. To her left Heidi carved what passed for meat into cubes and threw it into the frying pan, the fat sizzling and the kitchen buzzing with noise and work. By eleven in the morning Anja felt as if it was the end of the day.

The doors at the end of the kitchen opened and the guards came in, one carrying a clipboard, checking the women's names and prison numbers, hurrying past most but sometimes stopping at one, checking again then saying something, the women startled, hurrying to more guards waiting outside.

The guard stopped by her and consulted the list. 'Number 12975, Lehnartz. Outside now.'

What have I done, she began to ask, what's happening? The guards moved on, past the next woman and the next. The kitchen suddenly tense and the women frightened.

'Number 26748, Prost.'

Six, seven of them had been pulled out, the other women looking at them as they walked past the cookers and sinks. Shower, change into your own clothes and collect your property, the guard told them, other guards surrounding them. Buses in twenty minutes. The orders were always without explanation. Anyone late stays. They were hurrying, collecting their bags. An amnesty, someone whispered, something about political prisoners being released. They pushed the meagre items they had been allowed to keep into their bags and hurried to the courtyard.

The buses were waiting, single-decker and dark green, the fumes bellowing from their exhausts and the lines of men and women already forming beside them. It really is an amnesty, Anja tried to stop the hope, they really are setting us free. She clutched the bag to her and shuffled forward, Heidi behind her. The guards came down the lines, checking the names again, reallocating some prisoners to other lines. Who put me on the list? What did I do to deserve such luck?

'Anja Lehnartz.' The guard came to her and checked the lists.

'Is it true we're being released?' She clutched the bag even tighter and heard herself ask the question.

The guard repeated her number and name and did not reply.

'I want to see my mother. I want to go home to Berlin.' I don't want to be sent to one of the industrial towns, she meant, I don't want to go where I don't know anyone.

The guard crossed her name off the list and pushed her to another line. The checks were finished and they edged forward, on to the buses. Anja saw Heidi and tried to wave goodbye, climbed on to the bus. I'm going home. She sat down and looked through the window. I really am going home to see Mamma.

The door of the coach was pulled shut. Anja looked at the faces of the men and women round her and heard the shout, glanced out the window. Heidi had broken from the other queue and was running towards her.

'We're going to the West. Today. Now.' She was shouting, ignoring the guards around her. 'You're on the list but you're on the wrong bus.'

The prison gates opened and the coach for East Berlin pulled away.

The girls were in their early twenties, one blonde and the other brunette and both attractive; Hans-Joachim Schiller and Assad

Hussein had met them the night before and arranged to see them again. The evening was warm, mid spring, the tables spilled on to the pavements on the Kurfurstendamm and the violinists wandering between them. The girls excused themselves and went to the cloakroom, the two men watching as they weaved between the tables and went inside. One was tall, long hair and close-fitting dress, the other slightly shorter, also slim.

'I've found you a car.'

'How? You're as broke as I am.'

'Friends.'

'What sort?'

'What sort of friends or what sort of car?'

'What sort of friends.'

'Newspaper man.' The answer was honest though Hans-Joachim doubted whether Edward Daley had told him the entire truth.

'What sort of car?'

'Merc, of course.'

'What do you want in return?'

'Some people out occasionally. Not often and not many. One or two a month, no more.'

'Your friends. Do they know about it?'

'No. All they know is that they've given me money. They know what it's for, of course, but they don't know of you and they don't know how exactly it will be used.'

'Who else would know?'

'You, me, the courier in the East who would bring the escapers to the pick-up point, though he or she needn't know the details, certainly not your name.'

'If I did it, you understand it wouldn't just be for the car?'

'I understand that.'

The girls left the café and came towards them.

'Okay.'

The evening was warm, the children playing on the pavement. Anja dragged herself along the street, turned into the hallway and up the stairs to the flat.

The day after she returned home she had reported to the local branch of the Volkspolizie. The following week her identity card had been taken from her and replaced with a card which not only removed many of her rights, including the right to travel to neighbouring countries of the Eastern bloc, but which singled her out as a dissident. The same week she had been informed that her previous job at the Humboldt was no longer open to her but that as a productive member of society she had been found another. It was twenty kilometres outside Berlin: each morning after that she left home at six and each evening she returned home at seven. Two months later, however, her former professor at the Humboldt had contrived her transfer to a library in the centre of the city. The man was a member of the Party, perhaps because the job required it, perhaps because he believed in its politics. Either way Anja thanked him and understood how much he had risked for her.

Her mother and aunt were waiting for her, the supper ready on the table in the kitchen. Anja kissed them both, went to the bathroom and splashed water over her face. I'm tired, Mamma. Each day they say they've given me back my freedom and each day they take a little more away. Each night I'm glad I came home to you and each morning I wish I had gone to the West. They're breaking me, Mamma, and I don't think I'm going to make it.

The door closed and she turned, saw her mother, the expression on her face.

'Someone came for you today. Not East German. I think from the West. She said she'd be back.'

'Who? What was her name?' She understood why her mother had told her in the bathroom, not let her aunt know.

'She didn't give a name. She said she was a friend of Heidi's.'

The supper was salad and cold meats. When they had finished eating and clearing up her mother suggested to her aunt that they might go for a walk. At quarter to eight they left the flat, at eight exactly Anja heard the footsteps on the stairs but still jumped at the knock on the door.

The woman was in her early twenties, good-looking and casually dressed so as not to attract attention. She carried a handbag and a folded newspaper. 'Your mother told you I'm a friend of Heidi's?' She sat at the kitchen table while Anja made them both coffee, neither of them relaxed.

'How is she?'

'She's well.'

Anja put the cups on the table and sat down.

'Tell me what happened the last time you saw her.'

Why should someone come from the West and ask about the last time she had seen Heidi? she wondered. She told the woman about the rush in the kitchen and the coaches in the prison court-yard, the terrible mistake which had cost her her ticket to the West. 'Now you know who I am, how do I know you are who you say you are?'

The woman opened her handbag and gave Anja a photograph. It was of Heidi; she was standing in front of the Berlin Wall, the unmistakable west face of the Brandenburg Gate behind her. In front of her, so that the front page was clear, even in the photo-graph, she held open a copy of that day's *Berliner Taggblatt*. The courier unfolded the newspaper she had carried and gave it to Anja. It was a copy of the *Taggblatt*, the front page the same.

'What do you want?' It was a strange question to put to the visitor, Anja would think later.

'If you want to come to the West, we can help you.'

Anja felt the surge of excitement and bewilderment. 'How?' The question was spontaneous, not thought through.

'That doesn't matter. The only thing is whether or not you want to come.'

She knew that she should ask her mother, knew what her mother would say anyway. Knew that if she was caught she would get eighteen years, plus the remaining five of her original sentence. 'Yes, I would like to escape to the West.'

It was the first time either had mentioned the word *escape*. The courier placed the photograph of Heidi in her bag and folded the newspaper. 'You have a telephone?'

Anja gave her the number of the direct line in the library.

'Someone will get in touch with you. It might be days, even weeks. If it's a woman she'll give the name Karin, if it's a man he'll call himself Klaus. You do exactly as they say.'

It was three weeks since the woman had come to the flat, almost four. Each time the telephone in the library rang Anja had waited for the name, each time she had feared it would not happen.

The telephone rang. 'Archaeology, Doctor Podelski is on his way over.'

She put the telephone down and carried on working. The phone rang again.

'Anja?' A woman's voice.

'Yes.'

'It's Freda. I wondered what you were doing this weekend.'

The library was busy, students and staff around; sometimes Anja was reluctant to discuss private matters on the telephone in case the authorities found out and used it against her.

'Can I phone you this afternoon?'

'Of course.'

She put the set down, picked up her bag and began to leave for lunch. The telephone rang again.

'Anja?'

'Yes.'

'This is Klaus.'

The world froze. She turned to the window so that no one would see the expression on her face. 'Yes.'

'You finish work at four thirty today?'

'Yes.'

'Perhaps we could have a coffee together. The café behind the Opera House.'

'That would be fine.'

She put the telephone down and left the building. Nobody speak to me, she prayed, nobody see that something has happened. When she returned her mind was still spinning. The hands of the clock on the wall seemed to stick. Two o'clock, God how the time was dragging, three, four. Four thirty. She cleared the top of her desk, packed her bag and left.

She should have suggested something on the telephone so they would recognize each other, she thought, remembered that the phones were probably tapped, knew why Klaus had behaved like an old friend. She reached the café and went inside. The man stood immediately and shook her hand.

'Anja, nice to see you again. When's the next party?' He was in his mid thirties, casually dressed. He waved to the waitress and ordered two coffees. The tables around them were empty. He leaned forward slightly, still smiling.

'You go to Rodenberg Strasse, behind the Gethsemane Church. You must be there at exactly eight o'clock. Scherenberg Strasse runs across it. You stand by the fourth tree from the junction, on the left as you face Schönhauser Allee.'

She felt the fresh fear and tried to remember what he was telling her. The waitress brought their coffees; Klaus thanked her and waited till she had gone.

'You face the wall and you don't look around. When you hear the order *Now* you turn to your right. A car will be parked there with its boot open. You get in the boot. Any questions?'

'No.'

'Repeat the details to me.'

She repeated them verbatim. When, she asked. There would be time to walk around Berlin, she thought, see the places she loved. Perhaps even to go to Leipzig, visit the school and the old apartment block, sit on the steps of the fountain in Marienbergplatz and say a prayer at the Nicholaikirche.

'Tonight.' He paid the bill and left.

Her mother was preparing supper. Anja showered – if she was caught tonight, she tried to joke, it would be her last decent one for more years than she would wish to count – then dressed and went into the kitchen. The woman was bent over the sink; her shoulders were thin and her body had a worn look.

'I'm going out.' Anja did not know what to say, whether she should say anything. 'I may not be back.'

Her mother crossed the room and embraced her.

'Don't say anything to Auntie Helga tonight, tell her in the morning. I'll get a message to you as soon as I can.'

'Good luck.' The tears brimmed in the woman's eyes.

''Bye, Mamma. Thanks for everything you've done.'

She left the flat and began to walk, half her mind confused and frightened, the other half clear and cold. It was five minutes to eight. She turned into Rodenberg Strasse, the street empty, only the sound of some boys playing football two blocks away and an S-bahn train rumbling past. She counted four trees back from the junction and stood facing the wall. It was eight o'clock exactly.

The light was fading, Checkpoint Charlie fifty metres in front of him and Friedrichstrasse stretching like a grey ribbon behind it towards Unter den Linden. The lamps on the watch-towers flicked on. Hans-Joachim Schiller sat at the window table in the Oasis

Bar on Zimmer Strasse and tried to ignore the nerves in his stomach.

'*Now.*'

Anja turned and saw the Mercedes, had not even heard it. Other than the car the street was still empty. The boot was open; she walked the eight paces and climbed in. The boot shut and the car pulled away.

The lights of the car came down Friedrichstrasse. Not his, Hans-Joachim knew. He would know when they were his.

She had been in the boot twenty minutes, Anja estimated, tried to stop the feeling of nausea in her stomach and her throat. The road had been straight for thirty seconds, almost forty. Unter den Linden, she knew. If they turned left they were on the run in, heading down Friedrichstrasse towards Checkpoint Charlie, right and they were going away from it. The car slowed and stopped at a set of traffic lights then pulled away again. Turned left.

Hans-Joachim saw the lights, knew it was his car, the headlamps bumping on the road surface and the beams slightly high because of the weight in the boot. The Mercedes was halfway down Friedrichstrasse, three hundred metres from the checkpoint. Two hundred metres, one hundred. Hans-Joachim saw the grille on the front of the car and the CD number plate below it.

Keep calm, Anja, breathe deeply, draw the breath into your lungs now. No way you can breathe when you're at the crossing, no way you can do anything which might rock the car and give you away. She curled tight, tried to relax, felt the car bumping then slowing.

Assad Hussein braked gently and pulled round the cars in front to the lane reserved for diplomats and those with special passes. Anja felt the car stop, did not move, did not even breathe. Hans-Joachim saw Assad Hussein wind down the window and hold up his diplomatic passport for inspection. The guard reached down, inspected it and straightened. Assad Hussein smiled his thanks and Anja felt the car pull away.

The Mercedes drove past the Oasis, Assad Hussein looking straight ahead. Too many Stasi in the East and too much security in the West to leave now, Hans-Joachim thought. Give it a few more cars or they would know it was the diplomat. He made himself sit back in the chair and order another beer.

The car had been driving for another fifteen minutes. Perhaps she wasn't in the West, the fear began to grip her, perhaps she still hadn't passed through Checkpoint Charlie. The vehicle braked and stopped, and she waited.

The back street was deserted. Hans-Joachim bent down and opened the boot.

CHAPTER TEN

THE MARRIAGE of Hans-Joachim Schiller and Anja Lehnartz took place in the town hall at Schöneberg. The witnesses were Heidi Prost and Hans-Joachim's stepfather, Lutz, and the best man was Rolf Hanniman, who had returned from Cologne for the occasion.

After her escape Anja had lived with Heidi in a small flat in the Charlottenberg area of West Berlin. On the night of her escape there had been a party at the flat, three days after that Anja had told Hans-Joachim that she wished to help in any way she could in the escape organization. A week after that she had helped pull the yacht out of the Wannsee for the winter. That evening he had introduced her to Christina and Lutz.

The reception was small and held in the flat on Vorbergstrasse; present were close friends, family and members of the organization. The only foreigner present was Edward Daley, of the *LA Times*, to whom – as the night and the celebrations progressed – they jokingly awarded honorary West Berlin citizenship. The previous evening the diplomat Assad Hussein had drunk champagne with the couple at the Brasserie restaurant on Wittenbergplatz. With him he had brought wedding presents from Anja's mother and aunt; two days later he would take them photographs of the wedding they could not attend.

After the formal speeches Hans-Joachim stood and asked his guests to raise their glasses in a special toast. 'Absent friends.'

The flight from Berlin Tegel to Frankfurt, in West Germany, the following morning took seventy-five minutes and the connection to Vienna another ninety. At the Hertz desk at Vienna Hans-Joachim and Anja hired an Opel and drove north-west to the border crossing between Austria in the West and Czechoslovakia in the East, near Neu-Nageberg. The countryside was lost in winter, the snow hanging in the pines and the sky grey and menacing. That night, in the Hotel Waldrand, overlooking the valley which ran to the border, they ate Bohemian ham and drank sparkling wine. The following morning Anja kissed her husband goodbye and watched as he drove east, the exhaust of the Opel hanging in the air long after she could no longer see him.

Berlin was getting too tight – the two of them plus the others who formed the core of the new organization had discussed the subject endlessly. In the end it had been Anja who had come upon the solution. Not come upon as much as made the remark which led to it. One of the penalties imposed upon her after her release from prison, she had said, was that the identity card she was given in place of the normal one restricted her freedom of travel. What freedom, Hans-Joachim had asked, what travel? Within the Warsaw Pact, she had replied; for those who could afford it certain travel between the various countries was permitted.

They had spread the map on the floor of the flat and clustered round it as Hans-Joachim drew the route. The escape run by train from East Berlin to Prague. The Czech border with West Germany would be as closely guarded as the East German, so they should go further south to the Czech border with Austria, where the security might be slacker. And when that became tighter, as it inevitably would, they would run escapers even further south, through Hungary and Romania, even through Bulgaria into Turkey.

The road wound through the valley, dropping slightly, the hills on either side covered with pine forests and the wipers snicking the snow from the windscreen. The valley widened slightly, the road curved right, and Hans-Joachim saw the border crossing: the concrete and wire round the crossing point itself, control boxes on either side and heavy metal barriers striped red and white. Guards everywhere, greatcoats pulled against the weather and submachineguns on their shoulders, and the electrified fence stretching into the snow on either side. He pulled into the crossing and stopped behind the other vehicles waiting to pass into the country.

The Berlin Hotel was busy. Hans-Joachim walked through the foyer to the bar and ordered a Jack Daniels.

The bar was like the hotel and the hotel was like the city: whatever anyone wanted as long as they were prepared to pay. Even the spooks, perhaps especially the spooks. Each intelligence community with its strongholds, the British at the Olympic Stadium, the Americans on Clay Allee and the French in Reinickendorf, each with their outposts, their safe houses and their dead letter drops. Plus the Soviets. And, of course, the Stasi. Everyone denying it, yet each day the overt intelligence groups passed formally through the checkpoints and each evening they sat in the Berlin Hotel, or the Golden City Bar in the Hilton, and wore their professions like armbands.

Berlin was the same, covering its past yet flaunting it. The East colourless and grey, the historic splendour along streets like Unter den Linden where the tourist buses went, yet drab and still bomb-damaged even one block away. The West bright and brassy. The end of the K'Damm, the huge new Europa Centre where the Romanisches Café had once stood and the remains of the Kaiser Wilhelm Church floodlit in front of it; the S-bahn curving behind it across the Spree from Friedrichstrasse in the East to the Zoo Gardens in the West, the neon lights of the sex shows and strip-joints flashing around it.

And himself. Calling himself a student yet not a student for longer than he cared to remember. Forgetting everything when he and Anja made love yet the next morning crossing into the East at Neu-Nageberg. Pretending to himself and the world that neither he nor his organization existed yet sitting here now, waiting for a contact so he could hustle him for funds.

Edward Daley arrived five minutes late. Hans-Joachim stood to greet him and called for two Black Labels.

'What's running?' The newspaper man hung his overcoat over the next stool, his hair glistening with wet snow.

'Why should something be running?'

'Because something's always running when you buy the first round.'

The bar was beginning to fill.

'I need funding.'

The reporter raised his glass and laughed. There were other escape organizers, most of them professional and charging heavily for their services, the profits invested in bank accounts in Switzer-land or villas in Spain. There were also some who insisted on cash up front then left their clients penniless and stranded in the East. To his knowledge Hans-Joachim Schiller was one of the few, per-haps the only organizer, who did not charge. For this reason he came to people like Edward Daley for help, for this reason Edward Daley was prepared to help.

'How much?'

'As much as I can get.'

For the next fifteen minutes they discussed finances, stopping twice when other journalists spotted Daley and sauntered across to talk to him.

'There's a story that someone's running a diplomat.' Edward Daley changed the subject. 'No one's quite sure who or how, but a lot of people are interested.'

'And you think I'm involved?'

'Some people have made the connection.'

The next meeting with Assad Hussein was three days later. The Brasserie was busy, six of the eight stools at the bar taken and half the tables filled. They left and walked to the Hawaii Bar on the K'Damm.

'No more runs.'

Since Hans-Joachim had bought him the Mercedes Hussein had brought out eight groups of escapers.

'Why not?'

The Hawaii was quiet but would become busy later. They sat at one of the tables on the right side of the door, facing the bar.

'There's a rumour in West Berlin that someone's running a diplomat.'

'How does that affect us?'

'Because if the West knows about it the East is bound to.'

The snow had gone from the hills and the first hint of new green was in the trees. Anja stood at the front of the hotel and breathed in the air. It was evening, but still light, the early April warmth hanging in the valley.

Seven days ago the couriers had crossed into the East and made contact with those at the top of the escape list. Five days ago she and Hans-Joachim had flown to Frankfurt, collected the car and begun the drive to Vienna and from Vienna to Neu-Nageberg on the Czech border. Three days ago Maddie, Markus and Tony had crossed into Czechoslovakia and made their way to Prague. That afternoon Peter and Jan had arrived in Vienna.

'Is it always like this?'

Behind them the sun sank red above the trees.

'Gets easier.' Hans-Joachim put his arm round her and lied.

At dinner that evening Anja hardly ate, picking at her food and smiling her apologies at the waiter. When they lay in bed that night she lay staring at the ceiling and holding his hand. The curtains were half drawn, the moon shining through.

'Wish I could come with you, wish I could do more than just organize things this side.'

'No way you can cross the border. If I'm caught I do three or four years before the West buys me out. If you're caught they'll keep you for ever.'

The moon was three-quarters full, the light a primrose yellow through the window. Anja lay staring out at the ceiling, sensed Hans-Joachim was awake beside her. It doesn't get easier, she knew, not for him, not for any of them. It was four o'clock, five, the light changing, almost six. She felt the sickness in her stomach and throat and went to the bathroom, leant over the basin, body heaving and hands gripping the white of the porcelain.

Hans-Joachim wet a flannel and wiped her face. 'Nervous?'

She nodded and tried to smile.

'Don't worry. If anything goes wrong I'll pull out.'

The vial of Ketamine was wrapped in a polythene bag so that the dogs could not smell it and taped to the side of the compartment by the petrol tank. The salesman's case was in the back seat, the samples in boxes beside it. Hans-Joachim Schiller wore a dark suit and the diary appointments with the firms in Prague had been made from Vienna in case the border guards checked.

The drive to Prague took four hours; by the time he arrived it was early afternoon. He parked the car off Wenceslas Square and went to the café on the corner of the Smetana Theatre. The square – more a boulevard than a square, long and wide with the shops and cafés on both sides – was busy, the flowers speckled across the grass and already filling the beds at the side.

Maddie was sitting at the corner table; she was wearing a light blue pullover and loose-fitting denims. Contact on the hour every two hours, they had agreed. She saw him, lit a cigarette to indicate that everything was in order, and lifted the glass. Ten minutes later she paid and left, Hans-Joachim following her and checking there was no tail.

*

The light edged through the curtains. It was strange being alone in bed, not having Hans-Joachim beside her. Nearly five. Anja had not slept all night, worrying about Hans-Joachim and running through the arrangements in her mind: the place she would meet him after he had brought the escapers out, the *pension* in Vienna where she would hide the family till the other escapers came over. She tasted the bile in her throat and ran to the bathroom.

Hernan saw the family the moment they stepped from the train, made sure they did not see him. The couple were in their early thirties, the man wearing a brown windcheater and grey trousers, the woman with the yellow cardigan buttoned up the front, the boy and girl in their arms, the boy four and the girl two. The single bag the husband carried was tartan, frayed at the corners. The courier identified them to Hans-Joachim and left; thirty seconds later Hans-Joachim passed them on to Marcus.

'*I've always wanted to see the statue of Wenceslas in spring.*' Hernan had told them the code and the reply the day before in East Berlin. '*We wanted to show it to the children before they grew up.*'

By ten in the morning Wenceslas Square was already busy. Three sets of eyes watching and the first possible contact at eleven, the family eating ice-cream at the café by the National Museum.

'Excuse me, do you have a light?' Maddie leaned across from the next table, the cigarette in her hand.

'Of course.' The husband felt in his pocket for the matches.

'I've always wanted to see the statue of Wenceslas in spring.'

It was the wife who realized. 'We wanted to show it to the children before they grew up.'

'We'll go now.' Maddie's voice was calm and confident. 'Pay the bill and go outside. I'll be waiting. Follow fifty metres behind me.'

She thanked the man for the light and left, the family following her across the square. No tails, Hans-Joachim confirmed with the others and signalled to Maddie. She acknowledged the sign and headed towards the Old Town, waited for the family to catch her up. The children were confused, clinging to their parents. They turned into the side street and saw the car, the man leaning apparently nonchalantly against it and the engine running.

Hans-Joachim shook their hands as if he was greeting old

friends, opened the doors for them and they got in, the children sitting on their parents' laps in the back and Maddie in front, and drove off. Fifteen minutes they left the city and turned south and west. Three hours later they passed through the town of Sobeslav. The Opel was parked by the side of a café on the outskirts. As they passed it the two men walked to the car and fell in three hundred metres behind them. The afternoon was warm, the man and woman in the back falling asleep then jerking awake with nerves, the children dozing on their laps. Shortly before five Hans-Joachim pulled off the road into the woods and switched off the engine. The birds were singing and the sun dappled through the trees.

'We're three kilometres from the border.' He helped the family from the car. 'There are some things we have to do.'

The man and woman had been given no details of how they would be spirited into the West. They heard the sound of an engine and turned. The car swept into the woods behind them, blocking their way out, the two men already opening the doors and coming towards them.

Hans-Joachim saw the horror on the father's face. 'It's all right. They're with us.'

Behind him Maddie slipped off her sweater and blouse, removed her bra and put the blouse back on, only half the buttons done up; then she took off the denims she had been wearing and pulled on another pair, low cut and tight, the shape of her thighs and the contours of her crotch clear and obvious. Her hair had fallen loose; she shook it over her shoulders and put the clothes she had taken off in a rucksack.

'From here on you have to split up.' Hans-Joachim gathered the family around him. 'One adult and child per car. We need ten minutes to get things ready.'

They watched as he pulled out the rear seat, exposing the shell of the car beneath, the screws and welds of the wheel arches and petrol tank apparently rusted into place. The spare wheel was in a cavity in the floor of the boot, held in place by three clips. He unlocked the clips and removed the wheel. Then he put the clips back in position, turned the one closest to the front sharply to the right, unlocked the mechanism holding the panel of body shell at the side of the petrol tank, and revealed the hiding place beneath. In the second car Peter and Jan did the same.

The cavity was small and slightly bent to accommodate the contours of the bodywork. Hans-Joachim reached inside and took out the pack taped to the inside. Then he undressed and put on the suit he had worn the day before, knotting the tie but leaving it loose.

'It's time.'

The man and woman kissed each other goodbye, the father taking the son and the mother the daughter.

'You'll see each other in an hour.'

They kissed the children and walked to the cars, the man to Hans-Joachim's and the woman to the other.

'You lie in the compartment.' Hans-Joachim showed the man the space. 'Hold the boy against you. It looks tight but there's plenty of room and air.'

We're going to help you to sleep for a while, he told the boy. He broke the vial, drew up the Ketamine and injected it into the muscle of the boy's arm. The man climbed into the space and Hans-Joachim handed him the child. 'Good luck.'

He slid the panel back into position, locking it into place by reversing the process he had followed earlier, and lowered the rear seat into position, then put the salesman's case and samples on the ledge of the rear window and the rucksack on the seat itself. The other team were ready. They wiped the mud and leaves from their shoes and left the woods.

The crossing was quiet, two lorries coming the other way and one leaving, the border guards clambering over and under it. Hans-Joachim pulled behind it, switched off the engine and opened the door. To his right Maddie got out; he pulled the rucksack from the rear seat and gave it to her. Never cover the compartment, he calculated, never make the guards think you're hiding something. Maddie looked at him and shook his hand, the guards suddenly looking at her. Her breasts were large and heavy, they could see the shape through her blouse, could see that she was wearing nothing underneath. She glanced at the guards, walked to the control box, dropped the rucksack on the floor and handed the official her passport. The second car drove into the crossing behind them.

The guards were still looking at the woman, the length of her legs and the way the denim folded between them. The official trying to see down her blouse, imagining what lay below the next button, his actions automatic. Entry visa checked, passport stamped. He looked at her again, waved her through and turned to Hans-Joachim.

'Lucky bastard.' They all heard Peter in the second car. Hans-Joachim straightened his tie and confirmed what they all knew. The official was still looking at Maddie, her breasts floating beneath her blouse and her buttocks swaying as she walked. He turned back to Hans-Joachim and took his documents, glanced at him. Peter and Jan left the second car and entered the control box. The official pushed Hans-Joachim's passport back across the ledge, watching as he followed Maddie out and dumped her rucksack into the car again. Peter and Jan slid their passports in front of the man, not even looking at him, seeming to look only at the woman as she ducked into the car. The official laughed with them, stamped their passports, and they followed Hans-Joachim through to the West.

Three days later the next escapers left East Berlin for Prague.

The marriage of Werner Langer and Gabi Ullman took place in the civic offices off Alexanderplatz; the witnesses were his mother, Eva, who had travelled from Leipzig the day before, and her father. The reception was held immediately after. A band played in the corner and the refreshments included belugga caviar supplied by the Friends from the Soviet embassy. Although the formal wedding ceremony was attended only by close friends and family, the guest list for the reception was larger. When Eva Langer raised her champagne in toast she noticed that the men on her left spoke in Russian; when she looked at the names on the cards accompanying the gifts on display she recognized several members not only of the Central Committee but also of the politburo. When her son introduced her to his guests the one Eva remembered above all was the thin-faced man who bowed slightly when he shook her hand and whose name was Erich Honecker. Three hours later Werner and Gabi Langer began their honeymoon in Paris.

Three weeks after they returned Langer was informed of the trial date. He had known of the arrest for two months: the man was not as important as he might have wished but a deal was a deal and it would be investment in the future if it was known that he looked after his people when they were in trouble. He checked his timetable and telephoned Ernst Vöckel.

Anja took the call at five: it was from the West Berlin lawyer Stefan Pohl and he wished to speak to Hans-Joachim.

'He's out. Can I get him to call you back?'

The lawyer gave her a telephone number.

Hans-Joachim returned at seven. Anja gave him the message and he telephoned immediately.

'We'd like to see you.' Pohl never gave away anything on the telephone. 'Can you make tomorrow afternoon?'

'Of course.'

'My office at two.'

At one the following afternoon Hans-Joachim left the flat, at fifteen minutes to two he reached the offices on Pariser Strasse, close to the city centre. Even though he was early Pohl was waiting. Present was a second man, whom Pohl introduced as a colleague from the East. Hans-Joachim shook hands and sat down.

'Two months ago a Stasi agent was arrested in Hamburg, he goes on trial next week.' Vöckel came immediately to the point. 'The trial is expected to last three days, no more. He will be released for Max Steiner the following day.' He paused to sip his coffee. 'The exchange will take place at the Glienicker Bridge at two.' It was as if he was reading the terms of a business contract. 'There will be no publicity. I will not be present but you are quite at liberty to attend.'

'Does Max know?'

'Not yet. He will be informed on the morning of his departure.'

'Who'll bring him to the bridge?'

'The man in charge of his case.'

The weekend was unexpectedly cold and predictably long. On Monday Hans-Joachim was informed by Pohl that the trial in Hamburg had begun, on Tuesday he scoured the newspapers for details of the case, finding little. That night he stared at the ceiling and tried to sleep, knowing he would not.

'Can I come to the bridge with you?' Anja lay beside him, held his hand.

'Of course.'

Wednesday began cold, suddenly warming; Hans-Joachim

stayed in the flat and waited for the telephone call. At three, earlier than he had expected, he was asked to go immediately to the lawyer's office. When he arrived the receptionist welcomed him and hurried him upstairs. Vöckel and Pohl were standing together, each drinking whiskey. The East German poured him a glass and gave it to him.

'I'm sorry.'

'Why? What d'you mean?' The world blurred grey and slipped away. 'You said it was all arranged.'

'Democracy. The judge found a technical fault with the prosecution's evidence and threw the case out. We no longer have someone to swap for Max.'

The dinner began at seven thirty, the cabaret to follow. In keeping with the custom and practice of the Party, the celebration at the Distel Club was both informal and formal. Informal in that it was not an official occasion of Party, state or organization, yet formal in the sense that invitation to it and attendance at it signified position within the Party, at the present or the future. Mielke next to Honecker, Dieter Lindner and Heinz Moessner on the next table, Werner and Gabi Langer close to them and Gerhard Meyer and his wife also present.

Two weeks previously Erich Honecker had been officially named successor to Walter Ulbricht as Party General Secretary and therefore next head of state. A long road from Honecker's early days as a miner's son in Neunkirchen, Langer thought, in every way a hard one. Honecker was a good man, the right man for the leadership of the country. Ironic, of course, that his home town was in West Germany. A long road, he thought again, wondered how Honecker would rule the country and how and when his reign would end.

The first car came into the woods at five. In the past weeks they had done eight more runs, switching the cars and plates and alternating the crossings and covers, sometimes the drivers, but the basic procedure the same: the escapers into the secret compartments five kilometres from the border, the children drugged if necessary.

Jan's face was white, trembling. Sometimes they were like that when they were through. Anja had become accustomed to it: sometimes the pressure of what they were doing undermined them, yet sometimes they stepped from the cars as if they had been drinking champagne. She helped him out, pulled up the the rear seat, and opened the compartment. The eyes that stared up at her were wide with fright. Anja bent down and lifted the woman out.

'Welcome to Austria.'

Hans-Joachim came in ten minutes later, two men squeezed like sardines in the narrow space beneath the seat. Anja kissed him then watched as the two men shook his hand, would not let him go. A good moment to tell him, she thought, a moment he would never forget.

'How were things this morning?' Hans-Joachim put his arm round her and watched as the others reconstituted the cars. 'Getting better?'

She slipped her hand round his waist and led him away. 'You know the sickness?'

He nodded.

'It wasn't that I was nervous.'

'You're sure?'

She nodded and saw the crystal in his eyes. 'Positive.'

The cars were ready and the teams waiting. They walked back, arms round each other and the others looking at them.

'One more for the organization.' Hans-Joachim straightened and tried to retain his composure.

Maddie crossed to Anja and slipped her arms round her shoulders. 'Congratulations.'

The days were longer, hotter. Spring into summer. Soon the baby would be moving, Anja thought, soon she would be able to feel him. Funny how they all called him Little Hans, how they all assumed he would be a man like his father. Funny also how he was taking over. How sometimes all she wanted to do was to sit quietly with Hans-Joachim and enjoy the child she was carrying.

The days were cooler, summer into autumn. No more escapes, she sometimes wanted to plead with Hans-Joachim, at least not until the baby's born. No more escapes at all, she knew she really meant, no more risks. Not with the baby. The fear welled inside her again. Not a real fear – her thoughts were jumbled, confused – just the chemical reaction in her body now there were two of her.

Wenceslas Square was dark, the lights of the cafés sparkling around it. When Hans-Joachim had left the hotel for the final briefing the riot police were already gathering in the side streets. Student demonstrations, the porter at the hotel had told him, better keep off the streets tonight. Direct orders from President Novotny for the militia to crack down hard on any disturbances. Autumn gone, winter setting in, and Anja at home in Berlin. Sometimes he worried about her, how they were drifting apart, told himself that it was because he was away so much and she was concerned with the baby. Perhaps there was more than that, perhaps he was letting the worries show through. The checks on the borders were tighter now, there were stories of guards using sensors to pick up the body heat of concealed escapers, other reports of guards taking vehicles to pieces, measuring them internally and externally in an attempt to uncover hiding places.

The sounds of the demonstration echoed above the houses and the tear-gas drifted in the night. Not just a student demo, he had heard rumours, the first signs of opposition to the government, the splits between the old guard of Novotny and the reformers led by Dubcek. The tear-gas was acrid, drifting closer; five blocks away he heard the first sound of shooting. Cancel tomorrow's run, he decided. Contact the Schumanns when they arrived in Prague and send them back to Berlin, stop the others from leaving.

Anja heard the news on the radio. The previous night in Prague riot police and students had fought running battles through the streets. Unconfirmed reports suggested that the borders had been sealed. The baby was kicking. She made herself a tea and sat down, feeling him moving. Her stomach was large and she sometimes had trouble breathing. The escapers will be arriving now, will be going to Wenceslas Square – she checked the time – will have been picked up, be on their way to the border. In an hour they will be climbing into the secret compartments and running for the border, and at the border the guards will tear everything to pieces because of the trouble in Prague last night.

The telephone rang. She shuffled across the room and picked it up.

'Anja.'

She recognized his voice immediately. 'Where are you?'

'Vienna.'

She felt the relief and almost cried. There was nothing he could tell her, the telephones into Berlin were probably tapped, the line into the flat as well. Thank God he was safe, please God may the poor people who were trying to escape be okay. 'When will you be home?'

'Tonight.'

The meeting of those department heads sufficiently trusted to be informed of the decrees and edicts, sometimes the fears, from Moscow was due to begin at seven. It was almost Christmas. Perhaps tomorrow he could slip into the West and buy Gabi some French perfume, Langer thought. Perhaps Gabi was right, sometimes he spent too much time at work. He called for sandwiches and flicked through the additions to the reports which he had dealt with earlier.

Nothing further on the West Berlin rumours of someone running a diplomat, he noted. The possibility of infiltrating another informant into the science department at the university. A family called Schumann, absent from home in East Berlin for three days and their daughter now telling school friends about a train ride. He closed the files and went to the meeting.

The briefing was international rather than national: confirmation of policy decisions in the Kremlin, unrest in Poland and a potential leadership challenge in Czechoslovakia, the Slovak Dubcek already clashing openly – in Party terms at least – with First Secretary Novotny.

The briefing began at seven. It was chaired by the Berlin head of station but included specialists from Bonn and Langley. The cigar smoke rose in spirals and hung below the ceiling. Rossini sat in the rear row of those present and listened intently.

Washington was anxious to capitalize on recent movements in Poland and Czechoslovakia. They should be aware of fall-out in

Berlin. America involved in the student demonstrations in Prague, he assumed, possibly even the Company behind them. West Germany was probably involved as well.

The smell of Christmas was in the air, the windows of the shops and cafés on the Kurfurstendamm were covered with tinsel and coloured lights, the sound of carols in the streets. The flat was warm, the tree in the corner of the lounge and the decorations round the walls. Two weeks to the birth of her child, Anja thought. The cot was in the bedroom and the clothes were folded neatly in readiness. It was mid afternoon, already dark outside. She lay on the bed and enjoyed the peace.

Hernan had left for East Berlin at ten – the regular contact with the families whose escape had been delayed. At lunchtime Hans-Joachim and the others had gone to buy presents for the children and food hampers for their parents. An hour later she heard them laughing as they came up the stairs. Hernan returned from the East at seven. The moment he entered the flat Hans-Joachim knew.

'The Schumanns. Somebody informed on them. The Stasi are looking for them.'

'How'd you know?'

'The wife's mother.'

'Where are they now?'

'In hiding.'

His fault, Hans-Joachim knew, therefore his responsibility. Perhaps he could have got them over the border, perhaps he needn't have sent them back to East Berlin. Anja knew what he was going to say even before he himself had decided.

'Contact them in the morning. Arrangements as before. The night train to Prague tomorrow. The rest of us leave now. We'll make the pick-up as usual, come out through the crossing at Bystrice. We use one car. It'll be a squeeze but we'll manage. I'll drive it with Peter. Hernan makes the contact in East Berlin. Markus, Tony and Jan as back-up in Prague.'

'What about me?' It was Maddie.

'We need you in Prague, but Anja needs you here.'

The others left to collect their travel bags. Take care, Anja wanted to tell Hans-Joachim and understood what he was thinking.

'Sorry.' He put his hands on her stomach and felt the child stirring.

'Has to be done.' She laid her hands on his.

'Love me?'

''Course.' She knew what else he was thinking. 'Don't worry. Little Hans will still be waiting when you get back.'

Werner Langer entered and left West Berlin via the S-bahn at Friedrichstrasse. For three hours that afternoon he had shopped on the Kurfurstendamm, knowing that Gabi would enjoy the presents. When he returned to Lenin Allee the team leader in charge of the Schumann case was waiting for him.

'They've disappeared, parents and both children.'

'They're not with the husband's or wife's parents?'

'First thing we checked.'

'Prague again?'

'Looks like it.'

Nobody went to Prague in December. If you went to Prague out of the summer season it was for only one reason.

'Notify the Czechs. Give them a description, suggest they inform border crossings, and say we want first crack at them when they pick them up.'

The family arrived at nine, faces white with cold and fear, the courier identifying them to Hans-Joachim as they stepped from the train and the tail beginning.

The contractions began at nine twenty-five. Nothing to worry about, Anja told Maddie, it's supposed to happen like this. A few contractions to get you used to things then everything quiet for a few more days. Nine thirty, she thought, in Prague the escapers would have arrived at the Central Station, would be going to Wenceslas Square. The contractions were stronger, seemed more regular. In Prague they would be watching the Schumanns and looking for the tails. The contractions were rhythmic now, every five minutes, each lasting slightly longer, wrapping round her like a belt then slackening again. In Prague they would be picking up the escapers, taking them to the car, Hans-Joachim and Peter waiting. The contractions were harder, stronger. Anja stumbled into the bedroom and picked up the small bag she had kept packed. 'I think you'd better telephone the doctor.'

Hans-Joachim could not shake off the foreboding. Police on the corner of the square, just off the town hall, but not looking for them, not even looking interested in them. It was colder than Berlin, the snow hard on the pavements. He stamped his feet and saw Markus, the man, woman and child behind him, Tony and Jan in the doorways behind them. He opened the door and the family slid into the back seat. You go with the others, he told Peter, I'll take them by myself.

The contractions eased and Anja relaxed. The ward was cold and clinical; Anja could not help thinking of the interrogation room at Hohenschoenhausen, except that there was no pool of light beyond which she could see nothing, except that here the faces were friendly and smiling. Everything's fine, the midwife's voice was calm, warm. We'll take you into delivery soon.

The countryside was beautiful in a way Hans-Joachim had not seen before, the snow a haunting white on the trees and the pines stretching up the mountains, the road snaking between them and the water gushing through the ravine to his right.

Five kilometres to the border, he told the passengers, all change. He pulled into the wood and uncovered the compartment. Of course Anja's all right, of course Little Hans will wait. He started the engine again and reversed back on to the road. Three kilometres, two. One. Border crossing round the corner. Out of the bend and into the crossing. Two cars in front, lorry coming through the other way. Guards to left and right, waiting for him.

One nurse was in front, steering the trolley, another pushing, the midwife hurrying on one side and Maddie on the other. The next contraction tightened round her, the pain consuming her.

Almost there, Anja. She did not know whether it was her voice or the midwife's. Relax now, baby's doing fine. The contractions had stopped, she no longer felt the pain, only the fear of the calm which descended upon her. When I say push you push, Anja. When I tell you to stop you stop. She tried to smile. Push, Anja. Gently but firmly. Good girl. Baby's head's showing. Stop pushing now, Anja. Take a break. Baby's almost there.

Barrier down, shuddering into place. Eighteen years, might get out after ten. One run too many. He braced himself. Somebody had done it before, but that had been with a sports car and they had known the height of the barrier, let the air out of the tyres to lower the car and sawn through the supports of the windscreen. The guards were in front, submachine-guns pointing at him, waving at him to stop. Wonder how well built the car is, he almost laughed at himself, wonder how well the top half is connected to the bottom. Be seeing you, Little Hans. He slammed his foot on the accelerator and ducked his head.

Anja had never seen anything like the child before, skin so soft and hair so blond, almost gold; eyes so brilliant blue and face so perfect. 'Welcome to this world, my little thing.' She felt the skin against her own. 'Welcome to Berlin.'

The evening was quiet, the child lying by her side. Anja heard the door open and the nurse brought in a portable telephone. 'Your husband.'

Anja took it and heard his voice. 'There was no reply at the flat, I guessed where you were.'

Where are you, she asked, how are you?

'I'm in Vienna. I'm fine. Car's a bit of a mess but everyone's all right.' What about the baby, he asked, what about you? Are you okay?

I'm okay, Anja told him. The baby's okay. Everything's okay. The words tumbled out with the emotions.

And Little Hans, Hans-Joachim wanted to know. 'How is he? Does he have any hair? What does he look like?'

'She's fine. She's absolutely beautiful.'

Fourteen weeks after the birth of his daughter, Lisa, Hans-Joachim Schiller returned to Czechoslovakia. Because of stricter border searches, he had spent the first three months of the year researching, funding and converting a new escape car. The vehicle he eventually chose was a Cadillac, not common but not unusual given the number of US troops stationed in Central Europe. It was large, with a wide boot and massive bonnet. Most important, however, was the fact that a natural hiding place was provided by the car's design and construction.

The compartment was in two sections, the first horizontal in a hollow bulkhead running across the back of the engine space and the second vertical in the hollow wing of the vehicle, the escaper lying on his or her back in the bulkhead, legs hanging down inside the wing. Even if the border guards opened the engine space the bulkhead would seem to be too short for a person to lie in without bending and too narrow in which to curl or double up. The entrance was through the glove compartment and the unlocking procedure was such that if every part of the sequence was not done correctly, or in an incorrect order, the compartment could not be opened.

Because of the make of vehicle involved, there was one major difference in the team which entered Czechoslovakia on the second week in April. Whites, particularly young West Germans, would not normally drive a Cadillac. The driver was therefore West African.

Three months before, in January 1968, Alexander Dubcek had replaced the hard-line Antonin Novotny as First Secretary of the Communist Party of Czechoslovakia. Of the twenty-nine members of the new cabinet only four were Moscow sympathizers from the old régime. Censorship of the press was thrown out, wire-tapping made illegal, greater freedom of assembly, speech and movement were introduced and the powers of the security services drastically reduced.

Four days later the Cadillac made its first run. At the crossing at Mikulov it was subjected to a two-hour search; that evening it was christened Supercar.

Three weeks later Langer was informed by Dieter Lindner that the East German leader Walter Ulbricht had left Berlin for a secret meeting of senior East European communist leaders in Moscow. The agenda contained only one topic, the assurances given by Czech leaders that while embarking on a more liberal course in domestic policy there would be no departure from socialist principles. At the end of the month, Lindner also told him, the Kremlin would announce major exercises by Warsaw Pact troops on the Polish border with Czechoslovakia, as well as in Czechoslovakia itself.

Two days before the exercise began Michael Rossini was temporarily seconded to Prague. The situation building up, all the signs were there, something big about to happen. His first assignment was an assessment of six Eastern bloc diplomats and Party officials who had approached the United States with offers of information or friendship. The contact was at low level and the individuals concerned were in minor posts, leading him to assume that more senior approaches were being dealt with by more senior staff. The first two, he decided immediately, were Soviet plants, the third of little consequence and the fourth he was undecided about, though he agreed to see each a second time.

The fifth was a twenty-eight-year-old junior apparatchik at the Czech Finance Ministry named Josef Vlasak. The two men met at eight in the evening in a bar in the Old Quarter of the city. The Czech was tall, almost graceful in his movements and slightly expansive in his gestures, waving his hand to illustrate the points he was making.

Two evenings later he held his first meeting with the sixth man on the list. Milos Tomasek was a thirty-one-year-old Third Secretary at the Hungarian embassy in Prague. Unlike Vlasak he was short and small, Lenin-style goatee beard and round glasses, eyes darting behind them, and slightly balding. When he talked Tomasek sat forward, stabbing his right forefinger to emphasize his points.

On the day after his meeting with Vlasak Rossini requested access to all documents relating to the six men he was investigating, including the log-books in which had been entered details of their first approaches. When he had finished reading them he informed the filing department that he wished to retain the documents, signed a release form accepting responsibility for them, and locked them in the security cabinet which he had requested for his personal use.

The following week Prague newspapers carried what became known as the 'Two Thousand Words', an open letter calling for acceleration in the process of democratization and criticizing conditions in the Czech Communist Party prior to the January reforms. Two days later, on consecutive evenings and at different locations in the city, Michael Rossini conducted his second interviews with the Czech Vlasak and the Hungarian Tomasek. The following day the official Soviet newspaper *Pravda* attacked the letter, the week after that East European heads of state meeting in Warsaw stated that what they called reactionary forces were threatening to push Czechoslovakia from its socialist path but denied any intention of interfering in the country's internal affairs.

That afternoon Langer was summoned to Lindner's office on Lenin-Allee and informed that select officers from State Security were being sent to Czechoslovakia. His own orders were simple: he was to compile a list of those signatories of the 'Two Thousand Words' who might be especially dangerous to the state, and he was to avoid all contact with the Czech security services.

'Who else is going?' he asked.

Gerhard Meyer – Lindner lit a cigarette and told him.

'What's he doing?'

Lindner sat back in his chair and drew heavily on the Marlboro. 'He's liaising with a team trying to put Soviet plants into the Western camp.'

Berlin was hot, the water of the Wannsee a sparkling blue and the boats barely moving in the faintest of breezes. Hans-Joachim and Anja spent the day sailing, the yacht drifting gently, both of them laughing at Lisa's reaction when they dipped her feet in the water and allowing the picnic lunch to occupy most of the afternoon. By the time they returned to the flat it was ten, Lisa asleep in the carrycot. They put her to bed and opened a last bottle of wine. Hold on to such moments, Anja told herself, enjoy the times when you're together. The telephone call came at ten fifteen, Hans-Joachim taking it while Anja checked Lisa, then cupping his hand over the mouthpiece.

'Rolf Hanniman.'

'In Berlin?'

He nodded.

'Tell him to have supper with us.'

Fifteen minutes later they heard the footsteps on the stairs and the knock on the door. Anja allowed Hans-Joachim to open it, then watched as the two men greeted each other like old comrades, and laughed as Rolf came into the room and embraced her.

'Where's Lisa?'

She held his hand and they tiptoed into the bedroom. The child was fast asleep, breathing gently. In the doorway Hans-Joachim was looking at them. 'She's beautiful.' Rolf kissed Anja on the cheek. 'Just like her mother.'

For the next hour, over wine, cheese and salad, they talked

about the old days. When they had finished eating the two men sat in the lounge while Anja percolated coffee.

'So why are you in Berlin?' Hans-Joachim accepted the cup and made room for Anja on the sofa.

'To see you.' There was no hesitation in the reply.

Hans-Joachim waited.

'Two years ago I was recruited into West German counter-intelligence.'

Why, Hans-Joachim almost asked.

'But what about the tunnel on Sebastian Strasse, the fact that it was the BfV who set you all up?' It was Anja who spoke, Hans-Joachim still silent.

'We can look back, but it's better if we look forward. We all know why the police broke into the tunnel on Sebastian Strasse, we all know why the BfV arranged it. Don't forget I was there. I was inside the door thinking it was the East Germans who were coming in.'

'But what about the reports that Hans-Joachim was working for the Stasi?'

'We all know the reports were wrong, the BfV know that too, realize they made a terrible mistake.'

'So why are you in Berlin?' Hans-Joachim asked again.

'Czechoslovakia.'

'What do you want to know?' Neither of them queried the fact that he was now running his escapes through Prague.

'As much as you can tell me. Nothing that would endanger your set-up, of course. We've got military people in the country, but the things you get up to and the places you go might mean you see things they would miss.'

'What precisely?'

'Let's start with troop movements. The Warsaw Pact exercises have finished. Are they pulling out? If so how fast? Where? Which roads?'

Hans-Joachim sat forward, shoulders slightly hunched. 'Obviously I don't know what's happening to the north and east, where I assume most of the Warsaw Pact troops are supposed to have pulled out. Even on the roads I use, however, they're not moving. At least not very fast.'

'What? Who?'

'Tanks, armoured cars, troop carriers. Sometimes they're just pulled into the roadside, or in the woods. Sometimes they're moving, but if they are it's very slowly.'

'Why?'

'Perhaps waiting. Perhaps letting the Czechs know they're still there.'

'Nationalities?'

'East German near Plzen and Ceske Budejovice, Polish round Jihlava and Brno, Hungarian at Bratislava.' He fetched a road map from the desk and they began the details.

By the time they had finished it was gone four, the morning outside already light. Anja had made Rolf a bed in the spare room. When he woke it was almost ten; Hans-Joachim had already eaten and Anja was feeding Lisa. For the rest of the morning they talked and played with the child, then Hans-Joachim drove Rolf to Tegel.

If you ever feel like a change you know where to come, Rolf told him as they shook hands and said goodbye.

Michael Rossini's first meeting of the evening was at eight, in a café west of the Charles Bridge, in the Mala Strana quarter of the city, away from the prying eyes round Wenceslas Square. The Hungarian Milos Tomasek sat hunched in the corner as he had done on their first meeting, drinking Pilsner beer and explaining his country's position following the Bratislava statement.

'What will happen?' Rossini asked. 'Are the people right in their optimism?'

Tomasek sat forward, fingers holding the glass but not drinking. 'You know what happened in Hungary in 1956?'

'The reformist government of Prime Minister Nagy. Then the Russian tanks rolled in.'

Tomasek nodded. 'Until the end Nagy was talking about the ending of the one-party system and the coming of a full democracy. Even at the last moment he believed the Russians were agreeing to the withdrawal of Soviet troops.'

'And you think that what happened in Hungary is happening here.'

'Don't you?'

They stood to leave. As Tomasek rose he handed to Rossini an envelope containing the latest briefings from Moscow to Budapest, passed in turn to the embassy in Prague, on Kremlin thinking about the developing situation.

Rossini's second meeting was at ten, in a café in the Old Town. Josef Vlasak sat bent over the table, the bramborak and roast sausages in front of him.

'So what's happening?'

Vlasak pushed the plate away, the food untouched. 'What's happening to the Prague Spring, you mean?' His eyes were sad, almost mournful. 'Spring will never come to Prague until it first comes to Moscow.' He took the envelope from his pocket and slid it beneath the table. Inside, Rossini would discover when he checked in the safety of the US embassy that night, were the codes for messages between the Czech Defence Ministry and its armed forces.

The following morning Langer was recalled to East Berlin for what the order called consultation. The meeting with Lindner was at two.

'You've done a good job.' The intelligence reports were amongst a stack of documents on Lindner's desk. 'Both the Party and the Kremlin are pleased.' He took a single sheet from the stack and passed it across the desk. On it were six names from those Langer had highlighted as signatories to the 'Two Thousand Words'. 'Moscow passed these to Ulbricht and Ulbricht passed them to Honecker. Honecker consulted Mielke about who should do the job.' Lindner's eyes were slightly bloodshot and his face was tight. 'I recommended you and Moessner recommended Gerhard Meyer.' He took the cigarette case from his inside pocket. 'Mielke and Honecker decided you and Moscow agreed.'

Langer nodded and read the six names on the list. Two judges, one trade union official, two journalists and a playwright. 'What does Moscow want?'

'The six picked up. They're afraid they might disappear, possibly even go West.'

'When?'

'Tonight, between ten and two. There'll be an Ilyushin waiting at six.'

And by then it would all be over, they both understood. By then the tanks would have rolled and the Prague Spring would have ended.

*

Rossini's meeting with the Hungarian Tomasek was at nine. He passed the Bethlehem Chapel and made his way to the Medvidku, The Little Bears, on Na Perstyne.

Two judges, a trade union official, two journalists and a playwright – Langer did not need to consult the list of names and addresses. He stopped the car near the Hotel Zlata Husa on Vaclavske Namesti and went into the house on the left. The stairs were narrow, doors leading to flats off each floor, the stairs wooden and smelling of polish. The address was on the third floor, the door on the right. The playwright was at home – Langer had a photograph and the man had been shadowed all day. He knocked on the door, not heavily, not like a secret policeman – nothing to alert the man that anything was wrong. More like the knock of a friend. The door opened and he saw the face, jammed his foot against the wood so that the door could not be shut, saw the realization in the man's eyes and the woman and two children at the dinner table behind. Two of the team seized the man and bundled him down the back stairs, two more hurrying past and into the flat. No point in allowing the target to make trouble in the main street, Langer had already planned, no point in giving the family any chance to alert others.

The first of the journalists was at the café off Na Perstyne; the team trailing him had been reporting back every half-hour. The street was full of people, cars parked haphazardly along the pavement, some on it, and the lights from the bars and restaurants spilling on to the street. The target was at a table near the front of the bar with two other men, the three of them with glasses in front of them, though not drinking heavily. Enjoy it, thought Langer, and settled at a table along the wall. Twenty minutes later the target rose and made his way to the toilet at the rear. Langer followed him in. The toilet was small, barely enough room for more than three people, a cubicle in one corner and two urinals along the wall to the right of the door. The journalist was leaning forward, left hand holding himself and right supporting his weight against the wall, a cigarette between his fingers. Langer stood to his left and fumbled with his trousers, saw the door and the two team members come in, began to say something. The journalist turned to him, still urinating, attention away from the door. The first man hit him in the stomach, doubling him up, the urine splashing over his trousers and the second already holding the chloroform pad against his face. Langer pushed the penis back into the trousers and did them up. The journalist was losing consciousness, his body beginning to sag. The two team members draped an arm round each of their shoulders and half carried half dragged him through the bar to the car outside as if he was drunk.

Rossini's meeting with the Czech Vlasak was in the Plabana, opposite the Bethlehem Chapel. When he arrived the contact was waiting. Tonight, he knew by the man's face, as if he did not know already.

The address was on Vaclavske Namesti, close to the Hotel Zlata Husa. Langer slipped up the stairs and knocked on the door. A judge, he thought, yet a man who had lacked foresight and signed his name. The woman who opened the door was in her late fifties, grey-haired and well dressed, and holding a glass in her hand. He pushed past her, not speaking. The man was seated in an armchair, listening to Smetana. He was older than his wife, in his sixties, silver hair and distinguished face. As Langer entered the room he looked up, almost as if he had been waiting, then rose and kissed his wife goodbye.

At one Langer reached the fifth address, at one forty-five the last. The apartment block was quiet, no lights. A trade union official, married with three children. A small flat, Langer had also been briefed by the team assigned to the target, one of the children sometimes sleeping on a couch in the kitchen, and the man and his wife in the first bedroom to the right. He slid the knife between the door and the frame, eased open the lock and went in. Child asleep on left, he noted, turned to his right. The man sensed them and woke, his wife also waking and beginning to scream. One of the team hit her, knocked her out, two others holding down the man, the tape already over his mouth and the hypodermic in his arm. The body went suddenly limp, the woman beginning to moan and the children staring terrified. Two of the team lifted the man from the bed, flung a sheet over him, and carried him down the stairs.

It was two o'clock. Rossini received the confirmation that the first tanks had entered ten minutes later. He remained in the communications room for twenty more minutes then went to the filing cabinets in the office on the second floor.

Two fifteen, the water from the fountain in the centre of the square was arching into the night. Langer stood by the cars and listened to the thud of the tank engines drawing closer. A good job well done, he told himself, would tell the boys later. He rolled up his sleeves and washed his hands.

Two thirty, the embassy operating efficiently. Rossini unlocked the security safe and took out the documents he had stored there, then separated out those which contained even the smallest reference to the Czech Vlasak and the Hungarian Tomasek, beginning with the log in which the first approaches had been listed. The telephone was ringing. He ignored it, unclipped the spring binding, removed the pages on which the names of Vlasak and Tomasek appeared, substituted two clean pages from the back of the log in their place, and snapped the binding back into place. Then he entered the details from the original pages into the new ones, omitting the names of Vlasak and Tomasek, and fed the originals into the shredder.

It was three o'clock, Washington screaming for details. He cut himself off from the commotion and concentrated on the files containing the preliminary reports on the six men he had been ordered to investigate, as well as his own more detailed reports. The top sheet contained the names of all six. He retyped it, putting only four names and removing and shredding the original, then removed from the file and shredded the individual reports on Josef Vlasak and Milos Tomasek. The telephone was ringing again. He ran through his checklist, confirmed that he had missed nothing, and returned the files and log book to the security safe.

It was still too early for the sun, the morning grey and colourless. The cars swept along the perimeter fence of the airfield and slowed at the main gate. The tanks and jeeps were lined on either side, the soldiers looking at them. Russian, Langer noted, no tanks from any of the other Warsaw Pact countries; he held up his identity card for inspection and was waved through. The military Ilyushin was parked on the main runway, engines idling and a handful of men standing at the bottom of the steps to the main door. The cars stopped and the KGB colonel stepped forward.

It was six o'clock. 'On time.' He checked his watch.

'Of course, comrade.' Langer shook the Russian's hand.

'All six?'

'Of course.' Again.

'No problems?'

'Should there have been?'

Of course there wouldn't have been, the Russian knew.

The prisoners were moving slowly and uncertainly, as if drunk or drugged, the oldest of them still making a feeble attempt to walk upright and with dignity, and one wrapped in a sheet.

'See you in Moscow.'

The KGB colonel nodded and ran up the steps; the steps were withdrawn and the Ilyushin took off into the first orange of dawn.

The morning was quiet, the city under occupation. Rossini stood in Wenceslas Square and looked at the tanks and the soldiers in them, the people staring sullenly at the crews, the soldiers not returning their stares. The end of the Prague Spring and the onset of a winter that would last for ever. The colours gone and the square suddenly black and white.

The student was in his late teens, dressed in shirt and Levis. A strange smell, Rossini thought, and tried to remember what it was. The student stood looking at the tank crew, Wenceslas Square half filled with people, staring, forlorn, the news photographers trying to hide their cameras from the police. Petrol: he realized what the smell was. The student took the matches from his pocket.

Josef Vlasak was frightened, face tight and eyes darting. You have to be logical, Rossini told him; there's no point fighting the Russians, and even less fleeing the country. Remember the student Jan Palach, remember his sacrifice. If you believe in your country then you must make your own.

What sacrifice, Vlasak asked. What could compare with what Jan Palach did?

You remain in the Party. You embrace the new order, welcome the Russians. Rise in the Party until the day comes.

How long? Weeks? Months?

Years.

How many?

Who knows how many? Ten, twenty. But when the day comes you must be ready.

What about the files, my name on the papers in your embassy?

I destroyed them last night.

One hour later he repeated the conversation with Milos Tomasek.

It was snowing again, the flakes large, drifting past the window of the flat and sticking to the glass. The flat was warm, the Christmas decorations on the walls and the lights sparkling on the tree in the corner, the fire crackling in the grate. Hans-Joachim sat on the floor close to the tree, his back against an armchair and the child cradled in front of him. He was looking at her, talking to her, locked away from the world as if she was the world, Lisa grasping the small finger of his right hand, her eyes bright and dancing, laughing at him as he laughed at her. Only once had Anja begun to ask whether he was disappointed that she had not borne him a son, then she had looked at him, the way he stood in the middle of the room holding the girl and singing to her, and buried the doubt for ever.

A month before Hans-Joachim had made the decision and telephoned Rolf Hanniman, met the men from Cologne. A fortnight before he had made his last run. When Anja had asked him why he had described to her his feelings at the death of the student Jan Palach in Prague. He had grown accustomed to the fear and adrenaline of the escape runs, he had told her, but had never again experienced the anger he had felt at the spectacle of people climbing from the windows in Bernauer Strasse the week after the Berlin Wall had been built. Not until he had seen the look on the student's face and the calm deliberation with which he had set fire to himself. After that, he had explained to Anja, he had felt the overriding responsibility that when the opportunity presented itself – be it in ten or twenty years' time – he must be in a position to influence events rather than simply to help individuals. For this reason he had made his last run, for this reason Supercar now stood in a garage in the West, covered by a dustsheet. After Christmas he, Anja and Lisa would leave Berlin. In the New Year he would begin work for the BfV, the West German intelligence service.

The telephone rang. Anja wiped her hands and answered it.

'For you.'

'Who is it?'
'The lawyers.'

The drive to Brandenberg took two hours. Werner Langer left Berlin at eight, the morning quiet and the land white with snow, the sky a cold blue above it. The countryside gave way and he saw the outline of the prison.

Max Steiner began the day as he began every day: awake at five, the cell harsh and cold but still smelling of human bodies, breakfast, then the machine bench in the workshop. The prison was noisy and hectic; lunch break in three hours, he thought, for what the food at midday was worth, Christmas four days away. He concentrated on the drill and neither heard nor sensed the men behind him, only felt the tap on his shoulder and saw the supervisor and the two guards. He switched off the machine and walked between them out of the workshop and up the iron stairs to the cell block.

There was no point in asking anything, he knew.

They stopped at his cell. The clothes he had worn when he had been arrested were folded on the bunk, clean and pressed, shoes polished, a winter overcoat and a scarf beside them. When he had changed the guards led him from the cell, feet clattering on the floor, and down the stairs to the administration section. The window was halfway down, the bars across the glass. In the courtyard below he saw the three Ladas, the men lounging against them. The guards opened the door of the room and he stepped inside. The room was green-walled, a table across the centre, the man sitting on the far side.

'Happy Christmas, Max.'

Max Steiner recognized him immediately, would never forget him.

Langer signed the release form, closed the file and handed it to the prison official. Steiner was thinner, he thought, face leaner and eyes harder, but he hadn't worn too badly, would soon put on weight again. 'As I said, Max. Happy Christmas.'

The lights of the city were hidden by the snow. It was three months since Michael Rossini had left Prague, four since he had persuaded the Hungarian Tomasek and the Czech Vlasak to stay in place. His last Christmas in Berlin, he thought; in the New Year he would return to the United States. If he had bulldozed Tomasek and Vlasak into establishing the course of their lives so that, when the time came, they would be in a position to change their world, then he should do likewise. He swung in his chair and began mapping the next years of his life.

It's Christmas and you're out of your mind, he laughed at himself. In twenty years' time you'll be in your forties heading fifty. You'll have a comfortable law practice, an even more comfortable wife, and your only excitement will be running the kids to summer camp.

He picked up the telephone on the first ring.

'Al. My office. Right away.'

Something running. If it had been trouble the last word from Al Warner would have been *now*. *Right away* was different, something on the boil. The supervisor's office was already smelling of coffee and cigars.

'Just come through. The Glienicker Bridge this afternoon. Nothing to do with us but there might be somebody worth looking at.'

The flat was busy, Anja and Maddie cooking, Hans-Joachim and the others preparing the drinks, Lisa in the baby chair in the corner. The night before Anja had decided that she would go with Hans-Joachim; that morning, however, she had changed her mind. Eleven thirty, she saw Hans-Joachim glance again at the clock, almost a quarter to twelve. Nothing to go wrong now; he looked across at her and smiled, no last-minute call from the lawyers.

The wrought-iron supports were laced with white, the barrier across the eastern end striped red, and the river below was gunmetal grey. No one had crossed that morning, East or West, so that the snow was clean and unbroken. The engines of the cars were running and the windows streamed with condensation. In the West the BMWs of the BfV; away from them the Buick, American plates, the man standing beside it; next to it the Audi, the man also standing beside it. In the East the Ladas of State Security, the Mercedes close to them and the lawyer by the door. The noise of the world deadened by the snow, the flakes falling like feathers and settling on their shoulders and in their hair.

Two o'clock, the Glienicker Bridge, two lines of footprints in opposite directions. Max Steiner coming home.

BOOK THREE

CHAPTER ONE

THE OFFICE was on the fourth floor of the building on Lenin-Allee, the room swept regularly for bugs and the windows security-proofed against laser-surveillance. The desk which ran at right angles from the main desk at the top of the room sat three people on either side. To the left of the main desk was a security cabinet, a bank of telephone monitors on the desk itself. For the meeting a 16 mm cine projector had been installed on a separate table to the left, the screen across the bottom of the room by the door.

'Operation Claudius.'

In the last five years Werner Langer had aged slightly, his face and eyes occasionally showing the strain of the workload imposed upon him, though the eyes were still bright and flashing and the face more often taut with adrenaline than fatigue.

East Berlin, 1976.

There were only two other men in the room: the department head dealing with operations in West Germany and the case officer, both personally appointed. Within his area of responsibility Langer now controlled three departments, each divided into sections and each operating separately and interacting only through him.

'The target is Fritz Herbert. Aged thirty-four. Occupation: computerized electronics designer. Fled to the West in November 1973. Wife Ann-Marie, aged twenty-seven, left him eight months ago. Daughter Anna aged five.'

In the file photographs Herbert was round-faced and slightly overweight; his wife was pretty, large eyes and dark hair.

'Two suggested reasons for fleeing the GDR: he wanted freedom to travel and she wanted a Merc.' The information had come from the agents assigned to Fritz Herbert once he had been targeted.

The department head moved quickly through the next points. In 1974 Fritz Herbert had secured employment at the MBB aircraft complex in Ottobrunn. Despite his background, perhaps because he had made great play about his escape, and also because of his hard work and undoubted talent, Fritz Herbert had been promoted, moving between departments three times in fifteen months. The last promotion and move had taken him into classified work. It had been during this period that his wife had left him, at first taking their daughter with her then allowing him custody.

The case officer took over, dealing quickly with the progress of the assignments in the West. Reinhard Wagner, fellow worker at MBB, who had suggested the works trip to Amsterdam, without anyone even remembering it had been he who had made it, and who had persuaded Fritz Herbert to join the group. Klaus Giese, in place as a drinking companion at the bar which Fritz Herbert used. Wolf Mackowitz, theatrical agent and occasional lover once Herbert's wife had been located in Düsseldorf; responsible for her realization that the Mercedes for which she had fled the East was within her grasp, as well as the filming session in the luxury apartment hired for the weekend. Peter Heinemann in the projection room of the See-Through in Amsterdam.

Everyone ran every conceivable inducement to recruitment, Langer was aware: blackmail, bribery, intimidation, sex. He had considered the first three and decided on the fourth, though not in the way most would have contemplated. A honey trap, but in reverse. He had been careful, of course. Overseas operations were normally the domain of the international directorate run by Marcus Wolfe from the MfS headquarters complex on Normannenstrasse. Langer had quoted internal security, and even then had only informed Lindner.

'Better see it I suppose.' He drew the curtains.

The film lasted twelve minutes. When it was finished Langer pulled the curtains back and let the light into his office.

'Where the hell did you get the man who played the photographer?'

'Plenty around if you know where to look.'

'Just don't tell my wife.'

They laughed.

'So when do we do it?'

'Saturday.'

'And everything's ready?'

Everyone played their games. This was not the only one he was playing, not even the one he had spent most time on. But the one

from which he derived most satisfaction, the one he always knew
would come good.

'Yes.'

'You'll let me know as soon as it goes down.'

The following week he, Gabi and Nikki would go on holiday.

'Of course.'

*For Werner Langer the decade of the 1970s effectively began on Monday, 3 May
1971. On that day Erich Honecker replaced Walter Ulbricht as General Secretary
of the East German Socialist Unity Party, the head of state of the German Democratic Republic. One week later Erich Mielke introduced his first changes in the
upper echelons of State Security. Two days after that Dieter Lindner and Heinz
Moessner were promoted to generals in charge of the Berlin and Leipzig regions,
with full seats on the Collegiate. Among the promotions noted further down the
career ladder were those of Werner Langer and Gerhard Meyer.*

*In the summer of 1970 Gabi had borne him a daughter, whom they had called
Nicola. The evening he had been informed that his wife had been taken to hospital
and that delivery was imminent, Langer had excused himself from a meeting saying
that the Party would meet again but that his first child would only be born once.
The following morning, showing a humour not suspected in him, the chairman had
sent Nicola a bouquet of flowers together with a note asking her permission to
reconvene the meeting. It was the first time Nikki Langer intervened in the life of
her father, and it would not be the last.*

The briefing on Operation Claudius and the target called Fritz
Herbert lasted two hours. That afternoon Langer attended four
similar sessions. The last list he consulted that day was of Party
officials and politicians. Not those already known, already in positions of power. Those who were on their way up, who might one
day provide the politburo. The list of names from whom
Honecker's successor might come in fifteen, twenty years' time.
Verner and Naumann. Felfe and Modrow. Krenz and Schabowski.

By the time he reached home it was gone seven. They had
moved to the house following his promotion. To Langer it was a
base and a home, the rooms were comfortable and the garden
large. To Gabi it was also a status symbol, an indication of his
rising importance. Most of the time he was glad of the effort she
made for him: at the cabarets at the Distel or the weekends in the

country dachas. Sometimes, however, he was aware of the strain his work was putting on the marriage, of the tension between his commitment to his work and Gabi's to his advancement.

He kissed her, helped himself to a drink and went into the lounge. Nikki was watching television. 'Homework done?'

The girl was slim like her mother, blonde hair like her grandmother in Leipzig. For the past eighteen months she had been a student at the special high school for the children of the Party élite.

She nodded, hardly looked away from the set.

The Montreal Olympics, the East German successes every day, the victory ceremony that afternoon for the women's two hundred metres. He sat on the sofa, Nikki cuddled beside him, and watched the victory ceremony. The anthem militaristic yet haunting in the air, the red, gold and black flag, the symbols upon it, rising into the blue of the sky above the stadium. The young woman standing to attention, the gold medal round her neck and the first tear in her eye.

Nikki's face was shining; she looked up and pulled his arm round her. 'Do you think her mum and dad are proud of her?'

'Very proud.'

'As proud as you were of me?'

The week before he and Gabi had attended the school's annual presentation, clapped as Nikki had walked forward to accept the first year mathematics prize.

'I shouldn't think so.'

The MBB Sports Club arrived at Schipol shortly before five, the thirty-strong group squeezing into six cabs and reaching their hotel two streets from the Dam Square in the city centre by six. They would stay in Amsterdam for the Friday and Saturday nights, returning late on Sunday afternoon. Although the trip had been open to both sexes – at least officially – all the group was male. That evening, after drinking for an hour in the hotel, they shared a rijsttafel in an Indonesian restaurant two blocks away, washing the meal down with lager.

By the time they finished eating it was gone ten. They left Dam Square and walked down Molensteeg, the evening still warm and the atmosphere suddenly changing. One moment the shop windows were filled with chocolates and fur coats, paintings and books, and the next moment with women. Different colours, most of them slim and attractive and all of them almost naked. The sweet unmistakable smell of marijuana drifted in the air. The lights above the strip joints and sex shows were dazzling, touts in doorways and more women in more windows, some of them still girls.

The man called Reinhard Wagner glanced at Fritz Herbert. The target to be in the upstairs bar of the See-Through between ten and ten twenty the following evening, he had been instructed, the timing crucial.

They turned along Oudezijds Voorburgwal, the cobbled streets which ran along each side of the canal, packed with tourists. Fritz Herbert looked round, bemused, and fell behind the others.

The girl in the window was Eurasian. Thin blouse and suspenders, nothing else. Firm breasts and tight little nipples, Fritz Herbert thought. He hesitated again and saw the others were moving on, the girl folding and unfolding her legs. The others stopped at one of the strip joints, Frank Kummer haggling over prices, neon lights and cabaret shows for as far as Fritz Herbert could see. How could anyone do it? Fritz looked again at the woman in the shop window; how could anyone simply walk in and pay? Someone entered the door to the right of the window and the girl stepped behind the curtain. He ran after the others and looked at the posters outside the club. Looks good, he whispered to Reinhard Wagner. Let's go in here.

The last of the group returned to the hotel just before six, no one managing breakfast until gone ten. Tonight, thought Fritz Herbert, the little Eurasian. He sat at the table and tried to remember which window, where on the street. Good time last night, he told Frank Kummer, we owe you a vote of thanks.

'Special rate at the See-Through.' It was Reinhard Wagner.

'Special rate for what?' Frank Kummer was a good club secretary.

'Whatever you fancy apparently.'

What was that place, Frank Kummer asked later. What place, Reinhard Wagner replied. The place with the special rates. Forgotten. Perhaps it wasn't Reinhard after all, Frank Kummer thought, perhaps he would ask around.

That evening they ate again in the Indonesian restaurant off Dam Square then went to the red light area of the Oude Kerk.

The streets and side alleys were filled with tourists and sailors. The beer was cold and cheap, and the women all beautiful and painted. They stopped at the Go-Go and took in a pornographic film at the Vaudeville, the group splitting up, then stopped for another drink further along.

Reinhard Wagner was close to Fritz Herbert, talking to Frank Kummer. Guiding them. Taking them where he wanted them to go.

'That's it. Over there.'

'That's what?'

'The See-Through.' Frank Kummer led them over the bridge, through a group of American sailors. 'Good rate there, special discount for parties.'

The front of the club was red, the windows boarded and a light pulsing from the door. They went inside. There were two minders by the pay desk and photographs of women in a range of poses round the walls.

'Upstairs or down?'

'What rate for both?'

They paid and went downstairs. The room was twenty metres by fifteen, the tables packed together and the stage slightly raised at the far end, the lights strobing and the music loud. They ordered beer and settled down. On the stage a stripper was moving round a mock cobra, sliding it over her body and slipping it inside the flimsy loin-cloth. The lights went out and she cleared the stage, the spotlight suddenly coming for the next act. Strip, simulated sex, another strip.

'Fancy upstairs?' The suggestions were always to the club secretary. Three of them stayed, eight went to what the signs called the movie parlour on the first floor. It was almost ten o'clock.

The seats were as in a theatre, there was no bar. As they entered one film was half finished. They settled in the fifth row from the back and watched. The films were in a range of languages, no translations. Each began with a theme – a painter and decorator and a housewife, two students working for an older woman, a film producer selling a movie script – and each ended in a similar way, the shots in each only slightly different. The room was hot and stuffy.

'Fancy a drink?' Suggest they stay and Fritz would want a drink, the Stasi man knew from experience; suggest a drink and Fritz would want to stay.

'One more.' The movie ended and they waited for the next.

'Get yourself a beer.' The man called Peter Heinemann drifted into the projection room and put the briefcase on the floor. 'I'll manage here.' The arrangements in the club were informal, the staff frequently covering for each other.

'Thanks.' The projectionist was sweating, the wet pouring through his vest. 'Everything's ready. Alternate projectors. You know how to lace them up.' He picked up his coat and left.

The man calling himself Heinemann unclipped the reel from the second projector, opened the briefcase, took out the can of film and slid the roll into place, checking the sound sync.

Five past ten, Wagner checked. Must be soon now, whatever it was. Two seats away Fritz Herbert glanced at him.

'Beer after this one.'

The film began. Better shot than the others, Wagner thought, better quality. The apartment block looked expensive and the car the two men drove was a Porsche. One was a photographer, the cameras slung over his shoulder, the other was smarter dressed, smoother. The woman let them into the apartment and showed them the antiques. A drink, she asked. She was well dressed, tight-fitting dress low over the shoulders and high-heeled shoes. Antique dealer, the plot developed, valuing the set of Chinese vases, the photographer taking brochure shots for an auction. The woman opened a bottle of champagne and poured three glasses.

'Stand there.'

The photographer placed her in shot against a vase. Even after the first glass she was relaxed, laughing.

'Closer.'

She moved closer to the vase. More champagne, her dress slipping slightly.

'I said closer. Make love to it.'

The woman laughed again and slid her arms round the vase, hands round the neck.

'Much better.'

The second man was behind the woman, unzipping her dress. The woman was turning, sliding off his coat and shirt, her dress falling to the ground, nothing underneath. The photographer finished one roll of film and snapped another into the Nikon. Something wrong, Wagner thought, saw that Fritz Herbert was fascinated. Everyone was looking at the details of the sex act, the penetration of the various parts of the woman's body, the way she was fondling the man. Something the others had not seen and he himself had missed.

The woman was against a window, profile lost in the sunlight and her sex partner in silhouette, the photographer bent close to them, camera clicking. The woman's eyes, mouth, tongue along lips, vagina. The details of the ejaculation, the woman apparently not satisfied, reaching up towards the photographer. His midriff was taut and bare, trousers baggy. Fritz was nodding, urging the photographer on. Something about the woman, Wagner realized. She was still reaching for the photographer, unbuttoning his trousers, the man naked beneath them. Her face. He hadn't seen the woman's face.

'Jesus Christ.'

He heard Fritz gasp, looked at him then back at the screen. Even though it was not erect the penis was long and thick, the woman stroking it then taking it in her mouth. The organ was longer, thicker, the veins along it purple, throbbing. The woman was holding it, running her hands and fingers along it, emphasizing its dimensions. Go on, Wagner heard Fritz Herbert, give it to her. The photographer was pushing the woman on to the floor, was on her; she was holding the organ, stroking it against her vagina, against her stomach. Christ, Wagner heard Fritz Herbert again. The woman reached for the oil, the penis now fully engorged and massive. She massaged the oil into it and placed it against the mouth of her vagina, arching her back and sucking slowly into her. Fritz Herbert watched, willed the photographer on. The woman's body: stomach throbbing, breasts, neck. Mouth gasping and lips opening in amazement. The last image of the column sunk deep into her before Fritz Herbert saw the woman's face.

The water was blue and the sand golden. Langer sat at the top of the beach and watched Nikki splashing with the other children in the surf. Gabi disliked the sand, preferred the pool at the Party hotel. Sometimes, he thought, the thing Gabi preferred most was the cocktail party which began each evening. The beer was ice-cold and the sun hot; he stretched back and wondered how it had gone in Amsterdam.

The grass round the pool was neatly trimmed and the surface of the water shimmered in the heat. Gabi lay back, eyes half closed, listening to the conversation round her and reaching for the orange juice.

'A message for your husband.'

She looked up. The waiter was young, dark hair and slim. She took the note from him and smiled. Sometimes, her mind was half thinking, Werner was so tired or busy that he no longer even had time or energy for sex.

'Thank you. I'll give it to him.' She pulled on a pair of sandals and walked to the beach.

'There's a message for you.'

Langer looked up. 'When?'

'Five minutes ago.' She gave him the note. 'They want you to call.'

He pulled on a shirt and slacks and shouted to Nikki that he would be back. Sometimes, Gabi thought, he only seemed happy, only seemed alive, when he was working.

The telephone was answered immediately.

'How's the sun?'

'Hell.' Either good news or bad, he knew, nothing between. 'How was the film?'

'Won an Oscar.'

The bar was quiet. Fritz Herbert sat by himself; his head was slumped in his hands and the glass in front of him was half empty. He had not shaved or changed his shirt for three days.

'What's the trouble?'

'Nothing.' He remembered how he had left the club in Amsterdam, how he had vomited into the canal, explained to Frank Kummer that it had been the food. How he had walked the streets all night so that they would not see him crying.

'How long have you been here?' Klaus Giese sat down and ordered two fresh beers. 'Frank said you weren't at work today.'

Fritz Herbert mumbled a reason, his voice incomprehensible.

The man who would be his controller sat still, not speaking.

'Thanks, Klaus.' They had been sitting for two hours, almost three, the beers untouched.

'Thanks for what?'

'For listening.'

Klaus Giese reached for his beer. 'You haven't said a word all night.'

The smile touched Fritz Herbert's face. Not the smile of pleasure or of relief, the smile like the cold when the first frost of winter has set. 'It wasn't her fault, you see. She didn't want to do it. They made her. You understand that, don't you? They tricked her, turned her mind so that in the end she didn't know what she was doing.' The frost set harder.

What did they make her do, the man called Klaus Giese might have asked. How did they trick her, he asked instead, the words unspoken, all in Fritz Herbert's mind. He thanked Giese for the question and the friendship and understanding it showed.

'All she wanted was a Merc and they said she could have one. Every night on the television from the West. Come over, they said, we're the land of freedom and opportunity. We're the land of plenty.'

It was going to be so easy, the controller knew, wondered what they had done to turn him so completely and effectively.

'Come to us and all is yours. Come to us and it will be like it is on the television.' The frost was hardening. 'Come to us and you can live in Dallas, have a suntan all the year, drink Martini dries. Come to us and we will give you your Merc.'

'Who?'

'The West.'

'What did the West do to her?' The timing was incisive and the words perfect. 'What did it want in return for a bloody little car?'

The cold in Fritz Herbert's face was deep blue, permafrost. He screwed up the courage and told his only friend in the world everything.

That afternoon it had rained, breaking the long dry heat of summer and settling the dust, giving the streets an almost fresh smell. Anja packed the last case and half pulled, half carried it to the car. Behind her Lisa struggled with the bag she and Anja had filled with dolls and toys for the journey, then held it up for her mother to put in the back seat. Every day, it seemed, Lisa was growing, her face losing its roundness, though not its smile, and her blonde hair curled at the ends. Anja picked her up, hugged her, and they went back inside.

She and Hans-Joachim had booked the holiday in France in April – two weeks on the canals. For four months they had looked forward to it; in the last few days Lisa had not stopped talking about it.

'What time will Daddy be home?' Lisa stood with her thumb in her mouth.

'Soon.'

On 6 May 1974 the Social Democrat Willy Brandt resigned as Chancellor of the German Federal Republic following the arrest of his personal aide, Gunter Guillaume, on charges of spying for East Germany. Guillaume, an East Berliner, had entered West Germany as a refugee in 1956, joining the Social Democrat Party in 1957 and the SPD staff at the Chancellery in 1970. Since that appointment Hans-Joachim Schiller had been one of several BfV officers who had argued that because of his background Guillaume should be considered a security risk. The day after Brandt's resignation Finance Minister Helmut Schmidt was elected Chancellor. One week later Schiller was promoted to major.

Increasingly – partly because he was rarely at home due to the pressure of work and partly because she could not settle in Cologne – Anja had contemplated leaving him and returning with Lisa to Berlin. That she did not was due to a loyalty she felt to him, despite the increasing distance between them, and the understanding that he was under a pressure about which he could not tell her but because of which he needed her support. The day she heard of Willy Brandt's resignation she understood.

Hans-Joachim was due at five; at five fifteen Anja heard his car. Not bad, she thought, almost on time. As soon as she saw his face she knew.

'I'm sorry.' He did not know what to do, whether or not to pick up Lisa. 'Something's come up at work; I only just managed to slip out for an hour now.'

'So what about the holiday?' He saw the look in her face. Something always comes up at work. Isn't there anyone else in the department, in the entire bloody organization? Every time you do this to me.

'Tomorrow, Sunday at the latest.' Sometimes he did not know which devastated him the most: the anger she threw at him or the ice which said that for that part of her life he no longer existed.

'Fine. We'll see you on Sunday.' They both knew it would be the Monday or Tuesday, even the Wednesday. If they were lucky. 'You can't phone us, so we'll phone you.'

The barge was small but comfortable. Anja reached the basin where it was moored at eleven the following morning. That afternoon she and Lisa cycled to the village two kilometres away. It was only that evening, when Lisa asked, that Anja thought again about Hans-Joachim.

On the Sunday they waited near the barge; on Sunday evening, when Hans-Joachim had not arrived, Anja and Lisa again rode to the village, and Anja used the telephone in the local bar to phone Cologne. There was no reply at the house, and the office told her only that he was out. On the Monday Anja left the basin and headed the barge south, following the route she and Hans-Joachim had planned. Without him, however, the locks were difficult and there always seemed to be jobs to do and Lisa to look after.

At the end of the first week, when they telephoned him as they did every evening, he said he might be able to join them on the Monday. When he finally arrived it was Friday. The following day the holiday ended and they returned to Cologne.

New York was frenetic, Senate elections in four days and, more important to the majority of the city's citizens, the Jets at home to the Patriots. Rossini was at his campaign headquarters by seven in the morning, at eight he was briefed by his campaign manager on the latest opinion polls, as well as issues which were receiving attention; at nine he left to go on the stump, the round of speeches and media appearances in shopping malls and train stations which would dominate the last stages of the campaign.

After his return from Berlin Michael Rossini had studied law, graduating with honours then joining the Wall Street law firm of Dunleavy, Bailey and Schuster, becoming a partner after three years. During those years, and despite pressure of work, he had entered local politics, spending time cultivating his Italian background, as well as maintaining contact with former colleagues in both the military and intelligence fields. In the winter of 1973 Michael Rossini had married Sally, also a lawyer; in the spring of 1975 she had borne him a son. In November 1976, with her full support and backing, he ran for the US Senate. A week before the election, and in line with national trends, he was trailing second; with five days to go the gap had closed slightly, though not significantly. In the past twenty-four hours the statistics had remained unchanged.

The telephone call from the Pentagon to the newsroom of CBS's evening news programme came at eleven. The reporter who took it, Adrian Whitman, was twenty-six years old and had been on the show two years.

'You're interested in Rossini?' The caller had met Whitman when the reporter had been temporarily assigned to Washington the previous summer.

The newsroom was hectic; Whitman waved for silence and pressed the telephone close to his ear. 'Depends.'

'Ask him what he was doing in Berlin.'

Nobody ever gave good news about an election candidate, Whitman knew. Shit happens, he thought. The last Friday before the Tuesday election – the alarm bells should have rung but did not – the last day to exert any genuine influence. The right story on Friday with pick-ups over the weekend and you might just buck the trend, a pollster would have said. But it would need to be one hell of a story.

'Why?'

'Find out about the Berlin Wall. Couple of guys called Buffalo and Axe; the best man to ask is Fats.'

Whitman was scribbling the names. 'Where do I find them?'

'Buffalo and Axe might be difficult, Fats works at the Presbyterian Hospital. His last name is Walker.'

'Thanks.' Whitman put the phone down and hurried across to the news editor. 'Might have something about the elections, something about Rossini.'

'What?' The news editor was conducting a second conversation on the telephone.

'Dunno, but the source is good.'

The news editor checked the time. 'Three hours to stand it up, otherwise it doesn't make.' Give Whitman time and he'd piss in the wind all day going for a Pulitzer, give him a deadline and one day he'd win one.

Go for the man called Fats, Whitman thought, confront Rossini later. He checked the directory and telephoned the hospital. 'This is CBS Television, I'm trying to contact a Mr Walker.'

'Fats Walker?'

Minesota Fats the white pool player, Whitman thought, Fats Waller the black singer, and wondered which Fats Walker had been named after. 'Yes.'

'Putting you through.'

Fats was scrubbing up, he was told. Who wanted him?

'Adrian Whitman. CBS Television.'

'What about?'

'Tell him it's about Berlin and Mike Rossini.' The use of the familiar *Mike* was deliberate. He heard the words repeated, then the voice again.

'Can you call back this afternoon?'

The alarm bells still did not ring. 'I have to see him this morning.'

He heard the conversation again but could not pick out the details. 'Fifteen minutes.'

Gotta crew, he asked the programme organizer, running for the door.

'Stand-by camera doing nothing. Where'd you want them?'

'The Presbyterian Hospital.'

By the time Whitman reached the hospital it was twenty minutes after his initial call. An orderly was waiting for him at reception; emergency C-section, he explained. Whitman was rushed with military precision to the second floor, led into a dressing room, and given a green surgical gown and cap, lint mask and plastic slip-overs for his shoes, then taken across the corridor. The woman was stretched on the table, the screen in front of her and the epidural in her spine.

'So you want to know about Rossini.'

Whitman saw the surgeon glance at him above the surgical mask. 'Yessir.' It did not sound like his own voice.

'About Rossini in Berlin?'

'Yes.'

The surgeon completed the incision and felt carefully for the child. 'About the time Rossini went over the Wall and almost started World War Three.'

Christ, thought Whitman. 'Uh huh.'

Fats lifted the child in his hands and Whitman heard the first cry. Then watched as the surgeon tied and cut the umbilical cord, walked round the screen, and showed the child to the woman. 'She's a beaut, Jude.' Fats gave the child to a paediatrician and began to stitch up the wall of the womb. 'Off the record.'

Whitman had never before seen an expression like that on the woman's face as she looked at the child. 'Agreed.'

Fats finished the stitching, spoke gently with the mother again and returned to the changing room, Whitman following him. He threw the mask, cap and slip-ons into the waste can. 'So what do you want to know?'

'Whatever you can tell me about Rossini in Berlin.'

'Nothing much to say really. We were on patrol, place called Waldemarstrasse. Couple of guys made a break for it. One made it, one didn't.' The surgeon was stripped to his underwear, the muscles rippling across his back and shoulders like the fullback he had once been. 'When we got there the kid had just been shot, he was screaming his head off and dying fast. The West didn't know what to do and the East were just looking. We gave him covering fire and Mike went over.'

Jesus Christ, Whitman almost said aloud. 'What about Axe and Buffalo?' He was against the wall, held in the air with his feet off the ground, before he realized the surgeon had moved.

'Off the record?' It was the second time Fats had asked.

'Off the record.' Whitman was still in the air.

'I mean not to be used.'

Not to be used, agreed Whitman.

'Axe died, Buffalo's on skid row. All their kids are being taken care of. You leave them out.'

'How?' How are their kids being taken care of, he meant.

Fats lowered him to the floor. 'A trust fund.'

'You?'

'Doctors don't earn that much.'

'But lawyers do.'

Fats Walker shrugged. 'So what do you want?'

'An interview.'

'No Axe or Buffalo.'

No Axe or Buffalo, the reporter agreed.

By the time Whitman returned to the newsroom it was three. At three thirty he finished the script, laid down the commentary and telephoned the library for all material on the Berlin Wall in the mid sixties, especially shootings and deaths. At four fifteen he showed the producer of the day and the news editor the rough cut.

'Introduction's wrong.' The producer sat back. 'Set him up more before you take him to Berlin.' He swung in his chair and dialled the on-air studio. 'Drop the trailers for tonight's show, we're sending you a new one in ten minutes.' He redialled and spoke to the lawyer. 'I think you should come up.'

The first trailer was shown at five, the second at five thirty. At five forty-five Rossini was informed. At seven he sat feet up in the campaign office and waited, the election staff around him.

The first shots were of him campaigning, smiling and shaking hands. On paper the commentary would have been neutral and factually correct. 'Michael Rossini: lawyer and family man. Michael Rossini: local politician and charity supporter.' Spoken, however, the commentary had an edge. This is the Michael Rossini you know. The intonation was clear. This is the Michael Rossini you *think* you know.

The next shots were of Berlin, the Wall in the early days, the escapers running through the wire, ripping their clothes and skin as they scrambled to freedom. Then the Wall as he remembered it, the library footage in black and white, almost grey. 'Berlin in the early sixties.' The edge was still in the voice. 'Rossini was seconded there from the élite Eighty-Second Airborne. His job was to patrol the divide between East and West.' Slight exaggeration, the candidate almost laughed; he dropped his face in his hand and leaned on his elbow, saw the photograph of the jeep and the four men in it. 'His companions were called Fats, Axe and Buffalo. On a cold November morning, two young East Berliners broke for freedom at a place called Waldemarstrasse. One made it, the second was shot down. That day Michael Rossini broke orders and went over the Berlin Wall.'

The campaign staff looked at him in amazement.

The item continued, the interview with Fats, the doctor in surgical green and a gauze mask hanging round his neck. More shots of the Wall, the sound effects of shooting and someone screaming.

'Only when he knew the escaper was dead did Michael Rossini cross back to the West.'

The item ended and there was silence in the room, then the first telephone rang.

'Is it true?' The campaign organizer ignored it. 'What do I say to the press?' All the phones were ringing.

'Confirm I was in Airborne and that I was seconded to Berlin, but that I won't comment on anything else.'

The man was still looking at him. The *New York Times*: one of the staffers was standing, waiting, hand cupped over the mouthpiece. NBC *Meet the Press*, another told him. Sunday morning prime time live, normally reserved for heads of state, presidential candidates and recognized high-flyers.

'But is it true?'

'Yes.' Rossini picked up his coat and prepared to leave.

'Martin Schumaker.' His secretary held the phone towards him.

'Yes, sir.' A long time since he had shown the then junior senator round Berlin, he thought, since they had stood in the window of the flat on Liesenstrasse looking into the cemetery in the East, since they had ended the night in a bar off the K'Damm.

'Just phoning to congratulate you on your election to the Senate.' Schumaker now deputy chairman of the Senate Finance Committee, already powerful on the Hill and going places.

'The election isn't until next Tuesday.'

'Bullshit.'

The first tinge of autumn hung on the countryside, the hint of brown on the trees though the leaves not yet falling. Werner Langer and his daughter watched from the window of the train, the girl sitting so that she was facing forward.

Normally his mother celebrated her birthday with a glass of wine and a cake shared with the neighbours and the local committee of the Party. It had been Nikki who had suggested they go and Nikki who had asked if they could go by train. Gabi would not be able to make the trip, he had explained to Eva, Gabi had a Party meeting that weekend which she was committed to attend. Gabi, he knew, could not bear to stay in the small flat above the courtyard off Rosenstrasse, could not understand why Eva had not used her position in the Party, or her son's power in it, to move to a better flat and a better area.

The platform was busy but Eva saw them immediately: Werner a little older, the touch of grey in his hair; Nikki so much bigger than the last time Eva had seen her, so pretty, beautiful blonde hair. She swept the girl into her arms and kissed her, laughed at the way Nikki wished her happy birthday even though her birthday was not until the following day. They left the station, Nikki between them and holding their hands. Something about her, Eva thought, something which takes me back twenty years but which I cannot admit even to myself.

'Can we take the tram?'

He could have arranged a car but knew what Nikki would ask. 'Of course we can take the tram.'

The flat was smaller than he remembered; he sat in the armchair and breathed in the familiar smells, the reassuring warmth of the place. His mother had redecorated it but it was still the same, the table in the centre of the kitchen, the sideboard and fireplace, the photos on the wall. Perhaps it had always been small, he thought, watched as Eva and Nikki busied themselves, unpacking the girl's case, fussing over supper.

'I told people you were coming.' Eva laid the plates on the table, Nikki the knives and forks. 'They'd like to see you.'

'I'd like to see them again.'

They began supper, Nikki telling her grandmother about school and their holiday, the big cars which brought her father home, Eva remembering the wedding reception, then the conversation gradually turning, Eva telling Nikki how her father had played in a tin bath in the courtyard, about the school, the river where he had gone fishing.

They cleared the dishes and went to the neighbours, the committee members first, everyone admiring Nikki then asking Langer about his job at the Finance Ministry. The branch chairman was wearing his best suit, his breathing rasping and shallow where his lungs had been seared by the furnaces at the foundry where he worked. A good man, Langer thought, a cornerstone of the Party.

The next day Nikki insisted that her father take her to the school and the river and the streets where he played. Eva watched as the two of them stood looking at the school, as they crossed Marienbergplatz and sat side by side on the steps of the fountain and watched the boys playing football. As they walked to the Nicholai-kirche. The girl, bubbling, always talking, her eyes flashing and her blonde hair catching the sun.

That afternoon, when Werner Langer and Nikki had returned from the river and Nikki had washed and changed into her party dress, the three of them celebrated Eva's birthday, a handful of neighbours joining them, Eva cutting the cake her granddaughter had brought from Berlin.

'Is that Grandad?' The neighbours had left, Langer and Eva were washing up, Nikki standing by the table and looking at the photographs on the wall.

'No, that's not Grandad.' Eva turned and wiped her hands. 'This is Grandad.' She took the second photograph from the wall, brushing her hand across the glass as if to wipe the dust from it.

The girl nodded as if she understood. 'And this is you and Daddy.' The third photograph was of a young woman, her dress freshly ironed and her hair brushed, a child – only days old – in her arms.

'Yes.' Eva took it down and knelt by the girl. 'This is me and your father.'

As long as the wireless was on and the music was playing Eva knew she was safe; only when the music stopped did she turn and listen – for the warning of the bombers and some indication which city would suffer that night. The contraction eased and she relaxed again. The cot was by her bed in the next room and the suitcase was already packed in case she had to go to hospital. It was mid evening; she lay on the sofa and told herself it would not be tonight.

The next contraction started. Five minutes between the two, she calculated, nothing to worry about, not due for another two weeks, just a rehearsal. The contraction was sharper, like a band around her. Nothing to panic about, she told herself. Four minutes between them now, perhaps just three. Suddenly painful in a way she could never have imagined. Her hands were trembling, she was hot, cold, was not sure. Another contraction, almost making her scream.

The staircase outside was dark. She left her door open so that some light at least would guide her and held the banisters for support. The woman heard her immediately and came out. Eva was sitting on the bottom step of the stairs outside, her fingers were gripped round her knees and her face was pinched with fear.

'I've started.'

'I'll get the midwife.'

'*Don't go. Don't leave me by myself.*'

'*We'll go next door, they'll look after you while I get help.*'

The street was empty, the buildings like ghosts around them. The door into the hallway was unlocked; they pushed it open and went inside. The light wasn't working; they felt for the banisters and stumbled up. In the dark above them they heard a door open and saw the shaft of light, heard the rasp of the man's breathing.

'*Who is it?*'

'*Eva.*'

'*Wait there.*'

Another convulsion shook Eva's body. His hands and arms were large and strong. He waited till the contraction eased then helped her up the stairs.

'*Too late for the hospital.*'

The two women were already preparing the bed; in the corner of the room the boy woke and rubbed his eyes. He was just over a year old, his father in one of the tank divisions. The man sat Eva on the edge of the bed, helped take off her coat and shoes, then laid her down. There was a break in the music from the wireless in the kitchen, and they turned and waited.

'*I'll get the midwife, collect the suitcase on the way.*'

'*Bring the photographs and the cot.*'

The contraction was no longer round her body, was lower, across the bottom of her abdomen. Still tightening, building. Eva held the midwife's hand, searched for the other woman's, already afraid, the pain spiralling. The scream echoed round the room.

On the chair in the kitchen the man rocked the boy in his arms, holding the boy's head close to his chest.

The pain and tightness began to ease and she relaxed again, her body straightening on to the bed. '*Sing with me.*' The woman's voice was low, her head next to Eva's. What the hell do you mean, sing with you, Eva thought. The pain was beginning again and the room moving round her, the light bulb blurring.

> *A hundred green bottles, hanging on the wall.*
> *A hundred green bottles, hanging on the wall.*

Sing with me, Eva, it'll help you. Just follow me with the words. The contraction was tightening, the pain growing. Trust me, Eva, sing with me.

> *And if one green bottle should accidentally fall.*

Her hands were gripping the woman's and her body was arching again with the pain.

There'd be ninety-nine green bottles hanging on the wall.

The words are silly, Eva. What children sing. But they'll take you through it.

Ninety-nine green bottles hanging on the wall.

The scream died in her throat and the pain began to ease.

The music on the wireless stopped and they heard the voice. 'Air-raid warning. Enemy bombers approaching. Air-raid warning, enemy bombers approaching. Go to shelters now.' In the streets outside the air-raid sirens began to wail. They had five minutes, ten at most.

'Too late, Evie. Can't move you, you're too far gone.'

You go, she told the other woman, take the boy. The sweat was pouring from her forehead and drenching the pillow.

Can't leave you now, Eva.

You must, not for you, for your son. The man came into the room, the boy in his arms already wearing his coat. Quietly, so as not to disturb them, the man lit the oil lamps, bringing a third into the bedroom and leaving only one in the kitchen.

The contraction gripped her. Eva tried to sing and felt the fear as the pain enveloped her. She tried to control the scream and knew she could not.

The woman heard it and hesitated, was carried down the next flight by the rush of people. The front door was banging, the boy crying in her arms and the wail of the siren drowning everything, the scream from her flat almost lost in the pandemonium. In the street, she knew, in the safety of the bomb shelter, she would not hear the screams. The first markers drifted from the dark above, the memory of the scream hanging in the passageway. The first bombers would be arriving in two minutes, she knew. She clutched her son to her and ran back up the stairs.

A hundred green bottles, hanging on the wall.

Thanks for coming back. Eva clung to her hand and tried to smile. The first bombs fell on the city, the sound of the planes in the sky above them, the warning siren still screeching. The walls shuddered, the crockery on the sideboard trembling. The sound of the planes and the bombs was above them around them, never-ending. Ninety-eight green bottles . . . they were all singing.

Baby's head's showing, Evie. Push when I tell you. She felt the sudden peace. Baby's coming, Evie.

The electricity was gone and the oil lamps were flickering in the dark, the noise all round them. The bombs were as the contractions had been, wave after wave, mixing into each other, the building and the room shaking and the plaster on the ceiling cracking. Ninety-seven green bottles, they heard the man's voice above the hell.

It's a boy, Eva.

The thunder was all round them. Closer than it had ever been, everything shaking. The dresser in the kitchen crashed to the floor and the plaster fell round her from the ceiling. She lay back and heard the other sound, the sound of her son crying, clearing the mucus from his lungs. The umbilical cord was still intact. The midwife lifted the child, not yet cutting the cord, and laid him on his mother's stomach.

'Welcome to this world, my precious thing.' Eva wrapped her arms gently round him and kissed the top of his head, marvelling at the softness of his skin. 'Welcome, my little Werner Langer.'

The hoses of the fire-engines ran like snakes across the streets and the smell of burning hung in the air. The man and woman left the flat and walked around the square, past the trees in the middle of the square, neither speaking. On the corner a crowd had gathered. They stood in silence for five minutes then returned to the flat.

'What is it?' Eva pushed herself up in bed.

'The building where you used to live. It's been destroyed. There's nothing left.'

'What else is it?'

'The air-raid shelter on the corner. There was a direct hit. Everyone was killed.'

The following week Eva took Werner to have his photograph taken. Viktor was working the early shift; as an afterthought she asked whether he would like to go with her. When he came to collect them he was wearing a suit, dark grey with a fleck of blue in it, the collar of his shirt neatly starched, and a matching tie. After she had posed with the baby Eva insisted that he also have a photograph taken.

The proofs were ready three days later. Eva ordered prints of her and the baby for herself, Werner and Werner's parents – her own parents were dead – then studied the other photograph. At first it seemed formal, the man upright, almost Prussian. The more Eva looked at it, however, the more she saw the hint of a smile on the face and the laugh in the eyes. She ordered one for him, and one each for herself and the others.

CHAPTER TWO

THE NEW Year's Eve party was at Ernst Vöckel's. When Werner and Gabi Langer arrived at ten the house was already crowded. 1977 going into 1978.

The year had ended as most years now ended: with the usual mix of hope and scandal, politics and violence. In Czechoslovakia the organization Charter 77 had been formed to call for civil rights in the country. In West Germany the Red Army Faction had escalated even its level of violence. In America Jimmy Carter had ended his first year as President. In Russia the crackdown on the human rights movement had been tightened, particularly the campaign against the so-called Helsinki Group of dissidents. Amongst those arrested, but hardly noticed amid the welter of other activity, was the physicist and – since 1973 when his application to leave the Soviet Union for Israel had been rejected – the refusnik Antonin Shevienko.

At one minute to midnight Langer joined the circle of people linking arms in the lounge, the circle slightly misshapen and extending into the other rooms but the line unbroken.

It was almost two years since he had begun the game with Fritz Herbert. The Russians were happy with the material the man was providing, and if Moscow was happy then Berlin was delirious. But now it was time to move the game on.

CHAPTER THREE

IT WAS Lisa's birthday. Sometimes it seemed incredible to Anja that her daughter was ten years old; it was a long time since the runs from Czechoslovakia, she thought, a long time since a lot of things. Hans-Joachim was busy, often away from home. She still resented the time he gave to the organization, and the time he did not therefore give to her and their daughter, yet in a way she also admired him for it, even envied him. Sometimes, she also thought, it was inevitable that they would one day part.

The table was laid for the party, the doors to the garden open and the summer sun pouring in. She closed the door and fetched Lisa from school. By the time the girl had changed her friends were beginning to arrive, excited and chattering, Lisa opening the presents they brought. The telephone rang and Anja picked it up.

'Your grandmother.'

The girl took the set and sat on the foot of the stairs.

Schiller returned to his office at four, by four thirty he had cleared his desk and began to leave. That morning he had promised Lisa he would be home for the party, had sworn to Anja that he would not let them down. The telephone rang. He passed his secretary's desk and shook his head at her.

'Sorry, he's just left.'

He knew by her tone who was calling and hesitated.

'I'll check if he's still in the area.' She cupped her hand over the mouthpiece. 'Lensliger. Says it's urgent.' Lensliger headed the section which included the department which Schiller ran.

'How urgent? It's my daughter's birthday.'

'Urgent.'

He could see Lensliger and still be home in time, he thought. He pressed the switch for an outside line and dialled home. The number was engaged.

Lensliger's office was on the fifth floor, the blinds allowing in the light but cutting off both vision and sound from outside. The section head was sitting behind his desk, Rolf Hanniman in one of the chairs opposite. Schiller closed the door and sat in the other.

'Sorry about the party.' Lensliger was also a father and knew how much families suffered. His chair was turned sideways and he was rocking slightly in it. 'We might have a problem, we might have a break.' He stopped rocking and indicated that Rolf Hanniman should begin the briefing.

'It's possible we have an in on a network.' Hanniman sat forward. 'I spent this afternoon with an American contact. Apparently they've accessed someone who's running a number of people in the West. Russian or East German, I'm not sure.' Had to be Russian, Schiller thought, nobody was lucky enough to access an East German. 'One of the joes concerned is sending material out on a regular basis. Technical stuff mainly, I understand. The last batch contained a number of military items which might indicate an operation in West Germany.'

Ever since the Brandt affair, Bonn in general and the BfV in particular were especially sensitive of East German operations in the Federal Republic.

'Specifically?'

'Details of plans for a head-up system on the new European fighter.'

'Head-up?' Must telephone Lisa, he remembered, tell her I'll be home soon.

'A computerized method by which key data appears on the pilot's visor. Because he doesn't have to look down at his instruments he saves vital time. Especially important in low-level flying or air-to-air combat.'

'Why does this suggest an operation in West Germany?'

'Because certain parts of the research are taking place in this country.'

'The American source?'

'My man didn't know. High level. Code name Mateus.'

'Why'd he tell you? Why not go through official channels?'

'He owed me.'

'So where do we go from here?'

Lensliger straightened his chair and took the lead again. 'Rolf's people will handle the fighter bases where the system is being tested, yours the research and manufacturing companies involved.' They settled in their chairs and began the details.

By the time Schiller returned to the house it was almost ten and Lisa was in bed. I'm sorry, he tried to explain to Anja, wanted to wake Lisa and tell her. I was leaving when something came up. It always does, he saw the expression in his wife's eyes. 'I telephoned as soon as I knew but the line was engaged.'

'Of course.'

The following weekend Anja took Lisa to see her grandparents in West Berlin; Christina and Lutz met them at Tegel and drove them to the flat off Bismarckstrasse. That evening they ate ice-cream and walked along the Kurfurstendamm. By the time they returned to the flat and Lisa was asleep it was almost eleven; Christina and Anja sat in the lounge while Lutz made coffee.

'So why have you really come?' Christina sat in the armchair opposite.

The last months had been terrible and the arguments bloody, Lisa listening to them in her bedroom as they shouted at each other through the nights. In the end the decision had been clinical, merciful though merciless; in the end, when she had finally made it, Anja had felt the relief but the emptiness.

'I'm leaving Hans-Joachim. I'm bringing Lisa back to Berlin.'

'We thought that might be the case.'

'He's a good man, still devoted to us both, but he's never at home.' She had needed someone to talk to, had talked to no one. 'I no longer have a life of my own, I spend all my time waiting for him, and he spends all his time at work.' Anja tried to smile and wiped her face.

Christina sat on the sofa with her and put an arm round her. 'If that's what you've decided then that's what you must do, but you must tell Hans-Joachim yourself. Lutz and I will support both of you, we won't interfere or take sides, but you know we're always here.'

'Thank you.'

Lutz put the coffee on the floor and bent down. 'You all right?'

Anja nodded. 'Fine.' She looked at both of them, side by side as she always remembered them. Christina in her early fifties now, the first strands of silver in her hair and her face slightly fuller yet still attractive; Lutz one or two years older. 'He really is a good man, but you don't know how it is waiting for someone when you know they're not coming back.'

The line of women ran down the rubble and along what had once been a pavement. Every fifteen minutes they moved along one, so that each took it in turns to bend and pull the bricks from the debris. At the end of the line more women cleaned and stacked them.

When she had begun the work Christina's hands had been raw and bleeding, now they were hard with calluses across her palms. Sometime, she told herself, she should get a proper job; tonight she would ask Viktor to make enquiries at the factory where he worked. She straightened her back and tried to ease the pain from it. At least she was earning money, at least they were rebuilding the city.

Berlin, 1947.

The rumour was brought by someone who had run from the Zoo Gardens. More trains expected in an hour, more men coming home. The news passed up the line, the women stopping work and clustering together. How many? Where from? East or West? What time? The questions were urgent, incessant.

The woman did not know, had merely heard the rumour. Already some women were leaving, those whose husbands had returned or who had been notified that their husbands were dead wishing them good luck. Perhaps Hans, Christina thought. Perhaps today.

Each night she prayed. For her husband to come home. For the letter from one of the camps telling them that he was still alive, even the formal notification that he was still being held prisoner. Each morning she told herself that today would be the day. There was hardly anyone left on the line. She smiled nervously at the handful of women remaining and ran to Bremerplatz.

Hans-Joachim was playing outside. Christina pulled off her work clothes, washed and dressed, then stood in front of the mirror and combed her hair. Her stomach was churning and her hands were shaking. She locked the flat and hurried to the station. The entrance was blocked with women, the platforms above packed.

'Where from?'

East, West. Nobody could be sure, just as nobody had been sure the last time or the time before. The rumour swept through that there were no trains after all, that the information had been incorrect. The crowd sagged, still waited. Just as they had all waited in the snow of the last two winters, as they had waited in the heat of the last two summers. Three trains, the next rumour began, two from the East, one from the West. She felt the shiver of expectation and anxiety which joined them together.

They saw the train, two engines, green, the oil and grease streaked across the boilers and the steam bellowing from its stacks. Coming slowly from the west, the carriages behind it, swinging slowly over the bridge and into the station at the Zoo Gardens. The crowd saw the men, leaning from the carriages, waving, the women suddenly waving back, some holding up children. The first train drew into the Zoo Gardens, a second behind it.

Please today, Christina prayed, squeezed past the entrance and made it to the beginning of the platform. The first men were getting off the train. Two years after the war had ended, the anger was always with her, and still the bastards had not told them whether their men were dead or alive. She heard the cry behind her, almost a scream, felt someone pushing her away, pushing them all aside. One of the moments they all waited for, for someone else if not for themselves. The woman was almost frantic, shouting to be let through, afraid. The man saw her and dropped his bag, pushed through the crowd. Please may Hans come home today.

The second train came in and the other men began to get off; the crowd was bigger, thicker. She dropped her shoulder and squeezed closer, managed to reach the top of steps to the platform beneath the lines. The steps and the entrance halls were jammed. She stood on tiptoe so that she might see him and he might see her.

The crowd began to thin; she had been waiting almost two hours. Still the women waited. Christina left the Zoo Gardens and walked back towards the flat. It was late afternoon, already the streets were filling with soldiers. She turned off the K'Damm and saw him. A hundred metres in front, crossing towards the square. Right height, right body build, shoulders held back in the same way. Army greatcoat, even in summer. She broke into a run, the shout drying in her throat. The soldier was walking with a limp, as if a wound had not healed properly. She was fifty metres from him, still trying to shout. Right colour hair, right everything. He reached the square, hesitated, then turned right.

The disappointment annihilated her. Hans would not have turned right, Hans would have known the flat was to the left. She stopped running, tried to get her breath back, and went to the flat.

Tomorrow, she told herself. Next week, next month. Sometime. Tonight they would have meat with their potato, tonight she would open one of Nick's precious cans even though she and Viktor had agreed they were to be saved for winter. The footsteps went up the stairs. Tonight she would ask Viktor about getting her a job at the factory, tomorrow she would make the arrangements for Hans-Joachim to go to school. The footsteps came down the stairs and stopped.

She heard the knock on the door, dropped the tin, dropped everything. Was wiping her hands, brushing back her hair, opening the door.

The soldier she had seen in the square looked down at her. His eyes were dark, ringed by uncertainty. His hair had been cut short, disguising his age, and his body sagged. 'Frau Schiller?'

She nodded.

'*My name is Lutz, I was with Hans.*'

'*Come in.*'

He followed her into the kitchen.

'*Hans. Is he alive?*'

He tried to look her in the face but could not. '*No.*' *He managed to shake his head.* '*He's dead.*'

'*How?*' *They sat at the table.*

'*We made it through. Looked after each other.*' *He laughed, a bitter laugh, remembered a moment.* '*He died of malnutrition in the prison camp six months after the war ended.*'

A numbness settled upon her. '*You're hungry?*'

'*Yes.*'

'*In that case you must eat with us tonight, meet Viktor and Hans's son.*'

That night Christina cried for the first time. The next morning, when Viktor left for work, she was still crying.

The roof was leaking again and the walls were beginning to buckle. Lutz and Viktor had repaired them as best they could during the winter, now they had given way again. During the summer the weather had been fine, but soon autumn would come and after it another winter. Then the roof would finally cave in, they all knew, and when the roof came down the whole building would crumble with it.

August 1948.

'*He's coming.*' *Hans-Joachim was looking out the window.*

'*Has he got the ladder?*'

'*'Course he's got the ladder.*' *He ran down the stairs to help.*

Lutz and Hans-Joachim got on well together, Viktor and Lutz as well. Sometimes they went drinking together, took Hans-Joachim fishing.

A month after his return to Berlin Lutz had found a job. He had also found himself a corner in a room in the Neukoln area of the city, just big enough for his bed-roll and the suitcase in which he carried his few possessions. Most weekends he saw them, sometimes staying the night on the sofa in the kitchen, Viktor now sleeping in the second bedroom.

That summer the Americans and the British had introduced a new currency – the Deutschmark – in their zones. That summer the Russians had sealed off the city and tried to starve it into submission and the Allies had begun flying into Berlin the thousands of tons of food and fuel which the city needed every day to survive. Yet still Berlin was one city, governed by one council, meeting in the City Hall on Parochialstrasse in the Soviet sector. Three weeks before agitators from the East had tried to stop councillors from West Berlin taking their seats.

She heard the laughter outside and the man and boy came into the kitchen.

The next day was Saturday. Lutz and Viktor Wischenski spent the entire morning in the roof space, doing what repairs they could with the few materials they had managed to find. In the afternoon the two of them, plus Christina and Hans-Joachim, took the S-bahn to Wannsee and went fishing. By the time they returned to Bremerplatz it was almost seven, the evening still warm.

'Why don't you two go out tonight, have a drink?' Viktor glanced at Christina. 'Do you both the world of good.'

You don't know how much I want to, he could hear her voice as if they were alone. You don't know how much I want to get out of the flat and forget about everything. Don't know how frightened I am of what Hans-Joachim will think.

'I've only got my working clothes.'

Christina heard Lutz and felt the relief that she did not have to decide, yet with it the flush of disappointment.

'Borrow my bike. You could be home and back before supper's ready. Stay the night. That way we can get an early start in the morning.'

'Okay with you, Hans-Joachim?' Lutz turned to the boy.

'All right with me.'

The cafés on the Kurfurstendamm were crowded, the tables spilling on to the pavements. Even though the French and British and American soldiers were everywhere, it felt again like the old Berlin. Near the remains of the Kaiser Wilhelm Church a man was playing a barrel organ, the hookers lounging nearby.

'You're looking nice tonight.'

'Thank you.' She dusted an imagined speck from his suit and slid her hand through his arm. The sound of the piano drifted at them from the side street on their left, detached, almost ghostly, lost for a moment as the train rumbled across the viaduct over the road.

The bar was tucked under the railway bridge itself, the walls were covered with yellow embossed paper stained with cigarette smoke and covered with framed photographs, and the tables were heavy and varnished. As they entered the barman looked towards the door, as if expecting to recognize their faces, and waved at them anyway. The first room was packed; they laughed back, not even realizing they had done so, and pushed their way through the arch to the second room, on the right, and found a table. The pianist was in the far corner, seemingly absorbed in his music, bowing his head at whoever had bought him a drink. Christina allowed Lutz to take her coat and tried to imagine why she thought she knew the man. Something about the place, about the people, something about the feeling the place stirred in her. The pianist was playing Gershwin. He was in his early thirties, black hair swept back and slightly long, his fingers running casually along the keys.

The old Berlin, the thought caught Christina unaware, the Berlin which neither Hitler nor the bombs nor the Russians had managed to destroy.

The waiter waited for their order.

'Beer.' Lutz looked at Christina and she nodded. 'Two.'

The pianist came to the end of the tune and began another.

'What is it?'

She shook her head. 'Nothing.'

'You're thinking about Hans?'

'Yes.'

'Same here.'

The waiter weaved through the crowd with their drinks. In the dark of the corner the pianist bent over the keyboard; his hair was falling slightly forward and his evening suit was worn with age.

'The pianist. Ask him if he once played violin for the Berlin Opera. Ask him if he played on the last night, if he remembers the woman who gave him a rose.' Christina pulled a handful of notes from her handbag. 'If he says yes, buy him a drink and ask him if he would play it again.'

That's all your money; she saw the bewilderment on Lutz's face, play what again? I'll explain later, she told him.

The waiter looked at her. 'You were there?'

'Yes.'

'So was I.'

He pushed the money back into her hand, went to the bar, and returned with a bottle of champagne and four glasses. He poured one for the pianist then brought the bottle and other glasses to the table.

The pianist raised his glass to them, sipped from it, bowed his head slightly to Christina then leaned forward, hands and fingers poised over the keys. She could sense the expectation, see again the conductor raising his baton, could hear again the Russian guns closing on the city. The fingers touched lightly against the ivory and she felt the ice down her spine, the first notes unmistakable, lingering in the air. A woman on the next table was telling a joke and beginning to laugh. The man with her rested his hand on her forearm and motioned for her to stop. May 1945, the guns pounding in the evening air and the Berlin Symphony's final act of defiance at the Schauspielhaus. The silence fell upon the table and spread to the next, then the next, the entire bar silent.

Beethoven's Ninth. The beginning of the last movement. Even when the pianist stopped the tension hung in the air, then the moment was gone and he broke into New Orleans jazz.

'What are you thinking, Christina?'

'I'm thinking that I'd like to dance.'

*

The investigation based on the information provided by the agent code-name Mateus was thorough and the conclusion swift and clear-cut. Within four weeks an original list of six German companies dealing with the technical data which had been passed to the East had been reduced to three. Within these companies a total of five departments were isolated as having details of the head-up system; within these departments one hundred and thirty-five men and women were further short-listed and intensive investigations begun on every aspect of their lives. Political and family backgrounds, financial arrangements, sexual inclinations, school and university, sports clubs and leisure activities. At the end of two months the list was reduced to five, three men and two women.

'Any preferences?'

Rolf Hanniman and Hans-Joachim Schiller sat with Franz Lensliger.

'Fritz Herbert.'

'Why?'

They went into the details.

'If he's from East Germany how the hell did he get such a sensitive job?'

'Because his first job at MBB wasn't sensitive. He was a good worker, promoted several times. He moved into the section before the work on the head-up system was allocated to it.'

'But now?'

'But now he has access to a lot more.'

'Jesus Christ.'

They moved on: family details, the level of his overspending, the payments into a range of accounts from sources other than salary.

'What about his wife?'

'On the game. We found her on the Reeperbahn in Hamburg last week. Normal story, comes West, picked up by a pimp without even knowing it. Spot of fun then a few photos, at least one movie, then downhill from there. Her arms are like pin-cushions.'

'Talk about her husband?'

'She wasn't asked.'

'So what's the timetable?'

'We pick him up on Friday after work, gives us the weekend before anyone misses him.'

'What about the daughter?'

'She'll be taken care of.'

'The others on the list?'

'We still don't know that Fritz Herbert's our man.' Once on the security computer in Cologne, never off it.

'Good.'

The Friday shift finished at four; Fritz Herbert collected his car and drove home. He felt relaxed, almost carefree: no formulas entered on the pocket computer he carried, no photostat sheets or microfilm concealed in the false bottom of his briefcase. He had always been careful, put the extra money in the other accounts. And methodical, always worked out in advance what he was doing and how he would do it.

The hallway was empty and smelt of polish. He stepped into the lift, pressed the button for the second floor and felt for the keys of the flat. The apartment was an extravagance perhaps but he had been careful again, made sure he could pay for it out of his salary, covered his tracks as they had instructed. The lift stopped and he stepped out.

'Fritz Herbert?' The two men appeared from nowhere.

'Yes.'

He only half heard their next words and barely saw the identity cards they showed him before they bundled him down the stairs. The door at the rear was open and the minibus reversed against it. He was in the back of the bus, doors shutting and windows blackened, the driver accelerating before he even brought himself to speak.

How much do you earn at MBB, where do you bank, how much do you pay for the flat? What holidays do you take? Where? How often? No money other than in the one account? The room was dark outside the pool of light and he could barely see the men. What about the account in Zurich, the summer holiday in Corsica? The skiing holidays in Austria and Switzerland and the trip to Disneyland? Where'd you get the money, Fritz? Why the extra accounts? The paperwork and the computer print-outs to back up the questions, make his denials ineffectual, almost obscene. Where were you trained, Fritz? What about Ann-Marie?

They saw the weakness and closed on it like sewer rats. The men in the back rooms checking the simultaneous transcripts of the tapes, the computers whirring, cross-referencing, seeking the connections and guiding the interrogators.

Ann-Marie leaving him and taking their daughter. The Mercedes his wife was driving the afternoon she returned the girl to him. Amsterdam: the club outing, the bar in the Oude Kerk and the movies upstairs. We know you've told us once, Fritz, but tell us again. The computers accessing the works files at MBB and referencing back.

You were set up, Fritz. The men moved from the dark, no longer sat opposite him. Sat beside him and gave him coffee, offered him a cigarette.

You're a scientist, Fritz. Work it out for yourself, take as long as you want. What do you call it; the law of probability, isn't it? How many strip clubs and blue joints are there? What are the statistical chances of your being in the right room, in the right club, in the right city, at exactly the time they play a blue movie featuring Ann-Marie? Reinhard Wagner's disappeared, Fritz, the Reinhard Wagner who suggested the trip to the sports club. Mackowitz as well, the dirty little pimp who set Ann-Marie up to it, he's gone as well. Only Klaus Giese left, only your controller. It wasn't us, Fritz. It wasn't the West. It was the East. They set you up. Ruined your poor little Ann-Marie so they could get at you.

The office was quiet, the smell of cigarette smoke and coffee in the air and the sandwiches stale on the plate. Two o'clock on Sunday morning. Lensliger had flown in that evening, now he sat at the desk and read through the reports, the twenty pages of initial statement which Fritz Herbert had made and signed.

'Good job. Open and shut case. He won't stand a chance in court.'

'Why take him to court?' It was Hanniman who asked.

'What else do you suggest?'

'Turn him. Run him as a double.'

'Security problems?' Lensliger turned to Schiller.

'Containable. That was the first thing we made sure of.'

It would go down well in Bonn, they all knew, especially after the Willy Brandt fiasco.

'Why not?' Lensliger sat back and lit himself another cigarette. 'Why not give it a run?'

CHAPTER FOUR

THE NEW Year's Eve celebration at Party headquarters was the type of function which Gabi enjoyed; she had spent the afternoon at the hairdresser's, now she mixed effortlessly with the other guests. All the hierarchy present, Langer noted, plus those who would take their places in the decades to come. Honecker and his politburo; Mielke, Lindner and Moessner. Krenz and Schabowski amongst those drawing closer to the centre of political power; himself and Meyer climbing the ladder of State Security.

The year 1978 ending with duplicity and violence. The Vietnamese boat people in South-East Asia, the Red Brigade in Italy, and the demonstrations against the Shah in Iran. In Russia – he was marginally aware of the fact – the scientist and refusnik Antonin Shevienko, accused of treason, espionage and anti-Soviet agitation and propaganda, had been sentenced to three years in a close confinement prison and a further ten years in a strict régime labour camp.

And Fritz Herbert. Turned by the West Germans and everyone congratulating themselves. The game going well, he knew. Time to take it on a stage.

CHAPTER FIVE

THE STRETCH limousine crossed the Triborough Bridge, headed down East River Drive, then turned off at East Seventy-First and along First Avenue. Michael Rossini sat in the rear seat and watched a fishing cutter butting against the tide and the wind of the East River.

'Reminds me when I was a boy.' The Senate Intelligence Committee chairman had grown up on the shores of Chesapeake Bay and still kept a house there. 'Your son sail?'

'Only on vacation.'

'Bring him down sometime, he'd enjoy it. Sally as well.'

After Nick junior had been born Sally had continued her work as a lawyer. Because of the pressure of their two jobs, and the fact that Rossini spent considerable time in Washington, they insisted on spending weekends together, and taking as long a summer break as they could.

'You're off to Europe?' The Senate Foreign Affairs Committee chairman glanced across.

'Monday.'

It was the standard tour: Bonn for the politics, Berlin for the flag-waving and Vienna for the opera. Plus Prague. Something to make the Czechs understand they had not been forgotten, the State Department had suggested. No contact with Charter 77, though, for God's sake nothing provocative.

The limousine pulled under the canopy in front of the members' entrance of the United Nations building and they hurried inside, already late. The reception was on the fourth floor, the formal suits of the Western and European delegates mixing with the dazzling colours of Africa, the crystal white of the Arab *disdashes* contrasting with the immaculate khaki of the Third World Marxists. The waiters weaving between them, the silver salvers above their shoulders and the champagne flowing like water.

'Who's that?' Rossini stood with the American ambassador and an aide.

'The Hungarian ambassador to the UN.'

'The man with him?' The man was small, Lenin-style beard, eyes sharp behind the glasses.

'Special Party adviser, just in from Budapest to make sure they toe the official line.'

'High-flyer then?' It was the reputation for attention to detail which the ambassador and his staff had been warned the senator enjoyed on Capitol Hill.

'Very high.'

'Introduce me.'

The ambassadors shook hands, both known to each other, and introduced their guests.

'First Secretary Tomasek, from Budapest.'

'Senator Rossini, from Washington.'

The next morning Michael Rossini and his family travelled to his parents' home in Boston. The weekend was special, Nick and Hanni's wedding anniversary. At seven he and Sally changed for dinner; when they came downstairs Hanni was sitting on the sofa in the living room, her grandson by her side, showing him the photographs of old Berlin.

He glanced over their shoulders and saw the snapshot of the soldier and the young woman in the Kurfurstendamm, his arm round her shoulder and the blackened remains of the Kaiser Wilhelm Church behind them. 'Good-looking couple.'

'You bet.' His father stood beside him and gave him a glass of champagne.

When the other guests had gathered they went through to the dining room. The linen was sparkling white and the table immaculately laid, the caterers hired for the evening.

'Ladies and gentlemen, may I welcome you tonight and thank you for joining us on this special occasion.' He stood up and smiled at those around him. The guests were long-time friends of his parents, some of them from the legal world, others not. 'Just before you came this evening, I caught Hanni showing my son some old photographs from the family album. She was a good-looker then, I still can't believe she's old enough to be a grandmother.' The guests laughed. He raised his glass. 'May I ask you to join me in wishing Nick and Hanni a happy anniversary.'

The flat was quiet, Sunday morning; the boys were upstairs and the women sat round the table, the coffee cups in front of them.

'There's something I should tell you.'

'About how you get the money for the food?'

Hanni realized it was why they had conspired to be alone with her.

'Don't worry. We know.'

'How do you know?'

'We're not fools, Hanni. We could see what you were doing and what it was doing to you.'

'Why didn't you say something?'

'Because we thought you would be ashamed of yourself and we would lose you.'

'Why have you told me now?'

'Because we don't want to lose you.'

She sipped the coffee. 'Everything's changed.' *She was not sure what to say, how she should describe Nick.* 'I have a boyfriend.'

'We know that as well.'

'How?'

'Because you're different.'

'That's where I get the stuff now.'

'Do you do it with him?'

'No.'

'Then why does he give you the cigarettes and the food?'

No answer.

'Do you want to do it with him?'

Again no answer.

'Other men?'

'No.' *Why are you asking me, she wanted to know, why are you treating me like a criminal?*

'Why not?'

'Because now I've met him I couldn't, even if we needed the food for ourselves and the boys.'

'Does he know that?'

'Yes.'

'Have you told him?'

'Yes.'

'*Sorry, Hanni, but we had to be sure you were sure.*'

The next weekend Nick borrowed a jeep from the motor pool and drove them to the lakes at Wannsee. The water was crystal blue, the woods rising around it and its shores deserted. After they had unloaded the jeep they collected brush wood and made a fire.

By the time they had finished eating it was still only three thirty; they left the lake and followed a track south, the sun on their right. In front of them was a clearing, grass-covered, the sun dappling on it. Nick sat down and picked a blade of grass, held it in his mouth; lay back on the grass and stared at the sky.

The gust of wind came through the trees, warm, the scent of the pines from below. She had never smelt anything like it, breathed it in. The scent was powerful, almost intoxicating. She lay down, next to him, her hands under her head. The perfume drifted away on the wind, came back again. He leaned over, left elbow on the ground, his body weight on it, lips brushing against hers.

He was looking at her, the fingers of his right hand undoing the buttons down the front of her dress. His fingers were running lightly over her body, round her sides and along the top of her pants, stroking her, nails leaving delicate trails across her.

'*Sit up.*'

She sat up and leaned forward, slipped the dress from her shoulders. He leaned behind her and undid her bra, slid it off, so that only her pants remained.

'*Give me time, Nick.*'

He smiled and laid her back on the ground, watched her as she looked up at the sun through the trees, as her eyelids closed and she breathed in the scent of the pine. He kissed her, gently, their mouths wide open, lips almost still, barely touching. Kissed her ears, throat, neck. She stretched, arms above her head, felt his mouth and tongue on her breasts, teeth nibbling her nipples. '*What are you laughing at?*' She was relaxed, had never been so relaxed before.

He held her breasts, firm and full, drew the nipples between his teeth. '*You. I thought you were a skinny little thing the first time I saw you.*'

The scent of the pines hung in the trees, in his hair. She pushed him over, on to his back, and unbuttoned his tunic. '*Sit up.*' He leaned forward. She pulled the tunic over his shoulders then laid him on the ground, teeth biting gently at the lobes of his ears and fingers running round his nipples. She reached down and pulled off his shoes and socks, unbuttoned his trousers. He lifted his buttocks and slid off his trousers so that he was naked, and lay *again on his back. She moved slightly and held him with both hands, stroked him, scratched him delicately and carefully, laughed at the noises he made and the way he moved. He rolled over and lifted her buttocks, slid off her pants.*

'Not yet, Nick, I still need more time.'

They lay side by side, fingertips brushing again, looking at the trees. The war, the city, so far away they did not exist. The sun passed over them, she could still smell the scent of the pines and hear the rustle of the wind in the treetops. Her arms were round his neck, holding him, pulling him on to her. She felt his body weight on her, stomach against hers, legs against the insides of hers. They were kissing as they had kissed before, mouths open, lips barely touching. She was aware of the slight change of weight as he reached down and held himself close to her, the head of his penis stroking her, entering her slightly then withdrawing, teasing her, lubricating her, the lips of her vagina folding over him, drawing him in a fraction, not even taking the whole head, teasing him, making him even harder.

She knew he was about to come into her and waited for her muscles to contract, for the fear and hurt to take over. Felt the moment he began to move, slowly and gently, coming into her, filling her, the way she took him, soft and relaxed.

'Okay?'

She tried to nod, could only blink, realized she was shaking her head at him, knew he understood. He began to move, slowly at first then faster. He laughed at her again and stroked a hair from her face, kissed her. She felt the waves running through and over his body, felt them take over hers, her body and her mind, smelt again the scent of the pines. Clung to him, moved with him. Rolled him over again and sat astride him, watched his face as she moved up and down on him, felt his fingers scraping her back as she had scraped his. He held her shoulders, rocked her backwards, pulled her down again, kissing her face and her breasts.

He was supporting himself on his hands, no weight upon her, as if he was floating, as if they were both floating. His movements were stronger, longer. She could not believe it, could never have imagined it. The sun was spinning, treetops swirling in circles, the waves pounding through her body and the salt of their sweat stinging her eyes.

She felt her entire body beginning to stiffen, muscles tightening, arms clamped round him. No sun any more, no trees, just the light. Body stiffer, muscles tighter, harder. Body even stiffer, acting of its own accord. Her legs were locked around him, arms clasped round his neck. Teeth clamped tight.

'Now, Nick. For God's sake now.'

*

276

Bonn had been predictable, Vienna would have its colour and Prague its shadows, but Berlin was still Berlin. Of course there had been changes, of course the old lady had plastered on the face paint, powdered over the old cracks and tried to ignore the new. But in the end she was still the same whore that his father had fallen in love with and to whose door he in his turn had come.

The afternoon session at the Mission was short, the CIA head of station suddenly and inexplicably unavailable and the section itself strangely quiet. Something running, he knew, something to do with the fact that Al Warner was in town. They had met Warner two days ago for his background on European intelligence, Rossini and the other members of the Senate and House Intelligence Committees in the group receiving an additional briefing, as would be expected, when the rest had left.

Warner was in his late thirties with a frame like the Penn State halfback he had once been, short hair slightly balding, the squareness of his face offset by his gold-rimmed bifocals. Rossini had worked under him in Berlin in the late sixties, both men remembering the other. After the second meeting in Bonn, when the other members of the Intelligence Committees had rejoined the rest of the party for dinner, the two of them had spent the evening together, discussing nothing in particular but allowing the Jack Daniels to remind them of the past and prepare the ground for what – perhaps in retrospect – they both assumed would be the future.

Now Warner again. The briefest glimpse of him at the end of the corridor. In Berlin when he should have been in Bonn.

They began to leave, Senator Naborski – the senior member of the group – expressing their thanks to the ambassador and the few words fast becoming a speech, the drivers of the cars which would take them on their conducted tour waiting patiently. Rossini left the group and went to the cars.

'We go along the K'Damm?'

'Yes, sir.' The driver wore the uniform of the Marines.

'Drop me at the Europa Centre.' It was time to renew old acquaintances, those who had helped him in the past and whom he might still call upon in the future. Time to see how the Hilton was looking now it had been expanded and renamed the Inter-Continental, how it felt now that the old Golden City Bar had passed into history and probably mythology.

'You're not coming with us, sir? You don't wanna see East Berlin?'

'What's your name?'

'Corporal Mancini, sir.'

'First name?'

'Andy, sir.'

'Still run the patrols along the canal, Andy? The Hole in the Wall still open?' The others were coming down the steps, two of them checking their cameras. 'Still park the jeep up and go in the back door? Still get the radio blackout near Sebastian Strasse?'

The Marine laughed. It was something to tell the boys later, some senator who looked and sounded like all the other dudes but who knew about the patrols and where the best ass in town used to be. 'The Hole got shut down last year. Public health hazard. Know somewhere else though.'

'Not this time, Andy, but thanks anyway.'

The Congressional party arrived in Vienna at eleven the following morning. By twelve thirty they had checked in at the Hilton International on Am Stadt Park, and been driven to the United States embassy. There was a glint of bifocals in the corridor light. Bonn, Berlin, now Vienna.

'Hello, Al.' What's running, Al? What's going on?

'Afternoon, Senator.'

Out of bounds, Rossini knew Warner was going to say. You weren't dealt in on this one. The station chief changed his mind, the nod deliberate. Loose yourself from the others and join me when you can.

The party filed into the room on the second floor and settled in the chairs round the briefing table. The Second Secretary coughed politely and Senator Naborski rose to make his customary speech. Rossini left the meeting and hurried along the corridor. Three minutes later he was collected and taken to the Keep, in the centre of the embassy complex. The room was clinical, no decorations on the walls and no windows, and had been swept five minutes before. As they entered the man at the table looked up. He was in his forties, dark hair neatly cut, white shirt and blue tie, coat over the back of his chair.

'Senator Rossini, Bob Selly.' Warner saw the puzzlement in

Selly's eyes. 'It's okay, Mike used to be with the Company. Langley cleared him two minutes ago.'

They sat down at the table.

'Someone's coming out. Long-term penetration and they're finally on to him.'

'Who?'

'Code-name Mateus.'

'How's he coming?'

'Through Czechoslovakia. Passport already at a drop in Prague, stamps to be filled in en route.'

Passports were stamped on entry into the Eastern bloc and it was impossible to leave without the relevant stamp. The stamps themselves were changed regularly – colour, pattern, code for time and place. Mateus had the passport but not the stamp. Someone would therefore go in, collect a stamp and transfer it to the passport already held by Mateus. But because Mateus was being careful, the passport would be blank when the stamp was transferred, Mateus himself entering his personal details and photograph after.

'So?'

'Mateus is adamant that the duplicate stamp is to be passed to him on the train. He also insists on knowing the details of the person doing the run.'

'So what's the problem?'

'The person collecting the stamp. We gave Mateus his photograph and the name he would be using through a small article in the European edition of the *Herald Trib*, plus details of which train he would be on.'

'So?'

'The run is tomorrow morning, the information was in today's paper.'

'But?'

'The courier was killed in a car crash after the edition went out last night. Stupid bastard wrapped himself round a tree. Nothing and nobody else involved. First thing we checked.'

'Options?'

'There should be two: cancel the run or send someone else. Unfortunately neither applies. According to Langley Mateus is already running and knows he's been missed, and there's no one else he knows.'

'Easy.' Langley would have to be informed. Langley would kick up hell then Langley would agree.

'How?'

'Use me. Small piece in tomorrow's *Trib* reporting the death of the last courier, same place in the paper so the implication's obvious. Plus a report next to it of US Congressmen visiting Vienna and Prague, goodwill and that jazz, with photograph of some of them. If the *Trib* is the point of communication he's bound to check, just make sure the Europe edition is flown into Prague tonight.'

'Impossible.'

'Why?'

'A US senator would stand out a mile.'

'Persuade some of the others to make the trip by rail as well and use them as cover, tell them they need to experience the border first-hand.'

'How will Senator Naborski react?'

'Put Stan in the middle of the photograph and he'll love it.'

The train left Franz-Josef Bahnhof at seven seventeen. Thirty minutes later it passed through the Iron Curtain into the East, the guards joining it and the border officials checking and stamping passports.

Fifth carriage, third window seat on the left from the front – the instructions had been specific and the seat reserved. Rossini was to remain in it for two minutes after the station at Breclav. The passport would be taped behind the towel dispenser in the toilet at the end of the carriage nearest the engine. He should complete the forgery by Brno, forty-three minutes later. The morning was clear, the sun rising to his left, the train curving into the valley and through the trees. Forty-one minutes to lift the entry visa; he wished he had more time, had had more time last night to practise.

The train pulled into Breclav: the platforms were busy, guards and police everywhere, a few people leaving the train and others getting on. The porters closed the doors and the train pulled away. Eight twenty-three, he checked his watch and looked at the people passing in the corridor. Mostly men, a couple of women, one brunette, attractive-looking, the other in her early thirties, blonde hair and good clothes but severe expression on her face. Plus police and guards.

The rest of the Senate group were looking out the window. Rossini excused himself, took the briefcase from the luggage rack and squeezed past the soldiers in the corridor to the toilet at the end. The train was slowing, following a river along a valley bed. He locked the door and felt behind the towel dispenser. The passport was in a polythene bag, taped to the wall. No photograph or details in the passport yet, he noted, Mateus a pro. He opened the briefcase and took out a toilet bag. The train was picking up speed again. He placed the shaving cream and razor on the side to the left, half filled the basin with water and splashed some shaving cream in it, in case he was interrupted. Then he took out the soap box, toothbrush, the hand torch, roll of Elastoplast, bottles of aftershave and cologne, and the plastic container of dental floss, and placed them carefully to the right. The train was rocking slightly.

He removed the plastic strip and frame of negative film from the dental floss container, opened his passport and laid the film on the new stamp. Plenty of time, he told himself. He took the sunglasses from his pocket, removed the ultraviolet filter which had served as the right lens from the frame and fitted it over the end of the torch, then he removed the roll of Elastoplast from the metal ring which surrounded it, put the ring on the negative, switched on the torch and placed it and the filter on the ring directly above the film and stamp, holding it tightly in position.

Interesting, he had suggested the night before. Stone Age, Selby had retorted, but no time for anything else.

After ten minutes Rossini opened the soap container, removed the bar of soap – still wrapped in its paper – and placed the two halves at the top of the washbasin. Then he removed the torch from the negative, opened the bottles of aftershave and cologne, poured the chemicals from each into the respective halves of the soap container, and placed the negative in the chemicals, timing the duration in each chemical precisely. When the image of the stamp appeared he washed and dried the negative, took the plastic from the dental floss container, laid the negative on it and the torch and ultraviolet filter on the negative, again separating them from the plastic using the Elastoplast ring.

Twenty minutes gone, he checked his watch, almost thirty.

Twelve minutes left before the train reached Brno.

He removed the plastic, held it under the tap, and began to scrub it with the toothbrush, the hard plastic which had absorbed the image from the negative remaining intact and the softer material around it washing away. After three minutes the stamp on the plastic was clean, the lines neat and well defined. He felt in his inner jacket pocket for the paper and fountain pens, selected the pen containing the ink which most closely matched the colour of the original stamp, rubbed the ink on the stamp and tested it on the paper. In seven minutes the train would reach Brno. He checked the copy stamp against the original, then entered the stamp in the passport Mateus would use, angling it to match the original.

Five minutes to Brno. He left the passport open, allowing the stamp time to dry, repacked his briefcase, taped the passport back behind the dispenser, and went back to the compartment, smiling at the other members of the group. Two minutes later the train pulled into Brno. The station was busy with people and luggage, military everywhere. On the platform opposite another train pointed towards the border.

'Would Frau Schelling please report to the information office where there is an urgent message for her.' He heard the announcement and thought nothing of it, watched the people on the platform. His job done, he wondered when Mateus would make the pick-up, and where and how the man would run. The doors were slammed shut and the train began to move. The platform was still crowded, people jostling each other, men and women boarding the train towards the border. He looked at the faces and saw the woman again – blonde hair and attractive clothes, the good looks marred by the severe expression.

'Would Frau Schelling please report to the information office.'

The woman stepped into the station office and he realized. Knew that in fifty-five minutes the woman would be back at the border, knew how she would explain why she was leaving the country only two hours after entering it; the confirmation by the information office at Brno of a sick relative in Vienna and the need for Frau Schelling to return immediately. The hounds closing in and Mateus running for home. He settled back in his seat and enjoyed the ride into Prague.

*

The reception at the American embassy began at eight, the ambassador himself at pains to introduce the Washington group to local dignitaries. After thirty minutes he took Rossini aside and briefed him, quietly and efficiently, on diplomats present and the Czech representatives to whom he should pay special attention.

The other man was putting on weight, Rossini thought, just the beginning of a midriff under the Party suit, but the eyes still sharp as hell and the handshake firm.

'First Secretary Vlasak, may I introduce Senator Rossini.'

CHAPTER SIX

THE SKY was lead-grey, threatening snow, and the station was busy, everyone laughing as they jostled to catch a train or checking the board for those arriving. In the West, Langer thought, they would be playing Christmas carols. The Leipzig train came in, the first doors opening and the people suddenly pouring off, struggling with suitcases and cardboard boxes. Nikki shouted and waved. Eva saw her, dropped the case and waved back.

That evening the four of them went to the theatre, Nikki and Eva sitting side by side, Nikki barely able to stop talking. The following day, Christmas Eve, following the German custom, they placed the tree in the sitting room, decorating it with candles and chocolates, gingerbreads and fruit. At five they opened the presents, then sat down to eat. On Christmas morning it was beginning to snow. Whilst Gabi prepared dinner Nikki and Eva put on overcoats and headscarves and went for a walk. The snow was falling harder and beginning to cover the pavements. Langer stood in the window and watched the two as they walked down the street. As they reached the corner he saw Nikki slip her hand through her grandmother's arm and ask a question, saw the way his mother looked back at the girl and reply. Wondered what Nikki had asked and what Eva had said.

'Do you still miss Grandad?'

'Of course.'

The morning was cold and the night before it had begun to snow. Tomorrow her son would be one year old; Eva lit the fire and heated some water. Six o'clock: the boys were still asleep, the cot and small single bed crammed high with blankets between the beds. The kitchen had lost whatever warmth they had managed to build up the evening before; the damp of the wood at the side of the fireplace permeated the flat, making it seem even colder than it was, and the wind cut through the window despite the newspaper they had stuffed between the broken panes. Moisture was already seeping down the walls, even though they had tried to repair the roof, and there had been no electricity since the previous afternoon.

The city was still being bombed and the war was going badly; in a way they already knew it was lost. Sometimes Eva wondered whether they should have left the city with the other evacuees; often she wondered why they had not. It was already gone six thirty. She dragged out her coffee and bread as long as she could, kissed Werner softly, taking care not to wake him, and left the flat.

Even though it was still an hour till dawn there were people in the square, moving like ghosts, pale grey against the last of the dark, their coats pulled tight round them and their limbs stiff. Some on their way to work, others coming home, all of them searching for the scraps and the chances that might help them survive. The streets were wet and the pavements were running with mud, the brown mixed with the ash which trickled from the burnt buildings. Already the cold was seeping through her shoes. The snow was settling on her coat and numbing her shoulders; she turned left at the remains of the church and crossed the rubble. The vegetable stall was tucked beneath the railway viaduct close to the station, the buildings on either side destroyed and the crowd of men and women grabbing at the potatoes.

'How much?'

The woman shook her head at the coupons. 'Fifty Reichsmarks a kilo.'

It was more than she could afford, but at least she had something. 'Six.'

'Kilos?' The woman scooped them on to the scales.

'Potatoes.'

It was growing light, the grey of the streets and smoke of the trains giving way to the colours, however bleak and drab, of day. She walked on, past the remains of what had once been the greatest and most famous stores and hotels in the city, buying what she could, the snow still falling and the string bag she carried barely half full.

The street was cobbled – the large rectangle stones rather than the small rounded ones – and the houses on each side were tall, built round huge courtyards and divided into flats, the cellars deep below them. Even as she passed the bar on the corner Eva could smell the bread. Please may there be some left when I get there, please may he take my food coupons.

The baker's shop was packed with people like herself, coats pulled round them and faces cold and anxious. She pushed her way in and shuffled forward, standing on tiptoe and trying to see, the man to her right trying to steal past her, the other women pushing him back. The fear began to grip her, her eyes suddenly darting like everyone else's, counting the loaves and estimating the number of people. The bread smelt fresh and hot; she remembered the old days when she and Werner would buy a loaf, tear off pieces while it was still warm, and eat it with cheese and beer. The baker took the last loaf from the shelf and the shop emptied. She stood in the centre of the floor still smelling the bread. The baker began taking down the racks from the shelves and dusting the crumbs from the counter.

'Two hours.'

'I'm sorry?'

'We had a delivery of flour last night. Another batch of bread in two hours.'

'I'll wait.'

'I'm shutting up.' His manner was brisk and he worked as he spoke. 'You'll have to wait outside.'

'That's all right.' At least she would be first in the queue, at least she would get some bread. 'It's my son's birthday tomorrow.' She did not know why she told the man.

'How old is he?'

'One.' She stepped into the street.

'Where's his father?'

Neither she nor the other women had heard from their husbands for two months. 'He's with the 78th Infantry.'

'Which regiment?'

'The 195th.'

'Eastern Front.' It was a statement rather than a question.

'Who knows for sure?'

The baker shut the door and slammed up the locks.

Eva stamped her feet and rubbed her hands together, a queue already forming behind her. Her feet were cold, almost frozen. She had been waiting ninety minutes when she heard someone whistle to her and saw the baker waving to her from a doorway ten metres down the street. She left her place and followed him through the large double doors into the yard around which the block was built, and into the rear entrance of his shop. The room at the back was hot from the ovens, the shop itself in front.

'Your boy's one tomorrow?'

Eva nodded. The smell of the new bread filled the room, someone carrying flour up from the cellar below. The baker pushed two loaves into her bag, then a small round birthday cake.

'Why?'

The man's voice was proud. 'The 195th. My son as well.'

The snow was still falling; by the time she returned to the flat it was almost two. They would have something to eat, her mind was already thinking ahead, then they would take the boys for a walk, look for some firewood. She went up the stairs and into the flat.

Christina was waiting for her, the thin grey telegram envelope with the black edging on the kitchen table. 'I'm sorry, Eva.'

The guests began to arrive at nine, sixty to seventy of them, a mix of colleagues, Party associates and friends. It had been Gabi's idea. Good for your career, she had suggested; a *quid pro quo* Langer had thought she also meant, you and Nikki have Eva up for Christmas, I have my party for the New Year. He checked that Eva and Nikki were enjoying themselves and poured himself another drink. Times changing; he glanced across at them again and waited for midnight.

In Russia the head of the KGB, Yuri Andropov, had been made Marshal, second only in power and status to Brezhnev himself.

In East Germany the former head of the country's youth movement, Egon Krenz, had been given his first politburo job. At *Neues Deutschland*, the country's main newspaper, Gunter Schabowski had been made editor.

In America – partly because he was a Jewish refusnik and partly because of his alleged connections with the United States – the campaign for the release of the imprisoned Soviet dissident Antonin Shevienko was already beginning to grow.

And the game, Langer thought. Going well and everyone happy. The West Germans because they'd turned Fritz Herbert. The Russians because they were still getting at least part of the genuine material they wanted. And the Americans because Mateus was out. Yet the game was still not finished, the best was still to come.

BOOK FOUR

CHAPTER ONE

WASHINGTON WAS bright, the morning sun beginning to warm and the first haze of heat and car fumes already rising along Pennsylvania Avenue. The wire machines were in the lobby off the chamber and the press gallery overlooking the floor. The first person to read the news was a senator from Iowa.

Leonid Brezhnev, President of the Soviet Union, one of the two most powerful men in the world, the man who had ousted Nikita Khrushchev in 1964, was dead. His successor would be Yuri Andropov, for fifteen years head of the KGB.

The 727 dipped over the Potomac on the river approach to runway eighteen, the office buildings of Virginia beneath the right wing, and passed over Key Bridge. It was six months since Andropov had become General Secretary, since the gaunt-looking man in the ill-fitting suit had emerged from the obscurity of the building on Dzerzhinsky Square. The public image of Andropov, the faceless man from the KGB, still hung in the diplomatic air, yet already there was the first hint of changes, already the splinters of hope that the frozen days of Brezhnev were over. The week before Rossini had been shown the assessments at Langley, the policy analyses and the political backgrounds of those now rising in the new Kremlin.

The cabs were in a line outside the terminal. The first driver opened the door for him; Rossini stood back and allowed the woman behind to take it, then called the second. Force of habit, he sometimes laughed at himself. Never take the cab waiting for you. Even in Washington. And especially when it appeared that you were being steered towards it.

By the time he reached his office it was ten fifteen. He spent the next two hours dealing with legislative correspondence and talking to his staff, then walked to the Monocle, the building isolated on the edge of the parking lot that had once been the Carroll Arms.

The restaurant was busy and the others were waiting in one of the small booths at the rear. A strange mix, he thought, nothing like the normal Washington pressure group. Jewish Lobby and American Episcopal Church, businessmen and academics, Democrat and Republican. He shook their hands and sat down, knew he was neither the first senator nor the last whose support they would seek to enlist. You don't have to buy me lunch, he told them, you have my support anyway. The leader of the group thanked him and brought the meeting to order.

'The imprisoned Soviet dissident Antonin Shevienko.'

The report came in at six. The Red Army Faction suspect Suzanna Albrecht, linked with the Lufthansa hijacking which GSG–9 had ended at Mogadishu, as well as a series of bombings and shootings in the years since, had been sighted in Frankfurt. More overtime to try to push through the system, Schiller knew, more nights and weekends away from home.

Not that it mattered since Anja and Lisa had returned to Berlin. He still remembered the night he and Anja had finally decided, the morning she had left and the gaping abyss into which he had dropped. Until Rolf Hanniman had talked him out of it and he had re-immersed himself in his work.

At least Lisa was doing well, he consoled himself; he spoke to her regularly on the telephone, to Anja as well now. Sometimes Lisa wasn't there, of course, even at the times she knew he would normally contact her. Extra lessons, Anja had told him, drama and English.

He and Rolf were having dinner that evening, talking through tactics for the policy meeting with Bonn the following day. Ever since the Fritz Herbert case their rise up the career ladder of the BfV had been rapid. He sat back and flicked through the agenda for the following morning.

The report on the West German Albrecht was one of twenty-three awaiting Langer's return from Moscow. For the past forty-eight hours, as part of an East German delegation to the Kremlin, he had attended the standard briefings and receptions afforded visiting dignitaries, including a twenty-minute address by Premier Andropov. On the second day, however, he had excused himself from the official rounds of caviar and vodka and spent five and a half hours in the offices of the KGB.

He read quickly through the information. Suzanna Albrecht: entered East Berlin through Checkpoint Charlie using a forged West German passport, reported to People's Police and handed immediately to State Security. Department 21, he assumed, the section dealing with recruitment and training of the overseas activists whom others called terrorists.

It was less than twelve months since Andropov had come to power – his mind was on Moscow rather than the report. When the KGB man had taken over at the Kremlin it had seemed that the system was more secure, more stable than ever, the continuity assured. Yet suddenly the Russian leader was thinner, gaunter, than when he had first seen him, the wide square shoulders now like wire coat-hangers and the body hanging from them like an empty suit.

He laid the thoughts aside as briskly as if he was placing them with the stack of files on his left, telephoned Gabi to confirm that he would collect Nikki, then called his driver and told him he would drive himself home.

The colony was reserved for the upper echelons of government and Party officials, the houses large and well equipped; they had moved there after his promotion. He parked outside the house where the birthday party was being held, locked the car and went in. The party had almost finished. Langer accepted a whiskey and talked to the other parents while the children collected their coats.

Not children, Nikki had corrected him the weekend before. Students. Soon she herself would be a teenager. He looked at her now, blonde hair over her shoulders, tall with long legs, still thin. It was hard to think she was twelve, even harder to think that soon she would be filling out, that in not so many years she would be a young woman. He waved at her and smiled as she waved back.

The icicles were hanging from the eaves of the Berliner Dom and the water of the Spree which flowed near it was an unwelcoming grey. February was cold, warming slightly for the snow then freezing again. Langer was informed by Dieter Lindner at eight.

Lindner had just returned from Mielke's office in Normannen-strasse; the thin line of smoke drifted from the Marlboro and the ashtray was full. His face was strained and the nicotine on his fingers had darkened.

'Andropov died last night.' He coughed slightly.

'Who's in charge of the funeral?'

It was still early for the politburo to have appointed a successor; traditionally, however, whoever played the public role at the centre of the funeral arrangements was the man likely to be the country's next leader.

'Chernenko.' Lindner coughed again.

'But he's over seventy.'

'Seventy-two.' Lindner poured himself a black coffee and lit another cigarette.

Anja left the library at five thirty and took the S-bahn to Charlot-tenberg. In a way she had been lucky: to find the job at the university, to find the flat, to re-establish contact with old friends and to make new ones. Money was a problem, of course, even though Hans-Joachim helped her financially. Sometimes she thought she would need a second job, even work in the evenings, but that would mean leaving Lisa.

She had grown weary trying to tell herself that perhaps all daughters were like it, perhaps all teenagers. It was hard to think that Lisa was already fourteen, tall and blonde, slim face and haunting eyes. Perhaps all children grew up too quickly and rebelled against their parents too often, perhaps they all thought they were adults too young. Or perhaps Lisa was getting her own back for the terrible times she had suffered in the last months in Cologne. Anja had seen the look in her eyes as she had watched her parents argue; Hans-Joachim, in fairness, had also seen it, tried to make up for the days away from home, but whatever he tried only exaggerated the disappointment when he let them both down the next time.

Goethe Strasse was cobbled, the pavements wide and lined with trees, the shops mixed with the cafés and the buildings along it six-storey. Anja let herself into the hallway, checked the post-box and climbed the stairs. The flat was at the top, a large sitting room in the front, its balcony overlooking the street, the kitchen and dining area next to it and the bedrooms and bathroom at the rear, overlooking the courtyard. Originally there had been only one bedroom but they had converted it into two and decorated the place together. Anja unlocked the door and went in, called to Lisa.

Drama class or extra English – she rehearsed the reasons she had invented to explain away her daughter's absence. It was not so bad at five in the afternoon, not like waiting for Lisa in the evenings when she was late. She dumped her bag inside the door and pulled off her coat.

'Hello, Mamma.'

Anja heard the voice and felt sick with relief.

Werner Langer closed the files, placed them in the security cabinet, and took out the briefing memo on his next meeting. The world was changing, yet at the same time the world was in a vacuum, as if the future was unsure and unclear, as it if was on hold. Waiting for Moscow, waiting to see what would happen when Chernenko finally stumbled into his grave.

His own world was also moving on. Soon he would be forty; soon he would hold the standard party and make the standard jokes. He and Gabi were still together, though increasingly it seemed as if they led different lives. His consumed by work, Gabi's by the social functions and privileges afforded by his position. And Nikki. No longer a girl but not yet a young woman, her mind and interests expanding faster than he could ever have imagined. And not just over the things he was comfortable with; sometimes the questions he supposed he had asked when he had been that age, sometimes the thoughts that could only come from a shining innocence.

An aide brought the coffee and another ushered in the men who had been waiting downstairs. Bordoff, tall and well dressed, State Security major; Ebner, also wearing a smartly-cut suit, liaison with General Secretary Honecker's security staff; Noffke, clothes slightly less well cut and wearing an anxious expression, from the mayor's office. Plus Seidel, branch secretary for the area involved, face strained and manners too eager to please.

It was the first time Seidel had been to Lenin-Allee, the first time he had been allowed into such a room or met a man with such power. Langer rose, shook their hands, and made a point of thanking him for coming.

'Tomorrow morning.' He brought the meeting to order. 'I've seen the arrangements. Everything seems straightforward. I just want to go through the details in case we've missed anything.'

The liaison officer from Erich Honecker's office opened his brief-case, took out the file, and began to detail the General Secretary's movements and timetable.

When Langer returned home that evening the house was empty. He poured himself a gin and sat in the lounge, the French windows open, looking over the garden. It was rare nowadays that he had time to himself, therefore enjoyed the occasional moment when it came. The house was quiet and peaceful. He took the glass and walked upstairs to the bedroom at the front of the house. The room smelt of the perfume which Gabi had chosen for the evening, and the day clothes she had discarded lay on the bed. He opened the wardrobe and ran his fingers along the lines of clothes, many from the West. The door to Nikki's room was slightly ajar; he pushed it open and stood in the doorway, looking at the teddy bear on the bed and the posters on the walls. Incredible to think that she was fifteen now, that she had grown up so fast. Sometimes he thought that Nikki was the only thing which kept Gabi and himself together.

The book was face down on the bedside table, the brown paper around it to protect the cover. He reached down and picked it up. Page ninety-six; the observation was automatic, bottom of book nearest bed, as if she had laid it down before going to sleep the night before. The page marked by a postcard. He scanned the pages, idly, not really noting the words, then turned to the front, confirmed the name of the author and the title. Alexander Solzhenitsyn. *One Day in the Life of Ivan Denisovich.* He looked at the postcard. Not a normal postcard but a photograph of a man. The Soviet dissident Antonin Shevienko.

Carefully, not disturbing the rectangle of dust he knew would have already gathered, he put the card back in the book, placed the book back on the table and went downstairs.

The exercise the following morning was timed for ten minutes past nine, the three shops – butcher's, baker's and grocer's – at the end of Dimitrov Strasse close to Prenzlauer Allee. Even though his presence was not required Langer arrived at eight thirty, parked two blocks away, put on the grey featureless mac he kept for such occasions, and walked back to the area of the shops. Dimitrov Strasse was still quiet, a handful of men waiting at the tram stop and a few women beginning their daily shopping. Yet the telltale signs were everywhere: the unmarked Ladas in the side streets, the people already looking out of the windows in the apartment blocks above and opposite, and the men and women moving towards the shops, the woman with the pram in position.

How should he ask Nikki about the book? he wondered, unsure whether he should ask her at all. Not that the book was banned in East Germany, of course, simply that it was not available. How should he ask her about the author who had been both honoured and pilloried in his own country, about the imprisoned dissident Shevienko?

The two young men appeared from nowhere, black mock-leather jackets and severe looks. Name, they asked him, why are you hanging around? He reached into his pocket and showed them his identification. Sorry, they began to apologize. No need, he told them, you were doing your job.

The cars appeared at the top of the road, the lead Lada travelling quickly, the second vehicle tucked behind it and the tail guard slightly into the centre of road. The ear sets of the shadows along Dimitrov Strasse buzzed with instructions. A tram was trundling down the centre, sparks flying from the metal rails and the carriages swaying. The three cars cut inside it and pulled up outside the shops, the doors opening even before the cars had stopped.

Honecker stepped on to the pavement, looking up at the apartment blocks and seeing the coloured curtains in the windows. Outside the shop the woman lifted the child from the pram. The General Secretary crossed to her and began asking about the child and where her husband worked, then went inside. From the shop came the smell of fresh bread, in the butcher's and grocer's next to it the shelves were filled and the shops busy with customers. For ten minutes Honecker talked with them, then, as abruptly as he had arrived, the head of state left and the shoppers drifted away. The people meeting their leader and their leader being satisfied that his people were well housed, well clothed and well fed.

On the pavement the branch secretary looked at the convoy as it disappeared, the relief that all had gone well clear on his face.

The shadows had gone and the unmarked Ladas had disappeared.

'Well organized, Herr Seidel.' Langer stepped across the street. 'Thank you.'

When he returned home that evening Nikki was sitting in the chair by the open doors facing on to the garden, hair hanging over her shoulders, legs bent in front of her and feet on the chair, the book with the brown paper cover against her legs.

'What's that?' The question was natural, innocent, the technique so much part of him that he was unaware of it. He took off his jacket and dropped it over the back of a chair.

'Solzhenitsyn. It's good, you ought to read it.' She slipped the photograph of Shevienko between the pages and closed the book.

'I thought it wasn't available here.' He dropped the ice cubes into the glass and poured in the gin and tonic.

'It isn't.' She moved the cushion so he could sit opposite her.

'So how did you get it?'

'Someone brought it back.' She reached across for the gin, took a sip and gave him back the glass. 'Have you read it?'

The question disorientated him, was the sort of question he would throw into an interrogation. At precisely the time he would have thrown it in. 'Yes.'

'What did you think of it?'

The first alarm bell should have rung, he would think later. What are you doing, my little Nikki? he should have replied. You know I'm a member of the Party, you think I hold a senior position at the Finance Ministry, yet here you are asking me my opinion of a book which is not normally available in this country and which you are openly reading in my house.

'I thought it profoundly moving.'

'Why?'

He was off balance again. 'I'm not sure.' He was honest. With her, with himself. 'Because of its dignity.' The details as well, he knew, the way a man or woman survived in one of Stalin's concentration camps in the Siberian wastes.

'They couldn't have them here, could they? They haven't had them here?'

'Of course not, that was Stalin's Russia.'

'But there *were* concentration camps here?'

He remembered how he had always been so proud of her when she had questioned things for herself, how he had taken such pride when her teachers had told him what a clear and advanced thinker she was.

'Forty years ago, under the Nazis.'

'Of course.'

He leant forward and picked up the book, expecting that she would take it from him, that she would try to stop him seeing the photograph of Shevienko.

'Interesting, isn't it?'

'What's interesting?' He looked at the photograph.

'That *One Day in the Life of Ivan Denisovich* is about a man sent to the work camps on a false espionage charge, and that's how they put Shevienko away.'

He put the photograph back, closed the pages and waited.

'You've been in Moscow?'

'Yes.'

'What's going to happen when Chernenko dies?'

He shook his head as if it was none of his business and gave her back the book.

The message for Rossini was left with his secretary at ten and was passed to him when he arrived at his office in the Dirksen Senate Office Building shortly before midday. A Mr Warner had telephoned. Lunch at twelve thirty the next day, Friday. The Kentmoor marina, on the western shore of Chesapeake Bay.

'Did he leave a number where I could confirm?'

The Company safe house at St Michaels, a few miles south of Kentmoor and on the opposite shore – the thought was almost subliminal.

'No.'

The two men had met three times since the Vienna–Prague incident, once when Warner had looked him up in New York and twice at Langley.

'Can I fit it in?'

'Just.' The secretary had already checked the diary.

On Friday morning he was due to attend a Senate subcommittee, in the evening a fund-raising dinner organized by Fats Walker. That weekend he, Sally and Jimmy had been invited to New Haven for the annual Harvard–Yale match. Part of the East Coast establishment, he knew, one power play on the field during the afternoon and another over dinner in the evening. He had checked with Sally and seen the list of other guests.

'I'd better let the subcommittee know I have to leave early.'

'I already have.'

The drive the following morning was pleasant; it was early fall, the leaves tingeing brown though not the mass of brilliant reds and oranges he associated with New Hampshire. He left Washington on Route 50, crossed the Chesapeake Bay Bridge, then cut right towards Romancoke on Route 8. The countryside was lightly wooded, the grass landing-strip on his right. At the end he turned right; a quarter-mile further on he came to the marina, the low white building facing the water and the restaurant at the end of it. He parked and went inside.

The restaurant was furnished simply and functionally: fish nets on the walls and brown wrapping paper on the square plastic tables. Al Warner was sitting at a table overlooking the bay. He was looking relaxed, Rossini thought, light windbreaker and a little less hair, the quiet confidence of a man who was winning settled on his shoulders. The woman was in her early thirties, good-looking and attractive figure, her blonde hair swept back and her trouser suit off-the-rail from Saks Fifth Avenue or Valentino's. Both were drinking Rolling Rock from the bottle.

The woman saw him enter and smiled at him. Rossini recognized her immediately and understood why he had been invited. He crossed the floor and shook Warner's hand. The woman's eyes were dancing, the severe looks gone from the face. Rossini held out his hand to her. 'Good train ride?'

The debriefing over and Mateus out of quarantine.

She stood and took his hand, kissed him lightly on the cheek. 'Great train ride. Thanks for making it possible.'

The shadow hung across the Yale Bowl and the sun was sinking. Yale on the Harvard thirty-yard line. Harvard three points up and Yale needing a field goal to draw but a touch-down to win. Seventeen years ago their host had played quarterback for the Elis, now he sat hunched and anxious on the senator's right, lips calling the plays as Yale huddled.

It was seven months since Chernenko had come to power in

Russia, Rossini thought. Not many more, according to the latest briefings from Langley, before he died.

First down. The Yale quarterback calling the play. Green Nine, Green Nine. *Hut, hut, hut.* Pitch play: the quarterback faked to the fullback, the fullback butting to the line and blocking, the quarterback handing off to the halfback and the halfback bursting through the gap created by the fullback for an eight-yard gain. Yale chewing up the clock. Rossini smiled at how even now the jargon came back to him. The Elis using the running plays to keep the clock moving, needing to score but also needing to limit the time Harvard would have to come back at them.

Football like politics and politics like football. Plan your move and try to see what the other side were planning, counter them just as they were seeking to counter you. Then wait and see who's got it right.

Second down and two. Off tackle: the quarterback handed off to the fullback but the Crimsons read the move and stopped him dead for a two-yard loss.

Ten years, he had told the Czech Josef Vlasak and the Hungarian Milos Tomasek, perhaps twenty. Sixteen had already gone and times were changing, time to be changing himself. Decide the game plan and see where he should be going, how he would get there.

Third down and five. One play left. Red Fourteen, Red Fourteen. The quarterback began calling the play. *Hut, hut, hut.* Harvard showed blitz, the quarterback reading it but too late to change the play. He took the snap, rolled out, saw the receivers were covered and threw the ball away. The clock stopped and the Yale crowd dropped their heads in despair.

Fourth down, time out called and Harvard still three points ahead. Yale within field goal range. Three points from a field goal to tie, but still time for Harvard to come back only needing a field goal to be in the lead again. Six points for a touchdown, plus one for the conversion. Seven points, leaving Harvard needing a touchdown.

So why was he thinking about politics at a football match, why was he worrying about what he had told Vlasak and Tomasek?

The field goal unit was lining up to go on, the kicker warming up. The quarterback off the field and talking to the head coach, the crowd on its feet. Yale going for a tie, the assistant coach nodding to the kicker and the quarterback arguing with the head coach, fist clenched. Any game was important, but this was not any game. Harvard and Yale. World War. Something about the quarterback, Rossini thought, something about the way he was shaping up, telling the coach what he wanted to do. No fun kissing your sister, he remembered the expression, no point in going for a tie. Only one thing worth playing for.

What's his name, he asked his host.

'O'Bramsky.'

'Tell him he has a job.'

Why, his son asked.

The coach nodded and slapped the quarterback on the shoulders. The quarterback turned and trotted back on to the field.

'Same play as last time.' Rossini turned again to his son. 'Pitch to the halfback. It's over.'

The Yale men behind him misunderstood, thought he was a Harvard man saying that the quarterback was about to throw the game.

Black Seven on one. They could see him detailing the call but could not hear what he was saying. Black seven on one. Play seven, snap on the first *hut*.

They lined up.

'You want a bet?' Rossini looked at the men behind him.

One of them nodded. 'Fifty dollars.'

'Make it a hundred.'

They shook hands on it.

'Black Seven, Black Seven. *Hut*.'

Snap. Tackle and end blocking. Guard pulling and kicking out the defensive end, fullback lead blocking to create the opening. The halfback saw daylight and turned on the afterburners, the safety coming at him too high, too late. The halfback spun out of the tackle and crossed the end zone.

Decide where the power lies now and where it will lie at the end of the twenty years. He was no longer seeing the game, not even hearing the celebrations as it ended. Decide how he would have that power when the time came and how he would bridge the period between.

He turned to the men behind him and held out his hand. 'Like I said. No fun kissing your sister.'

Dinner that evening was vintage East Coast: Maine lobster and

Montrachet, company and conversation to match. At one he and Sally finally went to bed, at four he woke, went to the kitchen and made himself coffee.

Constitutional division of power: it was almost as if he was dictating a memo, executive versus legislature, President against Congress. Each had power but the power each had was different. Executive power the innovator, initiator; congressional power the counterweight. Congressional power therefore no longer satisfied his requirement, but already there were difficulties with the executive. The first problems of the Reagan administration were already emerging: confusion over policies in Central America and the Middle East, an occasional suggestion of the two becoming mixed. The threat of being tainted by association if he moved too early but the danger of being left in the cold if he did not.

He heard the sound on the stairs and turned.

'You all right?' Sally was wide awake, the dressing-gown pulled round her.

'Fine.'

'So what are you doing?'

He shrugged.

'Want to talk?'

'Already talking.' He made fresh coffee and began the list.

By the time the others woke there were five jobs on it which he calculated would become vacant in the next six months. By the following Tuesday he had extended it to eight, by Thursday reduced it to a short-list of three. That evening Rossini dined with the chairman of the Senate Foreign Affairs Committee, the following day he took lunch with the White House chief of staff; the next weekend he, Sally and Nick spent the Saturday and Sunday sailing with the chairman of the Senate Intelligence Committee on Chesapeake Bay. That evening he made his decision. The next morning he talked to Martin Schumaker and began his lobbying, that lunchtime he made the telephone call. Two days later, without announcement and at his own expense, he flew to Berlin.

The dinner was scheduled for seven o'clock in the Boka Grill, a Balkan restaurant tucked nondescriptly on Fasanenstrasse, behind the K'Damm. Michael Rossini arrived five minutes early, Max Steiner two minutes later.

'Thank you for arranging tonight's meeting.'

The table was in the corner, away from the door, the lighting dim and the walls covered with deep red drapes, ethnic music playing in the background.

'You had no difficulty finding me?'

In the years since he had crossed the Glienicker Bridge Max Steiner had qualified as a lawyer and been appointed a partner in a West Berlin law firm specializing in international commerce. His face was still lean, Rossini thought, his hair smartly cut and his suit casual though expensive.

'None at all.'

'You were at the bridge when I came over, of course.' Max Steiner had spent the last two days in telephone calls to Bonn and Washington, asking about Senator Rossini though never explaining why.

'I was there, though I wasn't involved in the arrangements.'

It was early, only two other tables occupied. The cab stopped outside and Ernst Vöckel came in, Max introducing them. They shook hands, stiffly and rather formally, and sat down. When the waiter brought the menus they ordered *Sagerteller* and *Schultheiss* beer.

Three lawyers, Rossini thought. One East German, with contacts in Moscow as well as Berlin. One West German, former escape organizer and political prisoner. One American, ex-CIA, now politician. If there's ever a contract between us Christ help the poor bastard who has to check the small print.

'Pleasant though it is to meet you, I have to ask why.' Vöckel paused till the waiter had left them.

'Because you're the conduit between East and West. You're the man Berlin and Moscow trust when they want something done.'

'Perhaps.' Vöckel shrugged. 'So what do you want?'

'Not what. Who.'

'Who then?'

'Shevienko.'

The East German laughed.

On Capitol Hill, Rossini knew, it was difficult to find a Congressman who did not display a photograph of the man on his office wall.

Yet nobody else had knocked on the back door and asked what deal could be done, Vöckel thought. He laid his napkin on the table and sat back, chin in hand and fingers stroking his face. 'Wrong time.'

'Chernenko?'

'Yes and no.'

Chernenko on the way out and the battle already under way in the Kremlin over who would succeed him. 'How long's he got?'

'Who knows?'

'I'm told less than eighteen months, possibly even twelve.'

Vöckel neither confirmed nor denied the appraisal. 'And who do your people tell you will take over then?'

'Uncertain, but their money's on Gorbachev.'

'So?'

'So now would be the time to begin.' While everyone else was standing still and doing nothing – the suggestion was clear.

'There are three problems.' It was as if Vöckel had made his decision. 'The first is that even if things went the way you want it might be years before we secured anything.'

'Which is another reason for starting now.'

'The second is that Moscow will want something in return.'

'Agreed. And the third?'

'The third is that Moscow might not consider that even the position of senator carries sufficient weight to undertake such a negotiation.'

'Already solved.'

'How?'

'In three weeks I will be appointed United States ambassador to West Germany.'

The television pictures from Moscow were bizarre, Anja thought, almost disturbing. The burial of the Soviet statesman Mikolov and the old men from the politburo gathered round his grave. Chernenko, the Soviet leader, barely able to walk without support and hardly seeming to speak.

She locked the flat, took the S-bahn to the Zoo Gardens, and met the other members of the library staff at the Irish Pub in the Europa Centre. The Friday evenings with the others was something she looked forward to: a time she could relax and try to push aside her worries about Lisa. Perhaps she should talk to someone, either Christina and Lutz, even Hans-Joachim. Perhaps she should tell Hans-Joachim the truth, what she feared for the future. Whatever happened to Lisa was both their blame, she admitted, a punishment for what they had put her through, however unwittingly, in Cologne. She tried to push the worries about Lisa to the back of her mind, to forget about them even for a moment.

At nine they left the Irish Pub and went to a restaurant one of the others had recommended for dinner. The Brasserie was on Wittenbergplatz: she remembered having seen it before. The bar was busy but friendly; they sat at a table and ordered white wine. At eleven thirty, almost twelve, the two barmaids began to clear up and the owner arrived to collect the day's takings. When he had finished he sat with them drinking coffee. One of the women who worked behind the bar was leaving, he told them; he was looking for someone to take her place. Perhaps, he suggested, they knew a student.

'*I'll* do it.' Anja was surprised at herself. Something to break the routine, she thought, get her out of the flat. Take her mind off Lisa. As long as it did not jeopardize the fragile relationship with her daughter, as long as she was there when Lisa needed her.

'Done it before?'

No, she admitted. It might even be fun, she was already thinking, and she could do with the extra money.

'Friday evenings, Saturdays and Sundays. Start next weekend.'

The meeting with the Friends on Dzerzhinksy Square was routine, beginning at two, continuing during the afternoon and ending at eleven the following morning. At four Langer returned to Berlin. A year – even he was surprised at how little time his KGB associates had given Chernenko when he had taken Andropov's crown – then there would be changes in the Kremlin. Already, they had told him over dinner at the KGB club in central Moscow the night before, the deals were being worked out and the new man primed.

Who, he had asked.

Mikhail Gorbachev, they had told him, but the old guard are already plotting against him.

*

The morning was cold. The beginning of March, the rain and wind cutting across Red Square in Moscow and down Unter den Linden in Berlin. Dieter Lindner was smoking too much, Langer thought, one day it would kill him. He waited while Lindner lit another cigarette and knew why he had been summoned.

'Chernenko's dead.'

'Who's taking over?'

'It's between Gorbachev and Grishin.' Gorbachev, Chernenko's deputy, the man with the reputation as a reformer. Grishin the hard-line mayor of Moscow.

'When will it be decided?'

It would be at least twenty-four hours before the vote for the new leader could take place, the analysts in Bonn, London and Washington were telling their policy-makers. Three of the Soviet politburo were overseas including Shcherbitsky, the Ukrainian Party boss and the mainstay of the old guard, who was in America.

'Gorbachev's called the politburo for tonight.'

Shcherbitsky was not going to make it in time, Rossini knew; Shcherbitsky's presence was crucial in the last-minute lobbying which might determine the choice of the next Soviet leader, but Shcherbitsky's plane was delayed and he would not have made it anyway.

It was midday, Los Angeles. Rossini had flown specially from Bonn to meet the Soviet delegation and prepare the ground for whatever the future might bring. Now he watched as they hurried across the tarmac and up the steps into the Aeroflot Ilyushin. Shcherbitsky in a hurry to get home, yet some of those accompanying him Gorbachev men. Rossini had sounded them out and knew who was for the old guard and who for the new. Mid evening in Moscow, he calculated the time difference, the politburo already in session, the reformers already trying to push the vote through.

The official came down the steps, took Bukovski, one of Shcherbitsky's key advisers aside, and whispered something to him. Rossini studied the man's face. Bukovski a Gorbachev man, he knew. He saw the faintest trace of a smile, then the features froze again.

The State Department aide stepped close to Rossini and updated him on the latest information from Moscow. The politburo was still meeting, nothing was expected for at least two hours, perhaps three. Possibly not even until the following day.

Rossini was still looking at Bukovski's face. 'They've already voted. It's Gorbachev.'

CHAPTER TWO

THE MEETING with the Friends ended at one. In the three hours before he returned to Berlin Werner Langer visited those places in Moscow which he had come to know during the Andropov and particularly the Brezhnev periods. There was still little food in the shops and the queues still formed at the first rumour of fresh supplies, yet the city seemed different. It was June, going into July, the new General Secretary had been in power a mere four months, yet already the people walked and talked as if they lived in another world. In a bookshop off Red Square he bought the two publications Nikki had asked him to get. Mikhail Gorbachev: *The Time for Peace* and *The Coming Century of Peace*.

The Brasserie was busy. Friday evening, the regulars drifting in and out and half the tables filled with people eating dinner. Strange times in Moscow, Anja thought, wondered what was going to happen and whether the faith people were suddenly expressing in the new Soviet leader would be fulfilled.

At first she had been dubious about working in a bar, now she enjoyed the company. Different from the friends she had made at the library, but interesting. The men always wanted to talk to her, of course; she allowed them to buy her an occasional drink, after a while she had even gone for dinner with one or two of them. But always she went home alone, never mentioning her husband, other than that they were separated. Sometimes, on the days she came over from the East on a pensioner's pass, her mother had eaten at the café, sometimes Lisa came in, but that now seemed so long ago.

The group came in and sat at the empty stools at the bar. Two businessmen from West Germany, the men had it written all over them, plus a couple of women they'd picked up for the evening. She smiled at them and poured their drinks. Not businessmen, she decided, politicians. The group were laughing and talking. She smiled at them again and served the two men who came in after them.

Michael Rossini left his official residence at seven thirty and was at his desk in the embassy before eight. His diary for the day was full, almost hectic. The only time not accounted for was between three and three thirty that afternoon.

Max Steiner left Berlin Tegel at ten minutes past one, arriving at Bonn-Cologne at fifteen minutes past two. The embassy car was waiting for him. There were no frills, no time to waste, the return flight leaving Bonn-Cologne at four forty. Just like the old days, he almost smiled. The car slipped through the security check and into the compound.

A secretary met him in the foyer and escorted him to the ambassador's suite. The room was well furnished, Stars and Stripes and portrait of the President: mahogany desk, green leather top, at one end and chairs round the fireplace at the other for informal meetings. Rossini rose and shook his hand. The secretary disappeared and the formality evaporated. It was July, going into August, the world and its politicians about to slow down for the summer.

'Good to see you again.'

'You too.'

'Drink?'

'Coffee.'

They sat facing each other.

'Vöckel needs a meeting, he says it's urgent.'

'Are we there, Max?'

'Perhaps.'

Three days later, accompanied by the two shadows who were his constant companions, Ambassador Rossini flew to West Berlin, arriving at nine forty-five, deliberately late. Tegel was quiet, the light above the city electric blue, almost expectant. The car was waiting to take him to the safe house where he would overnight. He showered, changed and made the telephone call, then was driven to the Inter-Continental Hotel, the car staying outside and one of the shadows tailing him. The foyer was large, sixty metres long and thirty wide, the reception desk on the opposite wall and doors leading to the bathrooms and reception areas behind it.

Rossini walked quickly to the Six Continents bar, noting the presence of the concierge at the desk but not acknowledging him, and ordered a Black Label. Just like the old days, he thought, almost looked for Eddy Daley. The security gamble was calculated. Rossini had always assumed that there was no point coming to West Berlin with the security cordon which would normally accompany a visiting ambassador, yet he saw no point in not being protected, especially given the proven efficiency of the Red Army Faction.

The concierge left the front desk and walked quietly and unnoticed to the rear of the foyer. Rossini left the bar, crossed the foyer as if he was going to the bathroom, then turned right and through the first door, the shadow checking he was not being followed.

Dieter Wernz was waiting. Wernz had been doorman at the old Hilton and become concierge when the hotel had changed. Even now he remembered the young Rossini, then the senator who had seen fit to visit old friends on his returns to the city. Had made sure that Rossini had his home telephone number in case he needed help in a hurry.

Rossini followed him through the bowels of the hotel to the service door at the rear. 'Thanks, Dieter.' They shook hands.

'Any time, Mike.'

Max Steiner was waiting, the engine of the BMW ticking over and the second shadow in another BMW behind. At ten twenty-five they slowed and picked up the first shadow, then drove to the 17th June, the pavements busy with hookers and the cars kerb-crawling. To his right, near Lützow Platz, Rossini could see the big wheel of the funfair whirling in the sky, the coloured lights bright against the black. Ernst Vöckel was waiting by the round-about at Grosse Stern. They stopped, door already open; the lawyer stepped in and Max pulled away, the second car tucked behind him.

'They've agreed.'

'Why now?'

The conversation was functional, none of them revealing their feelings.

'Two reasons. The West's pressure on human rights; Shevienko will be a showpiece.'

'And the second?'

Rossini and Vöckel were together in the back seat.

'Gorbachev's pushing Moscow faster than the old guard wants and needs an international coup.'

'So what does he want in return?' He could see the lights of the big wheel again, could imagine the screams of the people on it.

'You're not going to believe it.'

'Try me.'

They reached the barrier across 17th June, just before the Soviet war memorial, and turned back west.

'A summit in Vienna. All the trimmings, all the publicity.'

In front of them a Mercedes pulled into the side and the driver wound down his window and began talking to two women.'

'What conditions?'

'Agreed agenda, guaranteed agreements at the end.' Nobody held a summit any more without agreeing in advance what the leaders would appear to agree only at the end.

'Complications?' Rossini assumed there would be.

'Moscow will want some people back in return.'

'Why?'

The traffic lights in front of them began to change.

'Because Shevienko was imprisoned on espionage charges and Gorbachev will need to give something to the old guard.'

'High or low level?'

'Not too high. He simply needs something to buy off an attack from the hardliners.'

The lights turned red. Max braked and stopped in the inside lane, next to the pavement. The woman misunderstood and stepped out of the shadows towards the car. She was young and ash-blonde, high heels and leather mini-skirt, matching handbag. Rossini heard the sudden acceleration of the tail BMW and saw the headlights, the driver swinging right on to the pavement and hurtling the car at the woman. Max Steiner realized, slammed the car into gear and accelerated through the lights. The woman was shouting, screaming. The tail BMW bumped off the pavement and tucked behind them again.

'Don't stop by the pavement next time, Max. You'll give the boys a heart attack.' He sat back in the seat and breathed deeply for ten seconds. 'But if Shevienko is swopped, it would be an admission – on his part and ours – that he really was spying for us, which he was not.'

'That's for you to sort out in Washington.'

'What time-scale?'

'As soon as Washington agrees and the details are worked out. Gorbachev wants the summit before the end of the year.'

The following evening Rossini flew to Washington. Of the thirty-six hours he spent in the capital eight were at the White House. On his return he met again with Ernst Vöckel, again in secret. The morning after that the lawyer took Washington's response to Moscow.

The request to see Langer was made at three and the meeting arranged for five. It was Friday afternoon, the weather warm and sunny, even State Security winding down for the weekend. Hentze was in his shirt-sleeves; Langer poured them each a coffee. If Hentze had asked to see him on a Friday afternoon it had to be interesting or important, probably both.

'Schiller.' Hentze was in charge of the surveillance units operating in West Berlin.

'What about him?'

'He married in 1968.' Schiller's career in counter-intelligence, as well as his personal details, was meticulously documented by Central Records.

'Yes.'

Hentze put the coffee cup on the desk and took a photograph from the folder he had brought with him. 'Two weeks ago one of the surveillance teams in West Berlin were tagging a couple of Christian Democrat politicians in from Bonn.' Normal routine, he did not need to say, hope they were indiscreet, perhaps nudge them towards a first sin if they were not. Low-level stuff, no one they were targeting important or Langer would have been informed. 'One evening they picked up a couple of girls, took them to a bar.'

'Our girls?'

'No, casual. At the bar the boys managed to snatch a photo of the group.' He slid the photograph across the desk. The print was grainy, shot on fast film in bad light conditions, a number of men and women sitting at a bar, profile or half-profile, none of them looking at the camera but their faces and therefore their identities still clear. 'These are the politicians.' Hentze stretched across and circled two of the men with a pencil, the lead not touching the photograph and therefore leaving no indication which people in the photograph were of interest. He walked round the desk and drew a similar circle round the head of the person behind the politicians.

The barmaid was cleaning a glass, half turning and smiling as if someone had spoken to her, perhaps as if someone had just ordered a drink. She was tall, in her forties, attractive, white blouse and blonde hair cut short.

Langer felt the knotting in his stomach and only half heard Hentze's voice.

'Only knew it was her because I was checking the file recently.'

Anja hadn't changed much, he thought.

'I assume they must be separated.' Hentze's voice was only an echo. 'No record of it in the files though.'

'Association with the Bonn politicians?' His own voice was hollow and his questions automatic. 'Either of them go with her after?' Socially or sexually, he meant, and wondered why it bothered him.

'No. They left with the girls.'

'So what do you make of it?'

Hentze sat down again. 'Could be a logical explanation. I'm not sure.'

'No suggestion in the report that we're being set up, that the politicians were a bait to lead us to the bar?'

The boss was reacting as Hentze had expected, clearly and analytically, asking the questions he had already asked himself. 'None at all. I haven't questioned them, for obvious reasons, but there's nothing to suggest anything other than the meeting with the girls and the choice of bar were random.'

'Any known connections between the politicians and West German intelligence?'

'None known.'

'The two girls?'

'No indication of their identities.'

'But we know where and how the West Germans picked them up?'

'The Irish Pub in the Europa Centre. It's in the report, plus photos.' So there's a chance we can check on them, Hentze knew the boss was thinking, at least begin to establish what the hell's going on.

Everything set up and himself the target, Langer thought. It was the only reason for Anja to be in the photograph, the only bait Schiller knew he would go for. 'Who else knows?'

'Only me. The team had no way of knowing. Nobody else has seen the report or the photograph.'

Not even Schiller would use his wife as bait for a honey trap. Langer felt the disgust. 'You have everything there?'

'Yes.' Hentze handed the file across the desk. His name on the list when the recommendations went upstairs, he knew – the boss was always fair about things like that. But it was someone else's case now. No need to mention it to anyone, of course, the second understanding was equally understood, no need even to ask about it again.

By the time Langer returned home it was gone seven. Gabi was in the bathroom and Nikki was watching television, flicking between channels to pick up the news coverage. As he came in she reached forward and changed channels to the West. Everyone watched West German television, he watched it himself. Ridiculous, he thought, the Party trying to keep to the straight and narrow, and the people only concerned with Dallas from the West and Gorbachev from the East.

Nikki glanced up and saw him. 'Cocktail party tonight, remember. Mum's already screaming that you're late.'

The woman at the passport control was in her mid forties but seemed older, short and hard-looking, close-cropped hair and the captain's pips on her shoulders. Nazi, Nikki would have said. You're her boss, he reminded himself, you're the second in command of State Security in Berlin, you have powers she could never dream existed.

Five o'clock, Saturday afternoon, the S-bahn station at Friedrichstrasse.

Langer wore a brown leather jacket, lightweight sweater, Levis and brown leather casual shoes, all bought in the West. In a small holdall he carried a toilet bag and change of clothes. He stopped in front of the woman and handed his passport across the desk. Lothar Kleiner, mechanical engineer, from Düsseldorf in the Federal Republic, the entry visa and stamp obtained an hour before from Operations. She tore out the visa and pushed the passport back. Langer walked through, past the booths on the left for those entering East Berlin from the West, and turned right up the stairs to the platform.

The kiosk on the platform was busy, visitors from the West buying the small bottles of cheap spirits with the last of their Ostmarks, breaking them open and drinking them.

An unexpected meeting in Frankfurt-on-Oder, he had told Gabi.

The train clattered into the platform, the pensioners piled off with their shopping bags from the Kurfurstendamm, and he stepped on and sat down. Five minutes later the doors closed and the train pulled out of the station and into the sudden space and the wide blank expanse of the Wall, the watch-towers and the death strip. In front of him a tourist glanced round and snatched a photograph through the dirty window.

The square in front of the Europa Centre was busy; at the Hertz office he hired a BMW 320, parked it on Wormser Strasse then walked to the Hotel Consul on Knesebeckstrasse, checking in using the name Kleiner, and went to his room. Twenty minutes later he left, taking his case. The night porter was already on duty; he took the man aside and slipped him twenty Deutschmarks. A friend of mine called Werner Langer is expecting a telephone call. I'd appreciate it if you and the switchboard could make a note if anyone calls asking for him. The porter slid the note into his pocket and nodded.

The pension was a hundred metres from the U-bahn station at Berlinerstrasse. The woman showed him the small bedroom at the rear and the bathroom and toilet along the landing, giving him the keys to the bedroom, the door of the pension, and the hallway door on to the street, but not asking for his passport. It was almost seven; he showered and left.

The Kurfurstendamm was even busier and louder, the buskers and musicians in front of the Europa Centre and the pavements filled with people, the spotlights already picking out the shape of the Kaiser Wilhelm Church against the night sky and the neon lights of the sex shops and strip joints flashing on the streets behind it. The Irish Pub was on the lower floor of the Centre. Langer bought himself a beer and began his wait for the two women in the photograph.

At eight thirty, almost nine o'clock, he left the bar and walked the three hundred metres to Wittenbergplatz. The square was large, the Brasserie one of a line of cafés on the south side, the tables and chairs still outside. For the next thirty minutes he studied the area, looking for the watchers and checking the BMW. No eyes, he thought, no need until he showed. He returned to the Irish Bar and bought another beer. At ten the two women in the photograph had still not appeared, at ten thirty he left the Europa Centre and walked to Wittenbergplatz.

It had been a long week, Tuesday to Friday at the university library, last night and tonight at the bar, tomorrow all day. Monday almost here, Anja told herself, then she would sleep until midday. Two of the regulars were talking about football and asking her what team she supported. She pulled another beer and began to dry some glasses, polishing them until they sparkled and holding them against the light to check, then placing them on the shelves behind the bar.

That day she had tried again to contact Lisa; had gone to the places she knew Lisa went in the hope of seeing her. The evening before she had gone to the house where Lisa now lived and tried to get in, had waited on the pavement outside for two hours in the hope that Lisa might return. Each day she did the same and each night she felt sick with worry and fear.

The door opened. Automatically she glanced towards it and smiled at the man who came in, then picked up another glass and began to polish it, looked at the man again. The glass slipped from her fingers and shattered on the floor. 'Werner Langer?' There was an incredulity in her voice.

'Anja Lehnartz?' He stood in the middle of the floor, the surprise equally apparent in his, and checked for watchers.

She began to laugh, shake her head in disbelief, wiped her hands on the tea-towel. 'I don't believe it.' Everyone in the bar had turned and was looking at them, at him. 'I really don't believe it.' She dropped the towel on the bar and came round, instinctively wiping her hands on her skirt and touching her hair into place.

Stood in front of him. No acting in her response, he knew, hardly any in his. 'Werner Langer.' She was shaking her head, still incredulous.

They were both laughing, both still shaking their heads. He kissed her on the cheek, she on his, hugged her. Realized that his hand had slipped round her waist and hers round his.

An old friend, she half turned and explained to the regulars, introduced him to them. My first boyfriend, haven't seen him for twenty-five years.

There were no watchers at the bar unless they were real pros, but Schiller would only send the A-team on this one. No reaction to the name either. Nobody would believe that the great Werner Langer would come over from the East and use his real name, of course. Except that he would have to because it was the name Anja knew him by.

'Drink?'

'Beer. You?'

'White wine.'

So many questions, he saw it in her eyes, his brain working automatically. The BMW forty metres from the door if he got that far, three ways out from where it was parked, pavements wide enough to drive on if they blocked the roads, straight over the square if necessary.

'You look exactly the same.' The words came out of their accord. 'Just as beautiful as ever.'

'You look good yourself.'

The bar had settled slightly.

'What are you doing here?' In this bar, she meant, in the West. How did you know where to find me? 'Tell me all about yourself.'

'I live in Frankfurt, I'm in Berlin on business.' He answered two of her three questions. 'I was walking back to the hotel and decided on a last drink. I couldn't believe it when I saw you here. I still can't.' In a way he meant it. 'And you, what are you doing here?'

'I've been working here eighteen months. I work at the university library in the daytimes and here at weekends.' It was almost as if she was a teenager again, as if they were both young again. For a moment she forgot everything, the library, the work in the bar, her life with Hans-Joachim. Even Lisa. For a moment she was young and happy and carefree again.

But what are *you* doing in the West, how did *you* get out of the East? The question was unspoken. Later, the expression said it all, when the bar is empty or when we're alone together.

She smiled at him again and served another customer. 'And you're married, you have a family?'

'Yes, I'm married. I have a daughter called Nikki.'

'How old is she, do you have a photo?' Anja was bubbling.

'Fifteen. I'm sorry, I don't have a photograph with me. What about you?'

'I'm separated, two years ago. We have a daughter, Lisa. She lives with me here.'

She searched in her handbag and showed him the family photograph. There was something about Anja when she talked about her daughter, Langer sensed, about the way she kept the smile on her face. 'And your husband?'

'He works in Cologne.'

Of course he works in Cologne, Langer thought, he's deputy director of the BfV, tipped to be head within the next two years.

They talked on, idle chat, about old times and old friends, old memories. About his job, what he was doing in Berlin, which hotel he was at. About her. The coincidence of meeting again after so many years. At midnight the owner came to collect the day's takings and to shut up. I'll be half an hour, Anja told Langer, there's a bar round the corner, the Calvados. I'll see you there.'

Langer checked the area for fifteen minutes then went in. The bar was small and white-walled, one room at the front and a second at the rear, the bar itself on the left as he entered, stools round it. It was past midnight, a handful of men and one woman seated on the stools, and an older couple at one of the tables. He ordered a beer, sat at the bar for two minutes, then went to the rear.

The toilet was on the right of a passage leading off the back room, a small window high in one wall. He stood on the seat and opened it, saw that it led to a closed courtyard at the rear. On the other side of the corridor a second door led into a kitchen; he pushed it open and went in. The other door was at the side of a sink; he opened it and found himself in a narrow alley, cobbled and unlit, a brick wall to the right and a street ten metres to the left. Back door out, he thought; but if it was a honey trap Schiller would have recceed the place and known there was a back door.

He closed the door and returned to the bar. Anja joined him twenty minutes later.

The older couple had left and the barman sat hunched in conversation at the far end of the counter. Quietly, sitting tight against him, Anja told Langer her story. The library job in Berlin, the arrest by the Stasi, the years in prison and the day she had been bought out but had gone home to her mother in East Berlin by mistake. How she had escaped through Checkpoint Charlie in the back of a car and married the man who had organized it.

'What's his name?' He reminded himself that he was supposed to know nothing of the man.

'Hans-Joachim.'

'What does he do?'

'He works for the government.'

'Doing what?'

'Paperwork. He's a typical bureaucrat.'

He asked the barman to use the telephone and dialled the number of the hotel. Business, he explained to Anja, he was expecting a message. No calls for Werner Langer and no one asking about him, the night porter told him. He knew by his voice that the man was telling the truth, and returned to Anja.

What about you, she asked, when did you come out? How? Why? I thought you were a member of the Party? Expected you to be a general by now. She was laughing, teasing, reminding him of the way they had always been together.

He explained how he had become disillusioned, had begun to see that although the leaders probably believed in what they were doing they had become isolated, had refused to listen to the people or take into account what the people wanted. And in so doing they had become even more isolated, even though they continued to believe that what they were doing was for the good. In the end, he said, he had come to believe that they were clinging to power, even though they were not aware of it.

Anja was looking at him the way she had looked at him on the steps of the fountain near the Nicholaikirche in Leipzig, head slightly tilted to one side and eyes challenging.

In the end, he said, he had also come to believe that the Party élite used their position and their power to enjoy a lifestyle denied to the people. That although many in the Party worked for the good of the state and the people, there were those in its upper echelons who merely used it as a cocktail round, who took everything from it but who put nothing back.

You've been married twice, Anja almost interrupted him. The second time to the woman with whom you have a daughter in Frankfurt, and the first to the woman you're now talking about.

'What are you laughing at?' He turned and looked at her.

'I'm laughing at you.' Her eyes were blue and flashing as he remembered them. 'I'm laughing at how much you once believed in the system, the way we used to argue. I'm laughing at the day you warned me that my politics would get me into trouble.' I'm laughing, though I wouldn't admit it, at the last time we saw each other, how the different things we believed in tore us apart. I'm laughing at how we're suddenly like the kids we once were.

They were tight against each other, looking at each other. Faces and mouths almost touching. So how did you get out, she pulled back, how did you get to the West?

He told her the details, had dealt with the case himself, only changed the identity of the escaper and the way it had ended.

'You're looking tired.' He realized he had put his hand up and stroked her face.

'I am.'

'Where do you live?'

'Charlottenberg. Too far to walk.'

She asked the barman for the telephone. Are you about to betray? He listened as she ordered a cab. Are you selling me to your husband? He was still unsure why he had crossed the Wall, why he come into West Berlin. Five minutes, she told him, sat by him again. What are we going to do, Werner? She realized she was touching him, her fingers playing on his hand. The cab stopped outside; they left the bar and stood on the pavement.

'I'm working tomorrow.'

'What time?' Are you going to invite me back, am I going to suggest it? If I do come back we'll end up in bed. Is that what Schiller wants, is that what he's planned?

'Eleven in the morning till ten in the evening. Will you come and see me?'

They were still standing on the pavement, still uncertain what to do. He glanced round, the movement natural, and swept the street for the watchers. 'Give me your number in case there's a problem.'

She told him the telephone number at the flat and wondered whether he would come back with her, whether she wanted him to. 'Goodnight.'

He checked again for the watchers and opened the cab door for her. 'Tomorrow.'

Wormser Strasse was deserted, no other cars. He started the BMW, accelerated past the Calvados Bar and turned left at the top, slowing only fractionally for the lights. The K'Damm was quiet, hardly any traffic. He caught the cab, confirmed its registration number and Anja's blonde hair in the back seat, and settled fifty metres behind it. The cab turned into Goethe Strasse and pulled to the right-hand pavement. The pavements were wide and lined with trees, the road cobbled and the stones glistening wet where the cleaning lorry had swept and washed them. Langer stopped the BMW at the junction and checked the street for watchers. Anja left the cab and went into the apartment block, fumbling at the front door for her key.

Why hadn't she told him, she thought. She unlocked the door of the flat and went in, automatically checking Lisa's room, hoping beyond hoping. Then she went to the bathroom and leaned over the handbasin, realized she was trembling.

Sunday morning was warm. Half an hour after Anja left the flat Langer entered it. At nine that morning he had taken the airport bus to Tegel and hired a second BMW, different colour. One car for the café, one for the flat. At ten he had collected the gun and ammunition from the drop in the wooded area along the Tiergarten.

The curtains were half drawn; he went from room to room, establishing the layout then began again, more thoroughly, checking for the devices Schiller would have installed. The feeling that something was wrong was instinctive. He worked slowly and carefully, not moving anything unless it was necessary, taking note of the exact position of objects he had to move and replacing them accordingly, looking for the security measures he would have built in if he had been running the operation. No bugs, he was confident, no surveillance from the building opposite. Something else. He began checking the rooms again. Doorway into small hall, kitchen and eating area on the right, then lounge. Bathroom on left then bedrooms.

One cup and saucer on draining board, one plate. Lisa lives with me here, Anja had told him. Perhaps Lisa had been out the night before, perhaps she was staying with friends. Food in the fridge for one, not two. There was a logical explanation again, he told himself, Anja had Mondays off and hadn't done the shopping. He walked through the hall into Anja's room. The bed had been made and the window was slightly open at the top, allowing in the air. He went into the other bedroom. The room was smaller, the window closed and locked, and the chest of drawers doubled as a bedside table. He slid open the drawers and checked each. Not as many clothes as he would have expected, all neatly folded and lying as if they had been there some time. He left the bedroom and went back to the bathroom. The washing was hung over the bath: blouses, a skirt, bras and pants. He took them off one by one and looked at the labels. One style, one size.

He left the flat, leaving it exactly as he had found it. There was no exit from the courtyard at the rear; he had already checked, the front door and hallway the only way in and out. The hallway was empty. Letter-boxes on left, mirror and ledge beneath it on right. Carpet running up centre of stairs, each tread down having a slight overhang, the carpet tacked tightly round. He knelt and prised the carpet away from the wood beneath the bottom tread.

If they came for him it would be upstairs. Normal routine: the body search to see if he was armed then the rush down the stairs and they would relax slightly, would know they had him. He took the Star from his jacket and slipped it into the right side of the hiding place he had created, butt out so that he could pick it up easily and safety catch off, and the spare clips into the left.

Four times during the next ten hours Langer checked the locations on Wittenbergplatz and Goethe Strasse; at nine that evening he went to the Café Brasserie, at ten he left; Anja joined him in the Calvados an hour later.

'When do you go back to Frankfurt?'

'Tomorrow morning.'

'And when will you come back to Berlin?'

'I don't know.'

She smiled at him and telephoned for a cab.

The entrance hall was dimly lit, one of the lights not working, and the flat exactly as he had left it, no sign of anyone having been there during the day. Anja switched on the lights, pulled the curtains, and showed him round.

'Just big enough for the two of you.' He stood watching as she made coffee. 'Where's Lisa tonight?'

'Out with friends, she'll be back later.'

'You don't mind me meeting her?'

Anja took the percolator into the lounge and poured them each a cup as if she had not heard the question. 'Tell me about Nikki.'

They were sitting at right-angles to each other, Langer in an armchair facing the window. Anja on the sofa to his left, the glass-topped table in front of him.

'If I tell you you'll say I'm like any father.'

'Tell me anyway.'

'She's attractive, top of her class, good at languages.'

'Which languages?'

English and Russian, he knew he should have said. 'English and French.'

'What sort of school?'

The school for the sons and daughters of the Party élite. 'The local school.'

The conversation had become abrupt, almost unnatural.

'Does she read much?'

'More recently.'

'What books?'

'Gorbachev, Solzhenitsyn.' He poured them each another coffee. 'Tell me about Lisa.'

'She's great. Terrific. Really terrific.' There was too much enthusiasm in her voice and too much of a smile on her face.

'And she's still at school?'

'College.' The eyes betrayed her.

'Of course. What's she studying?'

'Economics.' The slightest hesitation, barely noticeable.

'How's she doing?'

'Well. Really well.'

'No problems with homework?'

'Not with Lisa.' Too quick, too forceful.

'You must really enjoy having her living with you.'

She was looking at him, trying to avoid his eyes.

He took the cup from her and put it on the table. 'Tell me the truth.'

She broke. 'Lisa's a drug addict. She's living in a squat with some bastard who beats the shit out of her and treats her like a whore.'

'How long?'

'Six months.'

'What have you told Hans-Joachim?'

She was beginning to cry. No sound. Just the tears which rolled down her cheeks every night and the despair in her eyes. He tried to remember whether Anja had told him her husband's name and confirmed that she had.

'I haven't.'

'Why not?'

Her face was running wet, shoulders sagged and body shaking. 'I'm afraid to.'

He pushed the table aside and sat beside Anja on the sofa. 'Tell me from the beginning. Tell me everything.'

Langer's meeting with the man called Kronen was in a bar in the Treptow area of East Berlin. It was mid afternoon, the men who used it at midday and in the evenings still at work. The walls were stained and the tables were chipped Formica. They sat at the table in the corner, the glasses of heavy brown beer barely touched in front of them. Kronen was dressed in overalls and donkey jacket, despite the weather; his face was slightly grey and he was of that indeterminate age between twenty-five and forty.

Lisa wasn't his business, Langer had tried to argue with himself. Lisa was Schiller's daughter, therefore Schiller's problem, Schiller's responsibility to sort out.

Anja's daughter, Anja's problem, therefore his. He was still unsure why he had gone to West Berlin.

'There are certain conditions which have to be met, and the timing has to be exact.' He had used Kronen before and knew he was reliable. 'I therefore suggest you use one of the fentanyls. Swiss bank account as usual.'

The room was large, high ceiling, the plaster around it ornate and exquisitely cast. The candle burned in the jam jar on the box in the centre of the floor, even though the electricity had been rewired to bypass the meter. The single armchair was broken and lopsided and the mattresses around it were dirty and torn, the food in the tins half eaten. The needles were scattered amongst them and the Jif plastic lemons were misshapen and empty. Eleven at night, the windows were shuttered and the timber jammed against the door. The figures were like wraiths, thin, almost unreal; their hair long and lank, and their movements slow.

Kronen took the wrap of paper from his pocket and laughed, the sound seeming to echo round the room, the others laughing with him as he held it up for them to see, teasing them and seeing their eyes glow, turning it like a precious stone in his fingers. Access had been easy: he had met them in the tents by Potsdamerplatz, sold them some smack the next day and told them his name was Paul, moved the filthy blanket that was his bedroll into the squat a week ago.

The candle flickered, the flame just below the rim of the jar and the glass black with soot, the spoon and full Jif beside it. Kronen moved the spoon closer and unscrewed the top of the plastic lemon. Carefully, aware their eyes watching his every movement, he undid the wrap and showed them the pure white powder inside. The flame was halfway down the candle. He trickled the powder into the spoon, squeezed in some lemon juice and held the spoon over the flame, watching as the powder dissolved. The atmosphere in the room was tense, suddenly on edge, each of them needing their fix, each suddenly even more desperate. Kronen picked up a hypodermic, drew the heroin up and nodded to the girl leaning against the right of the chair. Poor little bitch, real doll once. Now look at her, eyes like piss holes in the snow and face like she was in Dachau. Body and soul broken, anybody's and everybody's as long as the slime in the chair could get a fix from it.

The girl leaned towards him, suddenly shaking, and rolled up her sleeve.

The reaction was sudden and terrible. The man in the chair jerked upright, smashing his hand across her face and pushing her arm out of the way, holding out his own in its place. The arm was brown with dirt and riddled with pinpricks, the veins standing out as the man pulled the makeshift tourniquet round the top and tightened it. Kronen inserted the needle into one of the veins and pumped the heroin into his body, the man slipping back into the chair, his breathing already shallower as he felt the buzz.

The first blood trickled from the girl's nose. She pulled the sleeve of her blouse down and tried to wipe it away.

Slowly Kronen went round the circle, the eyes still watching him and the anxiety showing that there was not enough, the faces laughing as he took the second and third wraps from his pocket.

He came to the girl, looked at her, took her arm. Poor bastards, he thought, none of them deserving where they were about to go. Not his job to question. Weber's orders. He had known the man for five years and still only knew him by that name. He pressed the flesh and saw the vein stand out, then he inserted the bloodied silver of the needle into it and eased the plunger.

The flame was flickering, the candle burning down, the journeys already begun and the eyes suddenly staring, twitching. The devils dancing and the snakes crawling into their mouths and through their nostrils.

The man in the chair lay open-legged, shirt torn and white flesh showing through. Kronen knelt back, pulled up the right leg of his trousers and pulled down his sock. Taped to his right ankle was a cigar tube. He pulled it off, spun off the cap and took the syringe and ampoule from it. The man in the chair was looking at him, eyes seeing nothing except the demons, mind screaming at him to push them away but arms unable to move.

Kronen inserted the needle of the syringe through the rubber septum of the ampoule and drew up the liquid, holding the needle in his right hand with the tip away from himself. Some silly bastard had got it wrong once, or so the story had gone: scratched himself with the needle and was dead before he'd done the job. With his left hand he held the arm of the man in the chair and pressed it slightly. There was no need to apply a tourniquet, the veins were already raised. Three minutes since he had given the girl her dose, he calculated, remembered the timetable Weber had insisted upon. He squeezed gently on the hypodermic and emptied the five milligrams into the vein.

The man in the chair was mumbling, the wraiths around him locked inescapable into his nightmares. Kronen eased the syringe out, put it and the phial back in the cigar tube, still taking care not to touch the needle, screwed the cap back on and taped it back on to his ankle. It was six minutes since he had given the girl her shot; he glanced round the room and left.

The telephone kiosk was three blocks away, the *out of order* notice stuck across it. Ten minutes, Weber had instructed, the timing crucial. Kronen removed the notice and dialled for an ambulance.

The telephone rang at three. Anja jerked awake and felt in the dark. Found the hand set by the bedside. 'Yes.'

'Frau Schiller?'

'Yes.' She fumbled for the light and switched it on.

'You have a daughter, Lisa?'

'Yes.'

'This is the central hospital. Your daughter has just been admitted suffering from an overdose. We suggest you come immediately.'

Schiller had been at work since seven and was informed at eight. Your wife on line two, an aide told him.

Anja's voice was calm, trying to be calm. Schiller listened, the winter descending upon his face and the hand suddenly cupped over the mouthpiece.

Get me the time of the next flight to Berlin, he told the aide. This afternoon, the man checked and reported back to him, the line to ground control held open. All morning flights after eight o'clock have been cancelled.

'The eight o'clock flight?'

The aide checked. 'Taxiing for take-off.'

'Bring it back.'

Lisa's face was chalk, shroud-like, as if her features were unreal and the lines and marks upon them had faded away. The tubes and drips ran from and into her arms, nose and mouth. Anja and Hans-Joachim sat together at the side of the bed, Anja holding Lisa's right hand and the doctor examining her, Schiller staring at him and then at the thin green line across the monitor. Eleven in the morning. A nurse brought them coffee and they thanked her.

'She'll be okay.' The doctor had been on duty nearly twenty hours and was grey-faced with fatigue.

The bed was in the corner of the ward, the curtains drawn around it and the sounds of the other patients barely discernible, the antiseptic smell of the hospital permeating everything.

'Tell me the details.' Schiller's voice was quiet.

'Your daughter is a drug addict. She's been living in a squat.' Sometimes parents took it badly, the doctor knew, sometimes they never even found the bloody parents. 'She was admitted last night suffering from an overdose. A number of others were also admitted.'

The father was calm – the doctor's thoughts would come later, when he had time to reflect – as if he was used to dealing with crises. Profession teacher, it had said on the form he had filled in shortly after his arrival. Except, the staff sister would tell him that evening, that the BMW in which he had arrived had driven through the traffic lights outside on red and that the young man who had opened the doors for him had got out before the car had stopped.

'Lisa was lucky, another fifteen minutes and it would have been touch and go. One of the others was dead when the ambulances arrived at the squat.'

'What about the others?'

The voice was still calm, the question almost understated, the doctor would think that evening.

'They're okay.'

'All from the same squat?'

'Yes.'

'What was she on?'

'Heroin. As soon as she and the others arrived we ran an immuno-assay screen for the normal range – opiates and barbiturates – and the opiates were positive. So we banged them full of Naloxone.'

'Naloxone?'

'An antidote.'

'How were they brought in?'

'By ambulance.'

'How was the ambulance summoned?'

The doctor turned to the staff nurse. Emergency call, she checked the records.

'You must get a lot of this.'

'Too much.' Good to have someone who understood, the doctor thought.

'Thank you for all you've done.' Schiller stood and held out his hand. 'You know how much we appreciate it.'

The doctor shook his hand. He would have told them anyway, he would think later, but would have told them differently. 'Lisa was lucky.' He had used the words before but meant them differently this time.

'How?'

'The way she was going she would have been dead by the end of the year.' He began to leave.

'You said Lisa was an addict?'

The doctor turned back. 'Yes.'

'So what happened last night that she overdosed? Was the heroin cut with something different?'

'Interestingly, no. It was almost pure.'

'So why should that have produced an overdose?'

'Because it was so pure. They were comatose almost immediately.' He shook hands again and left them.

The ward seemed quiet, the sounds from outside the curtains far away.

'How long since she left home?'

'Six months.'

'Why didn't you tell me?'

'I was afraid. I thought she might pull out of it. I don't know.'

He looked at Anja and saw how she was trembling, put his arm round and held her. Not your fault, we're both to blame.

That night, after Lisa had regained consciousness and he and Anja had talked to her, Schiller returned to Cologne. The following morning he flew back to Berlin. That day, after he had talked again with Lisa, he spent the rest of the morning and all afternoon with her friends, sitting on their beds and holding their hands as Anja sat holding Lisa's, occasionally talking, more often listening, giving them something to hold on to as the doctor had given Lisa.

It was an experience he would never forget. The whiteness of the uniforms and the sheets, the faces looking up at him, the smell, the whiteness again. Another face, smiling, trying to smile; eyes almost beyond hope, trying desperately to pull back. He held the boy's hand and talked to him about something, anything; felt the pressure of the boy's fingers and knew he would pull through.

'Tell me again what happened.'

'Do I have to?'

It was mid evening and he had been at Lisa's bedside since five, smiling at her when she looked at him and stroking her face as she slept. She was looking better, he thought, dark black almost purple rings round her eyes, lip split. Just the hint of colour in her cheeks.

Last time, he promised.

Lech, Walter, Siegfrid whom she called Ziggy and Monika were sitting round, she told him, Elli making coffee. Fritz and Bridget weren't there, were off somewhere trying to score. Elli coming back, no coffee. Paul pulling out the wrap and nodding to her for the first fix. Lech hitting her and pushing her arm away, taking the first fix for himself like he always did. Paul only giving her a fix at the end.

Lech the bastard who had ruined her, lying still and cold on the slab where he belonged. Ziggy, Walter, Monika and Elli doing okay; he tried to put names to the faces which had looked up at him from the white of the pillows. Eight names, plus Lisa made nine. The calculations began. One dead, four others plus Lisa in hospital. Two otherwise accounted for, eight. One missing.

'When did Paul come to the squat?'

'One, two weeks ago.'

'Where did you meet him?'

'Tiergarten, the Kurfurstendamm, Potsdam Platz. I can't remember.'

'How did you meet him?'

'Who?'

'Paul.'

'I don't know. One day he was just there.'

The flat was quiet; they had returned at midnight. Schiller made himself a bed on the sofa while Anja made the coffee.

Tell me about the last six months; he took the cup from her; tell me what's happened since Lisa left home.

She told him, about the contacts with Lisa, how she had tried to bring her home, threatened her, told her how much she loved her. Told him how, just once, she had found the courage to telephone him but he had been away.

Tell me about yourself, Anja, tell me what else you did in that time, where you went and who you met.

She told him about the university, the job at the bar, the bar round the corner where she sometimes went afterwards.

Tell me about the men and women you meet there. Do you go out with any of them, have dates with any? *What are you asking? Why are you questioning Anja as if she was a suspect?*

I don't go to bed with any of them if that's what you mean. They try, they're bound to try. Perhaps that's what they expect of someone in a bar. But I've never slept with any of them.

Anyone else, Anja?

I've told you I haven't slept with anyone else.

I don't mean that, I mean have you met anyone else?

The hesitation. Only . . .

Only who? What?

She wondered why she had not been going to tell him. One night an old friend turned up in the bar. I haven't seen him for years.

How many years?

Twenty, twenty-five. They both knew what that meant. Actually it was in Leipzig. He was my first boyfriend.

Tell me about what you did.

We didn't go to bed.

He held her hand and reassured her. I know you didn't go to bed with him. His voice was softer, comforting. I know you haven't been to bed with anyone.

Have you?

He laughed. No time.

She laughed back.

Did you tell anyone else about Lisa?

She shook her head.

Did you tell him?

Yes.

What was his name?

Werner Langer.

Schiller's meeting with Sonntag was in a café in the Kreuzberg area of West Berlin. The walls were covered with travel posters and the varnish on the tables was peeling. They sat in the corner, furthest from the window. Sonntag was in his mid thirties, short, with close-cropped hair and slightly round face. The denim overalls had grease on them and the plumber's bag was under the table. The only thing which betrayed him were his eyes.

'A wet job.' The waitress had spilt the tea into the saucer; Schiller tipped it back into the mug. 'The other side of the Wall.'

It was what Sonntag had somehow assumed.

Schiller passed him the envelope. 'No photograph. This photofit is up to date. I'm told it's extremely accurate.'

Too far this time, Langer. In the sixties it was personal but we were too young to realize. Then it was business; hard and dirty, but business. Now you've made it personal again, even though you should know better, now you've involved my daughter.

'Name?'

'Langer.'

'Problems?' There always was one.

'He's Stasi.'

It was early evening, the café not yet busy. Michael Rossini sat in the chair against the wall facing the door, Max Steiner on the other side. In the street outside they saw Ernst Vöckel arrive and rose to greet him. There was something about the handshake that evening which each of them would remember. They sat down and savoured the moment.

'You know?'

'The President informed me this morning.' Rossini rolled the wine round the glass. It should be French, he thought, vintage champagne, instead it was warm Bulgarian. He still remembered the first photographs, taken secretly in the camp and smuggled to the West. The thin face and the staring eyes, the head shaved. 'When?'

'Within the next two weeks.'

'Does he know yet?'

'No.'

'Any details?'

'Still being worked out. Minor things, there won't be any problems. As soon as they're finalized we'll be given a precise date and time.'

'How will he come out?' Aeroflot from Moscow, he assumed, either to New York or possibly straight to Israel.

'Through East Germany. The night before his final release he will be flown secretly to Schönefeld and will stay in East Berlin overnight. The next day he will be free to go to the West.'

How, Rossini asked again.

Vöckel turned to his left. The last piece of the jigsaw, the public face of the secret deal between Washington and Moscow. 'You should know, Max. You did it yourself.' He saw the look on the man's face and the memory of the moment. 'Antonin Shevienko will walk across the Glienicker Bridge.'

At ten the following morning Hans-Joachim Schiller was invited to take coffee with the Director-General. The meeting was outside their normal briefings and for one moment he assumed it was to do with Langer. In the next two weeks, he was told instead, Moscow was releasing the dissident Shevienko. No other details were available, though it was suggested that the actual release would be through Berlin. Effective from that moment he was to take personal charge of the security operations from the West German standpoint. Only he was allowed to know the identity of the man coming out, however; all others should be led to assume it was a straightforward exchange. That afternoon he selected the team he would use for the operation, that evening he flew with two of them to Berlin.

Lisa was looking better. Her face was still pale but the rings round her eyes had lightened and the eyes themselves had begun to lose the haunted look which so terrified him.

The assassin Karl-Heinz Sonntag dialled the number and waited for the ringing tone. The ringing stopped, he held the monitor to the mouthpiece and activated the answerphone. The system was simple and foolproof, a method by which clients could pass messages to him, the code to activate the machine changed regularly. The tram rumbled past the kiosk. Sonntag pressed the telephone close to his right ear and tried to deafen the sound in his other ear with the palm of his hand.

'Potential location. The Glienicker Bridge. Approximately two weeks. Date and time to be confirmed.'

At least he could begin his preparations, Sonntag thought; he left the kiosk and hurried away. The street was busy; he walked hands in pockets and clothes neutral, his whole appearance immediately forgettable. Long-range job, he was already calculating, wondered how the man he knew only as Wolf had obtained the information and when he would know the rest.

Langer was informed by Lindner at eleven. In the next few days the Soviet dissident Antonin Shevienko would be released; he would be flown secretly to Schönefeld, remain in East Berlin overnight, and be freed the following morning. Langer had overall responsibility for all aspects of the operation from the moment Shevienko's aircraft entered East German air space.

That evening he flew to Moscow. The briefing was at the Lubianka. It was fifteen years since Langer had first come to Moscow. In that time he had always taken back with him the same impression: the faces wrapped against the cold and the eyes unmoving and without emotion as they read the copies of *Pravda* on the billboards. The last time, however, had been different: six months after Gorbachev had come to power. Then he had returned to Berlin with an unmistakable sense of change, now it was confirmed. The Moscow spring. Like the Prague Spring of '68.

The twenty-four-hour permit allowing West Berliners to travel in the countryside immediately outside Berlin, including Potsdam, would expire at ten that evening. Karl-Heinz Sonntag stood as close as he could to the eastern end of the Glienicker Bridge and looked west, the East German control house in front of him, the Soviet next to the bridge itself, both sets of guards already becoming agitated.

He had already selected the weapon he would use. A self-loading Dragunov sniper rifle, 4.4-kilogram weight, short-stroke gas action and ten-round magazine, 7.62-mm-long rounds. Flash hider at the muzzle with telescopic sight fitted as standard. And Soviet manufacture – he had allowed himself a certain amusement at the thought. If he left the weapon at the firing point, as was quite probable, then Moscow would have a lot of explaining to do.

The guard was coming towards him, waving at him to move on. Sonntag had already surveyed the area from the west of the bridge – normal procedure where possible: survey target area from potential firing points, then select firing point from target area. There was only one place where he could be sure of seeing his target, he decided, the wooded ground rising slightly behind the last of the summer-houses in the Schloss Park to the left of the bridge as he looked west. Over five hundred metres away, nearer six.

No problem, he was confident. One-round head shot at two hundred metres – his sniper training in the military had been thorough – one-round body shot at six hundred. No need even to check that the target was down. Drop the weapon and get the hell out as soon as he pressed the trigger.

He nodded at the guard and walked back down the road towards Potsdam.

The briefing began at four. 'Aeroflot code Zulu will leave Moscow at sixteen thirty local time and arrive at Schönefeld at seventeen fifty-five local time.' Langer sat at his desk and looked down the conference table. 'The security convoy will be waiting. Lion will exit the aircraft by the front door and be escorted to the second vehicle of the convoy. He will then be driven to the Palast Hotel. A section of the third floor will be sealed off. He will remain there overnight. He will not leave his room.' Even to him it sounded as if he was planning against an assassination.

'The exchange is at two the following afternoon. The convoy will leave the hotel at one fifteen and arrive at the Glienicker Bridge at one minute to the hour. The exchange will be completed by five minutes past. From the bridge the security convoy will drive straight to the GSFG airfield at Zossen-Wunsdorf.'

Zossen-Wunsdorf was Russian military, therefore the prisoner code-name Lion was being exchanged for a Russian; the logic was obvious. They moved to the details.

That evening Hans-Joachim Schiller flew to Berlin. Anja was at the hospital. Lisa's face was tight, her cheeks protruding and her eyes slightly disturbed. Withdrawal, the doctors had warned them, the agony of coming off the drugs. Don't worry, she tried to smile at him, it'll be okay. When she fell asleep they stayed at her bedside.

'What are you thinking?'

Anja was staring at Lisa. 'Nothing. Everything. Just thank God that she lived that night. Thank God they got her to the hospital in time.'

'Something else?'

Anja nodded. She was sitting on the edge of the bed, hands clasped and the strain showing on her face.

'What?'

'Werner Langer.'

'What about him?'

Anja was ringing her hands; she tried to stop and looked at him. 'When I told you the name the night after Lisa was taken to hospital, it was as if you knew him.'

'So what are you asking me?'

'Do you know him?'

The ward was quiet, only the shallow sound of Lisa's breathing. 'Yes.'

'How? Why?'

He stood and helped her up. 'Lisa's okay, let's go for a walk.'

The sounds echoed along the corridor and the smell of antiseptic hung in the air.

'Werner Langer doesn't live in Frankfurt. He does come West, but not because he's escaping. Langer is a general in East German State Security. Not just a general, the youngest ever appointed; when the present head of State Security goes Langer's favourite to take his job.'

The words demolished her. 'How do you know?' It was as if she was drowning, as if the waves were engulfing her and she could not break clear to the surface.

'We try to keep tabs on them just as they keep tabs on us.'

'So *was* it coincidence that he came into the bar?'

'What do you think?'

The corridor was empty, a telephone ringing somewhere. They sat at the line of chairs next to the lift.

'But does that mean he's connected to Lisa's overdose?' She was still drowning.

'Yes.'

'How?'

'The man Lisa calls Paul, the man who gave them the heroin that night. If he was an addict he would have given himself a fix as well. If he was an addict he wouldn't have disappeared.'

The grey drained down Anja's face. 'But the heroin he gave them was pure, the doctor said so. Strong enough to kill them.'

'Yes.'

'So Werner tried to kill Lisa?' The shock in Anja's voice was like nothing Schiller had ever experienced.

'So it would seem.'

'Why should he want to kill Lisa?' The shock had turned to desperation.

'To get at me.'

The foyer of the Inter-Continental was busy, muzak playing in the background. Sonntag left his chair and went to the telephones.

'Location confirmed.' The voice on the recording was bleak, factual. 'Timing 2.00 p.m. Friday.'

If it was at the Glienicker Bridge it would be a spy swap – the suspicion had been at the back of Sonntag's mind all along. He returned to his chair and tried to work out the extra difficulties it would present.

The hotel room was quiet, the double glazing keeping out the noises of the street and the air-conditioning humming. Schiller poured himself a whiskey, the merest dash of water. It was two in the morning and the night half gone. Why would Langer seek to get at him through Lisa? How did he know about her? Just as he knew about Anja. So work it out. Why he came over, how he knew Anja was working in the café. There was no explanation, no way he could work it out. He pulled on a dressing-gown and paced the room.

Langer meets Anja, she tells him about Lisa. So he doesn't know about Lisa until Anja tells him. Wrong. Langer's a professional, just as you are; Langer knew about Lisa in advance and made Anja think he had learned it from her. He tipped the whiskey down the basin in the bathroom, rinsed the glass, and went to bed. Why Anja, though? Why risk going to Anja if he already knew about Lisa? And if he didn't know, then why go to Anja at all?

Four o'clock, soon it would be getting light. He turned in the bed and tried to sleep.

The library was quiet, most of the students would not begin to arrive until gone nine. Anja settled at her desk and stared at the paperwork, the horror of what Hans-Joachim had told her still screaming at her.

In her mind she could see the small boy who had been her first friend, the magician and the night of the school party, the second time the magician had done the trick and the moment she saw his downfall, the way Werner Langer had engineered it, even though she did not know how.

The numbness wrapped round her. Emergency telephone call at 11.07; she was barely aware she was running through the time-table the doctor had told them the morning after Lisa had been admitted. Ambulances at squat at 11.15 p.m. Lisa and others reach hospital at 11.28 p.m. Emergency treatment begins 11.29.

One of the other librarians brought her a mug of coffee. She smiled and thanked him.

The briefing began at ten. Schiller listened while the team-leaders detailed the vehicle movements and security measures. After collection the package code-named Tiger would be transported in the third car of the convoy. All road intersections would be closed and there would be helicopter surveillance overhead.

There was something he had missed. Six people excluding Lisa in the squat that night, five accounted for, one missing. He began to go back, to trawl through the details. Forget about it all, forget about everything except getting Shevienko out safely.

He leaned forward and asked for questions.

When the briefing was over he spent a further fifty minutes dealing with other items then drove to the hospital. Lisa was sitting up in bed, her face was still white and her eyes sunken.

'Thanks for coming to Berlin, Papa. Thanks for coming to see me.'

'Why wouldn't I?' He stooped and kissed her. 'You're feeling okay?'

'Sometimes it's bad.'

'Bound to be.'

Six in the squat that night, excluding Lisa. Four in hospital, one body, one missing – Paul, the man Werner had sent over the Wall to kill her daughter. Why, Werner? Why try to get at Hans-Joachim through her? Why try to kill Lisa? Anja spooned the sugar into the coffee.

Emergency telephone call at 11.07, ambulances at squat at 11.15. Lisa was lucky, the doctor had said, another fifteen minutes and it would have been touch and go. Lucky also that they had been warned and had everything on stand-by.

Someone was talking to her, a telephone ringing.

Why the emergency telephone call? The thought came from nowhere. Why send for help and tell the hospital exactly what to expect if you really meant to kill Lisa?

The other librarian was talking to her, Anja nodding, replying. Not even aware of the conversation.

No confirmation it was the man called Paul who had made the call, but no one else who could have made it.

'Excuse me.' She broke off the conversation, telephoned the hotel where Hans-Joachim was staying and was told that he had checked out. If he had left the hotel he was returning to Berlin, but if he was returning to Berlin he would go somewhere else first. She redialled, heard the switchboard operator at the hospital and asked to speak to Lisa's ward. When the sister answered she identified herself and asked if her husband was there. He's just leaving, she was informed, waited while he was brought to the telephone.

Lisa was fine, he told her; he himself was about to leave for Cologne. Her mind was whirring, trying to work out how she should tell him, whether she herself believed it.

'There's something I don't understand.' She knew suddenly what Hans-Joachim would think. 'I have to see you. Now.'

She telephoned for a mini-cab, and picked up her coat and bag. 'I'll be back in an hour.'

The hospital was busy. As she walked down the corridor she

saw Hans-Joachim sitting on the bed, Lisa half asleep. She kissed her gently, not waking her. 'Thanks for waiting.'

'What is it?'

They walked to the recreation room at the end of the ward and sat down.

'I don't know how to begin.' She knew she was wrong, that she should not have come. 'Werner sent the man called Paul to kill Lisa. Paul gave everyone in the squat a massive fix of pure heroin.'

Schiller nodded.

'Lisa's alive because of the emergency call.'

'Yes.'

'Who made the call?'

'No name was given.'

'Who else could it have been other than Paul?' She saw the first suspicion cross his mind.

'One of the others from the squat could have returned, then gone again.'

'Think what you're assuming if that's the case. That another addict turns up at just the right time, makes the right telephone call, gives them the right information. Think about the timings, about the telephone call. Think about the information in it and what it meant.'

Emergency call 11.07, correct details given; 11.15 ambulances arrive; 11.28 reach hospital; 11.29 treatment begins.

Not quite correct. Not wrong but incomplete.

Emergency call 11.07. Details not simply accurate but unerringly precise. Address, location of room in house, numbers involved, symptoms. Ambulances arrive 11.15. Not one ambulance, three. Enough for everyone. Not just ambulances, para-medics. Reach hospital 11.28, hospital already on full stand-by and medical teams on crash. Treatment begins 11.29. Incorrect. Para-medics had begun treatment fourteen minutes before.

'It's too calculated to be anyone but Paul. But if it was Paul then he was under orders. If it was Paul that was what Werner told him to do.'

Langer turned her even though she didn't realize it, Schiller thought. Langer slept with her.

'If Werner meant to kill Lisa, why the emergency telephone call to save her life?' Anja's voice was desperate, pleading.

You're wrong, he wanted to say, Langer's Stasi, a real bastard.

It was Langer who locked Max Steiner up for eighteen years and tried to kill me in the tunnel on Bernauer Strasse. Six names, one missing. Forget the one missing, concentrate on the other five. Four still alive, one dead. Coincidence? Pure chance that the body in the morgue was the bastard who'd torn little Lisa's life to pieces? Langer still playing his games, covering his tracks. The overdose. Those who had survived exhibiting the classic symptoms, the man who had died showing the same symptoms and the immuno-assay tests confirming the cause of death. The pieces all fitting together and logical.

'Tell me about the evening he came back to the flat with you. Are you sure he didn't know about Lisa before you told him?'

'I'm sure.'

Of course Anja was sure, Langer was a pro. 'When you told him about Lisa was there mention of Lisa's boyfriend?'

'Yes.'

'Did he know that or did you tell him?'

'I told him, he didn't know. He didn't know anything.'

Perhaps it was all for the best, the nurse had confided in him that morning. Perhaps Lisa and the others had suffered so much that they really were intent on rehabilitation. Perhaps the shock was the only thing that could convince them. Coincidence – the other thought was still with him. Pure chance that the only person to die was the slime who'd ruined Lisa's life?

What's wrong, Anja asked him, what are you thinking?

'I'm not sure.' He told her he would be back, went to the staff sister and asked to use a telephone. There was something about him, about the way he spoke. Use my office, she told him. The number he dialled was in Cologne.

'Professor Schramm. Yes, I'll wait.'

The forensic science laboratory was the one used by the BfV, Karl Schramm head of toxicology. Through the window of the office he could see Lisa, Anja with her.

'Karl, Hans-Joachim. I'm phoning from West Berlin.'

On an open line, Schramm picked up the implication, calls from Berlin liable to be tapped anyway. 'I understand.'

'Apparent overdose. If the OD was a cover, what are the other side using nowadays?' Langer still playing his game, the thought was persistent, Langer now making him play it.

'Depends on the circumstances. Ricin perhaps. Cyanide is still a favourite. How quickly did death follow?'

'Within minutes.'

'Rules out ricin, ricin takes a couple of days, so it could be cyanide. You've seen the reports?'

'Yes.'

'Any petechial haemorrhages?' The discolouring of the flesh around the throat and neck caused by the bursting of blood vessels due to the asphyxiation caused by the cyanide.

'No.'

There was a pause while Schramm thought it through. 'Give what else you can on the background.'

'A number of others were present, all admitted to hospital suffering from heroin overdosing, diagnosed by symptoms and confirmed by immuno-assay screening. The heroin itself was almost pure.' Schiller thought he heard the chuckle.

'The deceased was present with the others.' Schramm's summary was clear and incisive. 'The hospital knew the others were suffering from heroin overdoses and an immuno-assay screen on the deceased also proved positive for opiates. Therefore cause of death was a heroin overdose.'

'Yes.'

'The bastards.'

Schiller heard the chuckle again and waited.

'If anything else was used it sounds as if it could have been one of the fentanyls. Death is almost immediate, certainly within minutes, and the symptoms tie with an opiate overdose.'

'So why wasn't it picked up?'

'The immediate symptoms were obvious and confirmed both by the standard tests and the background. The hospital had a body, no suspicion of foul play, and what seemed a confirmed cause.'

Open and shut, Schiller thought. Everything neat and tied up.

'What else do you want?' the toxicologist asked.

'You in Berlin.'

'When?'

'Now.'

Of course; the agreement was unspoken. 'We'll need GC/MS.' Gas chromatography/mass spectrometry. 'There are two departments in West Berlin with the facilities, one at the Institute of Forensic Medicine at the university and the other in the Polizeipräsident on Gothaer Strasse. I suggest we use the latter, it's more secure and I have a contact there. I assume you want me to arrange everything, keep you out of it.' They had worked together before.

'Yes. How long will it take?'

'Half a day to extract and clean up the blood. The more extraneous compounds we can remove the faster and easier the final analysis. Plus half a day to set and tune up the equipment for maximum sensitivity.'

'If I was pushing you.'

Schramm laughed. 'Late this evening. I'll phone my man and get him started.'

'Thanks.'

'Don't thank me yet. Just find out if they've cremated the body.'

Schiller smiled at the sister as she went past and dialled a second number. Max Steiner's secretary informed him that the lawyer was in conference with clients and could not be disturbed; after that he had meetings all afternoon. That evening he was dining with more clients and the following morning he was flying to Paris for thirty-six hours.

'When does the conference end?'

'In about an hour.'

It was two fifteen. 'Thank you.'

The meeting finished ten minutes early. Max Steiner thanked the three men and one woman who had flown from Stuttgart and telephoned his secretary to confirm that the firm's car was standing by to take them to Tegel airport.

'There's someone waiting for you.'

'Who?'

'He's called Schiller. He phoned earlier. I told him you can't see him but he's sitting here now.'

He escorted the clients to the car and returned to reception. There was something about Hans-Joachim when he was moving fast, he thought, even the way he sat. They shook hands and went into his office.

'If I needed to get a message to Langer in a hurry how would I do it?'

'No one else to know, I assume.'

'Correct.'

'Through Ernst Vöckel.'

It was what Schiller himself had considered. 'But then Vöckel would know.'

'Not if he thought it was me who wanted to contact Langer.'

'But would it be safe for you to go over?'

'We won't know until we try.'

The target at the Glienicker Bridge, two o'clock, Friday afternoon. Schiller remembered the instructions he had left. Still time to contact Sonntag and abort the operation if he was right – he had worked through the possibilities on the drive from the hospital – but always the chance that Sonntag had an alternative, might take Langer before he could cancel the order. Always the chance he had been right in the first place.

'It may not be necessary, I'll know tonight.'

'What is it?'

Schiller told him.

'What time tonight do you expect the forensic results?'

'Ten, possibly eleven.'

Steiner lifted the telephone and dialled his secretary. 'Dinner tonight and Paris tomorrow. Could you cancel both.'

The afternoon was warm. On the rise overlooking the Glienicker Bridge Sonntag peered down the telescopic sights. Immediately after the hit, he assumed, the entire area would be sealed off and all vehicles checked. On the day of the hit, therefore, he would take the train to Wannsee and walk the rest. And if he couldn't clear the area quickly enough he would go underground and stay hidden as long as necessary. This afternoon he would make the necessary preparations. The guards at the other end of the bridge changed shift. Nothing different, he noted, no sun in his eyes and no shadows across the area where his target would stand. The timing made no difference to his vision or his plans. He left the position and walked back to the schloss.

Mid evening and the light outside failing. The poison fentanyl and it would be Langer taking out the man who had wrecked Lisa's life, giving Lisa a chance. Why, Schiller wondered, why the hell did Langer do it? Perhaps it needed to be someone else, the thought did Langer do it? Perhaps it needed to be someone else, the thought haunted him, perhaps he himself would not have had the courage to do to his own daughter what Langer had done.

The print-out chattered on the computer; Schramm left his seat, pulled the sheet out, looked at it and walked back across the room to Schiller. The lines of most of the graphs were constant, one graph outstanding.

'Tri-methyl fentanyl.'

'How much?'

'More than enough to kill him.'

'Any attempt made to conceal it?'

'None at all. Whoever did it was letting you know.'

The lights blazed over Checkpoint Charlie, the shadows of the guards dark and menacing, and the watch-towers of the Wall strung out on either side. Even as he turned off Koch Strasse Max Steiner knew they were watching him, focusing the night glasses and reporting back. Just like the old days, he almost thought, hasn't changed much really. He stopped the car and walked to the offices on the right.

'Late for crossing.'

He shrugged.

The corporal behind the security screen checked his passport and looked at him, tried to intimidate him. There were four men in the room, two border guards behind the mesh and a third close to him, a fourth man in civilian clothes near the door.

'Five Deutschmarks.'

The official stamped his entry visa, folded it inside his passport, and slid the passport back under the grille. Someone had made a telephone call, Max understood, made sure that he got through quickly, that there was no trouble. He walked outside and started the BMW. The barrier in front of him lifted and he drove into East Berlin.

Vöckel was waiting in the KaminBar of the Palast. The bar was busy, mainly tourists but some businessmen. Max Steiner shook his head at the cocktail waiter and came immediately to the point.

'I need to see Langer urgently. Can you contact him for me?'

'Shevienko?'

'No.'

'How urgent?'

'Tonight.'

Vöckel left the bar; Max Steiner sat back and tried to spot the men from State Security. Three minutes later the East German returned.

'The Luxemburg bar behind the museum in twenty minutes.'

Unter den Linden was quiet, a single tram clattering its way towards Alexanderplatz, little traffic except an occasional Trabant or Lada of the People's Police. The bar was off a courtyard entered through an archway, trees on the pavement outside. The room was empty, Langer sitting at the third table on the left.

'Long time.'

They shook hands and Max sat down.

'Drink?'

'Coffee.'

Langer ordered two. 'Don't worry, the place is clean. I'll see you back across myself after.' Spoken quietly and confidently.

'Lisa.'

There was no reaction.

'Hans-Joachim sends you his thanks.'

Still no reaction.

'But there's a problem. He worked out what had happened but got the motive wrong. He thought you tried to kill her to get at him.'

There was still no reaction, no indication that Langer knew what he was talking about.

'Someone's after you.'

The waiter brought the coffee.

'No problem. They won't have a photograph and don't know my movements.'

'He has a photofit and a location.'

'Where?'

'The Shevienko release.'

'How do you know about Shevienko?'

'I helped set it up.'

'And Schiller?'

'In charge of security when Shevienko crosses over.'

The symmetry of it all, Langer thought. 'So what does he suggest?'

'He has a way of contacting his man, did so tonight, ordered him to abort the operation. As soon as he has confirmation that the message has been received he'll let you know.'

'Through Vöckel through you?'

'Yes. A simple code.'

'Give him my thanks.'

Karl-Heinz Sonntag made his check call at seven. An update on the target, he assumed, confirmation of time and place. Operation aborted, he heard the words with surprise, even regret. At nine the following morning Langer left Berlin for Moscow, Rossini was notified at nine thirty, at ten Schiller held his penultimate briefing.

'The exchange is confirmed for tomorrow. Tiger is on his way.'

The military Ilyushin 62 cleared Moscow control at five. The day was warm and the sky clear, the ground below changing its shapes and colours and the horizon curving around them. The Ilyushin was virtually empty, no civilian passengers. Langer sat by himself, five seats from the front. At twenty minutes past five the KGB colonel tapped him on the shoulder and nodded. Langer rose and walked to the man now sitting alone, as if he was in no-man's-land.

'Professor Shevienko.'

The man looked up. He was dressed in a light grey suit, collar and tie, his hair was cut short and his eyes were dark and expressionless, as if for many years he had concealed his emotions. 'Yes.'

He would always bear the haunted look of the camps, Langer thought. 'It is my duty to inform you that you have just left the Soviet Union. We are now in East German air space.'

The dissident turned from him and looked through the window. Langer waited and allowed the man his moment. Only when Shevienko looked up again did he continue.

'My name is Langer, I'm from Berlin. May I join you?'

'Of course.' Shevienko was looking out the window again, watching the ground below. Only after thirty seconds did he turn back and even then Langer waited a few more seconds.

'Until you enter the West tomorrow I am responsible for your personal safety.'

'That's very good of you.' There was almost a laugh in the man's eyes, as if he knew he was part of a game.

'You have been informed of the arrangements?'

'Perhaps you should inform me again.' It was as if he was accustomed to the state seeking to control his life. As if, despite that, he reserved at least part of that life for himself. As if, having been told what was happening by one official, he instinctively checked it with another to find if they were telling him the truth.

'You spend tonight and tomorrow morning in East Berlin. You cross to the West at the Glienicker Bridge tomorrow afternoon at two.' He went into the details.

'You've sealed off part of a whole floor?' Shevienko's voice was dry, the humour in it understated and testing. 'It sounds as if I am General Secretary Gorbachev.'

Langer looked at him and understood how he had survived. 'If you were we would have sealed off the entire hotel.'

Shevienko smiled for the first time. 'In that case you'd better tell me again what I have to do.'

The security convoy was waiting, the black cars already in position on the apron of the runway. The Ilyushin taxied past the control tower, turned left, away from the main buildings, and stopped on the far side of the airfield. The front passenger door of the plane opened and the steps were pushed into position. The black cars slid into place at the bottom and the men hurried up the steps and inside. It was dusk, the light fading. Two minutes later they left, packed around the man in the middle so that he could barely be seen, remaining grouped around him as he slid into the rear door of the second vehicle, then the convoy pulled away. Only after it had cleared the airport was the service truck allowed to stop at the foot of the steps and the men in green overalls permitted on to the plane.

The security convoy pulled to a halt outside the Palast Hotel and the men swirled through the foyer, the man again hidden amongst them and one set of lifts held open.

The service van left Schönefeld and turned for the city. Three kilometres later it pulled into the side street behind the waiting cars.

Do you always do things this way, Shevienko asked.

Habit, Langer replied.

They climbed out of the service van and into the Volvo.

When Langer returned home that evening Gabi was in the kitchen and Nikki was watching television. He spoke to his wife then heard the title music of the West German news programme and drifted into the lounge.

'There is increasing speculation tonight that after fifteen years' imprisonment the Russian dissident Antonin Shevienko is being released and allowed to leave the Soviet Union.' The newscaster's voice and face were tense, emphasizing the importance of the information. 'At ten this morning Shevienko telephoned a close friend to say that he was no longer in the prison camp where he has been held, but that he was in Moscow. At eleven he telephoned another friend to say that good news was expected. Since then nothing has been heard of him. The word in Moscow tonight is that he is already on his way to freedom.'

Nikki heard the noise and saw her father in the doorway. As she turned he saw the excitement in her eyes, almost a tear. 'Shevienko's coming out.'

It was a strange expression to use, he thought. *Coming out.* As if she was in the West rather than the East. He sat on the arm of the chair and watched the rest of the report with her.

The following morning was bright. Antonin Shevienko rose at six and walked for an hour in the garden; at seven he went inside and sat with Ernst Vöckel for breakfast. The previous evening Michael Rossini and Max Steiner had joined them for dinner.

The official announcement of the release was made at nine, the scheduling as precise and deliberate as the leaks the previous day. In time for the European and British early morning radio and television programmes, sufficient notice for the American breakfast shows to pull together major items on Shevienko. Just enough time for the networks to rush additional crews and anchor men in from Bonn, London and Paris, though many had anticipated the announcement and flown crews into Berlin the night before.

By ten the first cameras were in position, fifty metres back from the security line drawn by the phalanx of police already surrounding the western end of the bridge; by midday the numbers had packed the area set aside for them and spilled over. At one thirty the lines of police opened and the official vehicles drove into position.

Not the security convoy, Sonntag knew, wrong cars, wrong sort of men. The sun was hot on his back. Fifteen minutes to two. Secure, acquire, squeeze: the drill was almost a religion. *Secure – identify the target. Acquire – cross-hairs on head or heart. Squeeze – squeeze the trigger.* The routine was drilled so deeply into him that once he began it his actions would be automatic. He checked through the sights again. Ten minutes, five. He looked west and saw the BMWs coming in: looked east, the black cars snaking through the trees.

'*B'shavia Huzu a b'Yerushalaim.*' Michael Rossini practised the first words he would say officially to the Soviet Jew. 'This year in Jerusalem.'

The snow and the cold seventeen years ago, thought Max Steiner. Ernst Vöckel standing, waiting.

Secure target. Sonntag's response was instinctive.

Langer bending down and helping Shevienko from the car.

'Thank you.' The dissident straightened and shook Langer's hand.

'For what?'

'For giving me time on the plane to say goodbye to Russia. For last night.'

Acquire. The cross-hairs were on Langer's back, on his chest as he turned. The afternoon air was still, no need to allow for drift. Good photofit, Sonntag almost whispered to himself, good information.

Vöckel took Shevienko's arm and led him to the first metal of the bridge. Two o'clock. The Glienicker Bridge. The barrier lifted and Shevienko began the walk.

Squeeze.

'How does it feel, that moment?'

Max Steiner turned and saw Hans-Joachim Schiller standing beside him, looking again at the figure, small, growing larger.

'Like nothing I could describe.'

Pity really, thought Sonntag, and lowered the Dragunov. Five hundred metres away the figure reached the western end of the bridge and the man stepped forward to greet him, the guards closing in, the formal welcome then the BMWs screaming away. Pity Wolf had cancelled it. Not often you got the chance to take out Stasi. At least he knew he could have pulled it off. Lucky he hadn't loaded the mag, though.

BOOK FIVE

CHAPTER ONE

In NOVEMBER 1985, the first summit between President Reagan and General Secretary Gorbachev was held in Vienna. The year which followed was marked by a continually improving relationship between East and West, with Gorbachev openly criticizing what he called the wasted years of the Brezhnev period as well as improving the Soviet record on human rights. To many observers, including Rossini, Schiller and Langer, however, it sometimes appeared as if he was merely building a foundation for what was to follow. In January 1987, as the snows of winter settled across Europe, Gorbachev introduced the twin concepts of glasnost, openness, and perestroika, restructuring.

The interview was at three. At five minutes to the hour the two other officials on the board – a brigadier and a major – assembled in Werner Langer's office. Precisely on the hour the interviewee reported. He was formally welcomed, shaking hands with each of the men who would interview him, and took his place.

'You know the reason for this discussion. My first question is obvious. How do you assess the reform proposals of General Secretary Gorbachev?'

The State Security captain answered in an orderly but noncommittal manner.

The decision that every member of the Party, in every branch of the Party, be subjected to what the Central Committee described as frank and confidential discussions had been taken against a background of swelling reforms in Moscow and pressure for similar reforms in the GDR.

'And how do you assess the reaction of Party Secretary Honecker to these proposals?'

Again the captain answered without committing himself. Berlin was not Moscow, Langer thought as he listened to the man,

Honecker certainly not Gorbachev. After fifteen minutes he thanked the captain and offered him coffee.

When he arrived home that evening Gabi was at a meeting and Nikki was curled in her favourite chair, close to the window overlooking the garden.

A year before, he and Gabi had almost decided to split up and go their separate ways; in the last months, however, they had come to an understanding. She needed him for her social position, and he still needed her for his advancement within the Party. They had therefore agreed to remain together but to lead separate lives.

He poured himself a drink, walked across the room and glanced at the title of the book Nikki was reading. Mikhail Gorbachev: *Perestroika: New Thinking for Our Country and The World.*

'I thought that was banned in East Germany.'

Nikki looked up. 'It is.'

'So how did you get it?'

'Matti Seikmann bought it when she was in Moscow with her parents.'

Matti Seikmann was a school friend of Nikki and the daughter of a member of the Council of Ministers.

'May I ask you something?' Nikki closed the book but did not put it away.

Somewhere in the distance, too far away for him to take notice, he heard the alarm bell. 'Of course.'

'Russia is our ally and Gorbachev is our friend.'

'Yes.'

'So why is a book written by him about the policies he is introducing in his country banned in ours?'

'Why do you think?' He knew it was the wrong reply. Perhaps he was tired, he thought, perhaps he was amazed at the futility of the interview that afternoon.

'Because we're afraid.'

Langer shrugged and went into the kitchen, Nikki close behind him.

'Have you read it?'

'Have I read what?'

'The Gorbachev book.'

Of course I've read it, he almost said. He ignored the question and began to make himself dinner.

'What did you think of it?'

'You know I'm a member of the Party.' He turned on her. 'You know the Party has banned the Gorbachev book. Yet you bring it to my house, which is bad enough. Then you ask me what I think of it.'

'But you brought me back the other Gorbachev writings.'

'They weren't banned.'

'All right. I apologize.'

It wasn't like Nikki to apologize over something about which she felt so strongly, Langer thought.

'You can't comment on what Gorbachev has written, but what do you think of his reforms?'

More like Nikki, he almost smiled. 'I think that many people in this country agree with them.' It was as far as he would commit himself. 'I think that many people would like them here.'

Nikki looked at him, as if accusing him. 'I wonder.'

'You wonder what?'

She was still looking at him. 'I wonder how a man like Gorbachev could grow up in the system, be promoted by it, yet suddenly wish to change it.' It was not what she really intended to say. 'I wonder at what point in his life a man like Gorbachev decides that the system is wrong. How, having made that decision, he stays within the system until he is in a position to bring about the changes he thinks necessary.'

At one the following afternoon Langer reported to the office on the fifth floor and took his place opposite the three generals. Jensch, from Dresden; Heinz Moessner, Dieter Lindner's old rival and champion of Gerhard Meyer, from Leipzig; and Dieter Lindner himself. Lindner was suddenly looking older, Langer thought, the skin below the eyes shading grey and the cough worse.

'Thank you for coming; you know the reason for this discussion.' Lindner lit a cigarette and opened the session.

A charade, a farce to satisfy the idiots at Party headquarters; Langer wondered whether the questions and answers would have been so bland if Nikki had been sitting in his place.

When he returned home that evening Gabi was again out and Nikki was in her room doing her homework. He poured himself a drink and sat in the lounge. Nikki heard him and came downstairs.

'And what did you do at the Finance Ministry today?' The

question was a joke, the way she or Gabi always greeted him when he returned home.

Statistics, he knew he should have replied, continued the joke. Got the exchange rate wrong and wiped out half the country's foreign earnings. 'I had my frank and confidential discussion about the Party.' Why, he would ask himself later. Why did you not say what you always say? Why did you bring up such a subject?

'Who asked you the questions?'

'Three people above me in rank.' As soon as he said it he saw his mistake – *rank* not *grade* – and wondered if she would pick it up.

'And what did they ask you? Did they ask you about Gorbachev? Did they ask you why we don't have perestroika here?'

Nikki always so serious, he thought, so earnest; knew she had missed his blunder. 'They asked me a lot of things.'

They went through for supper.

'It's interesting, isn't it?' It was the way she often began a discussion.

'What's interesting?'

'Socialism. The relationship between the Party and the people.'

This is my daughter, the thought crept upon him. This is not how I planned to spend this evening, yet this is precisely the dialogue Gorbachev is encouraging in Moscow and what the Party is asking its members to have in East Germany. 'Why do you say it's interesting?'

'The Party says that socialism is the result of countless good deeds by millions of people, that it is the transition into the realm of true humanity, equality and fraternity, of peace and freedom.'

He recognized the quote from the 1966 new programme and poured himself another drink. Listened as she talked about the relationship between Party and people, about the need for the Party to protect the people but also to listen to them, to represent them.

What are you thinking, she suddenly asked.

Nothing; he tried to laugh it off. I'm thinking that another girl quoted the document you're now quoting. That she printed her thoughts and distributed them in the apartment blocks on Karl Marx Allee. That we caught her and sent her to prison for seven years.

'And now the Party is asking the people what they mean by

socialism, what they think the Party should do.' Nikki finished eating and pushed her plate aside. 'What the Party itself should be doing. What the Party itself should be.'

'Yes.'

'But what happens if, in their frank and confidential discussions, the Party members say that their definition of socialism is Gorbachev's and not Honecker's? That what they want in East Germany is the perestroika the people are enjoying in Russia?'

'Then the Party will do what its members want.'

'You're sure?'

'Of course I'm sure.'

Six weeks later the two of them travelled to Leipzig. They visited Eva at least three times a year now – Gabi at least made a point of coming once – but each September Werner Langer and his daughter made a special point of attending her birthday. In some ways the visit had become as important as Christmas.

The flat was small and warm, the smells and furniture familiar: the table in the centre of the kitchen, the sideboard and fireplace, the photographs on the wall. Langer sat on the steps overlooking the courtyard while Eva and Nikki unpacked, watching the children playing on the cobbles and waving to one of the women who lived opposite. The men came into the courtyard and he walked down to talk with them.

The supper was sizzling on the stove and the sunlight still shining on the door. Nikki would share a bed with her grandmother and Langer would have the room he had used after his own grandparents had died. Eva brushed the bedcover straight and went into the kitchen. Nikki was standing close to the fireplace looking at the photographs on the wall. As Eva watched she took one down, wiped the last dust from the glass with her sleeve, and looked at it.

'I wish I'd met Grandad.'

'So do I.'

'Was he like my father?'

'Yes.'

'During the war you were living here with his parents?'

'Yes, mine were dead.'

'So this is where my father was born?'
Yes, Eva knew she had to say.

The couple on the corner had the dog-weariness of people who had travelled far.
They were in their fifties, aged before their time. The man had once been tall, now
he was bent slightly, trilby hat and grey suit, the coat covered with dust and the
trousers baggy at the knees. The woman wore a coat over a simple floral dress. Their
shoes were sturdy, as if, when they had set out on their journey, they knew they must
complete it, and the case which the man had rested on the pavement was battered,
the corners reinforced and string tied round it in case the locks burst open.

Christina smiled as she passed them and saw how they appreciated it. For one
moment she thought they were going to ask her something, then the man picked up
the suitcase and they turned away. When she entered the hallway to the flat they were
shuffling along the far side of the square.

Berlin, autumn turning winter, 1945.

Supper was corned beef. They waited for Viktor to come home then sat down to eat.

The knock was hesitant, unsure. Christina pushed her chair back and ran to the
door. Knew you'd make it; she was already seeing her husband, arms round him,
knew you'd make it home to little Hans-Joachim and me.

The couple stood on the landing. The suitcase with the string around it was
between them on the floor and the man held the trilby hat in his hand, over his chest.
'Please, we are looking for Eva Langer.'

Christina felt herself sag. She should have known, she told herself. There were
always rumours when the men were coming. Always the women – herself amongst
them – waited at the station for the trains they hoped were bringing them home.

'Come in.'

Eva recognized them from the photograph and knew they recognized her, saw the
expression in the woman's eyes as she looked at the boy at Eva's side.

'We are Werner's parents. We have come to take you and the child home.'

No one knew what to do or say. It was Viktor who stood first, welcomed them in
and took their case from them. 'You have come far?'

The flat was clean and tidy, he understood the way the woman was looking round,
the two boys happy and well cared for. Saw both the sorrow and the happiness seep
across her face.

'Leipzig.'

'A long way.'

'Train, bus, part of the way we got a lift on a lorry. The rest we walked.'

Eva was still confused, dazed. She stood and kissed them both. So good to meet you at last, one of them was saying, such a pity we could not come when you and Werner married, the war restrictions and everything.

'Before Werner died he sent us little Werner's photograph and asked that if anything happened we should look after you both.' The man searched in the suitcase. 'We've brought the photo with us, and the letter.' He was anxious, uncertain, as if he felt an obligation to prove that they were who they were and that what they saying was the truth.

Viktor laid his hand on the man's arm. 'Later, now you must eat.' He gave them soap and a towel, and Hanni poured water for them to wash their hands.

'This is Werner.' Eva lifted her son from the chair and gave him to the woman. 'Perhaps you'd like to hold him.'

When the meal was over and the plates and dishes cleared, they sat around the table and showed each other the letters Werner had written from the front.

'We've made a room for you and the boy.' Her father-in-law was still anxious to please. 'We have arranged a job for you where Mamma and I work and organized the shifts so that one of us is always at home.'

They were so proud of what they had done, Eva thought, such good people. 'Let me think.' She tried to be sympathetic but knew she had to be honest. 'After Werner died this became my home and these people my family.'

The older woman leant across the table and patted her arm. 'Don't worry. We understand.'

That night Hanni slept with Christina so that the couple could sleep in her room; that night, when she thought everyone was asleep, Eva tiptoed into the kitchen to speak with Viktor. The man was sitting at the table, waiting for her.

'What should I do?'

'Only you can decide that, Eva.'

She listened while he told her what she already knew.

'We are your family, but so are they. We think of you and Werner as part of our family, they think of you and Werner as part of theirs. No side is right and no side is wrong.'

'But Leipzig is so far away. Leipzig is in the Russian zone. What will happen in the future?'

'Who knows what will happen in the future?'

Two mornings later Eva and Werner left, reaching Leipzig five days later. The following morning the three adults gathered wood from the bomb sites and warmed the flat. That afternoon Eva unpacked her case and settled into the small room off the kitchen which they had constructed for her and her son. The last things she packed into her case on the morning she had left Berlin, and the first things she unpacked and placed in position in the flat in Leipzig, that afternoon, were the photographs of her late husband and of Viktor Wischenski.

That evening, when they went to bed, her husband's parents heard her crying and told themselves that she was happy to be with them. When they realized the truth they did not know what to say.

'So this is where my father was born?' Nikki asked again, as if Eva had not heard her the first time.

'Yes, this is where your father was born.'

Nikki took the second photograph from the wall. 'And this is Uncle Viktor.'

Eva smiled. 'Uncle Viktor went with me when I had your father's first photograph taken; I persuaded him to have his taken as well.'

'And what's this?' Nikki hung the photograph on the wall and took down the third.

'That's where Uncle Viktor is buried.'

The girl picked up the photograph and looked at it. 'Shouldn't we put some flowers on it?'

Eva took the photograph from her and put it back in its place. Saw her son standing in the doorway. 'No.'

'Why not?'

'Because we can't.'

When he had been a child he had asked the same questions, Langer remembered. When he had been a child his mother had given him the same answers.

'Not even my father? My father can do anything.'

'No. Not even your father.'

That evening, after Eva and Nikki had returned from their walk and Langer had returned from his Party obligations, the mother and son sat in the kitchen, Nikki asleep in the bedroom, and enjoyed the last of the day.

The innocence of a child, I know, a daughter's belief in her father. Langer saw the question in his mother's eyes. But who are you, my son, what are you that you really can do anything? The birthday wine was on the table, the two glasses beside it.

'Why can't we put flowers on the grave?'

'Because the grave isn't in Leipzig.'

'Where is it?'

'Berlin.'

'Why didn't you tell me? I could have tended it, we could have visited it when you came to stay.'

'West Berlin.'

He poured them each a wine and waited for her to tell him.

'Your father was from Leipzig, I was from Berlin. We met there when he was on leave. We had a flat near the K'Damm. It was small but we made the most of it. During the war it was hard, your father was at the front, Berlin was bombed night and day, often there was no food. There were a number of us who were together, women with children, some without. Viktor was like an uncle to us, a grandfather to you.'

Later he would wonder why she had not told him before.

'Before your father died he wrote to his parents and asked that if he was killed they should take care of us. As soon as they could they came for us.'

'But my birth is registered in Leipzig.' He thought of the official records, the computer files on Lenin-Allee and God knew where else.

'After you were born I went to the town hall and tried to register you. It had been bombed. When we finally came to Leipzig I explained to the clerk and he said it was easier to say you were born here.'

'So I was born in Berlin?'

The flames from the fire were dancing in her eyes. 'Yes.'

It was no problem, he thought; many East Germans had been born in what was now the West, even Honecker himself. 'What about the others?'

'We lost touch.'

'Would you like me to find them again?'

'No.'

He leaned forward and poured them each another glass. 'What about Viktor's grave? Would you like me to put some flowers on it, make sure it's well tended?'

'But it's in the West.'

My dear innocent daughter, he thought. Asleep in her grandmother's bed with her thumb in her mouth and her hair like corn across the pillow. It is I who am the secret policeman, I who know everything about everybody. Yet in the end it is she who tells me what I do not know about myself.

'That would not be a problem.'

363

Eva smiled, as if a great burden had been lifted from her. 'Thank you.'

The following Wednesday afternoon Werner Langer crossed into the West via the S-bahn from Friedrichstrasse. In Uhlandstrasse, off the Kurfurstendamm, he bought a bouquet of flowers, then made his way to Südstern. The cemetery was quiet, the trees round the walls, some of the graves well tended but others neglected and overgrown. For fifteen minutes he walked up and down the rows till he came to the headstone.

Viktor Wischenski. 1894–1948. That he never be forgotten.

He placed the flowers on the grave and stood back.

The leaves were falling on the paths, the first browns and reds amongst the trees. Pity the flowers won't last, pity he hadn't known before. It was not the time to remember autumns and winters gone – his decision was logical and without emotion, built on his bedrock conviction in communism, the need to plan ahead – time only to think of the springs and summers to come. He left the cemetery and returned to the florist shop off the K'Damm. Perennials, he told the assistant, flowers that will bloom throughout the seasons, as many colours as you can imagine and as many as you have.

By the time he returned to the cemetery it was dusk and the gates were closed. He climbed over the railings, went to the grave, and dug the bulbs into the soil.

The meeting on the top floor at Lenin-Allee began at two; present were all senior officers of the Berlin region of the Ministry for State Security. An hour before Dieter Lindner had returned from a special meeting of the MfS Collegiate. Honecker responding to the moves in Moscow, Langer knew, the East German state about to follow the Gorbachev initiatives.

By two thirty the usual bureaucratic items had been cleared from the agenda and they turned to what was understood to be the main reason for calling them together: the confidential first draft of the Party's reaction to its internal enquiry.

Lindner's secretary entered the room and handed them each a photostat copy of the document the General had brought with him from Normannenstrasse. The Party about to announce its acceptance of the reforms initiated in Moscow. Langer opened the report. East Germany about to embark on a new future. He was aware of the growing dissatisfaction that the Party had not yet followed Gorbachev, could hardly not be aware of it, was also aware of how many people had argued for reform in the frank and personal discussions the Party had conducted with each of its members. Now the Party was about to reveal to the people the reforms they wanted; now the Party was about to show the leadership they all knew it possessed.

He skimmed quickly through the pages and tried to read the full wording of the introduction. Motivation was lacking, what it called the climate of trust was being weakened. Correct, he thought. The people still needed convincing that the Party had their interests at heart. Correct again. He turned to the recommendations.

In line with such conclusions the powers and resources of State Security would be expanded. The Ministry would seek more powers to deal as it saw fit with the subversive activities revealed by the Party's questioning of its members, and the Party itself would impose what it referred to as more demanding requirements on State Security.

The meeting moved from generalities to specifics. Item one: the financing of the additional resources to meet the expansion in power of State Security. Item two: surveillance of party members now considered unreliable or disloyal. Item three: increase in informant networks. Item four: additional remote control surveillance cameras at key points in the city. Item five: enlargement of departments to deal with the anticipated increase in information. Item six: further reduction of rights of individuals who had applied to leave the country and been refused. Item seven . . .

Michael Rossini's trip to Washington was part business and part pleasure. For the first five days he attended briefings at both the State Department and the White House on the implications for America and Europe of the new liberalism in Moscow, as well as the gradual build-up of resentment in certain of the Eastern bloc countries that such reforms were being denied them. Present at two of the meetings, he noted with interest and not a little pleasure, was the former agent code-name Mateus. On the sixth day he visited CIA headquarters at Langley. During the evenings of these days, as well as at two working breakfasts and a lunch, he had also held meetings with members both of the Senate and the House of Representatives.

Amongst the obvious topics for discussion was the direction of American politics now that the Reagan era was drawing to an end, the probable outcome of the presidential elections in November, and the new appointments which would follow. The lobbying was beginning – it was one of the reasons for the scheduling of his return – the power brokers working out the spoils. At State, therefore, he discussed the future of ambassadors appointed by Reagan; at Langley he discussed the future of the CIA and the list of runners from whom an incoming President would choose its new director. With Martin Schumaker, chairman of the Senate Finance Committee and therefore arguably the single most powerful man on the Hill, he discussed both.

On the seventh day he, Sally and Nick junior flew to Manchester, picked up a rental car, and drove to the cabin which his parents had bought when he had been a boy and where they had spent most of their vacations. Six months before they had decided that his father would retire from his legal practice; they would sell the house in Boston, perhaps retaining a small apartment, but aim to spend as much time as possible in the peace and solitude of New Hampshire.

When they arrived the packing cartons were stacked in the garage and the smoke from the barbecue was drifting across the grass and through the trees.

How long do you have, Hanni asked.

Two days then I have to head back.

What about Sally and Nick junior?

They'll stay and help.

On his last morning he stood looking at the cabin. Over the years they had built it up, added a porch on the front and rooms on the back, and made a study for his father.

'What're you thinking?'

'I'm thinking about how good it is here in spring, about the great vacations we had here when I was a kid.'

I'm thinking about another spring in another country twenty years ago this year.

He kissed Hanni and Sally goodbye, shook hands with his father and son, and began the drive back to Manchester. As the car passed through the trees Hanni saw him slow and look back, then the car passed from sight.

'You asked what *he* was thinking.' Nick stood beside her, an arm round her shoulder.

She looked up at him and laughed. 'Just thinking.'

It was six in the morning, still dark outside, three weeks since Eva and Werner had gone to Leipzig. Christina heard the outside door close as Viktor left then the second sound as Hanni left her room and went into the kitchen, heard the scuffle of a chair being knocked over then the retching. She pulled on her dressing-gown and went in to the kitchen. Hanni was bent over the sink, her shoulders bowed and her body shaking.

'*You all right?*'

Hanni tried to nod, looked up. The skin below her eyes was lined with black and the tears were running down her face.

'*How far gone are you?*'

'*Six weeks, almost seven. My last period was due three weeks ago.*' *She folded into Christina's arms, sobbing gently, with sickness or fear Christina did not know.*

'*It's Nick's?*' *She was not sure whether she asked for Hanni or for herself.*

Hanni was sobbing, clinging to her. '*Yes.*'

'*You're sure?*'

Hanni was nodding, face still buried in Christina's dressing-gown so that Christina could hardly hear the answer. '*I stopped with everyone else as soon as I met Nick, had a period after that.*'

The sickness was leaving her. Hanni allowed Christina to guide her to the table, then sat down while the other woman made them coffee. American coffee, she thought, coffee Nick had given them. How will I tell you, Nick? What will you say?

'*How long have you known?*' *Christina sat down.*

'*Since the sickness started. Even after I missed the period I hoped. Not any more.*'

Such a way to greet a child, Christina thought, remembered the day she had told Hans that she was pregnant and the celebration which had followed. '*When are you seeing Nick?*'

'*Tonight.*'

'*And what will you say to him?*'

'*I don't know.*'

The day dragged, drizzling grey, the morning seeming to last for ever then gone, the afternoon endless. At six thirty, when Viktor returned, Hanni told him as she would have told her father.

'*Don't worry.*' *Viktor was understanding, comforting.* '*We'll work it out.*'

Hans-Joachim was looking at her, not understanding why she did not play with him as she usually did.

'What time is Nick coming?'

'Seven. Give me an hour with him alone.'

'What are you going to tell him?'

The buzzing was still in her head and she was lost in panic. 'I still don't know.'

It was already seven. Christina, Viktor and Hans-Joachim left the flat and walked to the street. As they turned out of the square Nick's jeep passed them. Something's happened, Christina saw the expression on his face; God knows how but he knows.

Hanni sat at the table, elbows resting on the top and her head in her hands. Her hair was unkempt and her face was red from crying. 'I'm pregnant.' She looked at him only once, as she began to speak, so that by the time she finished the words were lost in a tangle of hair and tears.

'I'm going home.' He had thought all day about what he would say and how he would say it.

'When?' she asked. Heard only half of what he had said.

'Next week.' He was confused: by the way she had been sitting at the table when he came in, by her reaction to what he had told her, what he had asked her. 'What do you mean, you're pregnant?' It was as if her words had only just registered.

'It's yours, Nick. I know it's yours.' She left the table, almost knocking over the chair and went to her room, came back with the makeshift calendar and pencil stub. 'Look, Nick.' She was pointing at the calendar, marking the dates with the pencil, desperate, anxious. 'This is when I met you.' The pencil was thick, its mark heavy. 'The next week I had my period.' He was trying to stop her, take the pencil from her. The degradation was coming upon her again, the disgust and loathing she had felt when she had stood in the Kurfurstendamm and bartered over the price of her body.

'I know that you had a period then. I know there's been no one since.' He stopped her, held her hands firmly so that she couldn't move them. 'You didn't hear a word I said, did you?'

'No.'

'I'm going home to America. I want you to come with me.'

Perhaps it was Nikki's distaste, almost disdain, after the visit to Neunkirchen. Perhaps the girl on the Olympic rostrum with the tears of pride rolling down her face and the single detail about her mother and father that nobody was allowed to know. Perhaps it was the taste of the Moscow spring still lingering in his mouth. Langer stood at the bottom of the road and waited for the convoy.

The visit to Neunkirchen, the old steel town in the Saar, had been planned with precision. Erich Honecker's return to the town where he had been born. The two hours with the sister who still lived in the area and the silent minutes at the family grave, the television cameras capturing Honecker's genuine emotions.

But Neunkirchen is in *West* Germany, Nikki had argued.

The trip lasted only a few hours and was added to the end of a state visit to Bonn, he had felt obliged to argue back.

It doesn't matter, Nikki had borne down on him. How many East Germans have families and relatives there but are not allowed to visit them, how many East Germans were born in the West and would like to go home just once before they die? Honecker was using his power and his position to do something which he denies to every other person in this country.

You're wrong, he had argued, was aware of the first anger. Not an emotional or reactive anger, but cold and logical. Felt it again the night of the victory ceremony on television. The 1988 Olympics, the girl on the rostrum clutching the gold medal in her hand, the tears flowing down her face and the pride in her eyes as the red, black and gold flag was raised and the anthem played. Her mother and father denied permission to be present at the greatest moment in their daughter's life because of a rumour from a third-rate informant.

The convoy appeared at the top of the road, the lead car flashing its lights and the MfS shadows and police suddenly alert, the local branch secretary warning the shopkeepers.

There were more important matters, of course. The continuing demand for reform, even amongst Party members; the mounting crackdown but, conversely, the increase in reform demands which this itself produced. The people expressing their opposition more openly, leading to more arrests, support for the protesters coming from more and more places, including the Church. All triggered by the changes in Moscow and Honecker's iron insistence on maintaining the status quo.

Something wrong with the system, he knew Nikki would have said. But what could be wrong with a system which guaranteed housing and free medical attention, which gave its people education and jobs, he would have replied. Something wrong with the application of the system then, Nikki would have countered. Nothing wrong, and if there was, he would have conceded, though only to himself and then only when he sat alone at night with the glass of whiskey in his hand, then the Party would put it right.

The car radios crackled with instructions and the earpieces of Honecker's personal guards buzzed with fresh information. As abruptly as he had arrived the General Secretary left the shops and the convoy screamed away.

The appointment was at twelve. At ten thirty Hans-Joachim Schiller rose from his desk, pulled on the jacket of his suit, and left his office. As he walked through the outer room where his personal staff worked the men and women he had gathered round him over the years stood and watched. Two foxes in German history, they remembered: Rommel, the Desert Fox, and Schiller, the Fox from the Berlin Wall.

His shadow and driver were waiting. The Mercedes slid out of the security compound and turned for Bonn. It was snowing, the wipers flicking the flakes from the windscreen. At midday exactly he was shown into the Chancellor's office.

'Thank you for coming.' The Chancellor rose to greet him; they shook hands and sat down. An aide poured them each a coffee then left the room.

'As you are aware, the Director-General of the BfV retires next month.' The Chancellor was a large man, barely fitting behind the desk. 'It is my honour today formally to advise you that you have been appointed to take his place.'

A long way from the first escapes through the wire at Kommand-ante Allee, Schiller thought, twenty years since the decision to leave that world and enter counter-intelligence. 'Thank you, Chancellor.'

For the next hour they discussed the organization, the changes which Schiller would wish to introduce and the appointments he would wish to make.

'There is one other item we should discuss.' It was time for the Chancellor to leave. 'I myself wish to appoint a new personal adviser on security and intelligence, responsible for briefing me on overall matters. The appointment, of course, in no way diminishes your responsibility.'

'Of course.' The move was a continuation extension of existing practice. 'May I ask who?'

'Rolf Hanniman.'

A good day, Schiller thought, for himself, for everyone. 'I'm sure we'll be able to work together.'

'I'm sure you've had enough practice in the past.' The Chancellor shared the joke.

'When will you see him?'

'Tomorrow. I wanted you to know first.'

That evening Schiller spoke to Anja and Lisa on the telephone, the next day he lunched with Rolf Hanniman. At nine that morning Hanniman had been informed by the Chancellor of his new appointment. Though both men still preferred to drink beer when they met socially, that lunchtime they drank champagne. The next day Hanniman and his wife were going skiing. The topic had slipped naturally into the conversation when they had stopped discussing official matters, though even that discussion was limited for security reasons.

'Why not join us?' he suddenly asked. 'Even for a weekend.'

'Let me think about it. Where're you going?'

'A small place in Switzerland.'

'What's it called?'

'Lenk.'

'Never heard of it.'

'Exactly, neither has anyone else.'

Langer left Berlin at eleven; by two he was in Zurich, by three he was sure he was not being followed. At four he caught the Zurich-Berne express, leaving the train at Spiez and taking the branch line west, up the Simmen valley. The late afternoon was dark, the light failing fast and the fields and mountains an eerie white. In midweek the train was almost empty, only a handful of workmen going home and a few couples. At Zweisimmen he changed trains, waiting fifteen minutes for the connection. It was snowing again, the line following the river up the valley and the mountains suddenly lost in the black. At seven thirty the train reached the village of Lenk. He ignored the single cab waiting at the side of the station and walked to the hotel. The following morning he took the gondola to the Middle Station. The restaurant was quiet, almost deserted. Rolf Hanniman was waiting at a table in the corner.

*

The snow was knee-high in the park. Anja and Lisa finished the snowball fight, laughing and falling over each other, then shook themselves dry and ran to where Christina and Lutz were watching them. Each Sunday now they spent time with Christina and Lutz, took lunch with them whenever they could. It had stopped snowing, the day warm and the sky a brilliant blue. They left the park and began the walk to the car, Lutz and Lisa in front, Christina and Anja trailing behind.

'Lisa's well.'

'She's almost over it. Sometimes she gets depressed, but most of the time she's fine.'

They walked arm in arm, both of them looking at Lisa. The colour was back in her face and the laugh was in the eyes. Thank God for Werner, Anja had often thought, thank God that he had never come back.

'There's something you and Lutz should know. Hans-Joachim and I are getting divorced.' The week before he had telephoned and told her of his new job; the following evening they had spoken again and discussed the future. 'No one else is involved and everything is amicable. Lisa knows that she can spend as much time with her father as she wants.'

They walked on, the snow glistening in the branches above them and crackling beneath their feet.

'Sometimes it's necessary to know when to stop.' Christina smiled at her. 'Sometimes, however important something is, it's necessary to know when it's come to its natural end.'

The water ran along the top of the skirting board and the plaster was cracked. The families in the flat above had rigged a tarpaulin in the roof space, providing them with some protection but diverting the rain and snow which penetrated the roof down the side walls and on to the landing and stairs. The winter light poured through the gaping holes which they had mended only months before. Lutz checked the corners where the four walls met, then dropped back through the trap-door to the landing.

'Looks bad.'

They returned the ladder to the yard and went to the flat. The windows were stuffed with newspaper and wood where the glass had fallen out, the doors no longer shut properly because of the way the building was beginning to tilt, and the cracks were widening along the walls and ceiling. The electricity was off and the room was cold. The fire was laid but they did not light it, kept their coats on.

Christina poured the last of the coffee from the Thermos flask and sat with Lutz at the table. They were both wearing coats, the scarves tied round their necks. It was mid morning; Hans-Joachim was at school.

'It can't stand up much longer.' *Lutz had spent an hour in the roof space.* 'The side and end walls have come away from each other and the roof has had it.'

The winter seeped through Christina's coat and into her bones. Her feet were cold and her shoulders and back were stiff and aching.

'I've found a flat.' *Lutz looked at her.* 'The people who lived there have gone West and I know the landlord. It needs work on it, but it's dry and the building is safe. I'd like you and Hans-Joachim to come with me.'

'You're sure?'

Hans-Joachim and I would come with you anyway, even if there was no roof and we had to sleep on the floor.

'I wouldn't have asked you if I wasn't.'

Her shoulders were curled against the cold; Christina stood up and left the table.

'I also think we should get married.'

'I'll talk to Hans-Joachim this afternoon.'

'I've already talked to him.'

She began to laugh, knelt in front of the fireplace.

'What are you doing?'

'I'm fed up with the cold, I'm lighting the fire.'

They never lit the fire until the afternoon, until they were all in the flat. Her neck was tight with tension and her fingers trembled as she tried to strike a match. Lutz stood close to her and undid the top button of her coat, stroked her neck and shoulders. She felt the tip of his fingers, the tension draining away and the tingling which took its place, running down her spine and through her body.

Hanni, Nick and little Mike safe and well in America, she thought, Eva and Werner happy in Leipzig. Viktor dead and the flat in which they had shared their lives about to fall down. She would break the chain now, let them go their way and she and Hans-Joachim and Lutz would go theirs. She turned and put an arm round him, kissed him.

'Of course I'll marry you.'

The ice was spread across the copper roof of the Berliner Dom and the water flowing under the Marx-Engels Bridge was grey and cold. Werner and Gabi Langer glanced at the flurries of snow and hurried up the steps and into the Opera House. Tomorrow would be Christmas Eve; tonight, after the performance, they would dine out. They handed their overcoats to an attendant and went upstairs to where the reception was being held. The room was crowded and warm; most of the people present were known to them. As soon as they entered a waiter offered them champagne; they each took a glass and joined one of the groups. They had been talking for fifteen minutes, mingling with the other guests, when the five-minute warning bell rang and they drifted towards the auditorium. As they left the room an attendant confirmed Langer's identity and handed him a note. The other guests were moving past them, out the door. Langer read the note, folded it and put it in his pocket.

'Something's happened.' He took Gabi aside. 'I'll be back by the interval.'

'What?'

He saw the anger on her face. 'Dieter Lindner's been taken to hospital.'

The ward was quiet, the screens round the man in the corner and the doctors in constant attendance, the security guards discreet. Langer looked at the array of tubes and wires connected to Lindner's body and the oxygen mask on his face.

'What's wrong?'

'What do you think?' The doctor barely had time to look up at him. 'How many does he smoke a day?'

Fifty to sixty, Langer would have replied if it had been necessary. The telephone was ringing at the nursing station. The doctor moved round the bed and Langer stepped back to allow him space.

'If you want me to wait outside.'

'There's nothing you can do here.'

Langer stepped outside and looked for a chair. The sister came down the ward and saw him, knew it must be him – the only person in the ward wearing a dinner suit. 'You're wanted on the telephone.'

Only one person would be calling, he knew; only one reason why. He walked to the desk.

'How is he?'

He knew that Mielke was telephoning from the opera. 'Stable.'

'Will he pull through?'

'Yes.'

There was a pause. 'Until he returns to work I assume you will take charge.'

'Of course.'

*

Two weeks later, three days into the New Year, Langer was invited
to attend his first meeting of the Collegiate of State Security. Two
days before, the reports on the items to be discussed by the Collegiate, plus the accompanying appendices from all Stasi regions, were
delivered to him. That evening, after Gabi and Nikki had gone to
bed, he sat alone, the glass of whiskey in his hand, and familiarized
himself with them.

Decline in industrial output and Party membership; increase in
resentment due to lack of reforms and a rise in the number of
people applying to leave the GDR for the West. Pollution of the
environment, dissatisfaction amongst local managers at centralized
control from Berlin. Above all increasing unrest that the reforms
which were sweeping Russia were being denied them in East Germany. And the Church. Always and increasingly the Church.

He placed the glass on the arm of the chair. This is an area of
unrest – he was surprised at the frankness of many of the reports –
present or future, actual or potential. There are two ways of dealing
with it: either put right the basic cause or prepare now to face the
unrest which will follow if you do not. Between the lines, of course,
never clear and in the open. The reports written by intelligent men
and women, high-ranking State Security officers like himself.

The next evening, as he had done every evening since Christmas,
he drove to the hospital. For the first time since he had been admitted, Lindner was sitting up in bed, propped against the pillows. His
face was pale, almost a sheen on it, and his eyes were tired. When
he shook Langer's hand his own seemed large yet without substance, no indication in it of its former strength. For an hour they
sat together, sometimes talking, sometimes not.

'You're attending the Collegiate tomorrow?'

'Yes.'

'You've received the reports and appendices?'

For the first time since he had met him, Langer was suddenly
aware, Lindner was not chain-smoking. 'Yes.'

'Interesting reading?'

'Very.'

Lindner was growing tired. Langer told him that he would visit
him the following evening, after the Collegiate meeting, and rose to
leave.

'Give my regards to Moessner.' The smile was thin; even in the
past hour Lindner seemed to have shrunk a little, his body lost in

the white of the bed and his head frail on the pillows.

They both knew what Moessner would do and say at the meeting, how he would make a public point of welcoming Langer and offering his best wishes to Lindner, how he and Meyer would be conspiring against them both.

'Of course.'

By the time he returned home Gabi and Nikki had gone upstairs. He wished them each goodnight and sat reading through the reports again and planning what he would say if called upon to comment the following day. The old guard and the new, just as in Moscow. Yet perhaps the days of the old guard were numbered.

The Twelfth Congress of the Party was due in the spring after next, the spring of 1991; the elections to district, city, ward and parish assemblies also due within the next fifteen months. Then the people would have the chance to say what they thought about the Party; then the people would have the chance to respond to the crackdown following the Party's so-called democratic searching of its soul; then Honecker and the Party would begin to introduce the reforms the people wanted. He almost laughed. These are the thoughts which the Party considers a threat to state security. And those who have such thoughts are those whom the Party requires you to hunt down and arrest.

It was gone one. Perhaps it was a noise, carried on the night, perhaps a smell. In the deepest well of his mind – so deep it was almost subconscious – he saw a schoolroom, red-brick and poor, the fumes belching from the stove in the corner and the parents gathering outside. He unfolded himself from the chair and splashed more whiskey into the glass.

The meeting of the Collegiate was scheduled for ten, in the conference room adjoining Erich Mielke's suite on the first floor of House One in the MfS complex on Normannenstrasse, those generals resident outside East Berlin arriving in the city the evening before. Langer had been at work in Lenin-Allee since seven. At nine fifteen he put on the jacket of his suit and stood stiffly while his secretary brushed the last speck of dust from it. A long way from the NCO watching West German television with his stockinged feet on a barrack bunk and the Party delegation aghast behind him, he thought.

At nine twenty he left his inner office. Outside stood the men and women he had personally recruited and promoted over the years, a number of them coming from other MfS offices in the Berlin region to witness the moment. Langer, the youngest ever Stasi general. Langer, the youngest general ever to attend the Collegiate. One of the front runners for Mielke's job when he finally resigned. Already there had been suggestions that in the next elections Langer would be returned to the People's Chamber, opening his way to the General Council of the Party and from there to the Council of Ministers. Already there was talk of candidate membership of the politburo.

The Volvo was waiting. At twenty-five minutes to ten the car swung off Normannenstrasse and slowed for the barrier into the headquarters of State Security.

The complex itself was structured round an inner square, each side some four hundred metres long, with more buildings in the centre. Two sides were modern, grey-chip concrete and security-glassed, one of them – below which Langer now entered – housing Marcus Wolfe's foreign intelligence directorate, with its tower blocks reaching into the sky. The other two sides, along Frank-furter-Allee and the street at the rear, were older and appeared – from the outside at least – to contain apartments. In the centre of the square were more buildings, again grey and featureless, and the entire area was patrolled by armed guards and under constant video surveillance. The guards at the barrier were waiting. As the Volvo turned the barrier was raised and they snapped to attention.

In the centre of the complex – visible from the road if anyone dared to look, or knew what they were looking for – stood the building known as House One, the administrative and political head of the Ministry. Langer's driver drove the hundred metres to the block, swung slightly right then left behind the brick wall which prevented those arriving at House One from being seen.

Langer acknowledged the salutes of the guards clustered around him, and walked briskly up the steps, through the two sets of glass doors and into the reception area. The floor was marbled, the bronzes of Lenin and Dzerzhinsky to his left and the security desk to his right. The paternoster lift was also on the left – no doors and continually moving, one lift ascending and the other descending. He stepped on, staring straight ahead as the platform rose past the mezzanine floor, and stepped off on the first. The aide was waiting for him.

He turned left, through the first set of doors, past what he knew to be the conference room, and turned into the lounge area joining it. The other members of the Collegiate were already present, some sitting and drinking coffee, others standing and turning to welcome him.

At two minutes to ten they left the lounge area and went through the connecting door to the conference room. The room itself was simply decorated, windows down the right side as they now entered, dark wood panelling down the left, and the end walls lightly painted. The conference table which occupied the centre of the floor was T-shaped, three chairs at the head – the centre chair for Mielke and those on either side for two of the four deputy ministers at Normanennstrasse – and eight down each side – fifteen for the regional generals and the sixteenth for the overseas directorate.

Because he was the newest member of the Collegiate and because he was merely standing in for Lindner, Langer had assumed he would be placed near the bottom of the table. To his surprise, however, he was seated close to the top, only three chairs from Mielke himself, on the right side. The position which came with the power of the Berlin region, he partly assumed; the position which indicated a grooming for the place at the top.

Mielke opened the meeting, formally introducing the agenda.

'With your permission, gentlemen, may I say something before we start.' Moessner looked round their table, ensuring himself of the support of those present. 'May I welcome General Langer to his first meeting of the Collegiate, and may I express my sincerest best wishes to General Lindner on a speedy recovery.'

There were grunts of approval.

Right on cue, Langer thought. 'Thank you, General. Both sentiments are most appreciated.'

Moessner nodded and the meeting continued.

Most of those present were old men, grey-suited and grey-faced. Men who had shown loyalty and allegiance through the years, not just to the Party but to Mielke personally. Mittad from Magdeburg was speaking, commenting on the membership reports. Shoulders hunched and elbows on the table, hands clasped. Seventy years of age and a Miekle confidant from the beginning. Jensch from Dresden on the question of industrial output and the problems arising from it, thin face accentuating his bushy eyebrows.

'General Langer.' Erich Mielke looked from his desk. 'Perhaps you would care to comment.'

Langer had prepared a statement on each of the issues likely to be raised. Some, he began, might find it interesting that General Jensch had concerned himself with the issue of falling output. Dangerous ground; he sensed the frisson and saw Moessner smile: the Industry Minister is a friend of Mielke, as is Jensch himself. He himself also found it interesting, Langer continued, because it was precisely the type of issue to which the MfS should address itself.

Across the table Jensch nodded his approval.

Why, Langer knew Mielke was going to ask.

'It is not sufficient for State Security to deal with problems after they have arisen, it is also necessary to identify them in advance. It is not the role of State Security to give the Party solutions to problems like falling output, of course. What is important, however, is for State Security to be seen to be aware what is happening in the nation.' He continued in the same vein, summarizing and analysing, but never passing judgment, always the perfect technocrat.

So what *were* you saying, he asked himself when he sat alone at home that night. Where *do* you stand on the reforms so many people now believe we should inherit from Moscow but which the leadership is holding back? How much *did* he enjoy the power of entering Normannenstrasse that morning? he was aware he was also thinking. How much *had* he savoured the moment he had taken his seat on the Collegiate?

The following week Erich Honecker announced that he was bringing the Twelfth Party Congress forward from spring 1991 to spring 1990, next spring. The elections to district, city, ward and parish assemblies would also be held early.

Honecker setting up an occasion at which he would announce his retirement, the West German press speculated. Honecker preparing the ground for reform, Langer told Nikki that evening, planning to use the elections and the public forum of the congress to begin to make changes, bring some of the reformers like Hans Modrow, Party chief of Dresden, into the politburo. Honecker planning to use the spring to introduce perestroika to East Germany.

Dieter Lindner was thinner, weaker. His body was rested against the pillows and his eyes were yellow and watery. When he spoke it was as if his lungs could barely support the effort, and every thirty minutes he was given oxygen.

'So Honecker's brought forward the congress.' Sometimes it was an effort for Lindner to speak, as if he had to muster both his breath and his strength. 'The elections brought forward a year to this spring.' His head was nodding as if he had been giving the subject considerable thought. He propped himself up. 'You've seen the Collegiate report to the politburo by now, of course.'

Each week Mielke presented to the politburo a summary of the previous Collegiate's deliberations and the subjects discussed.

'Of course.'

'Still interesting reading?' The shrewdness had not gone from the voice.

None of the issues identified as problems in the MfS reports from the regions had been included. 'Very.'

Lindner relaxed for a few moments. Along the ward there was a hum of conversation and the slightly sharper voices of the nurses. 'And how is little Nikki?'

The snow had given way to rain, low and hard, cutting across the concrete bleakness of Alexanderplatz and down Unter den Linden towards the Brandenburg Gate. Remote-control surveillance cameras on the university and the library, Langer noted, as well as on most of the buildings in East Berlin, the grid covering sixty per cent of the inner city and the departments concerned working flat out. The country's answer to glasnost and perestroika.

He helped Gabi out of the official car and escorted her into the reception room off the banqueting hall of the Party headquarters. The annual presentation to Erich Mielke, the sort of occasion Gabi loved. The politburo and the Collegiate of State Security standing in two lines, lesser politicians and officials behind them, Erich Honecker in front. Mielke entered the room and they began to clap.

The Twelfth Congress and the May elections, he had told Nikki, then things will change.

The system is corrupt, she had argued back, the system is now a shell, built by and around Honecker and his clique to keep themselves in power. Honecker will not go in 1990, Honecker will tell the congress how wonderful socialism in the GDR is and everyone will applaud him.

The elections will begin the change, he had insisted.

Honecker will use the results to say he has one hundred per cent support she had rounded on him. In any case, why bother about the elections when we both know that the vote is compulsory and there is only one list of candidates. To vote for them all you have to do is collect your ballot paper and put it in the box. But to vote against them you have to go into the booth and cross their names off the list, so that everyone can see what you're doing.

Mielke was dressed in a light blue suit, thin-faced and smiling with satisfaction; Honecker also smiling. The General Secretary hung the medal round his security chief's neck and shook his hand, both men beaming. There was another round of clapping and Honecker and Mielke embraced then straightened. Two old men congratulating each other and pinning medals on each other's wheezing chests, Langer suddenly thought. Both of them fine young men in their time, fighting for what they believed in, now their time was gone. The ceremony ended and they went to the reception which followed it.

That evening, after Gabi and Nikki had gone to bed, Langer sat alone, the glass of whiskey on the arm of the chair and the games playing in his brain. What if change was both necessary and inevitable? He set out the parameters. But what if Honecker and the system prevented that change? How could someone – anyone – bring it about, assuming change was desirable? What conditions would have to be met – or created – to make such change possible?

The sound was a ghost in the night air. The schoolroom lost in the winter dark and the noise from inside of children and parents singing and laughing.

Dieter Lindner was looking better. There was a hint of colour in his face and his breathing and voice were stronger. On the table at the side of his bed was a vase of fresh flowers. The ward was on the ground floor, a conservatory off the far end facing on to the grounds. Lindner sat on the edge of the bed, swung his feet on to the floor and pulled on a dressing-gown and slippers.

'You want to sit outside for a while?'

'I thought we could.'

A nurse brought a wheelchair to the bedside. Langer saw the

way Lindner looked at it and knew how he himself would have reacted. 'We'll walk.'

The conservatory was warm. They sat in wicker chairs at the end furthest from the door and looked out on to the garden, the lawn and grounds illuminated in the evening dark.

'Nikki's a bright girl, we had a very good talk.' It was said with more emphasis than earlier. 'She's a good thinker.' The glance across was deliberate and the meaning clear. Like me when I was her age, like you when you were a young man. He raised his head slightly, as if he was looking into the black beyond the circle of lights. 'Don't ever forget to watch Moessner and Meyer, will you? Don't ever give them even half a chance.'

'Don't worry.'

'Good.'

Langer was staring into the darkness, aware of the sudden silence. 'Would you like a last cigarette?'

There was no answer. Lindner's chin was on his chest, and the chest was no longer moving.

The doctor was staring at them from the doorway; he was in his late twenties, his name tag on his lapel and his white coat hanging loose.

'General Lindner is sleeping.' Langer rose and stood in front of him. 'He is not to be disturbed for at least one hour.' The move of the head, taking in the doctor's name tag, was deliberate. 'After that time you personally are to deal with him. You understand what I'm saying.'

The doctor nodded. 'I'll see to it.'

'Good man. I need a telephone.'

'My office.' The doctor called a nurse and began his guard.

The room was along the corridor. Langer closed the door, dialled Normannenstrasse and confirmed that General Mielke was in the private suite off his office. Then he telephoned Lenin-Allee and spoke to the colonel who was his aide. It was nine o'clock.

'A meeting in my office at ten.'

'Tonight or tomorrow morning?'

'Tonight.' He dictated the list of senior officers in the Berlin region of State Security who were to attend.

'Which floor?' Since Lindner's illness Langer had operated both out of his own office on the fifth and Lindner's on the ninth.

'Ninth.'

He left the hospital and drove to Normannenstrasse, waiting for the barrier into the complex to be lifted and instructing the officer in charge to inform General Mielke that General Langer wished to see him. When he entered the reception area of House One an aide was waiting. The captain escorted him to the secretariat office on the first floor, knocked on the door to Mielke's office which led off it, and stood aside to allow Langer to enter, closing the door after him.

The office was panelled with light oak, Mielke's desk against the far end, a small conference table beneath the windows on the right, a chair at each end and four down each side, and five armchairs round a low circular table on the left. Mielke was seated at his desk, the bust of Lenin on the right and the portrait of Dzerzhinsky on the wall behind, next to the panelling which concealed his private safe.

As Langer entered he rose, shook his hand, and offered him a whiskey. Langer accepted, taking the glass though declining the offer to sit.

'I thought it right to tell you personally. Dieter Lindner died twenty minutes ago.'

Mielke nodded. Moessner ready to move as soon as Lindner died, Langer knew, could guess what Moessner had probably already recommended to Mielke: Moessner himself to Berlin as head of the region. Meyer, his number two in Leipzig, promoted to number one. Langer also promoted but moved to Brandenburg or Dresden, anywhere as long as it was outside the power of the Berlin fiefdom.

Langer raised his glass. 'General Lindner. A sword of the Party and a shield of the people.' It was an adaptation of the phrase Mielke himself liked to quote to describe the role of State Security.

'General Lindner.' Mielke raised his own glass. 'A sword and a shield.' He downed the drink, poured them each another, and waited for Langer to make his move, as he knew he would.

'When Dieter Lindner was taken ill, you said that you assumed I was taking over from him in his absence.' Langer was looking straight at Mielke. 'I therefore assume that, for the security of the state, I am taking over from General Lindner permanently.'

The Berlin region, Mielke understood. Lindner's major-general-ship and a full seat on the Collegiate. To be confirmed now, before Moessner even knew of Lindner's death. Langer's men probably already summoned to the office on the ninth floor on Lenin-Allee. Exactly as Lindner would have played it, as he himself would have done. Even the reference to the security of the state.

'Yes.'

'With your permission, therefore, and because of the great loyalty which the Berlin region had to General Lindner, I have ordered a meeting of key members of the region this evening, to inform them of his death.'

Before tonight there had been two contenders for his job when he finally laid aside the responsibility for maintaining the security of the nation, Mielke knew. Now the decision had been made. 'Of course.' He held out his hand. 'Thank you for giving me the news personally.'

The Washington morning was cold and brisk. Over the past week Ronald Reagan had closed his eight years of presidency with a series of parties in and around the White House. At ten thirty that morning his successor took the oath of office on Capitol Hill.

In the weeks that followed the new President began to prepare the series of nominations of those whom he wished Congress to confirm for the offices of state. On some even the initial debates were not merely bitter but public, considered by all concerned to be damaging not only to the individuals involved, but to the nation. On the issue of the new Director of Central Intelligence, however, the first discussions between White House and Congress were conducted not on the floors of the Hill but in private meetings between the representatives of each, as well as of the intelligence world itself.

At first there had seemed two front runners – the first an insider nomination, already a deputy director, and the second described by observers as a political ally of the incoming President. Both, however, had been discarded almost immediately. What was needed, said CIA headquarters at Langley, was a man with experience in the field, someone who understood the problems; what was needed, countered the White House, was a man with administrative experience who would hold the Company back from its sometimes more colourful ambitions. What was needed, suggested State, was someone with a special understanding of international politics, particularly of the new world being created by the changes in the Soviet Union. What was needed, Langley came back immediately, was someone with the steel to take advantage of those changes.

During the third weekend of the New Year the consensus began to form. What was needed, the various sides agreed, was someone who had served his country well during the previous administration but who had not been tarnished by issues like Irangate, El Salvador and the Beirut hostages fiasco. What was needed was someone who could be relied upon in an emergency, someone with proven foresight and vision. By Sunday evening the leaks began, on the Monday morning the *Washington Post* carried the names of two new front runners, on the Tuesday the *New York Times* reported that the President had invited the American ambassador in Bonn to the White House. On the Wednesday evening Michael Rossini was nominated Director of Central Intelligence.

The operation was low-key and unimportant. Langer only knew of it because he was passing through the department when the team went out. School teacher, fingered by an informant; MfS had arranged for a dental check-up for his daughter. While the husband was at school and the wife was guaranteed out of the house State Security would let themselves in and plant the material the People's Police would find when they searched the couple's flat that evening.

Nikki was waiting for him when he returned home. She seemed agitated, almost uncertain. After thirty minutes she told him. 'Matti Seikmann escaped to the West yesterday.'

'I know.'

'How?'

'It was mentioned.'

Matti Seikmann was the daughter of a member of the Council of Ministers. The previous afternoon she had crossed to the West using the privileges afforded her, then telephoned her parents and informed them that she did not intend to return. For the past twenty-four hours Langer's men had been scouring West Berlin for her.

'You knew Matti well, didn't you?' She gave you the Solzhenitsyn and Gorbachev books, he meant, you were at school together, you used to talk about glasnost and perestroika with her.

'Sort of.' Nikki sat opposite him, blonde hair to her shoulders, sweater and denims.

'Why did she go?'

'She was tired of the system.'

'But her family was part of the system, the system gave her everything.'

Nikki nodded, shrugged, said nothing.

'Are *you* tired of the system?'

A nod.

'Did you know Matti was going?'

Yes again.

'So why didn't you go with her?'

'Not because I was afraid of getting caught.' Her voice was raised, the edge of anger in it, as if she suspected her father had thought that was the reason.

'I know that.' So why didn't you go with her, the question remained.

'If you don't like the system there are two things you can do.'

This is what Anja said when she was your age, he thought, this is why she went to prison. Careful, my little thing, she saw it in his eyes. Careful because you don't know what you're saying or where it will lead you.

'Either you can leave or you can change the system.'

The night was dark, two in the morning. Langer refilled the glass and sat down again in the armchair. So how could someone change the system? The game began again as it did every night now. Obvious how someone would do it, he thought. Obvious, at least, how someone would create the circumstances under which change was possible.

What game are you playing? he asked himself. Why are you playing it? Because it was his job, he told himself. His responsibility was to counter people who played such games, and in order to fulfil that responsibility it was necessary to play the game himself.

He heard the sounds and saw the faces – the children and their parents in the classroom. It was a long time ago; he could tell by their haircuts and clothes, by the classroom itself; 1949, the party to celebrate the birth of the nation, the founding of East Germany. The schoolroom decorated, the food which the parents had prepared on the tables at one end and the stage at the other. The teacher introducing the magician and the magician scouring the faces for Anja's mother.

The results of the communal elections announced by the Council of State before Christmas were available within twelve hours of the polls closing. Official returns reported a 98.77 per cent turnout, with 98.85 per cent of the votes in favour of the candidates put forward by the so-called National Front, the umbrella grouping of the ruling Socialist Unity Party and the four other approved political parties.

That evening Nikki confronted him as Langer knew she would.

The validity of the vote had been challenged immediately by Church leaders, she said. In Berlin, she quoted the Church figures, the true turnout was 12 per cent lower, and the vote in favour of the government candidates 7 per cent lower.

You're wrong, he told her, the Church is wrong.

The true turnout was almost 20 per cent lower, he did not say, the vote in favour of government candidates 14 per cent less than what the people have been told.

Two weeks later, on the closing afternoon of the Twelfth Party Congress, Langer watched as Erich Honecker addressed the delegates. The speech lasted for eighteen minutes short of four hours; in it Honecker talked of the achievements of socialism in the GDR, and the great debt owed by the people to the Party. At the end he received the customary roses and standing ovation. At no point did he even mention reform.

A month before Heinz Moessner had moved from Leipzig to Normannenstrasse to take charge of the directorate which included D20, the new collation department, and Gerhard Meyer had been appointed Stasi chief in Leipzig in his place.

In Moscow the system was changing. In Poland Solidarity had been legalized and constitutional reforms were under way. In Czechoslovakia spring had been marked by demonstrations and the inevitable arrests. In Hungary the new parliament had begun the debate which was expected to lead to a full multi-party system. In East Germany, however, the system was going backwards, digging itself in. In East Germany the people running the system were tightening their grip upon it.

Even himself, Langer knew. The system admitting to him that it was corrupt, telling him how corrupt it was – the election results, the Collegiate reports still not being submitted to Honecker and his politburo. Yet at the same time the system asking him to perpetuate that corruption, sucking him more and more into it. More than that. He remembered the evening he had questioned Nikki about the Solzhenitsyn book, the way he had expected her to lie, the way he had expected her to lie over so many things. The system making him assume his own daughter would lie to him, yet all the time the system lying.

The whiskey glass was on the arm of the chair, his fingers round it. He felt himself beginning to sleep, fingers relaxing and the images beginning.

The magician asking for money and the woman's face drawn with tiredness, the girl by her side staring with fear. The classroom again, different, the children older. The musicians and the comedians, the children laughing and the magician waiting, his case of tricks safe in the other room. That's what I call magic, the man's voice from the back when it was done, took Frau Hildebrandte's one Mark and turned it into fifty.

If you're going to do it, he remembered what he had learned that day, do it before they even think about it, so that by the time they start looking it's already done.

One last chance, the deepest layer of loyalty pulled him back. One last opportunity for the system to prove that it was not lying to itself.

The shelves in the shops were full and the people were waiting; the pavements had been freshly swept and the fronts of the apartment blocks above and opposite were clean and sparkling. The woman holding the pram was beginning to worry and the child in it was beginning to cry. Mid morning in early summer and the weather already warm. Faces peering from behind the curtains in the block above the shops yet none of the windows in the block opposite open, the curtains drawn.

The convoy appeared at the top of the road, the security men suddenly alert and the branch chairman shuffling the people into place on the pavement and warning those inside the shops. The cars stopped and Erich Honecker stepped out. The branch chairman nudged the woman with the pram and she stepped forward, showed her son to the leader. He smiled and went into the shops.

Different route and location every month, Langer knew, identical procedure. Even the curtains the same, always blue, yellow or orange.

Honecker left the shops, the convoy screeched away and the pavements cleared. Langer crossed the street to the block opposite. The doors were freshly painted and locked. He left the front of the block and went to the street at the rear. You already know, so why bother to confirm it? Why use it as an excuse when you already know what you're going to do?

The Trabants were parked along the pavement and children were playing in the street. He went through the hallway and into the courtyard in the centre of the block, so that he was now at the rear of the apartments facing the shops which Honecker had visited fifteen minutes earlier. The doors and windows on the ground floor were boarded up, and the windows above were gaping open, most without frames and the glass in the others broken. The weeds were growing at the base, and the courtyard was scattered with broken bedsteads and iron, and smelt of cats.

He found a piece of metal, prised open one of the doors, and went inside. The hallway was damp and the plaster was peeling from the walls, the ceiling bulging. The staircase was to the left; he picked his way up it, keeping to the outside in case it was rotten, and went to the first floor. The doors to the three flats off the landing were hanging lop-sided, their hinges broken. He pushed one open and went in, knowing he would find the same in every flat in the block.

The paper was peeling off the walls, the electric wires hung naked from the remnants of the ceiling and the floorboards were rotten where the water from the tap had leaked on to them and the rain had poured through the broken window. He went through the kitchen and into the first of the bedrooms. The plaster was falling from the walls and there was a nest in the corner.

The system is a shell, Nikki had said. Part of it maintaining the delusion for Honecker himself that the system really was working, that his people were as well housed and happy as he probably genuinely believed them to be.

He left the bedroom and went to the room at the front of the block overlooking the street and shops. The floorboards were missing, the ceiling collapsed, and the square of brilliant orange curtain material was tacked neatly to what had once been a window frame.

There was no one in the world he could trust but two people he would need. He left the room, picked his way carefully down the stairs, and made the telephone call.

At two the next afternoon he met Max Steiner, Vöckel having arranged the meeting but unaware of its purpose. Three days later Max Steiner left Berlin for West Germany and the United States.

Michael Rossini's week had begun on Sunday afternoon; on the following Friday he was in New York and found half an hour for lunch with his wife. Beginning the next morning they would take twenty-four hours together on Martha's Vineyard.

We have a house guest, she told him.

Who?

Max Steiner.

How'd you know?

He called me at the office.

Why didn't he call me?

The Saturday morning was fine, only the slightest haze. Rossini flew the Cessna himself, landing shortly after midday.

The house was tucked discreetly between the pines and dunes on the eastern shore near Chilmark. He drove south then swung off the tarmac and down the unobtrusive track, following it for half a mile. In many ways he still preferred Oak Bluffs, the wood shingle house on Narangassett Avenue with the rocking chairs and hammocks on the front porch, where he, Sally and Nick had spent their early summers. Ice-cream from Mad Martha's and pizza take-outs from Papa's. Now, however, his position and the need for security dictated otherwise.

Max Steiner's rental car was parked in the shade at the side of the house and the smell of a barbecue was drifting from the beach. When the meal was finished the two men strolled along the edge of the water. Two hundred yards away the boys from the next house were rigging a catamaran. There was no one else near them.

'Langer wants a meet.'

'Why?'

'He didn't tell me.'

'When?' He wondered what game Langer was playing and how he might use it.

'As soon as possible.'

He found a small flat stone, crouched down and skimmed it across the water. 'Who else?' The stone bounced twice then sank, the first circles rippling from it.

'Hans-Joachim Schiller.'

'Where?'

'Berlin.'

What the hell was going on, what was Langer playing at?

'What parameters?'

'Absolute secrecy.'

'Schiller's agreed?'

'Yes.'

'Langer accepts that I'll have to bring a minder.'

'That's also what Schiller said.'

'But?'

'But absolutely no one else is to know.'

Rossini's last formal meeting in Washington before he left for Europe was the President's special advisory committee on Central Europe. That evening he flew from Andrews air force base. When he landed at Berlin Tegel it was nine in the morning, he recceed the location then snatched three hours' sleep.

The meeting was at four. He left the Kurfurstendamm at three and reached the location forty minutes later, twenty minutes early, standing in one corner, the shadow he had brought with him waiting discreetly in the street outside.

Schiller's last meeting was with the Chancellor's weekly intelligence briefing. That evening he flew to Hamburg, the following morning to Berlin. At three fifteen he left the Zoo Gardens, reaching the location fifteen minutes early and taking a position beneath the trees along the wall to the left, leaving his shadow outside.

Langer crossed to the West via the S-bahn from Friedrichstrasse. Off the main streets the city was quiet, basking in the early spring sun; he checked the area around the location, looking for the telltale signs of surveillance, then left. At a café on Körte Strasse he sat at a table on the pavement and ordered ice-cream and coffee, sweeping the street for a tail. At three thirty he returned to the location, checking the area again then waiting in the dark of a doorway at the top of the street and seeing the first man arrive, then the second, the shadows drifting in the street outside. It was four o'clock. Langer left the doorway and walked to the grave.

Schiller saw him first, through the trees and above the head-stones; Rossini picked him up moments later. The cemetery was quiet, some of the newer graves in neat rows and some of the older ones slightly overgrown, the trees hanging over them. By the bottom wall an old couple filled a watering-can, the man's hands beginning to shake as the can he was holding filled and the woman's arthritic fingers struggling to turn off the tap. Thirty metres away a girl knelt by a grave.

Schiller and Rossini beneath the trees, Langer assumed, waiting for him. The couple and the girl. No one else.

The headstone was rounded at the top, the only details on it the name and dates of birth and death of the person buried there and the one line of dedication. The grave itself was slightly raised, the grass on the sides and the flowers growing on the top.

From the cover of the trees they saw Langer crouch down, take the bulbs from the plastic bag he was carrying and dig them into the earth of the mound. Why this place? Schiller thought. What made him think that he should remember it?

Langer sensed the movements and stood, wiping his hands. 'Thank you for coming.'

The handshakes were formal, almost as if they were facing each other across a conference table.

'A long time since the Wall at Waldemarstrasse.' He looked at Rossini.

'Twenty-five years.'

The birds were singing, the sound of the traffic deadened. Fifty metres away the girl straightened and looked down at the grave she was tending. She was in her late teens, dressed in a skirt and blouse.

'Almost expect to see a ladder come over, for her to drop every-thing and run.'

The walls of the cemetery were red brick, worn with age, the ivy and brambles growing up and along them.

'Thank you for Lisa. Sorry about the misunderstanding.'

Langer shrugged. 'Before we begin there's something I should say. I have, and will continue to have, complete faith in the socialist system and integrity of my country.' What he was about to propose was political, not just intelligence, both Rossini and Schiller picked up the first tremors. 'I am, and will remain, a socialist.'

'Understood.'

He bent down again, his back to them. Interesting times, he suggested.

'In what way interesting?'

'Russia under Gorbachev, the changes in Poland and Hungary, the demonstrations in Czechoslovakia.'

Interesting times, agreed Rossini.

Except in East Germany, suggested Schiller.

'They *could* be interesting in East Germany.'

The others felt the breath of wind and waited.

'The problem in East Germany is not that people don't want change but that the system will not allow it.' The statement took them by surprise. 'The problem in East Germany is that Honecker has the system sewn tight. His people, myself included, are in the key positions. Until Honecker decides he wants change, change will not come. But unless change comes, then there will be chaos and bloodshed.'

Why should that concern us? He could read their minds. We oppose the system, therefore anything that damages it would be welcomed by us.

'But if there *is* chaos and bloodshed in East Germany, then the repercussions will be felt right back to Moscow.' Then the Moscow spring will be in danger, the implication was clear, then the reforms emanating from Gorbachev's Kremlin will be at risk.

'But Honecker doesn't want change.' It was Rossini.

'Precisely.'

'So what do you want from us?'

The birds were singing; from the tap came the sudden peal of laughter from the woman as the can filled and the water splashed over her husband.

'Help to get rid of Honecker.'

Jesus Christ, Schiller heard Rossini gasp. Honecker the archetypal Warsaw Pact leader, sometimes independent of Moscow but always a cornerstone of the Eastern bloc. Change in East Germany, he knew he himself was suddenly thinking, a democratic form of socialism like the Hungarians were trying to introduce, like Gorbachev himself was preaching.

'How?'

'By creating the conditions under which the pressure on him to go will be so great that he has no option. Conditions under which not only Moscow but his own people will no longer be able to support him.'

For twenty-five years of their lives they had opposed the East, now they were being asked to help change the system in order that it might survive. Yet unless they helped change it before chaos or the iron hand descended again in Moscow, they risked no change at all, the future as bleak as the past.

'If we did agree to help, how would we do it?' Both Rossini and Schiller waited for the catch, the moment Langer would spring the trap.

'Change is only possible if Moscow is confident that Russia itself is not threatened and that its borders are secure. The first stage, therefore, is for the West to guarantee to the countries of the Warsaw Pact, and particularly to Moscow, that it has no intention of interfering with the internal politics of those countries. That as far as the West is concerned the Warsaw Pact is the Warsaw Pact and will remain so.'

'And after that?'

'The last time East Germany was in crisis was in the late fifties and early sixties when so many people were leaving the country that it was in danger of losing all its key manpower.' It was why the Berlin Wall had been built. 'We create a similar crisis.'

'How?'

He had worked it through so many times, at first as if it was a game yet always aware of what he was doing. 'East Germans are allowed to travel freely within countries of the Warsaw Pact. Each year thousands go through Czechoslovakia to Hungary, this year a lot more will go. Most are young, the sort of person we lost before the Wall went up. If there was any way that they could go West, or any way they could stay in Hungary and not return, then the country would face the sort of crisis it faced in '61.'

'And Czechoslovakia?'

'Once the situation in Hungary became known, East Germans would start seeking refuge in embassies in other countries. The West German embassy in Prague is an obvious target. The Czechs would need to be persuaded not to interfere, and not to close its borders to East Germans trying to reach Hungary.'

'Then Honecker would go?'

'Perhaps.' If Honecker *did* go then there would be a new order in

East Germany, he saw they were thinking. And if there was a new order in East Germany there would be a new world in Central Europe. A Stasi sting, he was aware they were also thinking, knew what he would have to give them to persuade them otherwise and how much it would cost.

'But Honecker will only go if the situation you have described has an effect in East Germany itself, if the people there begin to rise.'

'Correct.' It was all in the reports, the bubbling dissatisfaction, still the fear to express it but the dissatisfaction nevertheless. The first hints of people speaking their minds and the first meetings. Only a few people and the meetings not on the streets, normally in the sanctity of churches. But the first signs nevertheless.

'And you want us to persuade the Hungarians and the Czechs.'

The girl had gone, only the couple left.

'I think they might find it a little strange if the request came from me.'

He would have to consult with the Chancellor, said Schiller; he with the President, said Rossini.

'You can't.'

'Why not?'

The old couple shuffled past them down the path, nodding good-bye. Langer waited till they reached the gate.

'Because once you do Honecker and Mielke will know and the opportunity will be gone.'

'How?'

It had taken so long; he remembered the game coming together, small and delicate, the pattern building up even when nothing appeared to be happening. 'You must still wonder how we arrested Max Steiner.'

'I assume he was betrayed.' Schiller knew it showed on his face even now.

'But by whom?'

'One of the organization.'

'One of the people working on the tunnel you were digging when we picked Max up?'

Obviously, thought Schiller, did not reply.

'You like blue movies?'

What the hell have blue movies got to do with it, Langer saw it in Schiller's eyes, what connection do they have with what we're discussing?

'You never saw Fritz Herbert's little epic, did you? Perhaps you'd like a copy.'

The case that broke on the night of Lisa's birthday party, Schiller remembered, the Stasi agent he and Rolf Hanniman had turned, the accelerated promotion for both of them which had resulted from it. He said nothing, confirmed nothing. Langer reached into the white plastic bag and handed him a video cassette.

'It's a bit dated now, of course, but still a classic in its way.'

What the hell are you going on about, Schiller wanted to know. What's the connection between Fritz Herbert and the arrest of Max Steiner?

'Who was in the Fritz Herbert case? Who started it, suggested you turn him once he confessed? Who built his reputation on the case, run all your double agents ever since? Who's now the Chancellor's special adviser on intelligence and security?'

He's setting you up, Rossini knew the West German did not need to be warned. That's what this meeting's all about.

'Who was in the escape organization right from the beginning, who knew about Max Steiner?'

Schiller knew who, knew it was impossible. His brain was working furiously, spinning like a computer through the facts. The bastard's setting me up, the alarm bells were ringing, that's what this meeting's all about.

'You know who.' Langer pressed on. 'The whole Fritz Herbert episode was a sting to get Rolf into the fast lane, put him where we wanted him.'

Impossible, he saw it again in Schiller's eyes.

'Your weekly briefing yesterday with the Chancellor. Item one, Red Army Faction. Item two, Middle East source for timing mechanisms found in bombs in Stuttgart and Hanover, the placing of the bombs not yet made public. Item three, security of senior civil servant involved in paedophile sex ring.' Langer's voice was calm, unrelenting. 'You, the Chancellor, and Rolf Hanniman. Definitely not you, presumably not the Chancellor. Only leaves one.' He paused. 'Think about it. Think who suggested you went into the BfV in the first place.'

Classic technique. Rossini stayed silent and watched the two men. Sow the seeds of doubt and create confusion. Just like the KGB did with the so-called Fifth Man in British intelligence. Put the entire organization in a spin for years.

Exactly what he himself would say if he was playing Langer's role, Schiller thought. But find the hole in the logic and the whole chain collapses. Not logical that Rolf betrayed Max, he saw it. Rolf was not in the organization when Max was arrested, had left one, perhaps two escapes before. Logical, he conceded, knew what he himself would have done if he had been Langer. Pull Rolf out, let one or two tunnels go through to maintain his cover, then go in.

'How?'

'A student called Willi Schultz: his girlfriend was on one of your tunnel lists but couldn't wait because she was pregnant so he tried to get her out through Checkpoint Charlie. We turned him and he named you all. Then we targeted Rolf.'

But how? How did you persuade Rolf to betray us? Unspoken.

'Your first run. Max Steiner into East Berlin because he was the only one with a West German passport, then the break through the wire at Kommandante Allee. Rolf Hanniman's girlfriend failed to show at the rendezvous, you remember. We made her an offer she couldn't refuse and she persuaded Rolf that Max didn't wait for her, that you both let her down.'

And after?

'After that it was easy; I think you call it capitalism.' Langer's voice was almost weary. 'He always was a greedy bastard.'

West Germany, he saw the relief in Rossini's eyes. Thank God not the United States.

'Good meeting in Washington before you came? Special discussion on change in Eastern Europe.'

Rossini tried not to flinch.

'President's special advisory panel? Top security clearance? Still breaking the budget at Saks and Valentino's?'

Who the hell are you talking about, Schiller wanted to know. He shifted his glance from Langer to Rossini then back to Langer. Something about the Fritz Herbert case.

'Enjoy the congressional trip to Europe in '79?' Langer's voice was again pressurizing, unrelenting. 'Interesting train ride from Vienna to Prague?'

The primary information source, Schiller remembered he had asked on the first night of the Fritz Herbert case, the evening of

Lisa's birthday. American, Rolf Hanniman had said, tipping us off. Seems they have somebody in deep. Code-name Mateus.

'Doing well for you in Washington is she? She's certainly doing well for us.'

How? He saw it in the ash of the American's face. How did you turn her, pull her round?

'No turning. She was ours from the beginning. Working for us before your people even thought they'd talent-spotted her. Pure coincidence that it was you who did the run, of course, though it certainly paid dividends.' He knelt again by the grave. 'You'll leave them both in place, of course. They're no use to anybody if we get wind you know about them.'

'Of course.'

'So when will I have your decisions?' Langer leaned forward and brushed the spring dust from the face of the headstone.

Viktor Wischenski. 1894–1948. That he never be forgotten.

'One week.'

A new East Germany – Schiller sat in his office and ran again through what was being offered. Honecker and the old régime out, perestroika-style reformers in. Possibly a known moderate like Modrow as leader. Rolf Hanniman, he also thought, could not shake off the nausea he felt. What was Langer playing at? What the hell was he doing tending a grave in West Berlin?

A new order in Eastern Europe: Rossini spun again through the implications. Major reforms in Poland and Hungary, protest but stalemate in East Germany and Czechoslovakia. East Germany the cornerstone, therefore the key. And if East Germany went . . .

He trawled again through his fears; Langer trying to compromise him. Langer working for the Soviets as the East Germans had always done. Langer causing him no end of trouble with Mateus. The classic covert operation – he went again through what was being offered. Removal of head of state by internal opposition. After Irangate the US Congress was opposed to any covert action, but Congress did not need to know. No one, because of Mateus, able to know. Ten years, he had told the Hungarian Tomasek and the Czech Vlasak, perhaps twenty. Now twenty-one.

He sat back, head cupped in his hands, and remembered the sun sinking below the west stand of the Yale Bowl. The Elis and the Crimsons. Fourth down and five. Last quarter, ten seconds on the clock. *Him* to call the play. The first chance, probably the last.

Black Seven on one; he was beginning to laugh. Pitch play. Tackle and end cross-blocking, guard pulling and kicking out the defensive end, fullback lead blocking to create the opening. No fun kissing your sister.

The meeting with Martin Schumaker was in a bar in downtown New York, Rossini deliberately avoiding Langley and Schumaker's office on Capitol Hill.

'The reforms in Hungary. Budapest is talking about closer economic links with the West. I need five major US institutions to bankroll them.'

They were both drinking Jack Daniels.

'And you can't set it up yourself.'

'No.'

'How soon?' Schumaker saw the glint in Rossini's eyes.

'Yesterday.'

Vienna was warm after the cold of winter, and quiet before the heat and noise of summer. The meeting with Milos Tomasek took place in a roadside café south of the city, on the side road to Eisenstadt.

'How many years did we say in Prague?'

'Ten, perhaps twenty.'

'It's time, Milos.'

The meeting with Josef Vlasak took place at six the following morning in a wood to the north.

'Too long, Mike.'

The birds were singing and the grass was still damp with dew.

'This summer, Josef.'

CHAPTER TWO

For reasons which even in retrospect were inexplicable, perhaps because of the events in China – the student occupation of Tiananmen Square and the threat it posed to the government – the decision from Budapest passed virtually unnoticed in the Western press. Quoting the desire to relax travel regulations for Hungarians, and the aim of creating a better economic climate with the West, the Hungarian Foreign Ministry announced at three in the afternoon that the following day the country would begin to dismantle its physical frontier with Austria.

By the following morning East Germany, Czechoslovakia and Romania had lodged strong objections. That afternoon Hungary began the massive task of dismantling the two hundred and sixty kilometres of twin barbed-wire fence and electronic alarm system which separated the peoples of the East from those of the West.

Two Fridays later Werner Langer and Nikki drove to Leipzig, reaching the tiny flat overlooking the courtyard, the wallflowers beginning to grow up the steps, shortly after ten.

What do you do at the Finance Ministry, Nikki asked during the journey.

'Classified.' He tried to joke it off.

'But what do you really do?'

'I deal with classified information, therefore I'm not allowed to tell you.'

'But you're fairly senior?'

'Yes.'

'You're also high up in the Party?'

'I have to be or we wouldn't be living in the colony.' Why do you ask? He turned the question and made her answer.

'I just wanted to know. You've never been really honest about what you do.' The older Nikki was, the more forthright and questioning she became. 'What do you think will happen in Beijing? Do you think the authorities will send the tanks in?'

The night before they had watched the West German television news reports of the student occupation of Tiananmen Square and the crisis it was causing in the Chinese government.

'No.' He hesitated and corrected himself. 'What I mean is: I hope not.'

'But you think they might?'

'Yes.'

'Why?'

It had been getting dark.

'Ask me what you really want to ask me, Nikki.'

'What if the same thing happened here? If the people took to the streets. What if Honecker gave the order to the army to fire on the crowd and you knew it? What would you do? What if I was one of the protesters?'

'I thought you were training to be an economist.' Langer took the back door out. 'You sound like a lawyer.'

When they arrived in Leipzig the *eisbein* was sizzling in the oven and Eva was waiting for them. The following day the three of them walked round the central market, then visited the graves of Langer's grandparents; on the Saturday evening they went to the drinks arranged by the local branch of the Party, not returning to the flat till gone midnight. At seven the next morning Langer heard a sound in the kitchen. He pulled on a sweater and trousers and left the bedroom.

Eva was sitting at the table; she had made a pot of tea and was buttering a slice of toast.

'You're up early.' Sometimes, he thought, his mother looked so isolated.

'I go to church now.' She fetched a second cup for him. 'I started a year ago.'

'The Church of St Thomas?' The large and imposing church in the city centre where Bach himself was buried and where the choir sang so beautifully on Friday evenings and Sunday mornings.

'Sometimes.'

In the months to come he would remember the moment, remember his mistake. That he had not asked her if she went to any other church, and if so which one.

'Why?'

'Perhaps I'm getting older, perhaps sometimes I get a little frightened.'

'Lonely?'

She nodded.

'It must have been difficult without my father.'

She nodded again.

'Whatever happens, thanks for everything.' He leant across the table and kissed her.

She left the flat and walked to the Nicholaikirche.

That evening, after Werner and Nikki had left, Eva Langer sat quietly and considered what she was doing. The next day she cleaned the flat, and did her shopping. At six on the Monday evening she locked up and walked again to the Nicholaikirche. The Sunday service served one function and the Monday meetings another. The Vopos were parked on the corner, the two Stasi further along, two more near the entrance to the church itself. She walked past them and went inside.

The candles were burning, the group who met in the church still small, no more than fifty. On Sunday mornings in the church they sang hymns and prayed to God; on Monday evenings they discussed politics and the need for reform. Not all those who attended were Christians, though the majority were. At first the police had appeared to ignore them, now they watched them: as they arrived and as they left. The priest recognized her and smiled.

The following Monday Eva went again. Each time it was easier yet more difficult. Easier because she knew what to expect; more difficult for the same reasons, because she knew that as she turned into Marienbergplatz she would see the unmarked Lada and feel the fear. Easier because each week the numbers in the Nicholaikirche grew; more difficult because as the numbers grew the authorities would have no option but to sweep them aside. She turned into Marienbergplatz. The Lada was there again. She passed the car, not looking at the two men inside, and made her way to the church.

The television pictures from China were stark and terrible. The tanks of the People's Army crushing the students in Tiananmen Square, the slaughter and brutality which accompanied it.

How far *will* Honecker go when he realizes, Langer wondered. Will he call in the tanks, will he order the army to fire on the crowd? Will it come to that? In four months East Germany would celebrate its fortieth anniversary; the security plans for the various activities had been under way for the past year. He switched off the set, wondering how Honecker would react if disturbances like those in China took place during the celebrations, and poured himself a whiskey.

The hard core of protesters were gathering in their small groups round the country, often in churches – he checked the Collegiate reports carefully now – but on the surface at least the country was quieter than last year. It was June, soon July. Then the colleges and universities would break up and the students and young families would begin the annual exodus south through Czechoslovakia to Hungary. Then they would realize.

On the third week of July Nikki informed her parents that she would be spending a week, perhaps more, with her grandmother in Leipzig. That day the university had closed for the summer and some of those with whom she now shared a flat had begun the drive to Budapest.

She left Berlin late on the Sunday morning, arriving in Leipzig in mid afternoon. That evening the two women walked in the park near the zoo, enjoying each other's company, sitting and talking, and taking a wine. On Monday they went shopping, Nikki watching Eva closely and waiting to see how she would react, Eva seeming to her to be increasingly worried. At five they had tea, at six Eva sat in her chair in the corner.

'Isn't it time for you to go?'

'What do you mean?'

'It's Monday evening.'

In a way, Eva would think later, she had always known; in a way expected it. 'How do you know?' She looked at the woman opposite her; not so long since Nikki was a girl.

'Everybody knows about the Monday evening meetings.'

How do you know *I* go, Eva had meant. She played with her hair, uncertain what to say or do.

'Why do you go? You know that one day it will be dangerous.'

'I find a peace there.' Eva sat still and tried to work out how she could explain. 'I go because I know it's right. I go because I consider the system in this country at this point in time is wrong. I go because I must at least stand up and say that it's wrong.'

And now I go I've found my peace. Forty-five years after I came to Leipzig.

'Come on then,' Nikki stood up. 'It's time.'

'You're coming as well?' Not Nikki, Eva thought. Not Nikki who is so beautiful and who has everything to live for under the system.

'If you go why shouldn't I?'

Eva was still uncertain. 'That's why you came to Leipzig, isn't it? You came for the Monday meeting at the Nicholaikirche.'

'I also came to see you.' Nikki wrapped the cardigan round her grandmother's shoulders.

'Does your father know?'

'Does my father know about you?'

The eyes were blue and flashing, hair blonde and face defiant. Like someone else, Eva thought.

The Lada was parked on the corner, a second near it; they walked past, Nikki's arm in Eva's. Soon it will change, Eva knew, soon they will not allow us this freedom. They crossed Marienberg-platz and stood in front of the fountain.

'Your father and Anja used to sit here on the steps.' The words came before Eva realized she had spoken them. 'You should have heard them argue. All the time.'

'Who's Anja?'

The Stasi on the right was moving towards them.

'Somebody.'

When they left the Nicholaikirche it was growing dark, the evening warm and wrapping around them. At The Teahouse, on the corner of St Thomas's, they took coffee, sitting at a table outside.

'Who's Anja?'

'A friend of your father's when he was young.' You don't know how glad I am that you're here, Nikki, you can't imagine how much it frightens me.

'What happened to her?'

'I don't know. She and her mother went away. No one saw them again.'

The family was from Dresden: Wolfgang, an industrial engineer and his wife Suzie, both in their mid twenties, their son Daniel aged two and a half. The pride of their life was the blue and white

Trabant car which they had bought through Wolfgang's father –
the waiting time for new vehicles was still ten years. The seats
were covered with mock fur, the bodywork immaculate, and every
Sunday morning for two hours Wolfgang washed and polished it.

Each year they came south camping: three years ago, before
Daniel had been born, they had gone to Czechoslovakia, last year
Hungary, this year Hungary again. Because Wolfgang was a Party
member there had been no difficulty obtaining the permits to travel
in other Eastern bloc countries. They had left Dresden eight days
ago and had another five left before they returned home.

The camp-site was on the side of a river, the banks sloping
gently to the water and the shale forming a beach where the
children played. The majority of the people on the site were Hungarian, though there were a number of East Germans, most their
age. They had arrived at the site knowing no one but making
friends almost immediately.

It was early evening. Suzie squatted by the fire, the sausages
and beans sizzling in the pan, and Daniel playing ten metres away.
Wolfgang had left that morning as he had left every morning for
the past three days. She heard the distinctive sound of the two-
stroke and looked up, saw the Trabbie bouncing across the grass.
Wolfgang picked up the boy and sat beside her.

'I've found it.'

'Is it true?'

'Yes.'

The next morning they rose at five; by six they had packed,
eaten breakfast and left the site, Daniel half asleep in the back.
The river so still and everything so peaceful, Suzie would remember later. Outside they turned left, followed the road north for five
kilometres then turned west, on to a side road, and swung north-
west. The morning was quiet, only the sounds of the birds and the
distinctive phut-phut of the Trabant. Three kilometres further on
Wolfgang swung left, on to a track, then through a small wood,
still following the track, and along the edge of a field.

How did he find this place, Suzie wondered, how can he find
his way back? 'How far?' The nerves cut through her stomach and
her throat was so tight that she could hardly breathe.

'Almost there.'

The track left the fields and ran between two hedges, the hedge
on the left higher and a dried river course beyond the hedge on

the right. The sun on their left, she thought, knew they were heading south. In the back seat Daniel woke and rubbed his eyes. Wolfgang slowed and stopped, then switched off the engine and got out, Suzie beside him holding Daniel.

'There.'

The sun was behind them and they were looking west. Thirty metres in front of them, like forgotten sentinels, were the posts of the border fence dividing Hungary and Austria. No wire, Suzie saw, stared wide eyed, no spotlights or alarms or guards. Just the posts stretching in a line to her right and left. At the official crossing points, she knew, the authorities were still turning families like them back; yet the same authorities had taken down the wire and were allowing people through where they could not be seen. Without speaking Wolfgang lifted the two bags and rucksack from the car. Suzie picked up the boy and followed her husband down into the bed of the river. The morning was still quiet, Suzie was not even aware of the sound of birds, the sun suddenly hot on her back. Wolfgang was two paces in front of her. They stumbled across the river bed and climbed the bank on the other side.

Everything was still so quiet, she thought, could not believe it.

They walked forward together, through the line of posts, and into Austria.

The figures were rising daily but were still too low. Schiller lifted the telephone and dialled the direct line of the editor of ZDF television's *Today* programme.

'Is he there?'

'Who wants him?'

'A friend.' He waited, then heard the man's voice. 'Something's happening on the Austrian-Hungarian border. You should get a crew there today.'

Who is this, the editor asked, how'd you know something's happening? Austrian-Hungarian border, he realized. Remembered. He cupped his hand over the mouthpiece and shouted for the news editor.

'How big?'

'About to be massive.'

The editor knew there was something else.

'You should also send crews to the West German embassies in Budapest and Prague.'

The television pictures were simple but dramatic. From Hungary the line of Trabants abandoned along the side of a cart-track just inside its border with Austria. From Czechoslovakia the East German refugees climbing over the fences into the West German embassies in Prague.

Soon her mother would object to their watching West German television, Nikki knew, soon Gabi would storm from the room.

More East Germans were crossing every day now, the reporter said. He was standing in front of a line of posts which marked the border. Any East Germans caught trying to escape by the Hungarians were given a warning; on a second attempt they were ordered to return to East Germany, their names reported to the East German authorities and their attempt to leave recorded on their documents. Behind the reporter the four figures rose from the hedge and crossed between the posts.

Gabi snorted and left the room.

'What do you think?' Sometimes her father showed no emotion whatever, Nikki thought; sometimes she wondered what he was really thinking.

'I think he paid them.'

She didn't understand and asked him what he meant.

'The figures we're supposed to think are East Germans escaping to the West behind the reporter. I think he paid them.' It was beginning, he thought.

'You're a cynic.'

Realist, he corrected her.

'What happened to Anja?' She hadn't meant to ask him, was only aware of the words after she had spoken them.

'Who's Anja?'

'Eva told me about her.'

It was strange, Nikki would think later, how she no longer called her grandmother by her family position but by her name. Her father had turned away from her and was watching the television again, the evening outside losing its light.

What happened to her, she asked again. Where is she?

Her father was still staring at the television. 'Anja's in the West.'

Nikki waited, said nothing.

Classic interrogation technique, Langer thought, the silence passing the responsibility to the other person, making him or her respond.

No emotion on her father's face, Nikki thought, never any reaction to anything.

'After she and her mother left Leipzig Anja went to Berlin.' He did not know why he told her. 'She became a political activist. Simple and innocent stuff, nothing that was ever going to bring the state down. Eventually she was caught and sent to prison.'

'How long?'

'Seven years.'

It was the first time her father had allowed her into even the smallest of his secrets, Nikki thought.

He was silent for a moment, thinking. 'After a couple of years she was bought by the West and released.' The wave of the hand, as if the details were irrelevant, as if Nikki knew them anyway. 'It was the way the state rid itself of undesirables, plus those the West wanted and was prepared to pay for.'

'Pay for?'

'Yes, there was a list.'

'How often?'

'When both sides decided it was necessary.'

'And the West paid for people to be released?'

'Of course.'

'How much?'

'Forty thousand Deutschmarks.'

'For all the list?'

He looked at her, as if questioning her innocence. 'Per person.'

She sat still, digesting what he had told her. 'How do you know all this?'

'It's common knowledge.' He smiled at her. Not his normal smile. 'Are you shocked that we sell people to the West?'

'I don't know.' I'm shocked at *you*, he knew she meant, I'm shocked that *you* were involved. That *you* sold people.

Why should you be shocked? he asked her. They wanted to leave and we needed the money. How else do you think we helped pay for the schools and the hospitals and the houses?

'You put her on the list, didn't you? You got Anja out of prison?'

He looked again at the television and did not reply.

'So Anja went to the West?' There had been a pause before the question.

'No.' Another pause after. 'For some reason Anja was returned to East Berlin.'

Nikki was devastated. 'But you said she was in the West?' She would always remember the moment, the way her father turned to her.

'Six months later she escaped.'

She felt the relief, almost the exhilaration. 'Eva said you used to sit on the steps of the fountain in Marienbergplatz and discuss politics. She said Anja never stopped talking politics.'

'Is that what Eva said?' Her father smiled again, she thought, as if remembering.

'Will I ever meet her?'

'I shouldn't think so.'

'Why not?'

'Because she's in the West and you're in the East.'

'Have you seen her since?'

'Not since the day I left Leipzig.'

Each day Langer studied the reports and looked at the television pictures from the West. Sometimes East Germans were crossing into Austria in ones and twos, sometimes in groups of a hundred. Already the embassies were filling; halfway through the month the West German embassy in Budapest had closed due to over-crowding.

Mid August.

The Hungarian and Czech governments were under mounting pressure, the Hungarians to seal the border again and the Czechs to stop the East Germans who were beginning to converge on the West German embassy in Prague, but neither government had so far shown any sign of conceding. Rossini, Langer knew, wondered how far back the contacts went.

Yet still there was no reaction. In the East, perhaps, because Honecker was preoccupied with the arrangements for the cele-brations marking the fortieth anniversary of the founding of the state, in October. In the West because it was assumed that both the state and the system were immovable.

*

On the third and fourth weekends in August Nikki travelled to Leipzig to attend the Monday evening meetings in the Nicholai-kirche with Eva. On each occasion there were more people, both inside and clustered outside after. At the end of the last visit in August, as they hurried back to the flat, Nikki told Eva of similar groups forming in Berlin. Because the numbers in Leipzig were growing, she said, she felt she should remain in Berlin and support the embryo movement there. The following morning the two women took the tram to the station. That evening Nikki went for the first time to the Gethsemane Church off Schönhauser Allee, in East Berlin.

The Collegiate meeting to discuss security at the fortieth anniversary celebrations convened at ten. The highlight of the celebrations would be a march past along Unter den Linden; the following evening there would be a banquet in the People's Assembly hosted by Erich Honecker. Among the foreign heads of state or friends of East Germany who would attend, and who would require special security attention, were Jarulzelski of Poland, the Czech Jakes, and Ceaucescu of Romania. Plus, of course, Mikhail Gorbachev. The Soviet leader himself would arrive on the afternoon of the sixth and stand beside Honecker at the march past. On the morning of the second day of his visit Gorbachev would meet the East German politburo, that evening he would again be at Erich Honecker's right side for the anniversary banquet.

The numbers of East Germans crossing into Austria was growing visibly, the trickle becoming a stream and the stream about to become a tide. The Hungarian authorities were now merely issuing verbal warnings to East Germans trying to cross the border into Austria. Six and a half thousand of the estimated two hundred thousand East Germans holidaying in Hungary had sought refuge in the special camps which had been set up for them, and many more had remained in hotels, camp-sites or with friends after their visas expired. In what had been described as an exceptional measure one hundred and eight East Germans who had sought refuge in the West German embassy in Budapest had been flown to Vienna. Their places in the embassy, however, had been taken immediately. In Prague the West German embassy had been closed due to the sheer number of East Germans occupying its room or camping in its grounds.

Any day now the system would react, Langer knew. Any day now it would take its revenge on the young people in Hungary and in the embassy in Prague by sweeping away those protesting in this country. But when the system did react it would only harden the resolve of the people in Hungary not to return. And once that happened the crisis would begin. Then questions would be asked of Honecker and Moscow would intervene.

From the outside the Gethsemane Church seemed sombre, partly because of the colour of its brickwork and partly because of the way it seemed tucked between the other buildings. Inside, however, the walls and ceilings rose in sweeping arches, the murals bright and colourful, and the altar giving a sense of permanence. Nikki Langer lit a candle and waited for the meeting to begin. There were not as many people as in Leipzig, but each week the number was growing. She came each evening now, knew the faces and some of the names, sometimes she went afterwards to the flat of the scientist Jens Reich, one of the leaders of the movement in the city. Everyone still suspicious about the Stasi, however, everyone looking for the agents whom they knew must try to infiltrate them.

Eva Langer reached the Nicholaikirche at six thirty. Tonight, for the first time, there were even people outside. A hundred and fifty, perhaps two hundred. She tightened the scarf round her head and went inside. There were more people this week, filling the pews and standing in the aisles. The meeting began and she looked at the young man next to her, saw the fear in his face.

'You haven't been before?'

'No.' He was little more than nineteen, the same age as Nikki, wearing blue overalls, as if he had come straight from work.

Welcome, she said, and saw the comfort he took from it.

It was strange being at the Monday meeting without Nikki; Nikki was someone to come with, feel safe with as they hurried home after. They had talked on the telephone the night before, the conversation guarded as always but specific enough for Eva to realize that the numbers in Berlin were still small.

Nikki saw the man slip through the door and whisper to Jens Reich, Reich nodding then looking at those around him. The meeting was almost over, the candles flickering in the gloom. He stood up.

'The police are waiting outside. We think they might have orders to arrest us.'

Some time they would come for us, Nikki thought, some time they were bound to move against us. Not many of us. She looked around: twenty, perhaps thirty. At least we didn't give in, at least we stood up and were counted. The others were moving towards the door. She buttoned her coat and walked with them. The police were lined along the pavement outside, spaced at two-metre intervals and facing the church. There would be no arrests tonight, she realized, the presence of the police merely intended to intimidate them. She walked through the line and returned home.

Enough of us, Eva thought, probably five, six hundred of us all together, those waiting and now those who had been inside. Enough to make us safe. The prayers ended and the priest led them outside. The speakers stood on the steps and began to address the crowd, the first asking that the authorities initiate democratic reforms, the second, a woman, that they address the political and social problems behind the current mass emigration.

The police came out of the side streets. Brandishing batons, grabbing the man or woman closest to them. Making directly for the steps, beating their way through the people to the speakers. The woman who was addressing the crowd continuing. People were turning, running. More police, as if they had at last been unleashed, as if the system had at last allowed them to take their vengeance on those who had goaded them for so long. The woman on the steps was being dragged off, hand clenched in the air, still speaking of reform. People panicking. Even more police. Eva turned to face them and they closed on her, batons raised, grabbed her, pulled her away. She was screaming, fighting back. The people around her rallying, trying to rescue her, more police grabbing her, pushing the people back. The figure came between them. Young, blue overalls. Throwing himself against those who were holding Eva. Run, she heard him shouting. Run now. They were releasing her and seizing him. Run, he was still shouting as they dragged him away. What's your name, she was shouting, tell us your name so that we know who they have. So they cannot deny having you.

*

The system had finally reacted.

Langer sealed himself off and reviewed the situation: the degree to which dissatisfaction was mounting throughout the country, as well as the rate at which it was suddenly accelerating, the malaise even spreading to State Security. The politburo knowing, everyone suddenly knowing, yet Honecker not reacting, not even offering to put the slightest problem right. The church meetings had suddenly become important beyond the numbers attending them. For the first time people could be seen to be standing up, the news not reported on East German television but seen anyway on the broadcasts from the West. He swung in his chair and remembered how he and Anja had sat by the fountain near the Nicholaikirche, wondered whether the people would have the courage to go there the following Monday.

The news from Budapest came the next day: the Hungarian government was suspending its 1969 bilateral agreement with East Germany under which citizens without valid travel documents were sent back. The implication was clear. East Germans in Hungary would not necessarily be forcibly returned to the GDR. That morning the East German politburo discussed restrictions on travel to Czechoslovakia and Hungary. That afternoon further requests were made to reduce access to the West German embassies in those countries. That evening Prague and Budapest again refused to comply.

Who the hell did Rossini have? Langer wondered. What the hell had he said to them to make them resist so much pressure? Everything now depending on the people, he also thought. Whether they had the courage to continue. All eyes on Leipzig, everyone waiting for the meeting at the Nicholaikirche the following Monday evening.

The night before Eva had not slept, since early morning her stomach had been knotted with nerves. Tonight she would not be so lucky, the foreboding grew in her; tonight, when she went to the Nicholaikirche, they would arrest her. *If* she went, she knew she was really thinking. Not many would go tonight, the personal risk would therefore be great. But if she did not go then the risk to those who did would be even greater. She put on her coat and left the flat.

The trams were running and the shops were still open. Strange how she assumed that the city would be different, that everybody would be watching the meeting at the Nicholaikirche. The police vans were in position, the Vopos were ringed round the square and the Stasi watching. She squeezed through them and saw the people. Five, six hundred, perhaps more. Double the number of the previous Monday. Eva went up the steps and through the doors. The church was packed. She lit a candle and prayed.

That night, after the prayer meeting, speeches were made to the crowd gathered in the square outside the church. That evening the police again intervened. That evening a hundred arrests were made. The following Monday the numbers of people attending the prayer meeting in the Nicholaikirche and the meeting in the square after had risen to nearly three thousand, the number and brutality of arrests increasing accordingly.

The Soviet Tupolev landed at East Berlin's Schönefeld airfield at ten in the morning. Its only passenger, other than the handful of civil servants accompanying him, was the Kremlim politburo member Yegor Ligachev, and the single message which he delivered publicly and sternly was simple. East Germany played a key role in the Warsaw Pact; anyone attacking the sovereignty and independence of East Germany should be aware that the Soviet Union was determined to keep to the letter of its agreement of friendship with the GDR.

The invitation from the KGB station head in Berlin came at four. Moscow was concerned with certain of the security arrangements for Mikhail Gorbachev's visit for the fortieth anniversary celebrations. Would General Langer be available to review them over a light dinner that evening?

'Formal or informal?' Formal and the Friends were indicating that he could notify Mielke, friend and ally of Honecker. Informal and he should tell no one.

'Informal; shall we say eight?'

'Eight would be fine.'

Someone in the East German politburo was moving, making the first tentative steps against Honecker. Langer crouched over the desk and drew up the list, trying to decide which, if any, of Honecker's politburo were plotting against him.

Krenz and Schabowski, he suspected. Egon Krenz, aged fifty-two, Honecker's crown prince. Career pattern remarkably similar to Honecker's. Former head of the communist youth movement and Central Committee secretary for security, youth affairs and sport. Gunter Schabowski, aged sixty. Former journalist now head of the Party machine in Berlin.

Three and a half hours later he left Lenin-Allee and drove to the Soviet embassy on Unter den Linden. The gate was opened for him immediately and an escort was waiting to take him to the ambassador's suite. The man from Moscow was waiting for him.

Vladimir Kryuchkov. Receding hairline and eyes close together, tight mouth despite the filling out of the face.

They shook hands and sat in the chairs in the corner, the table between them and no one else present.

'Thank you for coming.' Kryuchkov poured them each a vodka.

Vladimir Kryuchkov, confidant and ally of Mikhail Gorbachev. Vladimir Kryuchkov, head of the KGB.

'General Secretary Honecker, how is he after his stay in hospital?'

Vladimir Kryuchkov, later one of the conspirators in the anti-Gorbachev coup attempt in the summer of '91.

'I'm told he's fine.' He wondered how many listening devices were in the room.

'And he has no intention of resigning because of his health?'

'None that he has talked of.'

'But if he did decide to step down, who might take his place?'

The conversation was coded, Moscow still uncertain, Langer thought. Tell Kryuchkov what he needs to know, he decided, but make sure he covered himself.

'If General Secretary Honecker decided to step down an obvious candidate would be Hans Modrow, the Party chief in Dresden.' A leading reformer, he did not need to say, an advocate of perestroika and highly popular in the country.

'But the General Secretary has not seen fit to appoint Modrow to the politburo.' The Russian was sitting back, glass in hand, neither man drinking.

'No.'

'So what if it was felt more convenient for the successor to come from within the politburo?'

What if Moscow wanted change with continuity? The message

was again coded. What if Moscow decided to oust Honecker but considered that his replacement from someone outside the polit-buro would too closely resemble a coup d'état?

'If, for health reasons, the General Secretary decided to step down, then his successor should be a young man.'

'Agreed.'

The conspiracy in the politburo already under way, Langer confirmed. 'If it was decided, then the obvious candidates within the politburo would be Egon Krenz and Gunter Schabowski.'

'An interesting suggestion.' The man from Moscow had still not touched his vodka.

Krenz and Schabowski the conspirators, Langer knew for certain.

The figures were staggering. In September alone twenty-five thousand East Germans, most of them young and many of them highly qualified and well trained, had fled across the Hungarian border into Austria. Another two hundred thousand were still in Hungary. Nearly four thousand more who had been prevented from crossing into Hungary were crammed into the West German embassy in Prague, and yet more were in the West German embassy in Warsaw.

There was one other statistic. The previous Monday eight thousand people had marched through Leipzig after the now traditional evening meeting at the Nicholaikirche.

By the time Langer reached home it was gone nine. Thank God it was the weekend, he thought; thank God that by this time next week the fortieth celebrations would be almost over. The colonel who was his personal aide telephoned at ten.

'Honecker has just made a decision about the problem in the embassies.'

Honecker had no option, Langer thought: the world's socialist leaders about to fly in and the country facing crisis. 'Tell me.'

'He's agreed that the people in the embassies in Prague and Warsaw can leave. They'll travel to the West by train.'

Honecker trying to get the problem out the way before the festivities began, worried about what the nation would look like during the celebrations and papering over its cracks. Honecker still living in a world in which it was perfectly in order for entire housing blocks to be falling down as long as there were bright coloured curtains in the windows when the General Secretary passed by.

'When?'

'It'll take a day to organize, they leave on Sunday.'

'What else?'

'He has stipulated that the trains pass through East Germany.'

More delusion. As if the fact that they were leaving from East Germany would suggest that the state was letting them go, rather than that the state had no option.

'Which route?'

Honecker's going to order us to stop the trains, he sensed the colonel was thinking. He's going to order us to take the people off them.

'Dresden.'

Thank God it's not Berlin: he detected it in the colonel's voice, knew the man had made no effort to disguise the tone.

'Anything else?'

'No.'

'I'll see you in the morning.'

Honecker wouldn't pull the people off the trains. Not because he was incapable of it but because it would look bad, would look like the backs of the houses with the front doors freshly painted and the material tacked on to what had once been window frames. Honecker would save the crackdown until his visitors had left and the decorations of the anniversary celebrations had been taken down.

The final security meeting for the anniversary celebrations was held two days later in Langer's office. The briefing began at ten in the morning and ended at eight in the evening. At midday he was informed that the trains carrying East Germans from the West German embassy in Prague had left the city.

'How many on them?'

'Four thousand.'

At two he was informed that the train had entered the GDR, at six that it had passed through and was in the West.

'What happened in Dresden?'

'Another two thousand climbed on.'

'The embassy in Prague?'

'Filling up again.'

Two days later the politburo agreed to a second exodus of East Germans seeking asylum in the West German embassy in Prague. The following day, Wednesday – two days before the arrival of Mikhail Gorbachev in East Berlin – Langer instructed that he be informed regularly of the passage of the trains through the GDR.

At three he was notified that the trains had left Czechoslovakia and entered East Germany.

'How many trains?'

'Eight.'

'How many people on them?' He had already seen the West German television pictures.

'Ten thousand.'

At six he was informed that the trains were approaching Dresden, at seven that they were in the city and that a number of people were clashing with police.

'How many?'

'How many what?'

'How many are clashing with the police?'

There was a hesitation. 'Eight thousand.'

'What do they want?'

The hesitation again. 'To get on the trains.'

The crowd on the apron of the runway was two hundred strong – men, women and children; all of them were Party members and each had been carefully vetted. Honecker stood in front, his dark raincoat buttoned to the top, no hat, his silver-white hair immaculately brushed. Krenz just behind him, smiling as he always seemed to be smiling, the rest of the politburo and the official welcoming party close. Honecker was talking and joking with the press men near him, hands in pockets. His body movements were too quick, Langer thought, his responses to the journalists too rapid, too attentive.

The Ilyushin landed and taxied towards them.

Moscow was still uncertain. Langer tried to read the signs; either undecided whether Honecker should go, or undecided who would replace him.

The plane stopped in front of them. Honecker straightened his shoulders and drew his tongue along his lips. Krenz just behind him still, Langer noted, and looked for Schabowski. If they were going to replace Honecker then it would have to be a decision of the politburo, and if it was a decision of the politburo then Krenz and Schabowski would already have canvassed potential allies.

The steps were in place, the doors of the Ilyushin opened and Gorbachev walked out, his wife Raisa on his right, the mark of his birth on his forehead and the smile of the bear on his face.

The fortieth anniversary celebrations not just marking the past but mapping the future, Langer sensed. Amongst the champagne and congratulations of the next two days Honecker would be given his last chance. At the Palace of the Republic today and at his private meeting with Gorbachev tomorrow. Then Moscow would decide.

Gorbachev stepped forward and greeted Honecker. The diplomatic handshake then the fraternal greeting: the embrace followed by the three kisses – right cheek, left, right again. They turned, both men laughing, and walked through the crowd towards the waiting cars. The doors of the armour-plated Zil were open, the guards sweeping the crowd. Gorbachev stepped in and the convoy swept away.

The Palace of the Republic was overflowing, the vast auditorium arched round the podium at the front, the ranks of party and military apparatchnik looking down upon Honecker and Gorbachev as they took their seats. Behind them, emblazoned on the wall, were the dates 1949–1989 and the emblem of the Party. The national anthem began and they stood to sing, faces and backs straight and right hands on left breasts. The anthem ended and they sat, waited. Slowly, enjoying the moment, Erich Honecker rose, shuffled his papers slightly and began his address.

Langer looked round and studied the faces. Most of them attentive, ready to rise and applaud. Krenz straight-faced close to Honecker; Schabowski with the rest of the politburo, leaning slightly to his right, head resting on his hand; Gorbachev, accustomed to the endless monologues of the Soviet politburo, staring straight ahead.

The speech was predictable: the glories of socialism and the progress of the GDR, the future of East Germany in line with its past. There was nothing in it to signal change – Langer again looked at Honecker then at Gorbachev – no hint at all of perestroika. As Honecker finished and sat down the chamber rose to applaud him.

Two chances, one gone, the second tomorrow morning. Then Moscow would confirm what it already knew. He left the Palace of the Republic and confirmed that the security arrangements for the march past were in order.

Unter den Linden shook, the column of tanks five wide and seemingly unending, the rocket launchers following them, troop carriers then more armoured divisions. Nikki Langer did not know the titles and designations, looked only at the massive array as it trundled past her. This is the People's Army, she thought, this is what one day we will march against. The afternoon light faded and the military procession came to an end, the lasers piercing the darkening purple of the evening sky, and the parade of Party members began.

On the review stand she could see Honecker, face beaming and spectacles glinting in the lights. The ranks of socialist leaders around him, many from the Third World, the power base of the Soviet system like a phalanx close to him. Jarulzelski, Jakes, Ceaucescu. Gorbachev to Honecker's right, smiling, Raisa waving a white rose in time to the music beside him.

The procession of Party members seemed as endless as that of the tanks, the young men and women waving and singing as they passed the stand, red flags dipping. Yet more lines of Party members, the night darker and the flames of the gas candles each carried flickering in the sudden chill. This is the Party against whom we light our little candles, she thought, this is the system against which we battle. She looked again at the podium. They had placed their hopes on Gorbachev, the Russian was their inspiration, the man who had told them it was all possible. Now he stood alongside Honecker in East Germany's moment of triumph. She pushed her way to the back of the crowd and returned to Gethsemane.

That night the building in which the private meeting between Gorbachev, Honecker and their closest aides would take place was sealed off. The following morning, despite the fact that since three days before the beginning of the anniversary celebrations it had been a prohibited area, even to members of the Party, it was again searched, both physically and electronically. At ten minutes to ten Erich Honecker and his politburo arrived; five minutes later the Soviet convoy swept up the driveway to the white-walled building. At ten precisely the meeting began.

The room was in the front of the building, on the second floor. The conference table ran in front of the windows, Gorbachev seated in the centre of one side, his back to the windows, and Honecker immediately opposite him. The Russian's advisers on either side and the members of the East German politburo occupying the other seats. Krenz to Honecker's right, Schabowski on the opposite side of the table, four places from Gorbachev.

Even as the participants entered the room, however, the format of the meeting remained unclear. The meeting would be brief and limited to formal exchanges, Langer had been told by some of those attending. It would be open-ended, he had been told by others, the Soviet leader was fully prepared for a discussion of some length after the addresses by the two leaders.

A discussion on what, he had asked.

On change; the reply was unspoken.

Gorbachev's speech lasted a little over twenty minutes. In it he congratulated East Germany on its socialist path, paying special emphasis to its links with Moscow, then moving on to talk about the changing nature of that socialism, the message clear and unmistakable. When he finished he poured himself a mineral water and waited.

Honecker cleared his throat and began to speak, welcoming Gorbachev, then moving quickly to the history and achievements of the East German state, the glories of socialism and the future for East Germany in line with its past. It was the speech he had made in the Palace of the Republic; not necessarily the same words, though many of them similar – no acceptance in it of Gorbachev's suggestion for change, no indication that Honecker was anything other than totally inflexible.

Krenz's back was to him, so that Langer could not see his face; he looked at Schabowski then at Gorbachev. For one moment the Russian's eyes flicked up at him, then Gorbachev wiped his hand across his mouth and the smile of the bear descended again upon his face.

The speech ended and they waited. Honecker closed his document case, stood up and extended his hand to the Soviet leader.

Langer tried to see the faces of Krenz and Schabowski and followed the Russians and the politburo into the anteroom. The two sides were standing in distinct groups, not even the faintest suggestion that the meeting had been one of celebration. In the far corner Gorbachev summoned an aide, the movement barely noticeable. The official nodded, the movement again barely perceptible, and crossed to the KGB colonel on the edge of the group. The groups at last began to mix, the professional diplomats first, then the politicians.

'General Langer.' The KGB colonel had liaised with them on the Soviet leader's visit.

'Yes.'

'I was told to inform you of anything which might affect security. I understand that General Secretary Gorbachev might wish to leave his car during the return to his residence.'

Gorbachev's walkabouts were famous to the public and infamous to those who guarded him; Langer had already planned for them. 'I suggest the Memorial to the Victims of Fascism and Militarism. Security is already in place.'

'Good. What about television crews?'

'Which crews do you want?'

'East German, of course.'

'Of course.' Anything recorded by the East Germans would be censored before transmission. 'Who else?'

'American, British and West German.' The understanding was clear. Whatever Gorbachev said in his walkabout would be broadcast in the West and heard in the East.

'Fifteen minutes.'

The afternoon was busy, continued updates on security, the whereabouts of the various heads of state constantly being revised, the arrests of those even remotely suspected of any action against the celebrations. Langer turned on the television in the corner of the office and switched channels to the West Berlin station. The words Gorbachev had used had been reported to him ten minutes after the Russian leader had ended his walkabout; he wondered only how the man had said them and how they would come across on television.

In Dresden, he had been informed, the demonstrations which

had started when the trains from Prague had come through the city were continuing. An estimated five thousand people had been dispersed using water cannon and tear-gas.

The news programme began: Gorbachev's visit to East Berlin, pictures of the motorcade to the Honecker meeting that morning, the convoy of cars sweeping away after. The Zil passing the memorial to the Victims of Fascism and Militarism then stopping, and the familiar figure stepping out. Except that it was different. Except that Gorbachev was not smiling and waving, stopping to talk, but striding quickly through the crowd, face taut. The words themselves were seemingly in reply to nothing, the delivery short and sharp, as if he had suddenly grown both tired and irritated.

Moscow had not only decided; it had made its decision public. Langer wondered how the crowds in Dresden would respond, what the people who attended the Monday evening meetings in the Nicholaikirche would think, how the handful in the Gethsemane Church would react. The item ended. He returned home, showered and dressed, and drove to the banquet with Gabi.

Gethsemane Church was beginning to fill. Each day began the same way now: the first handful of women then the students; the small groups outside, some bringing food, then people moving inside as the afternoon wore on, the sleeping-bags and blankets on the cold stone floor. Then the afternoon would fade and the night vigil would begin. The candles fluttering in the dark and the riot police ringed outside.

Nikki sat with the group close to the altar and clutched the mug of coffee between her hands. Two hundred people, she calculated, perhaps three, the people still coming in. Sometimes, but especially in the early evening like now, she thought the church no longer felt like a place of worship, wondered what it reminded her of. Now she knew. A medieval castle under siege.

Behind her a woman began to tell a joke. She was Nikki's age, but had a small child strapped to her. Nikki turned and listened. Even in the comparative safety of the church the woman spoke quietly, all of them glancing over their shoulders.

Erich Honecker lies on the beach in the Baltic.
The sun rises above the early morning mist.

'Good morning, dear Sun,' says Erich.

'Good morning, General Secretary,' says the sun.
'I wish you a pleasant day.'

'How kind of you, dear Sun.'

The sun smiles.
'General Secretary, my only wish is to serve you
and the Party. I am delighted that my
greeting makes you happy.'

In the evening, as the sun sets, Honecker looks up.
'Thank you, dear Sun. I've had such a pleasant day.'

The sun looks down and smiles again.
'Kiss my arse, you old fool. I'm in the West now.'

They began to laugh. At the back someone pushed through and spoke to Jens Reich. They tried to listen and knew it would be bad news. Those standing next to Reich heard and passed the words on. That afternoon Gorbachev had spoken about the system in East Germany, commented on the fact that perestroika had not yet arrived in Berlin, criticized Honecker. It had been on West German television. They did not and could not believe it. Someone else found a radio set and tuned it to one of the West Berlin news stations.

On the steps outside the Party headquarters the cars pulled up and the heads of state stepped out; in the foyer Erich Honecker stood with his politburo to welcome them, the greetings always the same: the handshake then the formal demonstration of comradeship – the embrace and the three kisses. Right cheek, left, right again.

Langer introduced Gabi to the guests with whom they would share a table then returned to the foyer. Gorbachev had still not arrived, even though the formal dinner was due to start in fifteen minutes. Honecker was still smiling, welcoming his guests. Arafat, military uniform and *shamag*: Ortega, olive green uniform.

Langer left the foyer and went upstairs. A waiter offered him a drink; he shook his head and saw what he was looking for, the two meetings almost lost in the crowd. Krenz and Falin, the East German conspirator and the Soviet politburo member; Schabowski and Gerasimov, the second conspirator and the Soviet Foreign Ministry spokesman. As he watched the Russians nodded and left.

He returned to the foyer and waited. Honecker was still shaking hands and smiling, Prime Minister Willy Stoph next to him, Krenz and Schabowski joining the line.

The Zil stopped outside, Gorbachev entered the foyer and Honecker stepped forward to greet him. The procedure was formal and practised, they all knew: handshake, embrace, formal kiss of comradeship. Langer saw the Russian's eyes and could not believe that even Gorbachev would do it. Gorbachev nodded curtly, shook Honecker's hand, passed abruptly by, and stood in front of Willy Stoph. Handshake, embrace, the three kisses of fraternal comradeship.

Honecker was finished – Langer would remember the moment – the first chance for the coup de grâce would be at the politburo meeting in ten days' time, only the bloodshed of the last days of his régime to come.

Gethsemane was quiet, everyone listening, waiting. The bulletin began. In East Berlin, the newscaster said, Premier Gorbachev had had a busy schedule: a formal meeting with Erich Honecker and the East German politburo, a walkabout, then an afternoon's work in his official residence. Even now he was arriving at the Party headquarters for the banquet which would mark forty years of the East German state. A special report from their reporter with the Russian leader. They concentrated, no one hearing the words of the reporter, waiting only for the words of Gorbachev in Unter den Linden that afternoon. A fuller description of the motorcade, the sounds of the crowd outside the Memorial to the Victims of Fascism and Militarism. The questions, Gorbachev's answers. His voice curt and the answers short.

'What about East Germany, what about the last forty years?'
No reply.

'What about Honecker and his place in history?'

'Those who come late will be punished by history.'

Nikki hardly dared believe it. Gorbachev finally and openly criticizing Honecker. She crouched close to the set and waited for the next question and answer.

'What about perestroika? What about the fact that democracy has not yet come to East Germany?

The questions were staged, she realized.

'If you really want democracy, then take it.'

She straightened and allowed the words to sink in, wondered if Gorbachev had really said them, if he really understood what he had said and how his words would be interpreted.

They began to leave the church; later she would wonder who made the decision or whether it was spontaneous. Four hundred, she estimated, perhaps five hundred. The riot police were outside, facing them, shields and batons ready and visors down. They walked through the ranks and on to the street, turned down Schönhauser Allee. A thousand people, she looked round, fifteen hundred, the numbers suddenly growing, the people coming from nowhere, from everywhere. Mostly young, more coming from the side streets, joining them. They reached Karl-Liebknecht Strasse and turned right towards Unter den Linden. More police, still more people. The police were suddenly everywhere, armoured cars and water cannon. Stasi, pretending to be demonstrators. The mood was tense. On the far side of the road she saw the plain-clothes figures running, to her left two Stasi turned and smashed a television camera. The people still coming.

In the Palace of the Republic the national anthem ended and Honecker prepared to speak. To his right Gorbachev sat impassive.

'Dear comrades, friends and guests, members of the diplomatic corps.' Honecker's voice was clear and steady, the smile set on his face. God help us before we get him out, Langer thought, God help the people when they take to the streets. 'It is a great pleasure to welcome you here on this festive occasion.'

The aide picked his way through the tables. Langer sat back, apparently still concentrating on the Honecker speech, and turned his head so that he could hear the man's whisper.

'There's a demonstration outside; a few incidents but it's being contained. We can keep them away from the assembly, but it was felt you should be informed.'

'How large?'

'About seven thousand.'

Honecker finished his speech and raised his glass in toast. From all round the People's Assembly came the polite tinkle of glass.

Two hours later Langer watched as Gorbachev's Ilyushin took off from Schönefeld. At one that morning he was briefed on the night's disturbances, by the time he went to bed it was five. Already Sunday, he thought; in four hours Eva would be going to the service at St Thomas's. Tonight there will be trouble. Not Berlin, Berlin would be licking its wounds after the five hundred arrests. Probably Dresden, still fermenting after the demonstrations of three nights before. Then the Monday evening meeting in the Nicholaikirche. Leipzig on Monday would be the key: depending on the number of people who took to the streets and the reaction of the authorities.

At ten he spoke to Nikki by telephone, was surprised at his relief when she was in the flat where she now lived. She was fine, she told him, was busy doing her work for college. When the conversation was over she pulled on a coat and went to Gethsemane Church. The mood was a mix of fear and elation; she sat quietly, talking and listening, sometimes just sitting.

At five the first news came through from Dresden: thirty thousand were on the streets. They knew what was going to happen and waited. At six Langer was notified of emergency meetings of the politburo and the Stasi Collegiate the following morning. An hour later the service began in the Gethsemane Church, the elation gone and the fear hanging over them. At seven thirty the second news came through from Dresden. There had been no trouble, the police had not attacked, the people had dispersed after the authorities had agreed to meet a delegation for discussions.

The mood in the church swung again, the fear evaporated and the elation taking its place. Gorbachev had been right: if they really wanted democracy then they should take it. Today Dresden had fallen, tomorrow Leipzig would march. The two were different, the more cautious argued: in Dresden the Party chief was the reformer Hans Modrow, in Leipzig this was not the case. In Leipzig things might go differently. When the service ended Nikki informed the other members at the core of the Gethsemane movement that she would be out of Berlin for two days but would return on the Tuesday morning. Then she returned to the flat and telephoned Eva.

Nikki's train was due at three. Eva waited on the station, the chill of October in the air and the nerves eating through her stomach. Tonight there would be even more people than last week, tonight Nikki would be with her. Perhaps that was what was wrong, perhaps that was why she was afraid. That that night Nikki would be in Leipzig.

The Collegiate was informed at three; forty minutes later Erich Honecker arrived at Normannenstrasse and was escorted immediately to the conference room. Fresh coffee was served and Mielke's chair was moved slightly to accommodate one for Honecker.

The General Secretary was enjoying himself, enjoying playing with his power, enjoying playing with those with whom he had surrounded himself. 'The anticipated march in Leipzig tonight.' His eyes glanced again around the table. 'I have discussed the matter with General Meyer and we are in complete agreement.' There was a general mutter of approval, heads nodding at Meyer.

What have you done, Langer thought, what are you going to do tonight?

'This morning I ordered the People's Army to liaise with police and State Security in Leipzig.' Honecker looked at their faces again. 'Their brief is simple: to put down any disorder in the city tonight.' He sat up, abruptly, as if concluding the meeting the way he had concluded the meeting with Gorbachev. 'To this end I have today ordered that the tanks be moved into Leipzig and that the army be issued with live ammunition.'

The Collegiate meeting ended at five; immediately it was over Langer went to his office and telephoned Nikki's flat.

She was out, he was told.

Where is she, he asked. Nikki who was so strong and adamant in her views on the régime and the necessity of change. Nikki who had talked about staying in the East so that she could be part of that change.

'Still at the library. She normally gets back at seven. Any messages?'

'Could she telephone her father when she gets in.'

The street beside the Nicholaikirche was half full, no sign of police. The church itself was packed, people standing; Eva and Nikki found a place just inside the door and waited for the service. When it was over and they went outside the streets were filled, the people spilling into the squares and alleyways beyond.

We're safe, Eva thought. How many do you think, she asked Nikki. Five thousand, ten, twenty? Fifty thousand, the unofficial reports from Leipzig would state the following morning. With this number the authorities won't dare intervene, she told herself. But with these numbers they must.

The organizers began giving them instructions, telling them the route to follow. They left the church and began to walk, people joining them, in front and behind them. 'Not like the early days.' Eva laughed at Nikki, remembered how few there had been then.

There were more people marching, demonstrating in other parts of the city, the message was passed down the column. Police waiting ahead, the army as well and the tanks in position – it was incredible how the news travelled. They closed on the city centre, the night dark and the riot police suddenly blocking their way. Eva could just see them, above the heads of the people in front of them. The shape of a tank moving behind the riot police, muzzle suddenly swinging towards them. Soldiers to the left and right of them. Like Hungary in '56, she thought, Czechoslovakia in '68. Except these aren't Russians, these are our own people. The riot police came forward, slowly, deliberately, and stopped, three lines deep, visors down and batons drawn.

Keep walking, they heard the voice from the front line of the marchers, don't stop. The procession hesitated and slowed, then picked up its momentum again. A hundred metres between the people at the front and the riot police. More tanks, trundling down the street to their right, more soldiers. The police on the left charged, opening the lines of marchers, the first rows scattering but those behind holding firm. Sixty metres. The police charged again, more lines splintering away, running in panic. Fifty metres. Eva and Nikki were in the front line, suddenly and unexpectedly, nothing and no one between them and the riot police and the black dark hulks of the tanks.

Link arms, they heard the shout from the side. Eva looked across and tried to smile, saw Nikki try to smile back. The line was thirty metres across, the people close behind them, still marching, still moving forward. Prepare, they heard the orders, and saw the guns and batons go up. The line faltered and picked up again, linked arms tight so that nobody could let go.

The riot police came at them. The batons beat down, the riot police kicking and striking, breaking skulls, limbs, tearing through them. Nikki's right arm locked in Eva's left. Still marching, still going forward. Eva felt the fear, was unsure what to do. The batons raining down on her, right arm in the air, trying to defend herself. Nikki's arm still locked in her left.

The arm slipped away. Eva turned, saw Nikki as she fell, the blood streaming from her head and the batons still falling upon her. She crouched, knelt over her, took the blows on her back. Tried to protect her. The march was breaking, disintegrating, the people around her running in all directions. The riot police ran over those on the ground, began to chase those running away. Eva looked down and saw Nikki's face. Her hair was plastered in a dark brown-red and the blood was seeping from her nose and mouth, trickling across the white of her face. She laid the head down and tried to check if Nikki was still breathing, saw the blood on her own hands where she had cradled Nikki's head.

She heard the other noise and looked up. The tanks were advancing down the street, moving slowly, stopping for nothing. She knew she should not move Nikki, knew that unless she did they would be crushed, began to pull her to the side. The men were suddenly with her, lifting Nikki, helping her. Eva lost sense of time, direction, where they were or what was happening. One moment they were on the main street with the fighting still round them, the next they were in the quiet of a house, the young men reassuring her, telling her that Nikki was still breathing.

It's all right, they told her, we're medical students. One took Nikki's pulse and a second looked at her head. Eva not daring to look. Carefully the student eased back her hair and exposed the flesh and bone beneath.

'She might have a fractured skull. We have to get her to hospital.'

'You can't.' Eva heard her protests. 'The Stasi will find out, arrest her.' She knew she was right, knew also that unless they took her Nikki would die. Phone Werner, she thought, get his protection.

The car arrived outside. Carefully they lifted Nikki into the back seat, driving through the maze of back streets which were not patrolled by the police or the army, then smuggling her through a rear entrance of the hospital.

The doctors and nurses were waiting, other people also being brought in, medical students acting as lookouts. Quickly and efficiently they examined Nikki, cutting her hair away and taking her for an X-ray. Vopos on the way, already the reports were spreading, Stasi coming to the hospital. It's all right, the doctor confirmed, she's going to be okay. Bad gashes and concussion, but the skull isn't fractured as we first feared.

The first light came through the window and the room was suddenly quiet. Like the peace the morning after a bombing raid, Eva could not help thinking. The relief, the sheer joy, forty-five years ago in Berlin and this morning in Leipzig, that they had survived.

Werner Langer had been at Lenin-Allee since six. Already there were conflicting explanations for the army's failure to fire on the demonstrators in Leipzig. Honecker had relented. Krenz had persuaded him or had overruled him. Moscow had ordered the local commander of the East German units not to open fire, and begun pulling its own units out of the city.

Nikki was still not at the flat. He had tried twice the night before and begun again at seven. He put the papers to one side and began to telephone again, then changed his mind and dialled the other number.

Eva had fallen asleep in the armchair; she heard the ringing through the nightmare and struggled awake.

'It's Werner.'

'Nice of you to phone.'

'How's Nikki?' Already there was a subtext to the conversation. Is Nikki with you? Be careful. Remember that after last night the telephones to and from Leipzig will be tapped.

'Nikki arrived yesterday.' Confirmation that she was in Leipzig. 'She's still in bed, a bit of a cold.' Confirmation that they had been at the Nicholaikirche and the warning that Nikki had been injured.

'How bad?' How badly is she injured, what the hell happened?

'She'll be okay in a couple of days.'

'And you?'

Eva's back was striped where the batons had struck her, the flesh black and blue, turning deep purple, and the skin had been scoured from her arm where she had tried to protect herself. 'I'm fine.'

'I was thinking of coming down this evening.' His entire reaction was cold, impersonal; it would only be later that the anger and the guilt would come.

'I'm sure she'd like to see you.'

That afternoon he drove to Leipzig; that evening ten thousand marched in Magdeburg. The following evening there were more marches in Dresden, Plauen, Halle and other cities and towns across the GDR. It was as if the people had suddenly either lost their fear or were prepared to face it, he thought. As if the people had smelt the first warming wind of spring. Each evening after that, until the following weekend, the numbers and sizes of demonstrations grew; yet each night the police opposition to the demonstrations decreased. It was four days to the politburo meeting: still time for the system to respond, he told himself, still time for Honecker to realize and act.

The following Monday one hundred and twenty thousand marched in Leipzig, the first demonstration to be reported in the official East German media.

At ten the next morning Langer was contacted and invited to attend the meeting of the politburo that afternoon. It was as if the conspirators assumed he knew what they were doing, as if his presence would signal his support for them.

The information came through at eleven fifteen. Twenty minutes earlier, Prime Minister Stoph had been seen entering the Soviet embassy on Unter den Linden. The last pressures being applied and the last guarantees being secured. At eleven thirty Langer was again telephoned and asked if he had made his decision about attending the meeting that afternoon.

'Yes.' There was no hesitation. 'I'll be there.'

Three hours later he left Lenin-Allee and was driven to the Party headquarters on Karl-Marx Platz. The politburo were waiting outside the committee room, Krenz in one group, smiling as always, and Schabowski in another. As he entered they both looked at him and noted his presence. The door of the committee room was open; they went inside and took their places round the table, Langer sitting in the row of chairs placed against the wall on the right of the door. At the top Honecker shuffled his papers and prepared to open the meeting.

Abruptly, without warning or preliminaries, Stoph spoke. 'I propose to the politburo that Comrade Honecker be relieved of his position.'

It was as if the politburo was too stunned to speak, as if it did not react because – conversely – it had known what was to happen. Honecker's face did not change. Slowly he looked round the table, calling silently for their help.

'I propose we vote.' Again Stoph, again no preamble.

'Seconded.' From Schabowski.

It was cold and brutal, just as Honecker had done as a younger man.

'Those for.'

Stoph, to Honecker's left: arm raised. Krenz: arm raised. Mittag, the first of Honecker's guaranteed supporters: arm raised. It was done; Langer felt the chill of the excitement, it was all over. The vote came to Honecker. There were twenty-three members of the politburo, twenty-two so far in favour, tradition demanding that those concerned vote against themselves. For the last time Honecker looked at the ring of faces then raised his arm.

The room felt empty, the relief momentary then the sudden vacuum. Schabowski sensed the danger and moved against it. 'I propose that the politburo recommend to the Central Committee that Comrade Krenz be elected in the place of Comrade Honecker.'

For the second time that morning the vote was unanimous.

When Langer returned home Nikki was sitting in the living room. Her face was still drained and the plaster was taped across her forehead and down the left side of her face. Part of her skull was bald where the Leipzig doctors had shaved her head, the tape across the top, and she wore a woollen hat.

'Honecker's gone.' He sat down.

'How?'

'The politburo met this afternoon, the Central Committee will confirm it tomorrow.'

'How do you know?'

'I was there.'

'So we won.' She was looking at him, smiling.

Still Mielke and Moessner, Meyer as well, Langer was aware; still the old guard with their hands on the instruments of power. He smiled back and laughed.

The following day Erich Honecker formally resigned the three positions of power he had used to dominate the country for the past eighteen years: General Secretary of the Party, chairman of the Council of State, and chairman of the National Defence Council. In his last speech to the Central Committee he quoted grounds of ill-health, and at the end of it he received his last standing ovation. At the suggestion of the politburo Egon Krenz was then appointed General Secretary in his place, with his appointments to Honecker's other posts to be confirmed by the Volkskammer, the People's Parliament.

The afternoon after that Langer stood in the Party headquarters and watched as Egon Krenz formally welcomed the members of his new politburo. The occasion was attended by invited guests and filmed by the cameras of East German television, Krenz standing in the centre of the floor and the new members coming forward one by one and shaking his hand, dipping their heads to him. The new General Secretary accepting their allegiance and their homage.

That evening he sat at home, watching the ceremony on East German television. Gabi was reading a magazine and Nikki a book. He crossed the room and poured himself a whiskey. Already the mistakes were creeping in. One man again occupying the three key positions; the new cabinet gutted of Honecker supporters, but the reformer Hans Modrow still not a member. And Moscow.

The telephone rang and Nikki answered it.

'General Langer, please.'

She asked who wanted him and cupped her hand over the mouthpiece. 'For you.'

'Who is it?' He put the glass down.

'Egon Krenz.'

'I'll take it in my study.' The room was at the top of the stairs.

The new General Secretary thanked him both for his loyalty to the state and his conduct over the past years, and assured him of his position within the new East Germany. In order to maintain continuity, Erich Mielke would remain as head of State Security for the short term, but perhaps the two of them should discuss the longer term now that the leadership crisis was resolved. Of course, General Secretary, Langer replied. And congratulations. He put the telephone down and heard the sound at the door, saw Nikki.

'Bastard.' She was staring at him. 'Krenz called you general. But you're not army or police. Which leaves only one other thing.' Her face was white, her eyes still black from the beating, and the tape was still across her forehead and down her cheek. 'You were my father, the one person I could turn to. I told you about my friends, about what I believed in. I thought you shared my beliefs, that you agreed with them. I trusted you and all the time you were betraying me.'

He sat in the room, not bothering to close the door, and tried to work out what he could say. By the time he had even half decided Nikki had left the house.

The two women sat together. In the courtyard below the children were playing.

'When did you know my father was Stasi?'

'When you told me he arranged for Anja to be put on the list of those prisoners being sold to the West. Only the Stasi would have the power to do that.'

Eva's back and arms were still blue from the beating. She took Nikki's hand and stroked the hair away from her face. 'Perhaps you ought to talk to him. Ask him about it.'

'He's Stasi. How can I?'

The demonstrations were still growing; in cities and towns the Party itself was organizing mass discussions to debate the future of the country. The meeting in East Berlin was addressed by senior Party members including Schabowski and Marcus Wolfe, the former head of East German intelligence. In Leipzig the following week the number of marchers had risen to three hundred thousand. Each evening Langer sat alone reviewing the day's events and trying to see where they were taking the country.

The relationship between the people and the Party was changing, the people were now thinking more quickly than the Party, their political awareness advancing rapidly, daily. Yet at the same time neither the people nor the Party seemed coherent in their aims or their ideas. The people now enjoying a power they had never before dreamed of, yet something still troubling him. The vacuum in the country as dangerous as the vacuum in the politburo meeting after Honecker had been ousted. Have we gone so far that we cannot turn back? he asked himself. Have we gone far enough that the old guard cannot retake control or that the Soviets cannot change their mind?

The next morning he was informed that Egon Krenz had been summoned to Moscow. When he returned it was with the announcement that the reformer Hans Modrow was to join the politburo. Moscow was still running things: appointing Ulbricht in the first place and approving Honecker as his successor; assisting the overthrow of Honecker, now interfering with the decisions of his successor. Soon Moscow would be easing Krenz aside and bringing in Modrow. Fine as long as events in Moscow were stable, not so fine if the Moscow spring turned to winter. Already there were the first signs of challenge to Gorbachev, from both the conservatives and the reformers, and the first hint of the iron hand in the velvet glove of perestroika and glasnost.

It was three in the morning. He poured himself another whiskey. Of course the people of East Germany are on the move – it was as if Nikki was there, talking and arguing with him – of course the people want a new democratic form of socialism. But what good is that if we are still tied to Moscow? He could hear her, see her. Blonde hair and flashing eyes.

The sole function of the East German state in the Cold War was to be part of the border designed to protect the Soviet Union. But how has that changed? What makes you so sure of your own independence when the Soviet Union still has four hundred thousand troops in our country? The reformists are in power in Moscow now, so they've put the reformists in power in East Germany. But what happens if the old guard gets back in Moscow, what happens if Gorbachev is forced to change? What makes you so sure they won't bring the hardliners back again in Berlin?

Yet to do what you're suggesting we need change beyond what anyone is contemplating. To do that we have to make changes on such a scale that they can never be changed back.

Exactly.

But for that we have to change the whole basis on which East Germany is built. We have to destroy once and for all its position as a bastion of the Soviet frontier. We have to give the people what they do not even realize they want. We have to destroy the very reason for which the state of East Germany was created in 1945. Yet in doing so we give the reformers in Moscow a chance – the realization crept up on him like the first light creeping into the morning sky. Remove the outer protective wall from the empire and you at least give real change within the empire the possibility of survival.

At seven he telephoned Vöckel and arranged for Max Steiner to come East. Thirty hours later, shortly after midday, he himself crossed into the West.

CHAPTER THREE

THE SPIDER's webs were strung like nets across the ground and in the bushes, the morning dew glistening on them. Schiller had arrived in West Berlin at eleven the night before, staying at an address known only to himself. He climbed the wall by the gate and walked to the grave.

Viktor Wischenski. 1894–1948. That he never be forgotten.

There was something he should have remembered. Something about a boy standing alone at a grave, the rain running down his face, his lips turning blue with wet and cold, and the knuckles of his fists white. Schiller trawled back through his past and knew he was almost there, could not quite reach it. He left the cemetery and drove to his parents' flat.

His father had been up for an hour and his mother was preparing breakfast. Coffee and thick cream, black bread and cold meats. Over the years they had grown accustomed to his unannounced visits.

'Anja and Lisa are well?'

Since the divorce they had seen more of him, were glad that he saw more of Lisa. 'Fine.'

The photograph was on the sideboard. 'What was Uncle Viktor's family name?'

Christina glanced across at the photograph. 'Wischenski.'

'When did he die?'

'September 1948.' Why the interest, Schiller saw in her eyes, why the questions about Uncle Viktor?

'I was in Berlin a few weeks ago and went to the cemetery. The grave looked well kept.'

They smiled and nodded.

'I met someone there.'

'Where?' Christina lifted the jug.

'At the grave.'

'Who?' They both looked at him, voices and eyes suddenly sharper. 'Man or woman?'

'Man.'

There was the slightest disappointment in his mother's eyes. 'Who was he? Where was he from?' She poured his step-father a cup and began to pour his.

'He was from the East.'

'Where in the East?' She stopped pouring and looked at him again.

'Leipzig.'

'What was his name?'

'What do you think his name was?'

'Werner Langer?' There was an incredulity in her voice.

Werner Langer, he confirmed.

The first tears were in her eyes, her face breaking into a smile.

'Tell me about him.' He pulled a handkerchief from his pocket and gave it to her. Tell me why a general from East German State Security plants bulbs on the grave of Viktor Wischenski.

The meeting was at two thirty, the three men arriving within thirty seconds of each other.

'I would like to thank you both for the help you gave me earlier this year.'

They were standing at the foot of the grave, Langer on the right, Schiller in the centre and Rossini to the left.

'I am aware that the changes in East Germany could not have been brought about without that help. Perhaps, however, those changes are not going far enough.'

'How far should they go?' It was Rossini.

'Until East Germany is an independent country, till it is no longer simply part of the front-line defence for the Soviet Union.'

'And how would you do that while you're not only politically tied to the East but physically separated from the West?'

'By removing that physical separation.'

Jesus, he heard them both gasp. You know what we're talking about, you understand what you're saying.

'But you could only do that by bringing down the Berlin Wall.' Rossini kept the calm in his voice and summed up what both he and Schiller were thinking.

'Not necessarily bringing it down. Opening it up enough so that it can never again be closed.'

'But once you open up East Germany you redefine Eastern Europe. You redraw the political map of the world.'

'Yes.'

Langer was still running a scam; the distrust was ingrained in Schiller's mind. Despite what Christina had told him. Perhaps because of what she had told him. It was easy to assume the identity of another person, the East was doing it all the time. Yet Langer had been Langer long before he himself had become important, before he had become worth ensnaring. And then there was Rossini.

'What do you want from us?'

'Continued guarantees that neither of your countries will take advantage of the situation.'

'Agreed.' Rossini.

'What timetable?' Schiller.

Already Langer had sensed the conspiracies in the East, saw what was happening and who was at the core. 'It will have to be soon, before anyone takes control again.'

'How soon?'

'One week.'

For twenty-eight years the politicians had been discussing bringing down the Berlin Wall, Rossini thought. Now they were planning to do it in days.

'How?'

'Pressure on the new politburo, as before.'

'But can you hold the old guard off long enough?'

'Possibly.'

'Tactics.' It was Schiller. 'In the early days the people had a symbol. Honecker. Something or someone they wanted to get rid of. What we need now is another symbol. Something to unite them again, give them a purpose. Especially if that purpose is the opening up of the Wall.'

'What?' Langer.

'Or who.' Rossini.

A politician, they all assumed, someone like Hans Modrow.

'If Viktor Wischenski died because of the events which led to the Wall, perhaps he should play a part in those which bring it down.' Schiller watched for Langer's response.

How does Schiller know about Viktor? Langer tried to control the expression on his face. What does he know about how Viktor died? Obvious how the West German knew, he told himself. Noted the name and dates after the first meeting and ran a check. 'How did he die?' There was a sharpness in the question which betrayed him. Langer and Rossini unaware, Schiller knew, still could not believe it.

'He was killed by the East German People's Police at the Brandenburg Gate during the city council protests in 1948.'

'How do you know?' Eva didn't know. Eva had the photographs, one of the man he still called Uncle Viktor and the other of the grave, yet even Eva didn't know the circumstance of Viktor Wischenski's death.

'It was in the newspapers.'

'So what do you suggest?'

Schiller told them.

That night, after the arrangements had been finalized, Rossini returned to America. That night, after the first clandestine print runs were set up, Langer sat in his office on Lenin-Allee and called up Schiller's personal details on the computer.

The information was covered by the highest security classification; he typed in the first of the security codes, cleared the first check and punched in the code for the second. There had been something about Schiller that afternoon, even something about Rossini – he could not shake off the feeling. Schiller from the beginning, Rossini only at the end. He typed in the final security codes and accessed the file, ignoring the most recent information and returning to the past. Before August 1961. Before September 1948. Full name. Names of parents. Date and place of birth.

'Your father and I met when he was on leave in Berlin.' He remembered the evening Eva had told him. 'We had a small flat overlooking Bremerplatz. Not very big but we made it home.'

How the hell did Schiller know when he himself had discovered the truth only recently? What the hell was Schiller playing at? He closed the file, exited the computer, left Lenin-Allee and began the drive to Leipzig.

Eva was waiting for him even though it was almost midnight, the broth on the stove and the bread hot in the oven. 'Have you spoken to Nikki?'

'I've left messages but she doesn't phone back.'

Eva sat opposite him. 'Why didn't you tell her the truth?'

'What is the truth?'

The soup was as he remembered it as a boy.

So why didn't you tell Nikki the truth, Eva asked again.

'Perhaps Nikki is closer to the truth than she realizes.'

'What do you mean?'

He wiped the bread round the bowl and shook his head.

What are you doing, my son? She saw the smile on his face, remembered it from another time. The magician at the school so long ago.

The photographs were on the wall where they had always been. Langer washed and wiped his hands and took the one photograph from its place. 'You never told me how Viktor died.'

'I never knew. I still don't.'

'Why not?'

Eva shrugged. 'It was difficult. The people in the West who sent me the photograph were afraid of putting any information in the letter.'

'Would you like to know?'

'Of course.'

'He was shot by the People's Police at the Brandenburg Gate.'

She looked up at the ceiling, the tears filling her eyes and her fingers stroking her throat.

Tell me about Hans-Joachim Schiller, Langer said gently.

'Christina's Hans-Joachim?'

He remembered the parents' details on the security file. 'Yes, Christina's Hans-Joachim.'

Eva had dried her eyes and was looking at him again. It was almost as if she was not surprised, he thought, as if one day she expected it.

'He was there the night you were born, of course.'

Michael Rossini reached Andrews at eleven in the evening, the next morning he flew from Washington National to Manchester arriving shortly after nine. The rental car was waiting for him. He telephoned his parents to alert them of his visit and drove to the house. Fall had not yet given way to winter, the trees a quilt of reds, oranges and browns. He swung the car off the road and up the track.

Hanni was waiting for him in the doorway. 'How long are you stopping?' She kissed him and led him inside.

'Flying visit, lunch then away. Where's Dad?'

He was looking tired, she thought, as if he had not slept properly. 'Fishing, he left before you phoned. He'll be sorry that he missed you.'

He walked into the study; Hanni put on the coffee and followed him through.

The photograph was in a gold frame on the sideboard. He picked it up and looked at it. 'When I was a boy there was another photograph, a grave.'

She took the photograph from the drawer of the desk and gave it to him.

Viktor Wischenski. 1894–1948. That he never be forgotten.

'I was there yesterday.'

'Where?'

'At Viktor's grave.'

He turned to her and saw the look in her eyes. How did you know where it was? What were you doing there?

'I met two men there.'

'Who?'

'Who do you think?'

'How old were they?'

'My age, more or less.'

'Hans-Joachim Schiller and Werner Langer.'

He nodded and allowed her time, allowed himself time.

'But how could Werner Langer be there?' She sat down. 'Werner Langer is in the East. Eva took him to Leipzig when he was less than a year old.'

Tell me about them, he said. Tell me about Berlin in 1945.

Two weeks ago, Nikki thought, even ten days ago, and the mood as they waited to go on to the streets had been one of fear and foreboding; now it was one of triumph and expectancy. The Gethsemane Church was packed – students, parents with children, old and young from all walks of life. It was her first real day back. As she walked round the church the original protesters, men and women, came up to her and welcomed her. She sat with them and drank coffee, listened to the discussion about what was planned for that night.

'You're all right?' It was one of those with whom she had sat in the church when there had only been a handful of them.

She nodded. 'Why?'

'A special job. We need people we can trust.'

They left Gethsemane. Twenty minutes later they came to the printing works. More people she knew were guarding the back door; they recognized her and shook hands, then bustled her inside.

'A special poster, they're being printed and distributed throughout the country. We're using this press tonight and a different one tomorrow in case the Stasi try to find us.'

In case my father tries to hunt us down, she thought.

The others were arriving and the presses rolling.

'We hand out as many as we can,' the organizer instructed them. 'Tell people to put them on placards.' The first posters were ready; he picked one up and showed it to them.

The posters were in black and white, the image on them of a man, in his early fifties, good-looking but gaunt-faced, as if he had had little to eat. His hair was neatly combed, the style old-fashioned, and he wore a collar, tie and suit, also old-fashioned.

'Who is it?' someone behind Nikki asked.

A hero from the past, the organizer told them, a symbol of resistance to the régime.

Nikki saw the face and felt the shock. Tried to hide her confusion and her fear.

That night five thousand such posters were distributed in East Berlin, similar numbers in other locations where demonstrations were being held. Take them home tonight and make placards out of them, the people were told, there'll be more tomorrow. Already some people were nailing the posters on to wooden frames and holding them in the air. The following night the numbers of posters trebled, the television cameras picking them up, the following night a fifth of the people on the streets were carrying them. The night after that almost a third.

Why Uncle Viktor, the thought still pounded through Nikki Langer's head. What's going on?

The Collegiate met at three the following afternoon. In an hour the light would begin to fade and the people would begin to gather.

'Who is he?' Mielke ignored the official agenda and came straight to the point.

'We're trying to find out.' It was Meyer. 'We're only a matter of hours away from establishing his identity.'

The Honecker days were returning and the old guard regrouping, Langer thought. Mielke and Moessner behind Meyer, but no one acting alone. The hand of Moscow somewhere – one of the hands of Moscow. Probably the East German army and large parts of the Stasi. Himself to the side because of his presumed association with Krenz and Schabowski.

'So who's making and distributing them? Who's behind it?'

'We're close to finding that out also.'

The Chancellor sat behind his desk, the light fading and the reports already coming in from the East. Leipzig, where it had begun. Magdeburg, Halle, Dresden.

'How many?'

'How many where?'

'Berlin.'

'A hundred and fifty thousand.' Schiller watched Hanniman's face and waited for the Chancellor's next question.

'And he's there again?' There was something about the man in the photograph which haunted him.

'Yes.'

The Chancellor turned to the two people in the world he most trusted. 'Who's behind him and what do they want?'

The shadows hung like ghosts in the recesses of the Oval Office.

'Karl-Marx-Stadt, Plauen and Erfurt on the move.'

'Berlin?'

'Two hundred thousand.'

Satellite intelligence reporting major troop and tank movements in East Germany. Signals picking up heavy traffic between Moscow and Berlin. The Pentagon arguing readiness and the State Department counselling caution. Strategic Air Command querying Defcon Three status and recommending upgrade to Two.

The three men and one woman watched and waited. The heads

of NSC and CIA, the chairman of the Joint Chiefs of Staff, and the White House special adviser.

The next report came in. 'A quarter of a million on the streets of East Berlin and growing.'

'What did Trotsky say about Berlin?'

'It was Lenin.' The woman wore a slim gold band round her neck. Even now Rossini still thought of her as Mateus. 'The world was Europe, Europe was Germany, Germany was Berlin.'

And Berlin was the Wall, the President thought. He nodded and picked up the photograph. The man was in his early fifties, strong features but gaunt-faced, as if he had had little to eat. His hair was neatly combed, the style old-fashioned, and he wore a suit, collar and tie, also old-fashioned. The fourth quarter, the President remembered his college football days. Ten seconds on the clock and somebody going for the big one. One hell of a play, whatever it was.

'So where do we start looking for him?'

At the beginning, Michael Rossini might have said, but did not.

At six the following morning Nikki caught the train to Leipzig. Eva was waiting for her at the station. It was drizzling slightly, the weather cold. They took a tram to Rosenstrasse, the drizzle replaced by sudden rain, and ran across the pavement into the courtyard and up the stairs to the flat. Her shoes were wet, Nikki took them off and laid them by the fireplace. The photograph of her grandfather hung in its place on the wall above, two pale rectangles beside it.

'Why have you taken down the photographs of Uncle Viktor?'

'Why do you think?'

'But why is Uncle Viktor on the placards? Who decided it should be him?'

'I don't know.'

'But?'

'I think you should talk to your father.'

The item was on West Berlin television. No one read newspapers when they could watch television, Schiller had decided, and no one would watch East German television if they could watch pro-

grammes from the West. That morning, therefore, he had contacted the station and passed on the information, plus a copy of
the newspaper report containing the details of Viktor Wischenski's
death. The man on the posters, the programme said, was Viktor
Wischenski, a West Berliner shot dead by East German People's
Police at the Brandenburg Gate in 1948.

That evening the direction of the marches in East Berlin
changed, dramatically and suddenly. That night, for the first time,
the thousands began to close on the Berlin Wall.

The arrests had begun again. Quietly and efficiently, so that no
one even noticed. Starting in Leipzig and spreading around the
country, though not in Berlin. In Leipzig also, and again spreading
from there to other Stasi regions, the tank and other armoured
units of State Security not generally known to the public, including
the Felix Dzierzynski Guard Regiment, were placed on stand-by
and key divisions of the People's Army mobilized.

That morning Langer was invited to take lunch at the Soviet
embassy. Formal or informal, he asked. Informal, he was told.

The man from the Kremlin was waiting for him in the ambassador's suite. There were those in Moscow who were concerned
at certain tendencies now being exhibited in Berlin, the Russian
explained. While Moscow believed in and supported perestroika,
it viewed with concern the fact that the Berlin Wall had become a
key target of the demonstrations in Berlin. Moscow was confident,
however, that the problem could be resolved without undue delay
or notice.

'Of course.'

It was the same everywhere, he thought as he left, Berlin and
Moscow. The army, security service and police seeing their control
slipping away and planning how to retrieve it. The Party suddenly
afraid of losing its position and privilege and determined to retain
both.

Gerhard Meyer arrived in East Berlin at eleven, his absence from
Leipzig and his presence in the capital known only to his fellow
conspirators. The meeting took place at twelve and was attended
by senior ranks of the army, police and State Security, as well as

high-ranking Party officials. The only Stasi region not represented was Berlin, the personal loyalty of officers in that region to Werner Langer being considered a security risk.

For the first forty minutes they discussed the vacuum created by the removal from power of Erich Honecker and the public demonstrations and discussions which had followed. For the rest of the meeting Meyer led them through the plans already in hand to overturn the present situation and return the country to its former orderly existence.

'What about the Soviets?' The party official was from Magdeburg.

'The KGB is divided.' Moessner chaired the meeting. 'Originally it supported Gorbachev, now some of its members are not so sure. The Red Army, however, is becoming increasingly worried about the situation, particularly the demand that the Wall be opened.'

'So the Red Army in East Germany will not oppose us?'

Meyer glanced at the infantry general to his right. 'At worst it will remain neutral. At best, but only if necessary, it will support us.' He looked again at the general. 'That support, of course, will not be necessary.'

'When do we begin?'

'Tonight.'

'And Langer?'

'General Langer is being taken care of.'

The man in the off-green leather jacket had waited for Nikki all day. He noted her arrival then lost himself in the crowd inside the church as she talked to the other founding members of the movement. Traces of bruising to her face, he also noted; tape still in place presumably covering laceration. The sort of injury which might have been received in a riot, therefore something to be included in the report.

They left the church, joined the thousands along Unter den Linden, and began marching towards the Brandenburg Gate. Fifty metres past the Soviet embassy and two hundred metres short of the gate the road was blocked by Vopos, three deep and shoulder to shoulder, riot gear on and batons drawn. Behind and to the side of them were rows of troops, also in riot gear. Part of the crowd hesitated and stayed in Unter den Linden, circling aimlessly and suddenly unsure what to do. The rest turned for the other sections of the Wall where they had congregated on previous evenings. At each point access was denied, the People's Police and army stopping them at least one hundred metres away.

Langer was informed at eight. One week, he had told Schiller and Rossini. If he was lucky, he now thought. At eight thirty he left his office, collected his car and drove out of the compound surrounding the building on Lenin-Allee. The tails were parked five hundred metres away; as he passed them the light blue Lada pulled out and fell in fifty metres behind him. Two minutes later he stopped and made the Lada overtake him, saw the second ease into position behind.

When he returned home Nikki was in the lounge; her feet curled under her in the armchair. It was the first time she had come to the house since the Krenz telephone call.

'Let me look.' The bruising had almost gone from her face and the black round her eyes had disappeared, but the two thin strips of tape still ran across her forehead and down her left cheek. He lifted the woollen hat she wore; the hair on the top of her head was a short yellow stubble and the scars were ridged across it.

'I know.' She looked at him. 'Or at least I think I know.'

He smiled at her and poured them each a drink, white wine for her, whiskey for himself. 'How?'

'The man on the poster.'

'You've spoken to Eva?'

'I went to see her once I realized and she confirmed it was Viktor. That was all she said.'

'She's taken the photos down?'

'Of course.'

'So what do you know?'

'That you're not what I thought you were.'

He said nothing.

'The appearance of the posters had a unifying effect on the people and turned their attention to the opening up of the Wall.' Nikki sipped the wine and looked at him. 'Whoever was responsible for the posters and the story about Viktor on television knew what result they would have. No one else other than Eva knew about Viktor, therefore you were responsible for his appearance on the posters. Therefore it was you who directed the crowds and formed the single demand that the Wall be opened.' Confirm that I am right or wrong, the silence which followed asked.

'What else do you know?'

'I'm not sure.' Nikki hesitated, trying to pull the jumble of thoughts into a semblance of logic. 'I've often thought about how certain things – things we've all forgotten about now – just seemed to happen.'

What things? Unspoken.

'The Hungarian decision to dismantle their border with Austria; their steadfastness in not sending East Germans back after their travel documents had run out. The Czechs continuing to allow East Germans to go through to Austria. The West Germans running their embassies as refugee camps and the Czechs again, not keeping East Germans away from the Prague embassy.'

She was still looking at him. 'When people look back on this period they will talk about how Honecker was removed, probably about a politburo conspiracy against him, possibly the involvement of the Soviets. They'll talk about Schabowski and Modrow and Krenz and nobody will even know your name. But you did it, didn't you? You set the whole thing up.'

'I told you once you sounded like a lawyer. You still do.'

'You *are* a general in the Stasi, aren't you?'

'Yes.'

'Then why?'

Still no answer.

'How far do you want to go with the Wall?'

'Far enough that it can never again be closed. That it no longer bonds us irrevocably with Moscow, no longer puts us automatically under Russian control.' He looked up at her and laughed. 'Good that you're back.'

'Glad to be back.'

He left her and made the telephone call.

The morning was bleak. The moment he left the colony the tails picked him up. Langer turned off Blenkenburger Strasse into Romain-Rolland Strasse and began the game. Standard procedure, he assumed, two or three vehicle format, cars or bikes, vehicles behind or in front but none in contact for more than two minutes. He turned away from Lenin-Allee and picked up the radio.

'Operations immediately.' He used his code-name and was patched through within seconds. 'Foreign intelligence in city, travelling in three vehicles. He gave the details and the position. 'Suggest immediate interception.'

Stand by, he was told, all units being alerted.

Green Lada behind him, light yellow easing apparently innocently in front, blue out of sight. Green dropping back.

Update on locations, Control came through five minutes later.

'Gottwald Allee heading east.' Yellow turning left, blue moving up.

'Contact. Stand by.'

Blue slipping away, green in again.

'All units. Go.'

He turned off Gottwald Allee and drove to the meeting with Max Steiner.

At eleven Max crossed back to the West, by twelve he had spoken on secure lines to both Hans-Joachim Schiller and Michael Rossini. At six the marches began again. At ten that evening Schiller travelled secretly to West Berlin, half an hour later he was briefed by Max Steiner. Five hours before Rossini had flown equally secretly out of Andrews.

At three, Langer had been informed, Mielke and Meyer had been observed entering the Soviet embassy via the rear entrance. At four, he was also later informed, members of the Leipzig region of State Security had been placed on stand-by. At eight, he had observed for himself, the police and army had again prevented demonstrators from approaching the Wall.

The Gethsemane Church was busy, someone bringing soup for lunch and others organizing for that evening's march.

The man in the light green leather jacket, Nikki thought. In the church yesterday, on the corner this morning, in the church again now. No reason she should single him out from the hundreds now mingling around Gethsemane, she told herself.

When she looked again he had gone.

The three-day special session of the Central Committee began at ten the next morning at the Party headquarters on Karl-Marx

Platz. At twelve Langer was asked to attend a confidential session of the inner circle of the new politburo. The meeting began an hour later, in one of the many rooms in the labyrinth of the headquarters building.

That afternoon, he was informed, the Council of Ministers would declare an amnesty for those convicted of attempting to leave the country illegally. It would also formally legalize the protest movement New Forum. The following afternoon the main item on the agenda for the first session of the new politburo would be the relaxation of travel for the citizens of East Germany to the West.

'Too little too late.' His words were sharp and blunt, and took them by surprise.

'Why?'

'Because you're close to a coup d'état by the old guard.'

'How? What do you mean?'

Extra riot police and army reinforcements were being drafted into Berlin, he told them. Stasi units from Leipzig were also on their way. Moscow faces had been seen entering the Soviet embassy. Arrests had been under way for several days. The Felix Dzierzynski Guard Regiment and the other tank and armoured divisions of State Security had been placed on stand-by.

'What other tanks and armoured divisions of State Security?'

There are many things you do not know about State Security, he replied coldly.

'But the identities of the conspirators are known?'

'Of course.'

'Then why not simply arrest them?'

'Because that would precipitate the coup.'

'So what can we do?'

The atmosphere in the room was bleak.

'Simple. The purpose of the coup is twofold. Firstly, to maintain the positions and privileges of the Party, the army and State Security in the country. Secondly, to ensure that East Germany remains the front defensive line of the Soviet Union. The second is the more important. Remove it and you remove the rationale for Soviet support for the coup.'

'And how do we do that?'

He allowed them to wait. 'By opening up the Wall.'

But once you've opened it you could never close it again. He saw them face the dilemma. Yet in so doing you make it impossible for Moscow to intervene.

'If you would allow us a moment.'

He waited outside, two minutes later he was asked back. The item would be agreed at the meeting of the full politburo the following afternoon, he was informed. The decision would be unanimous and would be announced by Gunter Schabowski at a press conference immediately following the politburo meeting.

The tail picked him up the moment he left the building, crossing behind him to the Hotel Stadt Berlin and waiting beside him for the lift. The General was no problem, the tail thought, good in his day but past it now. The lift stopped and emptied. Eight people waiting to enter. Langer stepped into the lift and pressed the ascend button. The man closest to him jammed his foot in the door and began to object. Calmly Langer reached in his pocket, took out his State Security identity card, held it in front of the man, and shook his head.

Shit, the tail cursed, was already looking for the stairs and checking the panel of lights above the doors. Bastard, he cursed again, had pressed every floor, given no indication where he had left the lift.

The room at the foot of the service stairs at the rear was dark and smelt of central heating oil, the doors off it into the street and the intestines of the hotel.

'Hello, Werner.'

'Max.'

The eyes had been on her from the moment she had left the flat. She was being paranoid, Nikki rebuked herself, allowing herself to be dictated by her imagination. She left Unter den Linden and went to Gethsemane.

Max Steiner's meeting with Hans-Joachim Schiller and Michael Rossini was at five. For twenty minutes he briefed them on Langer's requirements for the following day, for the twenty minutes after that they discussed how they would meet them.

At five, on a secure line, Schiller spoke with the colonel commanding the West German counter-terrorist group GSG–9. The operation was priority and for political and security reasons could not be cleared with the Chancellor's office, he told the man. The two had worked together before and trusted each other. By five thirty the first teams were airlifting to Berlin.

At six Rossini met the officer commanding the American garrison in the city. The meeting had been arranged person-to-person, no one else being aware of it. For security reasons, he told the brigadier, the operation could not be cleared with anyone, not even the President. The brigadier had met him in Washington and still dined off the story that for once the politicians had got it right, that the man who knew the best whorehouse in town now headed the CIA.

One hour later Max Steiner crossed again to the East for his second meeting of the day with Werner Langer.

At the end Langer asked him one question. 'What do you want from me?'

'The safe house and the telephone number.'

At ten that night, as the crowds began to leave the streets of East Berlin, the aircraft hangar at Tempelhof in the West was sealed off and the run-throughs began, the details of the crossing marked on the floor, the Mercedes and BMWs of GSG–9 and the jeeps of the Berlin Brigade rehearsing and revising, checking and re-checking.

Opposition? One of the drivers asked as they stopped for a break at three in the morning.

Stasi in the East, he was told, probably Spetznaz in the West.

CHAPTER FOUR

THE MORNING was bright and cold. Langer rose at six, not having slept, and began the visits to those members of the Berlin district of State Security whom he considered would play key roles in the next fourteen hours. All were known to him and most were personal appointments. Because of the rapidly changing nature of events, he told each man, it was possible that certain units would receive different orders from different people. They, however, were Berlin garrison. They, therefore, would obey orders only from him. To avoid confusion, and for the purpose of confirmation, orders from him would carry the code Orange.

Berlin. Thursday, 9 November.

The shadows crossed at nine, on foot and individually, through Checkpoint Charlie or via the S-bahn to Friedrichstrasse. An hour later the first BMW passed through Checkpoint Charlie, the others at twenty-minute intervals, diplomatic plates prominent and Heckler and Kochs and Walthers concealed. At ten forty-five the Mercedes went East, Stars and Stripes fluttering from the wing, English-speaking GSG–9 driver and Max Steiner with American diplomatic passport in the rear. Just like the old days, he thought, same grim faces of the guards and same nerves in the pit of the stomach.

Langer met Nikki at eleven. 'This afternoon the politburo will vote to allow people to travel abroad. Effectively to pass through the Wall. The decision will be announced at a press conference at five. If anyone has the sense to ask, they will be told that the decision is effective immediately. The people will therefore expect to be able to cross this evening.

'The army and the Stasi are aware of this. Plans are already under way to stop this process. The Stasi Collegiate will meet at the same time to approve a crackdown. Because of who you are, and because they think they can get at me through you, you are therefore in danger.'

'I'm already being followed.'

'Of course.'

She waited.

'You're also being protected.'

She waited again.

'There's a telephone number, people waiting at it. If at any point from now on you think you're in danger you telephone that number. You ask for Klaus. You say your name is Karin.'

Old times' sake; he remembered how Max had laughed when he had passed on the instructions the night before.

'You'll be told that Klaus is out and asked to phone back. You go immediately to Rodenberg Strasse, behind the Gethsemane Church. Scherenberg Strasse runs across it. You stand by the fourth tree from the junction, on the right as you face Schönhauser Allee. A car will pick you up. You get in the boot.'

'What if anyone is following me?' She knew she had to ask but wished she had not, would never forget the ice on her father's face.

'If anyone is following you they'll be taken care of.' He told her the telephone number and made her repeat it, made her repeat the code-names and the address till he was confident she would not forget it.

'What about my mother?'

'Your mother is guaranteed political asylum in the West. If the time comes a number of embassies will be warned to receive her.'

'Thank you.'

'One last thing. You know you're being followed. We have people following you as well. If, at any time, they spot a danger they'll get you out. If that happens, the man in charge will introduce himself as Klaus. You do exactly as he says. Any questions?'

'Anja?' Nikki was unsure why she thought of the woman.

'What about Anja?'

'Who got her out?'

'A man called Schiller.'

'How?'

'In the boot of a car through Checkpoint Charlie.'

She nodded as if she understood. 'What else do I do?'

The ice had thawed from his face. 'Enjoy yourself. Today we make history.'

*

At two o'clock precisely the politburo met, the Central Committee also in session. At two thirty the crowds began to gather, earlier than usual, the winter light already fading and the expectancy in the air. At three the western end of Unter den Linden, close to the Brandenburg Gate, was sealed off by riot police and army, and the first rumours began to circulate of massive Vopo strength along the Wall. At three thirty Langer was informed that tanks of the Stasi's armoured units were closing on the city; simultaneously British and American units monitoring communications between Moscow and Berlin reported a sudden increase in radio traffic. At four police and army strength along the Wall, already massive, was reinforced.

The crowd was large, growing every minute. Nikki walked with the others from Gethsemane, sensing the feeling, the electricity in the air: the politburo meeting and the sudden police presence. They walked down Schönhauser Allee and along Unter den Linden. The man in the green leather jacket was close to her, looking away as she glanced at him.

The Mercedes was in the garage of the safe house, guards like ghosts inside and out, one GSG–9 man sitting by the telephone upstairs. You've done this before, he suggested. Once or twice, Max Steiner told him.

The man in the green leather jacket was still close to her, looking away again as she turned towards him. There was no reason to panic, Nikki reassured herself, no reason to call the number. The streets were packed, the number of people constantly growing. They left Unter den Linden and drifted towards the crossing in the Wall at Heinrich-Heine Strasse, unsure what to do or where to go.

Four o'clock. In the safe house near Rodenberg Strasse the GSG–9 man lifted the telephone and checked the dialling tone.

The politburo meeting ended at four thirty, the members returning to the Central Committee and a spokesman announcing merely that Gunter Schabowski would address a press conference at five.

Four forty-five. The crowd was packed around her, marching, moving slowly. The man in the leather jacket again: she had seen him this morning, plus another she remembered from yesterday. She felt the fear again and looked for a telephone box, knew there was no way she could get to one. More men looking at her, she thought. She was being paranoid, she told herself. Enjoy yourself, her father had told her, today we make history.

Langer left Lenin-Allee and was driven to Normannenstrasse. The other members of the Collegiate were already assembled. He smiled his greetings and took his place. Meyer opposite and Moessner to his left. Mielke opened the meeting.

In the committee room on the second floor of Party Headquarters Schabowski began his press conference. The table at which he sat ran the width of the room, slightly raised from the floor and the entire area was flooded with the lights of the television cameras. Quickly, almost nonchalantly, he dealt with the considerations of the politburo that afternoon: their desire for democracy, the importance of the election of Hans Modrow to the chairmanship of the Council of Ministers, the decision on travel. It was matter-of-fact, almost lost in the general discussion, the reporters and their camera and radio crews expecting nothing and wanting only to get back to the crowds on the streets.

'All border crossings to the Federal Republic of Germany and West Berlin can be used.' Schabowski's voice was slow and he read from a prepared document. 'Until new travel legislation can be enacted, those applying to make private journeys abroad may apply without meeting the previous preconditions. Permission would be given promptly.'

The television lights were switched off and the majority of reporters began to leave, only a few gathering round Schabowski at the top table.

'What sort of paperwork will be required?'

Schabowski shrugged. 'They will be given a stamp in their identity card.'

The room was emptying.

'That will be sufficient?'

'Yes.'

Even some of the reporters around the politburo member began to drift away.

'When will this become effective?'

Schabowski appeared to hesitate, then he consulted the briefing document and looked back up. 'From this moment.'

The telephone rang. Mielke answered immediately, listened, then pressed the conference button so they could all hear. Schabowski's statement and the decision of the politburo. Meyer rose, lifted one of the hand sets from the bank on Mielke's left and dialled a number. It was answered on the first ring.

'This is General Meyer.' He looked at Langer. 'Seal the Wall. All units in.' He dialled a second number and looked again at Langer. 'Meyer. Pick her up now.'

They heard it. The three hundred thousand suddenly silent, listening to the radios many of them held. *All borders to the Federal Republic and West Berlin are now open. All that is required is a stamp in the identity papers. The decision effective from this moment.*

The rumour swept the crowd as quickly as the news of the politburo decision: Stasi blocking off the Wall, the riot police and tanks already in position, stopping them going near the crossings to the West.

The man in the green jacket was moving towards her, another behind her, more in front. Nikki turned and tried to escape, more closing on her. The man was almost upon her, almost close enough to touch her, the others ringed around her. Stasi, she tried to shout, help me. She knew her voice was lost in the crowd and tried to push away for the last time. The hand took her arm and she turned.

'Hello, Nikki, I'm Klaus.'

More men, coming from nowhere. The first was steering her through the crowd, others in front of him cutting their way. The young men were all around her, shielding her, descending upon her like an impenetrable barrier. The man with the green leather jacket was trying to reach her, more Stasi behind. Someone moved in front of him, blocking him.

The car was on the edge of the crowd, engine running and doors open. She stepped in, the car already moving and the man sliding in beside her, another in the front passenger seat speaking on the radio. A Lada, she realized; Stasi, she thought, knew she had been tricked. It's all right, the man from GSG–9 told her, the limo's waiting.

'Blue. Contact.'

Schiller heard Max Steiner's voice and adjusted his earpiece. Radio silence broken only if they were bringing Nikki Langer out. GSG–9 only bringing her out if there was trouble.

'Repeat. Blue contact. Package picked up.' Package in place if Nikki had contacted the number at the safe house, package picked up if the GSG–9 shadows trailing Nikki had decided she was in danger.

The operations room was calm, almost cold, the images from the cameras overlooking Checkpoint Charlie flickering on the banks of monitors, the crossing in the foreground and Friedrichstrasse stretching like a ribbon beyond.

'Red. Received.' The voice of the GSG–9 commander.

Rossini sat down beside him.

The road was badly made and the street lighting poor. Nikki did not know the area, did not know where she was. The houses gave way to factories. The Lada stopped and she got out, saw the Mercedes. The man who stepped from it was older than the others, around her father's age, she thought. He opened the boot and she began to climb in.

'Good luck.'

'How can I thank you?'

Buy us all a beer on the Kurfurstendamm, Max Steiner told her.

Meyer was still looking at him, Mielke bringing the meeting to order again, issuing instructions and detailing actions. Langer left his seat and walked to the bank of telephones. Dialled.

'This is General Langer.'

'Yes, General.' The voice of the colonel in charge of the border crossings through the Wall.

'What orders have you received?'

'To close all exit points.'

'What else is happening?'

'The crowds are waiting to cross to the West, the riot police and the army are here in force.'

He looked at Meyer, at the Collegiate. 'You know what the politburo has ordered.'

'Yes, General.'

He was still looking at the Collegiate. Mielke. Meyer. 'This is General Langer. The code for today is Orange.'

*

The headlights blinked in the gloom at the top of Friedrichstrasse. Schiller looked at the monitors as the cameras zoomed in. The car was not his, he would know when it was.

'Your people ready?'

'Ready.'

Neither Schiller nor Rossini took his eyes off the monitors.

'Angels in place.'

They heard the orders of the American commander. German units carrying the colour code blue, American the colour green. In the street to their right the jeeps of the Berlin Brigade trundled apparently routinely into place.

'Movement at Gartenstrasse.'

There were lookouts at each of the major crossings through the Wall.

'Large crowds at Heinrich-Heine Strasse. Army and riot police in position between them and the crossing. Tanks closing in.' The observer was trained, professional. 'Crowd growing, jamming the road.' His voice was calm and analytical. 'Tanks moving into position.'

Schiller saw the headlights. As if he was sitting in the Oasis, he realized, as if he was not watching from the operations room but was sitting at the table in the bar of the corner of the building overlooking the East.

First BMW.

'Blue One. Coming home.'

'Green. Standing by.'

He saw the Mercedes, the twin beams slightly high, the woman in the boot curled like a foetus and praying to whatever God she believed in. The second and third BMWs.

'More movement at Heinrich-Heine Strasse. People coming forward, army and tanks stopped moving.' The voice was calm, detached. 'The people are at the control box, the guards are stamping identity cards. The barrier is still across the road. Christ. Oh Jesus Christ.' They heard the change in his voice, the sudden excitement, knew he was unaware of it. 'They're opening up the barrier. They've opened the Wall. They're coming through. The people are coming through.'

'Who? What? What people?'

'*The people*. Still coming. Hundreds already in the West. No one stopping them. The guards are standing back, watching.'

The lead BMW was fifty metres from Checkpoint Charlie. To the right of the Oasis Schiller saw the jeeps pull into position.

'Angels, stand by.' The voice of the American commander. 'Possible bandits.' Stasi moving into Checkpoint Charlie from the East and sealing off the route out, Soviet Spetznaz from the West. It was what they had expected, rehearsed against the night before.

The lead BMW swung right and left, through the first obstacles and into the diplomatic channel. The guards were coming forward, the driver winding down the window but not getting out. The passenger in the rear seat opened his window and waved his diplomatic credentials.

The Mercedes was at the bottom of Friedrichstrasse, the tail BMWs closing on it like wolves, entering Checkpoint Charlie. The border guard stepped back; in the control box a second guard reached for the button and lifted the barrier.

The alarm bell echoed in the night, the barrier half up then crashing down automatically, the men running from the other side. More men and guards, appearing suddenly from the shadows and closing on the cars. The lead BMW screamed forward, the Mercedes accelerating hard through the first obstacles, the tail BMWs fanned protectively behind it.

The jeeps screeched forward, lead vehicles hurtling into the no-man's-land before the checkpoint. Two cars coming up behind them, accelerating around them. Spetznaz, they knew. The jeeps spun into the cars and bulldozed them off the road.

The lead BMW slammed left and braked hard. The barrier crashed down on to the roof, the positioning of the car preventing it from closing. The Mercedes swerved right, the tail cars still protecting it, and accelerated under the barrier and into the West.

EPILOGUE

THE BOOKING was for eight in the evening. The restaurant was one of the most exclusive in the city, fully booked weeks in advance. Especially tonight. In the sky above the Brandenburg Gate the fireworks exploded in the black. On the streets on either side of the Gate the crowds stood and sang. In the concert hall three hundred metres away the Berlin Symphony waited.

Berlin. October 1990. Almost a year since the Wall had been opened.

The booking itself had only been made the morning before. That afternoon the owner himself had called to confirm the arrangements. That evening the manager had laid the table personally. The best table, the best champagne. At seven the violinist arrived. He was in his early seventies, with immaculately brushed white hair, and wore a dinner suit. For thirty minutes he played gently, his fingers moving quickly and sensitively and his face barely concealing his emotion. The restaurant was beginning to fill, both the head waiter and the manager nervous, anxious. At fifteen minutes to eight the violinist rose and went to the bathroom. When he returned a glass of champagne was brought to him, though he did not drink from it, and a single red rose was placed in his buttonhole. He stood silently, head slightly bowed and violin cradled in his arm.

'What were you playing?' The head waiter stood close to him.

The violinist looked at him and smiled. 'How old are you?'

'Thirty-seven.'

'Then you wouldn't understand.'

'Tell me anyway.'

'Before the war this area comprised tenement blocks and flats. Most of them were bombed, few of them survived.'

The waiter shook his head. 'And the tune.'

'Beethoven.'

The waiter was still looking at him.

In the street outside the manager saw the lights of the Mercedes, the doors opening and the young men getting out even while the car was slowing. The woman stepped out and walked towards the restaurant.

'It was forty-five years ago,' the violinist said simply. 'The Berlin Symphony at the Schauspielhaus. When we started the Russians were in Pankow, by the time we finished they were almost at the Brandenburg Gate. We played extracts from Verdi and Mozart, then Beethoven. The last movement of the Ninth. When the concert ended those in the audience with flowers in their coats took them off and gave them to us. I only played the last movement once more, in a bar under a railway viaduct for a woman who was prepared to give me everything she had in the world. After that I swore that I would never again play the Ninth.'

'But you're playing it tonight.'

The woman had almost reached the door. The violinist leaned forward and began to play, body swaying and fingers moving. In the street outside another Mercedes stopped, a second woman stepping out. In the semi-dusk the Lincoln drove into Bremerplatz.

'As I said, you wouldn't understand.'

The woman looked in her late sixties, still slim and attractive. She stood inside the door, looking at the musician as the manager took her coat. The violinist smiled, still playing, and dipped his head in a bow, the woman seeing the rose and realizing. The second woman entered the restaurant and heard the violin, then the third.

'Hello, Eva.'

'Hello, Christina.'

'Hello, Hanni.'

Ten minutes to midnight. The sky brilliant with lights and the city loud with celebration. That afternoon he had walked the length of the Wall, the woman at his side, from Heidelbergerstrasse in the south to Bernauer Strasse in the north. Rather, had walked what remained of the Wall, only the occasional section remaining, the gaping space between what had once been two halves of a divided city, the gypsy children near Heinrich-Heine Strasse and the Turks at Checkpoint Charlie and Potsdam Platz selling segments of the murals which had once decorated the west side, students selling tea and coffee in the remnants of a watch-tower.

The parade along Unter den Linden had only been a year ago, Honecker taking the salute and the other strong men of the Warsaw Pact at his side: Jaruzelski of Poland, Jakes from Czechoslovakia, Ceaucescu of Romania. All gone. Even now he could not believe it, the speed at which it had happened. All swept away in the flood that had followed the breaching of the Wall. And God only knew what would happen to the Soviet Union now its forward defences had collapsed.

The woman at his side had not spoken, allowed him his thoughts. It was five minutes to midnight. They left the Kurfurstendamm and crossed Wittenbergplatz.

The café was crowded, the people three deep at the bar and the tables packed. It had been the same all day, all evening. Everyone from Germany in Berlin, it seemed to Anja, everyone in Berlin in the Brasserie. It was almost midnight; Germany still divided, in sixty seconds one country. The beginning of the new order, not just in Germany, even in Central Europe. A whole new world. To her left someone ordered champagne; she took a bottle from the bin and reached for the glasses. The door opened and a man and a woman came in. She glanced across, hardly noticed the man, attention riveted on the woman. Like me when I was that age, the thought was barely conscious. Tall, long blonde hair, angry blue eyes. The thin grey line down the left of the woman's face.

Looking at me like I'm looking at her.

Midnight.

She waved the champagne in the air, saw Werner Langer nod and Nikki laugh.